THE BEAST OF NOOR

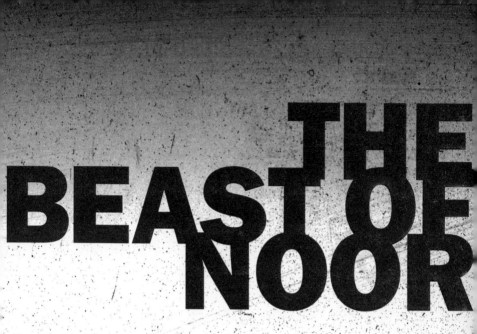

THE BEAST OF NOOR

JANET LEE CAREY

ATHENEUM BOOKS FOR YOUNG READERS
NEW YORK LONDON TORONTO SYDNEY

Atheneum Books for Young Readers
An imprint of Simon & Schuster Children's Publishing Division
1230 Avenue of the Americas, New York, New York 10020
This book is a work of fiction. Any references to historical events, real people, or real
locales are used fictitiously. Other names, characters, places, and incidents are products
of the author's imagination, and any resemblance to actual events or locales or persons,
living or dead, is entirely coincidental.
Book design by Michael McCartney
The text for this book is set in Centaur and NotCaslon.
Manufactured in the United States of America
First Edition
10 9 8 7 6 5 4 3 2 1
Library of Congress Cataloging-in-Publication Data
Carey, Janet Lee.
The Beast of Noor / Janet Lee Carey. — 1st ed.
p. cm.
Summary: Fifteen-year-old Miles Ferrell uses the rare and special gift he is given to
break the curse of the Shriker, a murderous creature reportedly brought to Shalem
Wood by his family's clan centuries before.
ISBN-13: 978-0-689-87644-8
ISBN-10: 0-689-87644-0
[1. Fantasy.] I. Title.
PZ7.C2125Bea 2006
[Fic]—dc22   2005017731

To Tom, guardian of Noor.

To the first intrepid Noor explorers in my
critique group: Peggy King Anderson,
Judy Bodmer, Katherine Grace Bond,
Dawn Knight, and Justina Chen Headley.

To Indu Sundaresan for
helping me cut to the chase.

And to my editor, Susan Burke, for her unfailing
ability to always "see the dog."

CHAPTERS

Author's Note

I owe great thanks to the fairy tales and legends of old, spoken across the world and woven through all cultures. From land to land many of these tales feature forest monsters, villainous wolves, and wild dogs. One legend from the British Isles tells of a phantom dog known by various names—Black Dog, Mauthe Doog, Padfoot, Barguest, Shriker, Gytrash, and so on. Charlotte Brontë describes the Gytrash in *Jane Eyre*, and Sir Arthur Conan Doyle seeks to hunt him down in *The Hound of the Baskervilles*. The phantom hound has existed long in legend and haunted many a tale. But the legend of the Shriker, which tells of Rory Sheen's betrayal and the Darro's curse on Enness Isle, is singular to the world of Noor.

We who work in fantasy today take the threads from all the storytellers of the past. From these ancient, many-colored threads we work to weave a new cloth. If the landscape, the characters, and the creatures here call up the old tales told beside the fire, when stories went from mouth to ear instead of page to eye, then I have woven well and the dreamer continues to dream.

Things are never what they seem,
Find the lost inside the dream.

—THE OLD MEN OF MOUNT SHALEM

In the shadow lands of Attenlore the Shriker waits. On the night of the dark moon he breaks through the great wind wall with a vengeful hunger that drives him back into the world of men. Finding passage from the Otherworld, he shape-shifts into a great black dog of monstrous height, taller than a woodland bear, broader backed and stronger. In the deeps of Shalem Wood he howls. And his moon call is a spell song for those who come to die in his jaws.

LOST POLLY

LOST POLLY

Do not wander in the deeps,
where the Shriker's shadow creeps.
When he rises from beneath,
beware the sharpness of his teeth.

—A SAYING ON ENNESS ISLE

THE FULL MOON DARKENED OVER AS POLLY CREPT THROUGH the trees. A sound had drawn her into Shalem Wood. A call so low and sweet it made her forget her sorrow over her lover, Tarn, who'd drowned at sea.

She stepped in rhythm to the call that filled her body and sang down to her bones. It was beautiful. So rich and deep. Who was the singer? Where was the song? Her heart beat in time with it. The green trees swayed with it. All dancing, dancing.

Polly began to spin, reeling round and round to the sweet, dark sound. She tripped on a root. Fell. Cried out. The sudden, sharp pain in her leg awakened her from her trance. She'd cut her knee and torn her sleeve in the blackberry hedge when she fell. Inching her way back to the trail, she came to a stand and looked about. She'd come into the woods alone at night, and in her sleeping gown! How had she gotten here?

It had been a full-moon night when she bedded down in Brim village, by the sea. Now the moon had eclipsed, and all was deep in shadow. Nothing but pale starlight to guide her.

Polly twisted the shell bracelet on her wrist. Think. She had to think. Taking a deep breath, she turned about. She'd retrace her steps, find the mountain road that led back to town. Aye, she could do that; she'd walked these woods by day before and knew her way well enough. Polly headed down the winding trail, never mind her sore knee.

An owl hooted from the pine branch above. Polly sped up her pace. There was a tale Gran used to tell years ago about a beast that haunted the forest on dark-moon nights like this. But it was just a story told to frighten little children and keep them out of Shalem Wood.

"Just a story," whispered Polly over and over as she

walked. Branches waved in the wind. Leaves trembled in the thornbushes. The broad-limbed oaks and pines creaked above like black-boned giants.

Halfway down the trail Polly stopped, heart pounding. This was the way back, wasn't it?

That call again. Her chest tightened. It was that call that had drawn her into Shalem Wood. Some kind of spell. It must be, for it didn't sound so lovely now. It sounded more like a *wolf's* howl. One wolf or many or . . . Polly took off running. She *had* to reach the road. It couldn't be far. But which way? It was so dark in the forest with the moon gone.

She fled through the bracken, gulping down the chill night air.

The baying sound came again. A wolf, surely, but it must be more than one; no single wolf could have such a monstrous howl. Polly rushed right, then left, then right again. She had to find her way out!

The sound of paws against the earth behind her. Fast. Faster. The beast was gaining. The pounding paws were too loud to come from a wolf. Not a wolf. Something *bigger* than a wolf.

The thing was bounding closer. Paw to earth. Paw

to earth. Pounding. Pounding. She ran fast, faster.

The beast pounced.

Miles awakened with a fright. Someone had screamed. He leaped off his cot and stood in his stocking feet, trembling, listening.

The scream was real, wasn't it? He looked out the window. Outside the full moon was eclipsed. Miles blinked in wonder. He'd never seen an eclipse before. How dark it made the barn, the dirt road. How black it made the trees in Shalem Wood.

Another horrible, high-pitched scream.

Miles started. The first scream *had* been real. Had his sister, Hanna, gone dreamwalking in the woods again? Was she badly hurt?

Miles tugged on his boots, grabbed his bow and hunting knife, and flung open his door. Halfway down the hall he ran into Da, who was already throwing on his cloak.

"Did you hear that?" asked Da.

"Aye. Where's Hanna?"

"She's in her room. I told her to stay put."

Someone else, then. Who was out there? No time

to think—they were already racing across the dirt road, the torch fires blowing back as they rushed along.

Starlight fell dimly on the treetops. The moon still hid in shadow. It was hard to see very far ahead, even with the torches.

"This way, Da!" They took the broadest trail through the whispering pines.

"Hello!" called Da. "Anyone out there?"

No answer. An owl winged overhead.

Miles splashed across a mountain stream, the cold water soaking into his boots. On the far side he saw something. "Look!" he called. They raced up the grade toward the blackberry bushes, where a bit of torn fabric flailed in the wind. Da held his torch up near enough to see the pattern in the cloth, white cotton stitched with violets.

Miles touched the violets. Small stitches like the ones his sister, Hanna, made.

"What is it?" asked Da.

Miles couldn't tell his da what he knew now, knew down in his bones, though he couldn't say why.

They'd find the girl—find her too late.

THE WILD HUNT

CLOUDS ROLLED IN FROM THE SEA, DARKENING THE ROCKY shore at the edge of Shalem Wood. In the green tide pool below the craggy cliffs Miles gathered mussels with Hanna. He plunged his hand into the cold sea water and shuddered. It had been a week since he'd heard the screams. But they'd found the girl, all right, after searching night till dawn.

It was Miles who saw the glint of white at the edge of the meadow. The bones nestled in the green grass were stripped clean, only a lock of golden hair and a shell bracelet left behind. He knew the bones were Polly's as soon as he saw the bracelet, for she always wore Tarn's gift. Why had she gone into the wood on such a night? Da had asked it as they searched the trail with torches, and Miles had wondered ever since.

Miles blinked. He'd try not to think of Polly though he'd thought of little else day and night this past week. And now they'd come to town, he'd heard the villagers talking of her death. No. He wouldn't think of that, either. He had dinner to help fetch.

Tugging three mussels from the crags, he dropped them in Hanna's basket, wiped his dripping nose on the back of his hand, and stood in the shadow of the cliff. He didn't mind gathering mussels for Mother, though he was fifteen now and the task was beneath him. He had hopes of being chosen to study magic on Othlore Isle. And if he got his wish, the years he'd spent herding Da's sheep and gathering food for Mother would hardly be worth his while. Only his studies with the Falconer would count for something to the wise meers.

Miles found the place in the sky where the dim white orb of sun was shrouded by storm clouds. *Othlore.* He longed to see the isle, though it was hundreds of miles away. "Soon," he whispered to himself and to the sea. He'd prove himself there. And when he returned home full of magic power, he'd make sure the village folk never talked down to him again, never reviled him or pushed him aside as they did now. They'd treat him with honor as they did the Falconer. He felt the pulse drumming in his ears just thinking of it.

Hanna dropped her mussels in the basket, licked the salt from her fingers, and glanced up at him with her mismatched eyes—one blue, one green—a feature she was ashamed of, but one he was used to and liked well enough. "It's time we got back," she said.

Miles let her words blow free between them. True, it was time to go. He didn't want to face the villagers yet, with their wary looks and blaming talk. Still, Hanna was right. Granda would have sold the wool by now, and he'd be waiting for them near the market square.

Hanna took up the basket and swung it back and forth as they started up the beach. Along the shoreline a fisherman's wife was heading for the tide pools with her little girl. The child flung out her chubby arms and took off, running toward Hanna.

"Effie!" her mother called. "Stay back!"

Effie raced up the beach.

"She's all right," said Hanna, touching the child's rosy cheek.

The woman raced up and grabbed Effie.

Hanna started and pulled back.

"I told you not to go near them!" the mother scolded, shaking the girl so harshly she began to cry.

"Go home with you!" she shouted at Miles and Hanna. "Go back where you belong!" She lifted her crying child and carried her back down the beach.

"I wouldn't have harmed her," said Hanna.

"It's not you she's afraid of."

Hanna kicked up the sand. "Not my eyes, then?"

"Not your eyes this time. I saw the farmwives and the shopkeepers today. They were talking in hushed voices behind their hands, but I heard them all the same."

"What are they saying now?"

A wave swept in, the foam licking the edge of Miles's boots.

"Tell me," said Hanna.

"You don't want to know."

"I do," insisted Hanna.

Miles looked over at his sister. She was small for

her thirteen years, but she had a stubborn strength that often made up for her size. "They're saying we're to blame for Polly's death."

Hanna stopped short. "What? But they *can't* be blaming us for that! All you did was find her and bring her . . . her bones back to town. It isn't right!"

"Right or wrong doesn't matter to them, Hanna."

Miles pulled up a piece of cordgrass, bit down hard, and sucked the sharp, green taste from the stem. It was just like the village folk to blame his clan for Polly's death. They'd always been outsiders, living ten miles from town, coming down mountain only once a month to buy supplies or worship in the kirk. The villagers had never warmed to them, but Miles had never felt their outright anger. Not until today. Fishmongers, farmwives, merchants, it didn't matter. He saw the piercing hatred in their eyes—the chill look of fear. Those who believed in the old legend were spreading rumors, saying the Shriker killed Polly Downs and that it was all the fault of his own Sheen clan, for the legend said it was a Sheen that brought the monstrous dog to Shalem Wood three hundred years ago.

Wind stung Miles's face and ears. Flies flew up from

the green seaweed, circling his head, buzzing. Crossing the beach to the cliff, they started for the narrow path where the goldenrod bowed tip to sand in the heavy wind.

The first raindrops fell, early warnings of the storm to come. Hanna stepped ahead of Miles, dug the toe of her boot into the foothold, and scaled the cliff rocks. The mussel shells made a clatter sound as her basket banged against the cliff.

"I'll take the basket," said Miles.

"I'm all right." Hanna grunted as she pulled herself up to level ground, then straightened out her skirt, waiting for him to follow. Miles grabbed a handhold, leaped up to level ground, and quickened his step to beat out the storm.

The dirt alley wound this way and that, with cottages to the left and right, some near the cliff edge looking out to sea, others facing the dirt road to town. Two women came into their backyards with their washing. At another cottage an old man was feeding slops to his pigs.

Hanna and Miles were fast on their feet, and they would have made it back to the market square before the storm if Gerald, Mic, and Cully hadn't caught them in the alley.

"Ah, look! It's the Sheens!" called Gerald.

"The shepherd boy and his sister, who talks to trees," said Cully.

"Watch out," warned Mic, "or she'll hex you with her eyes!"

"Which one? The blue eye or the green?"

Miles widened his stance and curled his right hand into a stony fist. The boys were all fifteen like himself, and each a head taller than him. Still, he would warn them off. "Out of our way, fish bait!"

"Fish bait, is it? You Sheens all stink of sheep!" Cully pinched his nose.

"You know that's not our name," said Hanna. "We're Ferrells."

"Your granda's a Sheen and so's your mother!" called Mic. "So the bad blood's in your veins!"

Hanna tried to walk around them, but Mic stepped in front of her. Beyond the fence the old man with the slop bucket took out his pipe and lit up. On the other side the women watched. It was three against two, and Hanna only a girl, but none of the grown-ups made a move to help.

Cully stuck his chest out. "My granda says the

Shriker killed Polly Downs, and all because of you Sheens. Your clan brought the Shriker into Shalem Wood long ago, and he hunts there still."

"Shut up, Cully," shouted Miles. "That's just an old story!"

"Aye," cried Hanna. "The mountain wolves killed Polly. Mother said so."

"Aye, well, your mum's a dirty Sheen herself, so she would say that."

"You'll leave our mother out of this if you want to keep your teeth in your mouth!" Miles shouted.

Mic snorted and knocked Hanna's mussel basket into the bushes. Miles howled. Bounding forward, he pounced on Mic.

"Miles, don't!" cried Hanna, but he was already punching Mic's belly, his chest, his face, wherever he could drive a fist home. Mic was strong, but he wasn't as fast as Miles. Already Mic's nose was bleeding, and he had a cut above his eye. The other boys grabbed Miles from behind and dragged him over to the fence.

Hanna shouted, "Help him!" The old man puffed his pipe and looked away. She rushed to the leaning fence.

"Stay back, Hanna," warned Miles. But she jumped on Cully's back and wrapped her arms about his thick neck.

Cully spun round, pried her off, and threw her down. Miles shouted, kicked Mic's shin, and pushed against Gerald and Cully's hold. Still, they forced him to the ground and held him there.

Miles writhed under their combined weight. If the Falconer had ever bothered to teach him a single spell, he'd have the power to beat the three of them for good and all. He'd use his magic power to turn them all to maggots. Crush them under his boot.

Mic straddled Miles's chest, hissing, "Dirty Sheen. This will teach you to come to town!" He punched him hard in the mouth. Miles roared and struggled under his weight. Mic struck again and again, punching Miles's cheek, his jaw. Miles tasted blood.

"Stop it!" screamed Hanna.

"Harder!" shouted Cully.

"Get off him now, boys!" Granda's stern voice came from somewhere above.

"Quick!" shouted Mic. "To the beach!" The village boys leaped off Miles and ran down the winding alley for the beach path.

Miles heaved a sickened breath, leaned on his elbow, and spit blood on the sand. Granda gazed down at him, his head seeming more than life size with the dark clouds rolling above. Granda sniffed. "You're all right, then," he said with a nod.

Hanna knelt down and brushed the sand from Miles's shirt. He pushed her off and jumped up. "I would have beaten them, Granda, if you'd given me the chance!"

"All three?"

Miles wiped his bleeding lip. "All three and more. They were talking after Mother, saying she lied about—"

"Boy." Granda placed a warning hand on Miles's shoulder. He tipped his head toward the backyards lining the dirt alley. Mrs. Nye and the other woman were still outside, watching, listening. So was the old man with the pipe. Granda's gesture said, *Not here. Not now.* He turned and helped Hanna pick up the spilled mussels. "Your mother will get a good stew from these," he said.

An hour later they were huddled around a small fire in a cave partway up Mount Shalem. On the way home the storm had caught them out on the road, the rain coming down in handfuls and the hard wind gusting first this way, then that. After tying the cart horse to an oak tree, they'd run into the thick forest till Granda found the cave he was searching for. It was a low cave and a small one, lichen-covered inside and out, but it was dry enough.

By the crackling fire Miles rubbed his swollen lip. It would be a while before he could play his flute for the Falconer without some pain, but the fight had been worth it.

Across the flames Granda coughed and wrung the corner of his cloak, letting the water dribble down to the rocky floor beside him. Steam rose up about his knees. "Well, the storm's blown us here. We're well away from other eyes and ears." He looked across the fire, first at Miles, then at Hanna. "I've waited overlong to be alone with you both this way." He tugged on his left ear and tipped his head. "It's now you'll be needing to hear the story."

Hanna wriggled by the fire. "Tell us about the Sylth Queen," she said. "How she comes to Shalem Wood on the Breal's Moon night."

Granda nodded. "A good story, true enough, and we'll all be honoring Breal's Moon soon, now that we've had an eclipse. But it's the Shriker's tale I'm bound to tell today."

Hanna's eyes grew wide. "No! Not that one!"

"Don't be such a sniveling baby," snapped Miles.

"I'm not!"

"Aye, you are."

"That's enough," warned Granda.

Miles rubbed the cut between his knuckles.

Hanna frowned across the fire. "The Shriker's tale is just a story, after all. Isn't it, Granda?"

Miles leaned forward, awaiting Granda's answer. Mother and Da said it was just a tale, but those who believed in the Old Ways said the beast was real—a man killer—and they blamed his family for bringing the monster into the world. "It's all because of what they're saying in town about Polly, isn't it?"

"Aye, her death has brought the Shriker's curse back into people's minds. And you can bet the tale is being told in every cottage on Enness Isle just now."

"Every cottage but ours," said Miles bitterly. "If Mother had only—"

"Mother said you were never to tell that story in her house again," warned Hanna.

It was true Mother had banned the Shriker's tale five years back, when Miles was ten and Hanna only eight. She'd returned from the market and caught Granda in the telling. No sooner was Mother in the door than she flew into a rage. "Never again!" she screamed. "Never again in my house! Outside with you, Da!" she shouted. And she slammed the door against her own da, her cheeks burning red, as if she'd been slapped.

In the dimly lit cave Granda ran his hand through his curling hair like a plow furrowing the ground, his fingers leaving combing lines behind. He cleared his throat and passed them each a worried look. "Your mother's sought to protect you children in her way, but I've held back far too long with the things I've got to say. You're Sheens and in some danger now. Someone in this family has to warn you."

"I can handle the village folk," said Miles. "If you hadn't broken up the fight today—"

"It's not *them* I'm worried about, boy."

Miles scooted back a ways. What was happening? First the townsfolk had turned on them, now Granda was snapping at him. The cave felt too close, the wind outside too wild. He touched his sore jaw and felt the tender swelling there.

"Do you trust me, children?"

Miles and Hanna nodded.

"Well, good then. You need to hear the family tale again—come to know it backward and forward and inside out." He sniffed and wiped his hands on his breeches. "The more you know, the better armed you'll be for what's to come."

Miles shivered, wondering what Granda meant by "for what's to come," but it was too late to ask, for already Granda's knobby hands were held out to the fire's glow to cast a shadow on the rocky wall. He moved his fingers this way and that until they took the shape of a great dog's head. The shadow grew larger. The jaws opened. Miles tensed. He pulled out his knife and shaved a long strip of bark off a bit of kindling.

Granda began, "It was many long years ago on a stormy winter's night, the Darro came riding across the sky with his pack of ghost dogs.

"All shadow and bone the Darro was, being Death's own man, and he rode his dark horse through the storm right here to Enness Isle."

Miles nodded, remembering well this part. He poked the fire with his newly carved stick. Sparks flew to the stone ceiling and parted in three directions like small flocks of sunbirds.

"The Darro came as he ever does, to hunt souls bound for death's passage and put them in his sack. The Wild Hunt it was called in those days, and whenever the Darro came riding, people were bound to lose their lives.

"Well, this hunt was no different from any other, and more than one poor villager died that night, but one man ran swifter than the rest of them, and his name was Rory Sheen."

At the sound of this name Miles waved his flaming stick in the air, and Hanna held the corner of her cloak out to the fire like a damp shield.

"Now, Rory was a shepherd," said Granda. "He knew the foothills of Mount Shalem well. And he had himself a faithful bear hound to help him mind his sheep. The dog's black fur was thick as a bear's hide, and he was strong as they come. He was a loyal hound, always looking to please his master. So when the Darro and his ghost pack came for Rory, he and his dog gave them great chase.

"Through Shalem Wood they sped, and the wind could hardly go faster. But after many hours the chase was over and the Darro won out, as he always does in the end.

"There in the deeps the Darro's ghost hounds surrounded Rory, some howling their victory and others snarling and showing their great, long fangs. But Rory's dog, who loved his master beyond all measure, leaped into the fray and fought the beasts to save his master's life."

Miles stopped his carving and looked up. "He was brave."

"Aye," said Granda. "He threw himself at their enemies while Rory cowered by the trees. But the dog was mortal and far and away outnumbered, so it wasn't long before he lost the fight. And he limped away to lie down at his master's feet with barely his own life."

"A good dog, then," said Miles thoughtfully.

"How could he be?" said Hanna. "With all that happened next?" For both of them had heard the tale before.

"He *was* good just then for defending his master."

Granda held up his hand and they quieted down. Rain angled in through the mouth of the cave. A few drops hit the flames and sizzled.

"Now, Rory was sore afraid," said Granda. "He

might have prayed to eOwey and found some help. But Rory wasn't a praying man, and he wasn't about to start now, so he put his hands together and begged the Darro to spare his life.

"The Darro was used to poor souls in their last earthly moment begging to be spared. Rich folk had offered him many a bag of gold and silver over the years in trade for their life, but he could see this man was poor. Still, he leaned across his shadow mare and said, 'What will you give me in return for your life?'

"Looking about, the poor man could think of nothing, and his dog, sensing Rory's end, nuzzled his master's hand to give the man a last bit of comfort before his death.

"'Take my dog,' he said.

"'Your dog, you say?' The Darro flicked his whip and considered the beast lying at his master's feet. 'Tell me his name.'

"'He's just a dog,' said Rory. 'He has no name.'

"The Darro laughed at this. Blood still dripped from the dog's teeth, and even now his own hounds were licking their wounds. No dog had ever fought the ghost pack before and lived.

"Now, it's rare the Darro will strike a bargain. But it was clear this man, this Rory Sheen, didn't know the strength of his own dog.

"'Done!' said the Darro. Then, putting out his hand, he pulled the dog up by the scruff of the neck. 'I name you Shriker. Shape-Shifter. Mighty Hunter. Your master has betrayed you. And through his betrayal man's best friend becomes his worst enemy.'

"He shook the dog until his bones rattled. 'Now you are cursed, and the thirst for revenge will drive you all your days until your thirst is quenched!'"

Miles poked his stick into the flames. He'd heard the Darro's curse before, but here in the cave, half dark from their small fire, the curse echoed rock to rock, and it seemed to go down into his very insides.

Granda put out his hands again and shaped them so the black dog's shadow fell across the granite wall. "Now the beast was cursed, the Darro dropped the Shriker to the ground. The beast turned upon the man who had betrayed him and attacked him to within an inch of his life.

"I say an inch and no more, for Rory had made a Darro's bargain, and so he lived. Ah, he lived, all right," said Granda, "if you could call it living, for Rory Sheen was maimed by the Shriker and driven to madness. Year on year the Shriker followed him, hunting Rory and no other. Times the beast shape-shifted to a wild cat or falcon or formed himself into Rory's own shadow when others were about, so the villagers would not see his true nature. But Rory knew who was behind him. And whenever the man went off alone, the Shriker shaped himself into a great black dog again. So that in the end all Rory could ever hear were the *pad, pad* sounds of the hound's great paws everywhere he went. And when at last his final hour came, on the night of the dark moon, he died a bloody death in the Shriker's jaws."

Granda rested his hands in his lap.

Miles let out his breath in a slow stream. He'd been holding it a long while, caught inside the story. This was the third time he'd heard the tale from Granda; still, his flesh pricked when he pictured Rory's death. And there was something else that made his breath catch, the part about the beast shape-shifting. He hadn't remembered that from before.

He was about to ask about it when Granda said,

"It was long ago this happened. Three hundred years at least, and for a time after Rory's death the Shriker was not seen nor heard of in all of Enness Isle, but now it's said he returns at the time of the dark moon to hunt more human prey in Shalem Wood."

LOST BROTHER

He returns at the time of the dark moon.

—The legend of the Shriker

Hanna shook despite her nearness to the fire. "Why did you end the tale that way, Granda? You never said before that he's returned."

"Is that the way they're telling the story in all the villages?" Miles asked. Hanna could hear the anger in his voice, and it unsettled her all the more.

Granda blew his nose, then folded his handkerchief. "I'm thinking they are, for wasn't poor Polly killed on the night of the dark moon, just like the story says? It'll be bad for us Sheens from now on, I'm afraid."

"But there's no reason the beast should return," said

Hanna. "He killed the master who betrayed him, so he *got* his revenge."

"Well, you'd think so," said Granda, "but remember, the Darro cursed him *all* his days until his thirst is quenched."

Smoke drifted from the flames to the rock ceiling. Hanna watched it part, curling back upon itself. *Until his thirst is quenched.* Was it a thirst for human blood? She tore a jagged nail from her finger and flinched. "Mother said Polly must have been half crazed to go to Shalem Wood at night."

"Aye," agreed Granda. "Especially on such a night. The beast always attacks when the moon eclipses."

"Why does he come then?" asked Miles.

"It's a mystery, that, but I've seen it time and time again. There'd been no sign of the Shriker since the days of Rory Sheen but fifty-odd years ago the beast came back. No one can say why, but ever since then he comes to Shalem along with the eclipse. And once the beast is back he hunts whenever there's a full moon. Some of his worst attacks were thirteen years ago."

Hanna took this in; people had died the year that she was born. "Who was killed thirteen years back?" she asked.

"Ah, well, you don't want to know that."

"You said the more we know, the better armed we'll be against what's to come," reminded Miles.

Granda coughed. "If you must know—the midwife was killed on her way home from Hanna's birthing. Her man died the next night when he came up mountain all armed and ready to slay the monster."

Granda closed his eyes. Opened them again. "Aye, that was a killing year for the beast, every time the moon waxed full, and many here on Enness Isle were slain. But the first was the midwife. Your poor mother didn't speak for a full year after that. None could heal her, not the Falconer, nor Old Gurty, nor Brother Adolpho with his kind prayers. All shamed your mother was because the townsfolk blamed her for the deaths. She was a Sheen, after all, and she'd lured the midwife into the wood."

"But she didn't!" cried Hanna. "Mother would never have done that! She only needed help with her labor and—"

"I'm only telling you what the Brim folk said. You know how cruel they can be."

Hanna drew her knees to her chest and put her

head down on them. She didn't know. Not really. Not until Polly's death. It was true the village boys had teased her all along about her eyes, and the villagers had never been generous or kind, except for Brother Adolpho and Taunier, the blacksmith's apprentice, who was still new to the isle.

The fire warmed the backs of her arms, her elbows felt too hot; still, she didn't move. No one had ever told her what had happened the night that she was born. Was that why Mother gave her strange looks sometimes? She'd always thought it had to do with her eyes.

Hanna gripped her knees tighter. All her life she'd wanted to belong, to have friends in town. And her eyes had stood in the way of that. So she'd wished for two blue eyes, or two green, or two brown. Two of *any* common color, as long as they matched.

Miles leaped up and started pacing. "If the village folk think our mother could have . . . if that's what they all think of us, we should leave this stupid isle behind!"

"And where would we go, lad? We're shepherds. This is our land, from Gusting Hill to Senowey River. Leave it and we lose our livelihood."

"But if every time someone dies in Shalem Wood

when the moon is full we're looked on as the ones to blame . . ."

"Not every time," said Granda. "It's only in the dark-moon years, and how often are they?"

Hanna thought of Hallard's grandson. Found in Shalem Wood last year. He'd been struck by lightning in the high meadow. No one had called that a Shriker's kill or blamed the Sheens for that.

Miles's shadow crept along the wall as he turned and paced the cave's length again. "There must be a way to break the Shriker's curse."

The words "break" and "curse" fell hard and sharp in the hollow of the cave.

"Ah," said Granda. "It would take some powerful magic to do that."

What kind of magic? wondered Hanna. She looked up at Miles. Golden firelight bathed his cheeks and forehead, but it didn't soften his fierce look. His face was as taut and gleaming as a bronze shield.

Hanna dug a little line in the dirt, drops from her rain-soaked hair staining the dust a darker brown. All this talk of death and curses frightened her. She wished she could go back to three months ago, when the last days of winter had dressed the mountainside with snow. When Polly had been alive and the Shriker's tale had seemed a story, a dark tale Granda wasn't allowed to tell in the house.

There were better stories then, happier ones about the Otherworld; about Wild Esper, the wind woman; and the Sylth Queen, who ruled the fairy world of Oth. Stories she could fill her heart and mind with. She believed them all, and always had, the Old Ways seeming right to her way of thinking. But she'd shut her mind against the shadow realm and the monsters that dwelled there, wishing, hoping they weren't true. "You can't have it both ways, Hanna," Granda said to her once. All the same, she'd swept the dark tales from her mind, quick and tidy, the way Mother went at the kitchen floor with her broom.

Granda had been talking with Miles while she was lost in thought, and she caught only the end of what he was saying.

". . . out in Shalem Wood at night?"

"I've gone out with the Falconer."

"Well, your teacher's a good soul," said Granda. "And he's a fine leafer. There's many on Enness who owe their life to his healing hand."

The old man coughed and cleared his throat. "So, you've not ventured out alone, then?"

Miles shrugged and sat again beside the fire. "A few times. I know the woods by day and night, and I always take my knife."

Hanna looked at her brother's face, his high brows, which shadowed his deep-set eyes. She thought of Polly's bones. "Tell him he shouldn't go out alone, Granda! Not with wild beasts out there and . . . and more . . ."

"Aye," said Granda. "You should listen to your sister. The woods are a danger at night now the moon's eclipsed. You'll have to watch Hanna closely too, boy. With her dreamwalks and all."

"I've always done so," said Miles proudly. "She never wanders farther than the garden or the well."

"She's older now and may begin to wander farther in her sleep."

Hanna blushed. They were speaking of her as if she weren't sitting right beside them. She wasn't a child anymore. She wanted to shout, "I can take care of myself, thank you all the same!" But she never knew when a dreamwalk would come or where her feet would take her in her sleep.

Granda sneezed and wiped his nose. "And you

yourself had best keep clear of Shalem Wood as well, Miles," he warned, "for once the Shriker's freed on the night of the dark moon, he comes back to hunt more prey on full-moon nights until the winter snows come to the wood. Some years three people die, some years seven, but never only one, so Polly Downs was only the first to fall this time around."

Miles kept quiet. He pulled out his knife again and stripped the bark from a fresh stick, the brown curls falling at his feet.

Granda gave a grunt. "You think you're man enough to face whatever's out there?"

"I know the mountain and the woods better than anyone else on Enness Isle, except for the Falconer," boasted Miles. "I can fend for myself all right."

"Ah, my boy." Granda sighed. "My brother, Enoch, thought the same. There was no one and nothing held him back. He had such a thirst to uncover the secrets of Shalem Wood and prove he could wield magic to overcome whatever lurked out there."

Miles dropped his knife and quickly picked it up again. "Did he ever . . . find a way?"

"It's hard to speak of even now." Granda coughed

and held his hands out to the meager fire. Hanna saw the old man was chilled and might come down with a fever if they stayed here any longer. "It's stopped raining," she said, coming to a stand. "We should be going home."

Granda sniffed and patted the ground. "By and by, Hanna."

She sat again and flicked a piece of caked mud from her boot.

"This won't take long, and we'll leave straight after that. You know what's been said about my brother."

"Aye," said Hanna. "You always told us he left Enness when he was a young man."

"Well, that's true enough, but there's more I've not told you. Here's the truth about him, plain and simple. I hope it'll be a warning to you both."

Hanna added the last bit of kindling to the lowsome fire. The wet wood hissed. Beside the rising cloud of steam Granda leaned back, raised his knees, and wrapped his arms about them. "My brother had a ken for magic. Enough so that he was chosen to study with the meers on Othlore."

Hanna peered through the flames at her brother. It was Miles's dream to go to Othlore. He'd told her so, and they'd kept it secret between them. His face changed in the dancing shadows. Surprise, hunger, jealousy, she wasn't sure. It might be one or all.

Granda went on. "But Enoch wasn't on Othlore six months before he was sent back home."

"Why?" Miles blurted out.

"Some disgrace, he never said what it was. Our da was angry enough with the lad. He'd expected Enoch to come home a healer. There were many sick on Enness Isle back then. Da wouldn't have him in the house, so he sent Enoch away to live in a shepherd's hut in the high pasture. There was a girl who used to visit him, bring him little cakes and cider. A real beauty she was back then, with bright green eyes and a grand face with a smiling mouth.

"I went there too to see him when I could. But Enoch didn't make for good company, being full of anger at the meers for dismissing him and rageful at our da as well. He threw me out of his hut the last time I came to call.

"After that day my brother vanished. Seven years I searched the mountain for my brother's bones. And then," Granda said with a sigh. "I found him at long last."

Hanna's mouth went dry. "The way Miles found Polly?" she asked in a strained voice.

"No, Hanna, not like that." Granda went silent and stared into the fire.

"What, then?" whispered Hanna.

"He wasn't dead. Enoch was lost . . . enspelled."

"Who enspelled him?" asked Miles.

"I don't know, son. Enoch was too fond of magical power and too fearless for his own good. Someone went after him and punished him for it. It may have been a meer, though the meers I know don't wield dark magic. It may have been one of the Oth folk, a sylth with great powers, like the Sylth Queen."

"It couldn't have been *her*," said Hanna. "She's queen of all the fairies, and she's beautiful and kind—"

"And dangerous if you cross her," said Granda.

"Why would she enspell your brother?" asked Miles.

"I told you it's a mystery." Granda sucked in his cheeks and lost himself in thought awhile. At last he said, "A horrible spell it was. My brother's imprisoned inside a tree."

Hanna shivered. "Can't he get out?"

"He never has done," sighed Granda. "The Enoch Tree is up on the high cliff, an isolated place where no one ever wanders. It's a hard climb, but I've a mind to take you there myself when I'm feeling stronger. For now you'll both abide my wishes and not go digging into things beyond your nature the way Enoch did, or bounding off alone like Polly. You'll stay clear of the woods at night. Say you will."

"I will," they agreed. Hanna didn't mind the promise, but she studied Miles's shadowed face across the fire and wondered why his dark eyes were glowing so.

Those who cause the curse must break it,
and the breaking's in the blood.

—A SAYING ON ENNESS ISLE

GRANDA NEVER DID GET STRONG ENOUGH TO SHOW Miles and Hanna the Enoch Tree. Nearly three weeks had passed since they arrived home from market day soaked to the skin. The old man was chilled from the storm. He went to bed and never got up again. No matter that the Falconer came with his healing herbs; that Gurty, the woods woman, brought twiggy smokes and teas; that Brother Adolpho prayed over him.

Miles pulled another river stone from his sack. A man's eldest son was supposed to lay stones about a grave two days after a father's burial, but Granda had no sons, so the honor fell to him.

He laid the last stone down and wiped his hands, then stood and sang the Crossing Over song under his breath. In the shadow of the great oak he cried alone for the old man, the warm wind at his back his sole company.

Climbing down the hill, he passed the shed where Hanna was leaning over the vat dipping the round candles for the Breal's Moon celebration. She didn't hear him pass, though he saw her well enough, her hair tied back in a yellow scarf, her hands reddened from work as she dipped the wicks into the wax.

He thought to speak to her. Say the stone circle was in its place, but the words were caught down in his throat. Turning the corner, he took his music book from its hiding place behind the woodpile and crossed the dirt road. He was off to the Falconer's to take what was needed. He must gather the kind of power only magic could bring to keep his promise to Granda.

On the night before Granda died, Miles had sat by the cot and held the old man's hand, the flesh dry as paper.

"You must look after Hanna and Tymm," said Granda, his eyes afire with the fever that was on him. "Don't let them go into Shalem Wood at night. Do all you can to keep them safe from the Shriker. Promise me now."

Miles gripped the old man's hand. "I promise."

"Good, then." Granda looked at him and smiled for the first time in weeks, and it was that smile above all he wanted to remember now.

Miles quit the road and hiked across the rolling hills for the Falconer's house. "A promise made is a promise kept," Da used to say. Today Miles meant to do just that.

Mother and Da still insisted it was the wolves killed Polly, but Granda had been certain it was the Shriker. If he was right, if the Shriker had returned, then Miles needed the strength to turn him back—a spell great enough to send the hellhound to the underworld for good and all. A spell like that might well be hidden in the Falconer's book.

Wading through the thick bracken, he adjusted the flute pouch strung over his shoulder and left the sunlit hills for the shadowy wood. He'd slept little in the past three weeks with Granda sick and the Shriker always on his mind. He'd begged Granda to tell him more about the beast when Mother wasn't in the room, and on the nights he took his watch over the sickbed, Granda told in halting breaths how the Shriker called some victims to himself with a doleful baying, and those that heard the call couldn't help but follow. "And never look straight into his eyes," warned Granda. "For he'll enspell you with them so's you can't even run."

Miles wished now more than ever that Mother hadn't banned the tale when he was ten years old. There was so much to remember. So many mysteries unsolved. Rory had died three hundred years ago, and the Shriker seemed to disappear with him. Why, then, did the beast return to Shalem Wood fifty years ago at the time of the eclipse? Who or what had brought him back? Granda couldn't answer that. There were more questions left unanswered: Why did the Shriker hunt some victims and lure in others with a call? How was it they heard the Shriker's howl? Couldn't those who heard it resist the call somehow? It was all a mystery still, and one he'd have to solve himself with Granda gone.

"Those who cause the curse must break it, and the breaking's in the blood." It was an old saying on Enness Isle, and it had awakened him with a cold sweat more than once since Polly's death. He knew what the monster could do. He'd seen Polly's bones lying in the green meadow, felt sick at the sight of them and her lock of golden hair. He *couldn't* let that happen to anyone else. He wouldn't. If Rory Sheen's betrayal had brought the Shriker into the world, then a Sheen must break the curse.

Miles gazed above the pines, midday and no moon out. Still, three nights from now, on Breal's festival, the moon would rise full over the mountain. Granda said once the beast was back in Shalem Wood he attacked each time there was a full moon. And if Granda was right, the Shriker would be on the prowl again. Miles leaped rock to rock across the shallow stream. On the far side he quickened his step. He had to arrive before the Falconer returned for their lesson so that he had time to go after the spell book, the only book the Falconer had forbidden him to read. He was driven now to take what needed taking, even if it meant going against his master.

Arriving at the ivy-covered door set in the hill, Miles knocked and waited. No movement from within. Good. He crept inside the hollow hill and felt the chill as he passed the empty hearth. He hadn't much time.

Passing the falcon's perch, where Aetwan rested when at home, he entered the open alcove that was his master's study. The room smelled of the dried herbs that dangled from the roots in the ceiling. Wiping his hands on his pants, he raised his arm and ran his fingers along the book spines, passing *Entor's Herbal, The Othic Art of Meditation, The Book of eOwey.*

He wouldn't have to steal a spell if the Falconer were more trusting with his magic. So far he'd taught Miles only music and herb lore, no matter how often he asked the meer to teach him spells. He'd asked the Falconer to share his magic book just two weeks ago while they were gathering herbs for Granda. But his teacher's answer was the same as ever: "When you're ready. When it's time."

Miles felt a tingling in his fingertips when he reached *The Way Between Worlds*, a book full of meers' magic.

He opened the window a crack to keep an ear out for his teacher, pulled down a music book, and layed his flute out on the table so that he could take it up right quick when the Falconer returned.

Back in the alcove he scooted his chair out a bit to face the main room and the door. Now, to find the spell.

Miles held his hand over the book. He would do it. No one else in his family had the means to stop the monster. Not Da, who was a Ferrell, after all, and didn't himself believe. Not Mother, who was full of fear. Not Hanna or Tymm, who were too young. It would take magic power. Granda had said as much that day in the cave, and Miles was the only Sheen with that kind of power close at hand.

Miles's heart pounded as he opened the tome. He blinked at the illuminations along the margins—quail, swallows, flowering vines, sprites. Fine pictures, but there wasn't time to look.

Spells. There must be a section on that. He flipped the pages in twos and threes: a lot of information on healing herbs. Farther on he spied a section filled with the legends of Oth, what Granda called the magical Otherworld.

Miles shook himself. Spells. Wasn't there a section on spell casting? What sort of magic book would leave that out? He flipped through the pages, searching, searching.

A crackling sound came through the window. Miles jumped up and peered out. Holly leaves trembled in the tree beside the woodpile. It was the wind, what Granda would have called one of Wild Esper's playful breezes. He sat again. On the small table the stray flurry turned the book pages. They fluttered like wings. *Rustle, rustle, hush. Rustle, rustle, hush.*

The pages settled down at last to a section on the Breal's Moon festival. The folk all over Noor were readying themselves for the festival now, and all were telling the mythical legend of Breal, who slew the serpent Wratheren and pulled the swallowed moon from the serpent's jaws.

Miles read the left-hand page. No spells there. He'd nearly finished with the right when he saw the words "Sylth Queen" in the bottom corner. Legend said the passage between the worlds of Noor and Oth could be crossed on Breal's Moon night, and that the Sylth Queen chose that one night of all nights to come out of the Otherworld into the world of men.

Turn the page. You need a spell. He tugged the corner, then paused, staring at the last two lines on the bottom of the page: "Cast this spell, and if you have the Gift, the way to the sylth folk will appear."

The first spell, the *only* spell he'd found. But it had

nothing to do with ridding the world of the Shriker's curse. Still, it *was* a spell; he'd memorize it quickly and move on. Miles read the spell three times and four, closed his eyes, and thought of it. He knew enough not to say it aloud, even in a whisper. He checked the words again, then read: "By the giant's-head boulder under Breal's moonlight look to the way that opens in the night." Giant's-head boulder. He'd seen a boulder shaped like a giant's head in the high meadow. A great head with deep-set eyes and mossy hair and . . .

A humming voice outside: The Falconer was back! Miles slammed the book shut and shoved it onto the high shelf.

THE SEED

THE SEER

At the end of the dark passage Kwium found the door all learned men pass through and chose instead to crawl in through the window.

—*THE BOOK OF EOWEY*

MILES RUSHED TO THE FALCONER'S MAIN ROOM AND dived for the table. He was counting out the time when his teacher stepped inside.

"Ah," said the Falconer.

Miles looked up at the figure in the doorway. The light behind the Falconer turned him to a standing shadow, his tall outline filling the open doorframe. Miles was struck again by his teacher's height. The Falconer was the tallest man on Enness Isle, close to seven feet, and old age had barely stooped him. The smaller outline of his falcon, Aetwan, seemed to grow up from the old man's shoulder, no features visible with the bright daylight behind.

Aetwan flew to his perch and fluffed out his wings.

"You're early today." The Falconer shut the door, removed his cloak, and hung it on a jutting root. He placed a stained leather bag on the table. "I've been gathering jessu root. Tell me what it's used for."

Already he was testing him, when they'd hardly said hello. "You can make a tonic with it?" Miles hesitated. "To . . . ,"—he screwed up his brows in thought—"to ease a bellyache."

The Falconer nodded and Miles sighed. It gave him such pleasure to please his master. He saw him clearly now in the soft window light and searched his age-lined face for a smile. There was none, but the meer's nod had been enough.

The old man searched Miles's face too, his golden eyes steady and piercing. Miles quickly turned to his flute, covering three finger holes. *The Way Between Worlds* was tucked up on the shelf again. There was no way the Falconer could know what he'd just done, unless . . .

Miles swallowed. It was true the man was a *seer* and read the future at times. Miles had seen him packing boneset to take to Hallard's barn when Jara fell from her horse. The leafer had known Jara's leg was broken, how it had happened and when, without a word from the farmer, and he'd been there to help reset the leg within the hour.

The Falconer crossed to the alcove and closed the window. Miles tensed. Stupid of him. He'd left the window open. Stepping back up to the table, his teacher flipped through the music book. Hummed the tune. "Try this one," he said.

Miles played it dutifully, though with little feeling, for it was the same song as the week before. Blowing a steady stream of air into his wooden flute, he fixed his eyes on the silver ervay that hung upon the wall. So beautiful. So perfect. And he was ready to play it. More than ready. So why did his teacher still make him use an old wooden flute?

The thought made his finger slip, and the note blew sharp and shrill.

The Falconer did not frown but simply said, "Hold your elbows so."

Miles lifted his arms higher. His hand slipped again. Another sour note.

The meer tipped his head. "Where are you, Miles?"

"Here."

"And where is the song?"

"It's here," said Miles, holding up the flute.

"It's not in *you*, then?"

"It *is* in me," said Miles, seeing at once his teacher's meaning. "But this flute is rough. I've grown past it."

The Falconer raised his bushy brows. "Have you, now? Well," he said, waving his hand. "Put it away, then."

Miles happily stuffed it in its pouch. He saw Aetwan eyeing him from his corner perch and ignored the falcon.

The meer stood and ran his hand along the book bindings on his high shelf. Miles willed his tapered fingers to stop at *The Way Between Worlds*, to pull it down, to open it at last and share the magic there. But the Falconer's hand passed the golden letters and stopped at *Entor's Herbal*.

"Sir," said Miles. "When will you be teaching me some magic?"

The Falconer sat beside him and rested his elbows on the table.

Silence.

He'd asked so many times to learn magic from the meer, and always his teacher held it back.

"You know why your mother and your da sent you here."

"Aye, to improve my music and to learn some ways of healing."

"Healers are needed all over Noor," said the Falconer, "and there aren't that many of us skilled enough to do the work."

"But I've studied that two years now, and I want more." Hearing the strength behind his words, he added a quick, "Sir."

"I don't think your mother would want that."

"I'm the one that's here," said Miles. "I'm fifteen now. She doesn't have to know." He wanted to say he needed a spell to break the Shriker's curse, but the Falconer had a wary look.

"I can see you're hungry to learn." He tipped his head. A ray of sunlight fell across his shoulder. "You have some promise of the Gift. But a man must know himself before he learns the ways of magic." He emptied the leather pouch and laid a circle of jessu root upon the table. "You're dabbling in things beyond your skill. Magic can be dangerous in the wrong hands."

Miles started. Was the Falconer saying he was

too young, too inexperienced, or was he saying there was something *wrong* with him because he was a Sheen? Everyone in Enness thought the Sheens were worthless, but the Falconer didn't think that, did he? Miles felt sick with anger. He wanted to shout at the old man. Claim his right to magic. He leaped to a stand and felt himself swaying. He looked at the Falconer's face, met a solemn frown, and lost his nerve. He'd already crossed a boundary line and stolen a spell from his book.

The Falconer pushed the willow chair away from the table. He took the empty pouch and his cutting knife. "Come, boy. The sun is high. We'll fetch some herbs."

They had walked for nearly an hour in the woods when the Falconer decided to gather elm bark. "You know the way to the grove," he said. "You may as well take the lead."

Miles felt a rising pride as he stepped ahead of his teacher. He walked as quietly as he could, so as not to disturb the woodland animals about. He hoped the Falconer would notice that.

The old man followed behind him with his staff. As they rounded a sharp bend, the Falconer said, "Knowledge of the trails is a good thing, son. But I'm sure you

know it's not safe to come here at night after what happened to Polly Downs."

Miles clenched his jaw and kept walking. The Falconer didn't know his plan to try to break the Shriker's
curse; he couldn't possibly know. "I'm aware of the dangers," he said at last.

The meer suddenly passed him and stood before
him on the trail. "Are you?" he asked sharply. "I hope
you are, boy." The Falconer's copper eyes were bright. He
looked down at him so fiercely that Miles's knees began
to quake.

THE ENOCH TREE

THE ENOCH TREE

Pier could not escape the Sylth Queen, though he ran two nights and a day. And when he fell exhausted to the earth, she gathered in her powers and turned the man to stone.

—"The Stone Man," a legend of Oth,
from *The Way Between Worlds*

Miles was still thinking on the Falconer's words two days later as he herded the sheep through the thick mist in the high meadow. The meer had never warned him so harshly before. Did the Falconer sense something about his plan?

He paced through the grass with his shepherd's crook. If he could hike to the giant bolder on Breal's Moon night, work the spell he'd found in his master's book aright, and find his way to the Sylth Queen, she might grant him a boon, a power spell to rid the world of the Shriker. If not, the very fact that he'd said the spell that opened the way to the sylth feast should prove he had the Gift and was worthy for Othlore. Once he arrived on the magic isle, he could search there for the spell. Either way he'd be sure to get his hands on the power he needed to break the Shriker's curse.

Hanna came up the hill with the lunch basket, her blue cloak floating ghostlike in the mist. Miles rested his shepherd's crook against an oak tree. "What have you brought me?"

"Mother and I baked all morning," said Hanna, puffing from her climb. "There's fresh barley bread and two kinds of cheese." She set the basket by the tree. "I've been just over the hill with Da's meal. He left most of the sweet cakes for us to eat." She started to unpack the lunch.

"Not here," said Miles. "Up there." He pointed to a sunny spot just above the mist, a high, stony cliff on the next ridge.

"Why so far up?"

Miles didn't answer. Instead he turned and went up the hill. He knew she'd follow, and soon he heard her footfalls behind him. He felt the need to flee the sheep and feel the sun on his face while he ate. The flock was safe enough grazing near the stream under the sheepdog's care. Koogan would bark if there was any trouble.

Climbing up the steep hill, Miles broke into the full sunlight, and it was like surfacing through lake water. He passed the maple and hiked a bit farther to the very top of the cliff. Above the fog light glinted off the cliff rocks. Higher up to his right the snow-covered peak of Mount Shalem sparkled blue white in the sun. Miles breathed in the fresh, green smells of spring as he looked out over the foothills. Here and there alders and pines poked out of the mist, but he couldn't make out Brim village or the harbor down below.

Miles licked his wind-chapped lips. He used to look forward to the monthly trip to town when he was younger, wishing with all his heart that he were a village boy, living near the harbor, where trade ships came to port, buying sweets on market day, playing games with his mates. He'd tried to make friends the few times he'd gone to town, but even in those days the village boys had been cold.

The one time they'd let him join their games, Gerald, Aven, Mic, and Cully had sent him back to "explore" a deep cave. Once he'd crept down the long passage, they'd run off laughing and left him in the dark. It had taken him more than an hour to find his way out. He shivered now with anger just remembering that.

He was glad the town below was mist covered. Glad he couldn't see the cottages, shops, and docks. "Come on, Hanna," he called. "The cliff is safe enough, and you'll like what you see." He thought to say, "You can't see Brim at all," but he decided to surprise her.

Down below Hanna stood in the sunlight, clinging to a maple tree.

"Come on up now, lazybones."

"I'm not lazy!"

"You are too!"

"I won't come, and you can't make me."

"Don't be stupid. It's a better view up here."

"Shut up, Miles!" Hanna lifted her hand and pointed at him. No, not at him, at something . . . behind him. The rocks underfoot made a grinding sound as he turned to see what she was looking at.

Miles's throat tightened. A stunted oak leaned over the cliff's edge. The tree was strangely formed, with thick roots snaking through the shallow soil, a broad trunk, two bent branches held aloft. But it was not so much the tree that held his gaze as what he saw inside: a man. It *was* a man, and not just the shape of one caught inside the tree. Miles was sure of that, for he could see the man's outline clearly, his arms outstretched inside the branches, his knees bent as if he were running, and all of him leaning forward like he was hell-bent on leaping off the cliff.

Blood sang in Miles's ears. *Run*, he thought, but his legs felt boneless.

"Hanna," he said in a hoarse whisper. Then louder still so Hanna could hear, "Remember Granda's tale of his brother, Enoch?"

No answer from below.

Miles cleared his throat. "I think we've found the Enoch Tree."

"Is he . . . dead?"

He peered harder at the oak. "Not dead—enspelled inside the tree. That's what Granda said."

A wind crossed the cliff, and the branches waved. Each ending in what looked like hands—wooden hands.

Miles's heart pounded in rhythm to the swaying arms. He couldn't stop looking at the form caught in the oak, but where was his face?

"Come away," said Hanna.

Miles didn't move. In the bright sun shadows from the windy leaves painted the tree trunk now gray, now black. As the shadows parted, a terrible face appeared. An old, cracked, wild-eyed face, the jaws open wide in a silent scream.

"eOwey protect us," whispered Miles through chattering teeth, but not so loud that Hanna would hear.

The breeze picked up. Branches creaked, and the face was swallowed in shadow again. Granda had said Enoch was sixteen years old when he was enspelled, but the man inside the oak looked very old. Had he aged right along with the tree?

He stared at his great-uncle, caught inside the tree, and shuddered.

"Come down by me," said Hanna.

Down the steep incline he met her under the maple branches. Hanna turned away from the Enoch Tree, gesturing toward it with her hand. "I can't look at *that* and eat, too." Miles took in her round face, her green eye and her blue. She hadn't run off, but was trying to be brave, and he was proud of her for that.

Hanna unpacked the bread. "It's not just a tree that looks like a man is caught inside?"

Miles turned. "Climb up with me and see for yourself." He was feeling braver now.

"Tell me." Hanna gulped. "Tell me it's just a tree."

"It's Enoch, Hanna. I'm sure of it."

"I don't want it to be!"

"It doesn't matter what you want! He's there. It's real and that's all."

Hanna leaped up and began to go.

"Wait," said Miles. "Don't leave." He sliced a bit of cheese. "Here, have some. We came all this way. Come on."

Hanna took the cheese. "I still don't like it," she muttered. She knelt down and tore herself some bread. "Granda never told us why . . . why it happened to his brother." She looked over at Miles. "The nights you took your turn sitting up with him when he was sick. Did Granda ever tell you more about Enoch then?"

Miles shook his head. She wasn't asking if they'd spoken about the Shriker, or his answer would have been different. "There's only what he said to us that day in the cave. That Enoch was banished from Othlore." Miles blushed with the thought. The shame of it. To be chosen for magic, only to be sent away from the meers' isle. He must have been a stupid boy to let his chance at magic slip away for good and all.

"Would the Sylth Queen imprison him for that?" asked Hanna.

"I don't see why she would hex him for something he'd done on the meers' isle. He must have done something here on Enness." Miles glanced quickly up the hill. The Enoch Tree leaned so far over the edge it seemed a single push would topple it right down. What was Enoch running from so very long ago? And why was he screaming?

He turned and chewed his meal. His cheeks swelled out with bread, but he felt a gnawing emptiness no bread could fill. Enoch's story was a mystery, like most of Granda's tales. Still, Enoch's ending was warning enough. If it was the Sylth Queen who hexed Enoch, he'd have to take extra care when he went to meet the sylth folk in Shalem Wood tomorrow night.

Miles tossed his crumbs to the ravens and watched the birds fight over them. The Falconer was so protective of his magic. If it weren't for that, he would never have had to steal the spell.

". . . must have been very bad," said Hanna.

"What?" Miles started. She couldn't hear his thoughts, he knew. He tried to see her expression, but her face was half hidden by her blowing hair.

"I said Enoch must have been very bad. Else why would the Sylth Queen have punished him?"

"Ah," said Miles. "Well, remember Granda didn't say it was her that hexed Enoch for sure." He needed the reminder more than she to keep up his courage to enter Shalem Wood.

Hanna peered up through the maple branches. "I know what Granda said was true," she said. "About the sylth folk and the magical Otherworld. I've always known it. But I'm not like you. I never wanted to be different or claim the part of Mother's clan with—"

"Magic in our past?" he said. "Don't you know how good magic can be?"

"How can you call it good? With Enoch caught like that inside a tree, with what happened to Rory Sheen and all that's come of that!"

"They were spoilers. They didn't know how to handle magic." Miles wanted to say, "It'll be different with me," but he stopped himself.

"It's not that I mind magic so much." Hanna paused and sent a single glance back at the Enoch Tree, then turned her head again. "It's the darker parts I mind."

She didn't speak the Shriker's name, but Miles knew well enough what she was thinking. Her face seemed pale, even here in the sun, and her brows were drawn. *I'll break the Shriker's curse, which holds us down,* he promised silently. *I'll free the Sheens forever.*

"The Shriker's not here, Hanna. It's daylight now, and if he comes at all, he comes only at night."

Hanna tried to brave a smile, failed, and started to pack up the basket. Miles leaped up and stretched against his tense muscles.

They left the island of sun for the misty lands below. The sheep baaed loudly when the two leaped over the shallow stream as if they were trespassers and strangers to the meadow.

DREAMWALK

DREAMWALK

*The dreamwalker finds the hidden way
when the world is dark.*

—A SAYING OF THE DESERT FOLK OF KANAYAR,
FROM *THE WAY BETWEEN WORLDS*

HANNA RACED THROUGH THE DARK FOREST. NOT FAR
behind she heard the pounding paws against the earth,
the ragged panting sounds coming from the beast's
bloody mouth. No stars or moon to guide her as she
flew. *Run faster now through the blowing trees! But which way?*
She ran uphill and down. The wind shrieked. The monster howled. The wild sounds clashed in the air. Joining
together, flooding Shalem Wood. The beast was nearly
on her. Paws pounding the forest floor, loud, louder.

"Hanna!" a child's voice called. She crashed head-
long into a tangled thicket. She was caught now, and the
beast was gaining on her. . . .

Hanna opened her eyes and found herself standing by the hearth, struggling with her wool blanket. She'd been dreamwalking again. Her little brother, Tymm, was crouched behind Da's high-backed chair.

"You called out," he said in a trembling voice.

"It's nothing, Tymm. I was only dreaming." She took his hand. "Come off to bed now." They crossed the room and climbed the creaking ladder to Tymm's sleeping loft. Cricket cages hung from the low ceiling, all woven by Tymm's deft fingers.

Tymm pulled the quilt up to his chin. "Why do you walk in your dreams?" he asked. "Is it because of your eyes?"

Hanna blushed. "It's nothing to do with that!" Her voice sounded sharper than she wanted. She took a slow breath to calm herself, then worked her face into a smile, the more to ease Tymm back to sleep again. "Now, it's off to the dream world with you, or Mother and Da will be angry with me for waking you." Tymm turned over on his cot, and Hanna climbed down the ladder.

Silence filled the cottage. She could wake Mother and Da and tell them her dreamwalk, but they worried enough over her strange visions. If Granda were still alive . . . Thinking of him made her eyes prick.

Wiping away the dampness with the back of her hand, she crossed the moonlit room and tiptoed down the hall toward Miles's door. It was rare to awaken from a dreamwalk without Miles at her side. Granda had taught him to listen out for her at night and follow her when she wandered off, lest she harm herself in some way. She often awoke in the garden with Miles's hand on her shoulder, a worried look written on his face.

It may have been the Breal's Moon celebration that tired him out and made him less attentive than usual. He'd played songs on his flute, recited the epic tale of Breal's heroic quest with Da over the twelve moon candles, lighted the flaming serpent's bread and shared it with the family after a day of fasting. But he shouldn't have been any more tired than she. She'd been the one to dip and form the round moon candles, each with a coin and cherry pit at its core—two days' work, that— and she'd gotten up at dawn with Mother to knead and shape the serpent's bread.

Turning the doorknob and sliding across the wooden slats, she felt her way along the floor.

"Miles?"

No answer. Hanna reached across his cot to waken him and found only a blanket roll. Her hand went cold.

Gone. Hanna worked to rein in her fear. It was nearly midnight by the moon's reading through the framed window. Where was he? Close by. He must be. He wouldn't have gone into Shalem Wood alone on a full-moon night, not after Granda's warning. Not after seeing the Enoch Tree only yesterday.

Through the thickened glass she watched for Miles's shadow crossing the garden and saw only her mother's wild roses waving in the soft spring air. There was hardly a breeze tonight, so why the keening in her dream?

Hanna paced the moonlit floor, the memory of the dreamwalk shadowing her. The thing that had chased her was larger than a bear, yet its howl was like that of a wolf. There was no living creature in all of Noor like that. A cur of monstrous size like . . .

The word "Shriker" came as a whisper, but it was strong enough to force her down. She bent over, placed both hands on Miles's cot, and let a series of shivers trail slowly up her spine. She wouldn't feel this chill fear if it had just been a dream, would she? Sitting on the bed, she pressed her forehead to the glass, closed her eyes, opened them again. "The dreamwalks aren't real," she whispered. But then there was the night last winter when she'd walked outside while dreaming and seen wild wolves attacking the fold. The next night a pack had come down the ravine and slaughtered fourteen sheep. Hanna's throat tightened at the memory. She'd seen the dead sheep lying in the field and smelled the rusting-metal scent of their spilled blood. That one had come true. But not all her dreamwalks had. She had to remember that.

Miles would help her settle her mind on the matter. Her vision might have been a wind dream, a forewarning of foul weather, only that and nothing more. She hoped it was so.

Tomorrow she was due to work in Brother Adolpho's garden, and she needed a full night's rest. Still, she slid the window open and felt the breeze whispering in. Miles might be around back by the well or just up the hill at Granda's grave. Feet over the sill and down to the earth, she closed the window behind her and crept outside.

The full moon glowed bright as a ship's lantern over Mount Shalem. Hanna tiptoed through Mother's garden, where the festival candles still burned in their clay pots, their waxen smell filling the night air.

Before Breal's Moon left the mountain, she had to find Miles, tell him her dreamwalk, rid herself of the strange, haunting fear that was pressing even now against her chest.

An hour later Hanna climbed back in through the window. Miles wasn't in the garden or by the well. He wasn't up the hill at Granda's grave. She'd checked the barn, too, and climbed the ladder to the loft; nothing there but piles of hay and a few startled owls. Back in her room she dried her damp feet, but the chill wouldn't leave her. Where was he?

*A sharpened weapon will not vanquish
the fear hidden in a man's own soul.*

—THE OTHIC ART OF MEDITATION

A MILE FROM THE COTTAGE, WHERE HANNA WAITED UP,
Miles crossed the meadow to the thick line of pine trees
guarding Shalem Wood. He watched the bracken for any
sign of movement, for golden eyes that might peer out
or the sudden gleam of teeth. But only branches stirred,
waving slow and sighing in the breeze as if swimming in
the deep of a dream.

Tucking his flute in its leather pouch, he checked
the trees again and adjusted the bow across his shoulder. He must wait a little longer to say the spell. He
played the words over in his mind, ancient Othic
words that were only sounds to him, and he wondered

not for the first time what they meant.

Once the spell was cast, there was to be some kind of magical path leading to the sylth gathering.

Miles skirted a fallen tree and leaped onto the flat gray bolder shaped like a giant's head. Standing on the moss that covered the stone like thick green hair, he gazed down the rolling foothills to the shore of Enness Isle.

A brisk wind slapped his cheek. Miles pulled up his hood. Midnight by the moon's reading. Time. Lifting his hands to the stars, he said the incantation, the words flowing smoothly from his tongue.

"*Evendera kalieanne. Mosura tan ahanaad.*" Taking a deep breath, he turned about. Nothing. No change. His body went cold. He didn't have the Gift. He dug his nails into his palms, his temples pounding.

Miles closed his eyes. Had there been more on the page? Had he . . . aye, he'd left out a word. He faced the sea again, lifted his hands, said the spell slowly, and with the new incantation he felt a warmth against his back. *By the giant's-head boulder under Breal's moonlight look to the way that opens in the night.*

Turning on his heels, he saw a gleam coming toward him from the woods. Across the hills and all the way to his boulder beads of light as large as stepping-stones spread in a long line before him, as if a giant's pearled necklace had fallen to the earth.

He laughed aloud. Here it was. The way to the sylth celebration. He had the Gift. He knew it!

Jumping down, he knelt beside the first glowing patch and touched the ground, half expecting to feel a soft roundness in the gleam, but his hands lit up and that was all. He took his first step onto the magical path. The soft light seemed to fill him as he walked, and set his skin to tingling. He followed the path across the grassy hill to the edge of the woods, then stepped between the tall pines and slender elms, his leather boots whispering against the forest floor.

With a knife hidden in his boot and a bow slung over his shoulder, Miles watched the edge of the path to his left and to his right. A rustle near the juniper bushes could mean sure battle with bear or wolf or mountain lion. But these were the least of his worries. It was the thought of meeting the Shriker that sent a blade of icy fear through his heart.

The farther he went, the more the trees drew close together, shutting out moon and stars. Soon darkness rose up all around him. It gave him a strange feeling, as if he were walking down a monstrous throat. The tall trees were spiked like rows of teeth. A wind's breath scoured past. He stopped to slow his heart and calm his fears. He had the beads of light to guide him to the sylth celebration, and that should be enough.

Magic awaited at the end of the light path if he had the courage for it. He was close now and couldn't turn back. The journey would be worth any danger if he found the sylth folk at the Breal's Moon gathering at its end. And if he should suddenly have to quit the woods? He spun round to check the way out and sucked in a shock of air. The pearling lights had all disappeared, and there was nothing but swallowing dark behind.

He must have cast the stolen spell wrongly somehow. Mispronounced it or left some other word out, else why would the lights be disappearing?

Miles turned and quickened his pace. Eyes watched him as he passed. Eyes he couldn't see in the pressing dark. And in the midst of the trees came a soft flutter, which could have been wings or branches waving in the wind.

The sense of increasing danger made him hurry along, as even now the lights before him faded. In this dense part of the forest he'd soon be completely lost without their soft glow. The cedars sighed along the path, and the myrtle bushes swayed.

A crackling sound from behind! Feet? Hooves? Paws? Miles raced ahead. The wind rose up, shifting from soft to sharp, knifing through the branches. It whistled like a boiling kettle, then pitched to a high scream. Like a wild woman with a broom, it beat against his back, driving him on and on until he ran into the deeps.

A granite boulder lay in the midst of the opening like a brooding giant hunched over in thought. Miles stood on the edge of the deeps, walled in on all sides by a circle of ancient trees. The pearl path faded, and night swelled up around him.

He drew his knife.

The blade had no gleam in the sudden dark.

*Ezryeah took up his walking stick
and left his homeland forever.*

—THE BOOK OF EOWEY

THE AIR WAS THICK AND COLD AS WELL WATER. MILES heard the sound of heavy breathing, which could have been his own or the close, cold breath of one ready to attack. The thought of coming face-to-face with the Shriker made him want to run, but in this dark to run was to stumble, and to stumble was to become sure prey.

Teeth clenched, knife drawn, he waited. His eyes had nearly adjusted to the dark when he saw sparkling lights darting in and out of the pine trees. He blinked, thinking these were but the lights that flew before the eyes when one was about to faint, but the vision did not change with the blinking. One, two, a dozen, more. They flew closer, until he was surrounded by sprites, each one no bigger than his hand. Their skin shone bright as candle flames new to the wick, their clothes were the leafing, flowering colors of woodland meadows. Some had bows, others polished swords that mirrored silver light.

In the cool air above the deeps, orbs began to bloom and lit the trees as if it were Noorfest Eve. Miles sheathed his knife and drew a breath to ease his shaking limbs.

A thrumming sound pulsed through the high branches. Something was coming. He could feel it, and though he didn't know what this thing would be, he felt a tingling run across his skin and down the backs of his arms.

Above his head sparks blew apart, then drew together again. Sprites swirled faster and faster, like bright leaves in the wind, and Miles saw a passage open high in the air in the very center of the deeps. Through the shining the sylth folk flew in twos and threes, making way for their queen. The sprites were two inches long, but the sylth folk were human size, as Miles knew they would be. But nothing in the common lore, nor anything he'd read in the spell book, prepared him for the sight of Queen

Shaleedyn borne up on her silver throne. Miles held his breath as the bearers, three on one side and three on the other, placed her throne on the high boulder in the center of the deeps. Light orbs drifted downward and hung in midair above her.

A soft wind encircled Miles, and he stood unable to move or speak, the presence of the queen washing over him, like a wave. Her dark hair was crowned in delicate purple blooms with shining webs strung between. A bracelet of pure sylth silver coiled up her left arm from wrist to elbow. Her skin shimmered, like stream water, and the colors of her gown were ever changing in the soft light. But it was the look in her lavender eyes that sent a sudden chill down his back. He'd seen that look once before, in the angry eyes of a mother mountain lion near her cub's den on Mount Shalem. Her eyes had been golden, and they'd held his death in them should he venture closer. The queen's eyes were night's answer to the pair of suns in the mountain lion's eyes, but they held the same wildness in them and had the same burning power.

Just below her crown a ruby-backed spider gently combed the queen's black hair. Its small legs worked carefully through her tresses; turning here and there, it wove silver threads prettily into the strands. Miles sighed watching the sprites and sylth folk gather beneath the forest canopy. It was as he'd dreamed it to be all the years of his life.

A deep howl broke the momentary spell, and he looked above the throne. The passage from Oth to Noor was swelling to greater size. The once bright tunnel was now bathed in red, and it seemed to be pulsing like an open wound.

The howl came again and louder. The stark call filled his ears like a lone wolf's cry; only the sound was deeper and more monstrous. The joining of a hundred wolves into one, the baying of the night itself when day has fled to the farthest end of the world.

A dozen sylths escaped the crimson passage, their faces drawn with terror.

"He's coming!" shouted one above the din. "Queen Shaleedyn! He's right behind us!"

The creature's howl echoed through the passage. It filled the deeps and the woods all round. Sweat spilled over Miles's brow. Was it the Shriker? Was he coming after them? He squinted against the salty drops, grabbed his bow, and tore an arrow from his quiver. Above him Queen Shaleedyn stood and twirled around, her dress flying out in a sudden, colorful waterfall. She held her hand up, calling, *"Kalass elandra!"*

Suddenly the passage shut with a thundering clap. The night's wound vanished, closing like a dungeon door, with the monster held behind.

The air shimmered. The sprites swirled over the queen's head like shooting stars, and the sylths all cheered, some lifting swords, *"Akabree tha Shaleedyn!"*

"Akabree tha!"

Miles felt like shouting too, though he did not know the words' meaning. Queen Shaleedyn adjusted her gown and sat again with a nod, as if she'd done nothing more than sweep a cobweb from the corner.

"Roses," called a sylth in a rust orange tunic. Seeds were tossed from many a hand. Some twisted scarves till droplets fell upon the darkened earth in a bright rain. Other sylths blew upon the earth about the stone, like bellows working to a fire. Then all drew back as a thick vine wended up the boulder and along the back of the silver throne; here and there wisteria bloomed among the roses.

The flowering brought others to the wood, as all around them tree spirits emerged. One by one the tall, moonlit deyas stepped out of their grandtrees. The tree spirits stood in a broad circle, some male, some female, each deya twelve feet high at least. Arms out and swaying, the deyas shimmered like a crown of fallen stars. The deyas bowed to the Sylth Queen. She, in turn, honored them with a single nod.

Miles tucked his arrow back in its quiver and went down on one knee, partly from respect and partly because he was trembling too much to stand. The queen's power awed him, and he could barely breathe in the presence of it.

"Human child. Who sent for you?" The queen's voice was clear as a dove's call, but there was a sharpness sheathed in the sound.

Miles found himself unable to answer. The queen's eyes narrowed. "If you have come uninvited from the world of men, show what gift you've brought us." She opened her hand.

Miles felt as if his bones were mash and his skin were no more than a water bag. He cursed his luck for having read only one page in the Falconer's book regarding the Sylth Queen. She expected a gift! Of course she would! Did she want gold or silver? He was poor, his pockets empty. All he'd brought was his flute. And it was hand carved, at that. He sensed her waiting above, though he could not gather the courage to look her once more in the face.

There'd been little he could steal from the Falconer's book, but Miles knew the lore surrounding the Sylth Queen. If she was displeased, she could freeze his flesh to winter's ice or root him forever within a tree, the way she'd imprisoned Enoch. He shook at the thought, his tongue already dry as a snake's, his skin suddenly wood-tight about his limbs. He licked his lips and said a quick prayer to eOwey before willing his stiff arm to move. Reaching slow with the weight of dread, he pulled the flute from its leather pouch. With trembling hand he lifted it in humble offering. *Let it be enough,* he prayed. *Let her understand.* For he still could not fetch any words from his mouth.

The queen gave a nod. "A musician," she said. "We have a human musician for the Breal's Moon dance!" She laughed, and all the sylths laughed with her. The sound struck him like the ringing of bells on prayer's morn. He felt a wave of relief, but still he kept his flute aloft, afraid to make a move just yet.

"Stand," ordered the queen. "You may yet be spared. Let us see what sort of music you have in you."

Miles stood, however slowly, on shaking legs.

Sweat broke out across his back. He found the notes and began to play. Not a single foot lifted, not a single wing fluttered. All stood planted as firmly on the forest floor as a row of wildflowers on a still summer's night. He took a breath and hesitated. The queen had said he may yet be spared. Spared from what? Miles glanced to his left, wondering if he could flee the dance and how he'd get back home without the pearling light if he managed to escape.

"Listen," said the queen.

Miles closed his eyes. A soft stirring then as he found, somewhere in the deeps, the faintest sigh of a breeze blowing a strange music through the woods. A dream-sung tune. The breeze blew about him, toyed with his hair, and filled his ears with sound. It was very soft at first, but it grew louder as he listened. Soon a steady beat filled his body. He chose a note and began to play, going he knew not where, but following the wind song the trees were bowing to.

He didn't open his eyes at first, but played on until he felt a rush of warmth brush past his face. A burst of color appeared when he dared at last to look. All around him sprites, deyas, and sylths were twirling. On the high boulder the queen sat swaying gently to his song. Miles flushed, feeling such a rush of pure joy that he nearly lost the melody. He shut his eyes again and danced his fingers along the wooden flute to find the tune. There it was. Strange. Beautiful. Like the Sylth Queen herself.

An hour passed, and two, and three, the best hours in all his life. He wanted more, but at last the queen held up her hand. The Oth folk and deyas settled in a great circle around her throne.

"I'm well pleased with the human boy." She reached out to adjust her silken sleeve, as if settling something in her mind.

"Speak your name," she said. "And tell us what you do."

"I am Miles Ferrell." He swallowed. "I am a shepherd." Miles winced. Why tell them that? He should have said he was studying to become a meer.

Silence descended, and Miles licked the sweat dewing his upper lip. What now?

"Turn around," said the queen.

Miles turned. *I will not tremble*, he thought, but a steady turning was hard won with his legs taut as spun rope and his feet suddenly heavy as well stones.

"Mileseryl," whispered the deyas. It was the first word he'd heard from them—his name blending into another sound, and he wondered at it.

Queen Shaleedyn surveyed the crowd. "The shepherd boy plays well," she said. "I shall bestow on him a gift."

Miles's heart leaped. A sylth gift was very rare indeed. This much he'd learned from the Falconer, when he'd spoken of such things. And now here he was, the chosen one! He stood at full attention, fearing to make a move or say a wrong word, lest she change her mind.

He passed his flute from his right hand to his left. In his mind the songs still echoed, and the happiness left a sweet taste in his mouth. What if she gave him an ervay, rarest of all flutes, made of pure sylth silver? Ah, what a gift that would be. One like the Falconer's or better! With a flute like that he could be a great musician and play in the palaces of kings!

Queen Shaleedyn clapped her hands. "Gather the rose petals," she ordered. The sylths flew up and plucked petals from the roses all about the throne. Then they busied themselves with tiny, feathered pens, and one by one the petals were writ with spells.

Not an ervay, then; it was a magical gift she had in mind. And that was so much better. If she gave him magic, there was only one thing he needed—power to destroy the beast that had haunted his family for the past three hundred years. He would choose that above any other wish.

A cooling wind blew through the deeps. Wings fluttered. The queen's dark hair lifted as if she were underwater. She tilted her head and listened to the breeze whispering through the green branches.

Queen Shaleedyn nodded thoughtfully, though not a soul had spoken, and she raised her hand. "The wind will choose the gift," she said.

Miles looked about. There were many wind spirits he knew: Noorushh, who rode the storm winds out at sea; Tygoss, from the southern reaches; and Wild Esper, who often rode the winds above Enness Isle. Was a wind spirit here to choose? No sign of anyone here, only a soft, lilting breeze.

The sylths held the rose petals in their open palms. With a wave of the queen's hand they tossed them high in the air. The breeze swirled, and the petals spun above the gathering, the golden letters showing against the rose red in the orb light. In a gentle gust they flew beyond the edge of night, but a single petal drifted down onto the queen's lap.

For a moment all was still.

"This is the gift, then," said the queen, lifting the petal from her gown. "Come kneel before me, boy."

Miles was relieved to be told what to do. He swiftly stored his flute and came to his knees before the queen's throne. He could not look away from her this time with the weight of his fate resting in her lap. Queen Shaleedyn held up the petal. She read the words silently at first, her brow shooting suddenly upward like a winged bird. It fell again suddenly but kept its thoughtful curve. The queen lifted the petal higher in the orb light, her dark hair still waving in the soft breeze. At last she seemed to come to a decision, and looking down at all below, she spoke the words aloud. "The spell is so written," she said. "He shall have the power to shape-shift."

Miles's mouth went dry. Shape-shifting was a rare

gift. In all of Noor few meers had ever had the power. But how could he use it against the Shriker? He wiped the sweat from his upper lip. His hand trembled as another thought struck him. The Shriker also had the power to change forms. Granda had said so.

There was a strange sound, like overlapping waves, as the sylth folk all through the deeps took a sudden breath. The sprites flitted in and out in agitation. And soon the sylths were whispering one to another, their wings lowered as if weights had been hung on the tips. Throughout the crowd Miles heard a single question repeated lip to ear.

"Who wrote the spell?"

And again, "Who wrote the spell?" Heads tipped. Hands were held to mouths. Still no one admitted to having written it. Miles kept as quiet as he could. His legs began to wobble. Indeed, he couldn't have stood just then if he tried.

The queen held out the petal and gazed down at her folk. "The wind has chosen," she said decidedly. The whispering stopped. Heads bowed, hands fell to their sides, the sylth folk tucked their wings behind broad backs and slender.

Queen Shaleedyn's face shone in the blue orb light. "Two things you must promise," she said to Miles.

"I'll promise anything."

"Anything?" The queen's eyes flashed. "You should not be so quick to promise when you don't yet know what I will ask!"

Miles's cheeks grew hot. Sylths murmured at his back. "I'm sorry," he said. "I didn't mean . . ."

"What do you mean, then, boy?"

"I mean to keep whatever promise I make," said Miles.

The queen observed him awhile, fingering the sapphires about her slender neck. The spider in her hair busily decorated the strands about her left ear. At last she gave a little nod. "First, promise me you'll use this power only in great need."

"I promise," said Miles.

"Second, promise you will keep this power secret."

Miles shifted on his knees. This was harder to agree to. How would the meers know to choose him to go to Othlore if he had to hide his power? If he couldn't even tell the Falconer? He would need to go there still. Go there soon to find the power to destroy the Shriker.

The gift the queen was offering wouldn't be enough to take the Shriker on.

"If you cannot promise this——," said the queen, folding her long fingers about the spell petal.

"I promise," Miles blurted out. He watched the tightly gripped petal half hidden in her hand, fiercely hoping she would not withdraw the gift. Another moment passed, and her hand opened outward, her fingers unfurling in the orb light.

"We follow the law of the Old Magic," warned the queen. "A promise made is a promise kept. Break it and our punishment is swift."

Miles trembled, thinking of Enoch. "I'll keep my word," he choked.

The queen gave a nod. "Stand and open your mouth."

Queen Shaleedyn leaned forward to place the rose petal on his tongue, and closing his mouth, he sucked the spell from the rose, swallowing its magic.

A slow fire filled his body. Miles swayed and closed his eyes. Crimson and golden colors pulsed behind his eyelids as the power and the heat flooded through him. The sylths began to hum a low sound like that of swarming bees. The deep-voiced deyas joined in. And from the throne above he heard the queen chanting:

"Follow where the blind are leading,
Listen where the mute are keening,
Where the deaf are storytelling,
Where the silent bells are knelling,
Take the road that splits asunder,
Nor left, nor right, but travel under,
Where the one self meets the other,
In the beast eye spy your brother,
One from two and strange combining
With the other intertwining."

Miles tumbled forward. His heart beat like the silent bells, his flesh parting as if a beast were pulling him asunder. He screamed, though no sound seared his throat. And the sylths all lifted suddenly to the sky like sparks flung from a fire.

Miles awoke to the shifting dark, felt his cheek and neck. The flesh fire was gone. His skin was cool, his heart now steadily beating. He stood up slowly, rubbed his arms and legs, and felt his strength return. The sylth folk, deyas, and sprites were gone, and the great gray stone was empty, but the scent of roses still filled the air. A single withered vine remained where the blooms had sprung up about the throne. It clung to the boulder, the leaves hanging dark and heavy as oiled hair.

Night was now far gone. Miles quit the deeps and took a path, narrow as a deer trail, in the silk moonlight. He followed a barely audible gurgling sound until he met a mountain stream. The night water was as golden black as spilled coins on a wool purse. He gulped mouthful after mouthful, then waited for the small pool to settle again.

In the stilled surface he studied his brown eyes, his lean face and disheveled dark hair. He was the same and not the same. The boy in the water trembled as a droplet fell from his chin to break the skin of water. Miles washed the smear of dirt by his nose and sat back on his haunches. A warm wind caressed his back. Something new was forming in him.

He closed his eyes. There it was. Taut and ready as a weapon to the hand. A new power. Coiled up like a serpent at the base of his spine.

Where the silent bells are knelling.

—SONG OF THE SYLTH QUEEN

HANNA LEANED AGAINST THE GATE AT THE EDGE OF THE kirk garden and watched the shell-white clouds cross the sky. Miles had seemed all gone over this morning. Hair askew and dark rings around his eyes, he'd walked unsteadily to the kitchen table, as if the floorboards were a rolling ship's deck and he must plant his feet to keep from falling.

At breakfast his eyes wandered here and there. He seemed unaware of Mother, Da, Tymm, or herself. Miles was usually hungry of a morn, but he hardly touched his oatmeal. He gazed at the tallow candle, then down at his dirt-stained hands. She watched him curl his fingers like a cat's claws, then sigh and look out the window.

"Where's your head, boy?" Da asked.

"Oh, here," said Miles, but Hanna could see it wasn't.

There'd been no time at all to ask Miles where he'd been so late last night or tell him her dreamwalk, and so she'd left the cottage troubled in her mind.

Across the busy garden Brother Adolpho handed Taunier a hoe as he talked around his smile. Hanna tried not to stare at the two of them, but she'd had a secret liking for Taunier, the fifteen-year-old blacksmith's apprentice, since he'd come to Enness Isle. Taunier's long hair was shining black, and his skin was brown as thool. He was both strong and handsome, but the real reason she liked him was because he'd greeted her often with a smile when she worshiped at kirk, and never had he commented on her eyes.

Brother Adolpho looked directly at Taunier, who was already as tall as the Brother. Hanna leaned against the gate. If she could take a moment of Brother Adolpho's time, she might speak with him today. Questions were crowding her mind, gathering many on many, the way the clouds were doing.

Taunier went to work with his hoe. Brother Adolpho entered the stone shed and came out with a trimming saw. Now was her chance. Basket in hand, she walked up the path past the workers. On the wood bench Brother Adolpho was cleaning the blade of his saw.

"Are you here to work, Hanna?"

"Aye. I brought my own basket."

He gazed at the other folk, who'd turned their backs as Hanna passed. "Well, let me see what we can do with you." He laid down the saw and rag, stood with a sigh, and rubbed his lower back. Hanna followed him into the shed, where he searched for seeds in the half dark.

"Marigold seeds," he mumbled. "And some poppies, too, I'm thinking."

They were alone now and she could ask him. "Brother Adolpho?"

"Aye?"

His back was still to her as he stepped into a single ray of light falling through the open door. She must ask one question first, before she could ask the others, but how could she put it into words? "Do you . . . believe in the Otherworld?"

He moved his hand along the shelves. "Do you

mean the peaceful afterworld of Eyeshala, where our souls go after death?"

She hesitated, and he turned and looked down at her. "Ah," he said. He peered through the door to see if they were quite alone. "You're speaking of Oth. A place full of sylth folk and sprites and unicorns and such."

Hanna nodded shyly.

"Why do you ask?"

"I need to know," she whispered. There was a fierceness hiding in her hushed tone.

"I see," he said. "Oth. Well, it's an unseen place, now isn't it?" He turned back to the shelves. "Not all the Brothers would agree with me, but it makes me think on the verse that begins, 'eOwey sang the worlds and in the song made all things seen and unseen.'"

Hanna remembered the verse, and her heart lightened. "And so . . . you believe?"

"I have faith enough to say it's a mystery." He reached for a cloth pouch. "There are so many worlds. More than just our own Noor. You only have to look at the stars to see that." He lifted his finger and stirred the dust motes floating in the streaming light. "A million suns and more, and many worlds circling them, no doubt." He handed her the pouch. "Marigolds," he said.

"May I have bluebells, too?" Hanna didn't want to leave the shed just yet and thought to make him search more.

"Bluebell seeds, is it?" he muttered, walking farther back into the shadows. The smell of turned earth filled the shed as he walked, a spring scent with the newness of life hidden in it.

Hanna swung the small seed pouch. She was glad to think the Brother had room in his mind for many worlds, the way Granda had, and she should have known he would, for the two had been close kith when Granda was alive.

"Bluebells, bluebells," Brother Adolpho sang to himself.

Hanna blinked in the dusky shed. It was a good verse he'd given her. She could believe that eOwey created all things seen and unseen. And she was content to think the great spirit made the sylths and the sprites, as much as the fish and fowl, and the animals and people of Noor. But then there were the others, and it was for them that she had come.

Waiting in the shadows, she felt the chill of her

dreamwalk visiting the shed. "Brother Adolpho?"

"I think these are the seeds," he said, turning round.

"If eOwey made all things," said Hanna, "what about . . ." She tightened her stomach against a sudden tumbling feeling.

"Ask," said Brother Adolpho. He said it gently, as if he could tell it was hard for her.

She licked her dry lips. "What about the evil ones?"

Brother Adolpho placed another small pouch in her basket. "You have more questions than I've got seeds today, Hanna."

She blushed and was glad for the half-light in the shed, making it too dim for him to see the color coming to her cheeks.

"I'll say this to your question. No creature begins evil. A babe is innocent enough when he comes into the world, though he may grow up to be a liar or a thief or worse." He walked into the sunlight, and Hanna followed him outside. They stood on the cobbles by the corner of the great stone kirk, where the stained-glass windows sparkled in the sun. "I know there's been talk in the town, but folk will always talk."

Brother Adolpho crossed his arms and smiled at all the workers in the foreyard. "Don't let your fears blind you to the beauty of the world, Hanna," he said.

Hanna tried to think on the beauty of the world a few moments later as she passed Mrs. Nye in the rows. "Sheen!" she hissed, as if the name itself were a curse.

"There goes the half-witch," said Mic behind her back. Hanna winced. *They can't harm me here in the garden,* she thought. But even as she made her way past Cully, she remembered the time last winter when the village boys had caught her talking to an oak tree and tied her to the trunk. "Well, now, we've captured the half-witch who likes to talk to trees!" they shouted, and, "We should burn her!"

Miles had come along and stopped their game. He was shorter than her captors but fiercer than all. He threw stones and sent most of them scurrying off. The last two he fought till they were bruised and bloody. But Miles wasn't here to fight for her today.

Hanna walked to the back side of the kirk, where Brother Adolpho wanted her to plant the seeds. He'd set her in a place apart. Was that to protect her from the villagers' cruel taunts? She crouched in the shadow of the bell tower, the bells all still and quiet now. "The beauty of the world," she whispered, but kneeling here so close to the back of the graveyard, where the woodland lost were buried, she felt this shadowed place like a hunger.

The graves set apart in the lone corner of the yard held the torn remains of the bodies found in Shalem Wood. The Shriker's victims, Granda had said. Some graves were three hundred years old, but the ones closest to the fence were newer. She wondered where the midwife's grave was. Was it close to Polly's?

No creature begins evil. Hadn't Brother Adolpho just told her that? Hanna spaded the soil. Thinking, and thinking more. In Granda's tale the Shriker was born a black bear hound, a breed raised up to guard the sheep on Enness Isle and Tyr. Bear hounds were fierce, but only to those who attacked the sheep or to strangers who came after their master. Loyal dogs, all of them, and born that way, so Da was fond of saying.

The Shriker was born a bear hound; it wasn't eOwey, but the Darro who changed him with his curse and turned him into a shape-shifter. She rubbed her temples, not caring that she soiled her face as she tried to dampen down the sudden pain. The thoughts were too big for her head, or too heavy to hold alone, especially here in the shadow of the hill. For no matter how he had begun, the Shriker was evil now. There were more gravestones here than she wanted to count. And these deaths were all his doing.

The sun began to dip behind the mountain in the rounding of the hour, and the day went darker gold. Hanna peered through the fence and saw posy of wild roses on one grave halfway up the hill. By its place among the others she thought it must be Polly's grave. Mother had told her that Brian Gowler had loved the girl, and he'd tried to court her after Tarn's death. But Polly had kept her shell bracelet like it was a wedding band. She'd stayed true to Tarn's memory, and she wouldn't have another.

Hanna lowered her head. The roses were Brian's, no doubt.

More seeds, and she must plant them for Brother Adolpho. She reached into the little sack. Behind her, wind sang through the branches of the apple tree—a strange sound like a woman moaning. Hanna looked up. Hadn't her dreamwalk begun something like this, with a low, keening wind just before the Shriker came?

Ezryeah could not speak for nine years after swallowing the fire.

—*The Book of eOwey*

Leaves fluttered in the apple tree. The wind picked up, and the song grew louder through the twisted branches, until it became shrill as a wolf's call. Hanna fought off a shiver as she plunged her spade into the ground. A long shadow came up behind her. She felt its coming with a rush of cold as the light disappeared. Leaping to her feet, she spun around and saw the tall, gray-caped figure of the Falconer.

Hanna gripped her seed basket and peered up at the old man. He was her brother's teacher, and a healer, but she'd always feared him, and whenever he came to visit their cottage, she stood apart.

"Daughter," he said. "You're all a-shiver."

"I'm all right," said Hanna, not letting on how unsettled she was. She straightened up as best she could, but the man was so tall her head still reached only to just above his middle. "I have a deal of work to do." She hoped these words would send the Falconer away, but he leaned against his walking stick, looking now and again up at the sky as if in watch for something.

"It's not the cold makes you shiver," said the Falconer, "but the nearness of these graves."

Hanna stood silent, unsure of what to make of his words. The Falconer raised his eyes to the sky once more. Then he lifted his forearm, which was wrapped in a thick brown leather band. A falcon soared from behind a spray of clouds. The bird slowly circled downward, growing larger as it flew closer to them. Then, with a flap of wings, Aetwan landed on his master's arm. She'd seen falconer and falcon together before, but never so close by, for Mother never let the bird inside the cottage. With the falcon sitting level to the old man's face, she saw now how alike they were. Both man and bird had dark eyes ringed in fiery gold, and both had heads that went from stillness to swiftness when they looked about, as if they saw invisible things moving all around them.

Hanna wanted to continue planting, but Aetwan stared at her with such wild eyes she couldn't move. Wind blew against the falcon's feathers and troubled the old man's hair. Both tipped their heads as if listening to a speech, though no one was speaking.

The Falconer leaned forward so close that his long nose nearly touched Hanna's brow. "You've heard the Shriker's call."

"I haven't." Hanna stepped back.

He kept her in his steady gaze. "Well, it's revenge he's after, and Sheens he's after more than most," he said. "You're to come to me when you hear the call."

Never, thought Hanna as the old man stood up tall again.

"Aye, you'll come to my place in the woods," said the Falconer. "I can see that much at least."

Hanna hoped he wasn't right, though some said he was a seer and could read the future. "I don't even know the way," said Hanna with a shrug.

"Your brother can show you, but not at night, mind. Make sure Miles brings you in daylight, when it's safe."

"Miles is busy most days," argued Hanna.

The Falconer laughed, then turned heel and disappeared faster than any old man had a right to. A cloud passed overhead, shadowing the grass at the old man's feet as he climbed the hill. Hanna felt a rush of anger. She swung her hands to and fro to rid herself of it. What right did he have to frighten her so? Why should he take it on himself to tell her what to do? She didn't have to go. She *wouldn't* go.

Lunging too quickly for the watering can beside the fence, she tore a long hole in her skirt on a rusty nail. "Oh, now look!" she cried to no one at all. Her best skirt torn, and she had only two. She couldn't risk walking past the teasing village boys in a torn skirt. She'd have to take the long way back to the road, where Miles would meet her with the horse and cart.

Hanna looked along the fence in the direction she would have to walk. It was the one way she didn't want to go, for it passed by the oldest part of the graveyard, and she could see it was a shadowed place.

WILD WOLF

The demons that followed them were as their own shadows.

—*The Book of Eowey*

AT SUNSET MILES HEADED DOWN MOUNTAIN TO MEET Hanna at the byway. His hands felt raw from his day's work trying to mend the broken cartwheel with Da. Hanna would be disappointed to see no cart to pick her up. It would be a long walk home.

High in a nearby fir tree a spinney bird sang out. It was a gentle tune, like one the Falconer played on his ervay. Miles stopped to listen. Spinney birds were rare, and each sang a slightly different song. The notes the male bird sang were clear and drawn out; they started high, then fell slowly, and as the notes cascaded down, Miles's heart fell with them. Then up they sprang again, the tune ending higher than it had begun. If he'd played a song like that for the Sylth Queen, what magic would she have given him then?

The bird's tune was left behind as the dirt road parted company with the forest and took him along the rolling foothills. Miles jammed his hands in his pockets. The full-moon had come and gone last night. There'd been no death in Shalem Wood. At least, he'd heard of none. In the deeps he'd seen the tunnel pulsing red, heard the Shriker's stark howl before Queen Shaleedyn slammed the passage shut. Her power and the magic flowing out on Breal's Moon must have kept the Shriker from his kill this once.

Granda had said Polly would be the first of many victims this time around if it was anything like before. But the Sylth Queen's power had bought Miles some time to gather the magic he needed to overcome the Shriker before his next return. He was grateful to the queen for that.

Miles quickened his pace, feeling the coil of power at the base of his spine the way he'd felt it in the deeps. Shape-shifting was a great gift, but he didn't see how it could be used to overcome the Shriker. He'd still have to sail to Othlore and learn more powerful magic to wield a breaking spell, but how? He couldn't impress the Falconer with his magical skill if he had to keep his power secret.

He was still puzzling over that when he rounded the bend and stopped to gaze down the broad dirt road. Hanna was at the byway, just as she'd promised to be, but there were others with her. Mic and Cully, he guessed, though only one boy held a torch. He was still too far away to be sure.

Miles started down the final hill. Mic and Cully were always after Hanna. Last spring they'd bound her to a tree, but he'd caught them in their game and beaten them hard till they both ran off screaming. He'd left the fight with a black eye, and he was proud enough to show it to Da, though it made his mother cry.

Near the north side of the high kirk wall Cully waved his torch. In the pale golden light Miles saw Hanna clinging to her skirt. The village boys had gone too far this time and torn it!

Mic danced around her, taunting, "A cape! The witch girl has a cape!" He came in closer. "Give us a kiss, witch girl!"

"Watch out, or she'll hex you with her evil eye!" Cully said.

"Ah," shouted Mic. "I'll have my kiss. She's a pretty enough witch." Hanna backed away, but he grabbed her torn skirt. "It's a cape. Take it off and wear it on your back!"

"Aye," called Cully, holding up his torch. "Take it off! It's not a skirt at all!"

Miles started running. He would pound them to the earth for this! He'd give them more than the evil eye! He'd blacken their eyes with his fists! He flew down the road, head throbbing, stomach churning. Skidding past a puddle, he fell, leaped up, regained his footing, and flung himself onward. Arms pumping, he raced till his skin began to burn.

Hot needles pricked his flesh. The strange feeling made him glance down. What he saw filled him with exhilaration and terror. Thick fur was growing along his forearms.

Miles sped up. More hot needles. Fur sprouted across his chest, his neck, his face. His jaw ached, as if a strong hand were tugging his teeth outward. His mouth grew longer and longer, forming a narrow snout.

Unable to run upright any longer, Miles hunched over. His hands curled to paws, and he fell on all fours. He should turn and run the other way before anyone saw him shape-shift. But anger drove him down the hill, and as he ran, he let out a warning snarl. Rounding a sharp curve, he pounded down the road toward Mic and Cully.

"Wolf!" screamed Hanna. The boys parted as if sliced by a knife.

Miles's nostrils filled with the thick, stark odor of their fear as he raced toward them. Cully waved his torch to frighten him off, but Miles ran fearless past the fire, heading straight for Mic, his brilliant, bounding muscles taut with speed. He leaped at the boy, knocking him to the ground. Planting his paws on Mic's chest, he went for him.

"Stop him!" Hanna screamed. "He's killing Mic!"

Miles tasted the blood in his mouth. He drew back, suddenly confused. Beneath him Mic was flattened on the road, clutching his bloody arm and moaning. He hadn't meant . . . This wasn't how . . .

A rock soared past.

"Get away!" screamed Cully. "Get away from him

now!" More rocks cascaded down, from Cully's hand, from Hanna's. One hit his back, another cut his neck.

"Hanna!" he cried, but it came out a yowl. Miles turned tail and ran back across the road, the long grass slapping his forelegs as he bounded uphill and down.

Cully tore after him, throwing more stones. "I'll kill you, monster!" he screamed. "Come back and see if I don't!" He chased Miles up to the tree line. Miles leaped over the bracken and bounded through the gorse bushes.

Feet pounded the forest floor behind him. Then from the road below he heard Hanna screaming, "Cully! Come back! Come help me with Mic!"

Miles kept running, one mile, two, though he knew by the silence in the woods behind that Cully had turned back long ago to help Hanna with Mic. He slowed his pace at last and sought cold comfort at Senowey River. Chest heaving, head bent, he lapped up the water, looking at his own wolf's eyes. His strange, long snout and shiny black nose. He drank again, washing the taste of blood from his mouth, then left the shore and waded out into the tumbling water.

He went in deep and deeper, until he was up to

his neck in the slow current. The heated wolf flesh slowly cooled in the swirling water. His arms and legs lengthened. His face softened. He stretched out his spine. Another moment in the rushing river and he knew he had changed back.

Rising up to a stand in the waist-high current, Miles touched his arms. He ran his hand along his smooth-skinned face and washed the blood from his wounded neck. The cut from Cully's rock stung, but it wasn't deep. He waded to a small pool near the shore, lay faceup in the shallows, then let himself sink down a second time. Through the water's surface the winking stars above wobbled like tiny chicks on unsure feet. Miles lay still a long while, as one dead. Finally, lungs aching, he burst through the surface and sucked in big gulps of air.

Back on shore he stood trembling. His legs felt thin. His knees wobbled with the strangeness of what had happened. Still, Mic had deserved the scare, hadn't he? He'd torn Hanna's skirt and called her a witch and . . . he'd been cruel. Cruel and stupid!

Miles shook the water from his hair the way he'd seen dogs do. Hanna always laughed when he did that.

But she wasn't here to laugh at him now. She was likely home with Mother and Da. At least, he hoped she was. He didn't dare go back down to the crossway to see.

The weight of the water clung to his clothes. On the rocky bank he pulled off his shirt and wrung the dense cloth, twisting harder and harder till the last drops stained the ground. He was dressing again when he heard a sound coming from a stand of copper beeches.

Miles pivoted, fear creeping up his back. It had been only one day since the queen gifted him with magic, and already he'd broken the first promise. He was to use his power only in great need. A torn skirt and teasing village boys couldn't be considered "great need." He knew they couldn't. But then, he hadn't willed the change. It wasn't so much that he'd used the power, but that the power had used him.

Looking to his left and right, he turned and retraced his steps, covering his paw tracks with the familiar shape of his own boot prints. He was all for the road now and with good reason. He remembered the look on Enoch's face there in the twisted oak, the terror in his eyes and his mouth torn in a scream. It was all that was left of a man who'd angered the Sylth Queen.

COVERING THE T

In the end all Rory could ever hear were the pad, pad *sounds of the hound's great paws everywhere he went.*

—THE LEGEND OF THE SHRIKER

TYMM RAN DOWN THE MOONLIT ROAD, WAVING HIS ARMS in warning. "Oh, you're in a deal of trouble!" he shouted. He ran once around Miles, as a puppy would, then tugged his arm to pull him toward the cottage. "Da's angry, and Mother's crying," he panted. "Hanna was attacked by a wolf while she waited for you at the byway."

Miles wanted to shout, "Not Hanna! I didn't touch her!" But he held his tongue.

"Da will likely whip you with the switch for being late to fetch her." Tymm skipped along happily. As the one who most often got a lashing, he seemed to welcome the idea of sharing the attention with his brother.

Miles entered the cottage and found Mother crying, just as Tymm had said. "Where's Hanna?" he asked.

"Where indeed!" boomed Da. "You were sent to meet your sister at the byway. What happened to you, boy?"

"I . . . I took a fall," said Miles.

"Look," said Mother, rising from her chair. "He's cut!"

"It's nothing," said Miles, reaching for his neck. "I washed the blood off in the river."

"And while you were having a little bath, your sister was attacked!" growled Da.

"And she was nearly kilt, wasn't she!" said Tymm, who now sat halfway up the ladder to the loft.

"Now, don't be saying that," scolded Mother. "The wolf only tore her skirt, but oh, to think what that creature might have done." She wiped a tear from her damp cheek.

Da crossed his arms and looked down at Miles, his face furrowed like a field before the planting. "I've told you time and again you're to care for your sister."

Miles wanted to shout, "But I *was* taking care of her. It was Mic and Cully who tore her skirt, and I ran down to help her." But he managed to clamp his mouth shut until the hot words cooled. Da turned his face away as if he was ashamed to look at him, and that hurt far more than a slap would have, or any stinging lashes with the willow switch, for that matter.

"Is Hanna in her room?" asked Miles.

"Aye," said Mother, "but she's likely sleeping now. I gave her some tamalla herb to calm her soul."

"I'll just go see." Miles took a candle from the table and went down the hall.

"Hanna?" he whispered, setting the candle down on the table by her cot.

Hanna turned over. "Oh, Miles. It was terrible. Where were you?" She blinked up at him, her eyes nearly matching colors in the candle's glow.

"I was on my way to you. But . . . the hour was late."

"Aye. Late. Did Da tell you about the wolf?"

Miles sat down on the edge of her cot. "He did. And more than told me."

"Aye, Da was terrible angry when Cully brought me home in the cart and told him what had happened."

"Cully?"

"He drove me home." She shook her head. "Poor Mic's arm was torn open, and broken besides. Oh, there was so much blood. His da had to send for the Falconer to medicine him. The Falconer had spent the night in Brim to tend little Effie's burns. He was only just on his way home when he turned back for Mic."

Miles put his head in his hands, trying to take it all in. He'd broken Mic's arm, and his teacher, his own teacher, had been called upon to cure him.

"How could you let Cully bring you home when he'd torn your skirt?" he asked hoarsely.

"He never did!" said Hanna. "Is that what Mother said? I tore it myself on the kirkyard fence."

"So Mic and Cully—"

"They were teasing me, as they ever do. I'd have kicked them in the shins if I could, but there were two of them." She frowned. Her face twitched, then she suddenly brightened. "But Cully was brave as ever in helping me stone the wolf."

"Oh, Hanna," sighed Miles.

She reached up and touched his arm. "I know you're sorry you weren't there to help me fight off the wolf, but Cully was there, so you needn't . . ."

Miles drew away from her touch and lurched toward the door.

"Where are you going?" asked Hanna. "I told you it's all right."

He half stumbled into the narrow hall, then shut his sister's door.

SPELL SONG

SPELL SONG

In the deeps of Shalem Wood he howls.

—THE LEGEND OF THE SHRIKER

HANNA ADDED BOILING WATER TO THE COLD WATER IN the basin, dipped a bowl in, and started to scrub. The water was too hot, but she dropped in the spoons with a clatter, working the suds to wash another bowl.

"Look now," said Da, scooting his chair closer to Miles. "My son's becoming a man."

"Whatever do you mean?" said Mother.

"Show her your neck, son," ordered Da.

"Ah," said Mother. "A beard's beginning. Come see, Hanna."

"Me first," shouted Tymm, leaping from his chair. He put his hand up to his brother's neck.

"Get back," warned Miles, slapping his hand away.

"Oh, let him see," said Mother. "It's not every day a boy gets a beard."

Hanna wiped her wet, raw hands on her apron and peered at Miles.

"Strange color," said Mother. "It's almost gray. And it's growing right over that cut you got a few weeks back."

"It's very thick for a starter," said Da proudly.

Hanna agreed with Mother. A strange-looking beard. Not dark brown like Miles's hair, or even red brown as she'd seen on many a farmer and fisherman. It didn't look so much like a man's beard as their sheepdog Koogan's thick fur. She frowned to herself, then catching Miles's wary eyes, lifted her lips to smile.

Tymm was dancing round the table, chanting, "It's not every day a boy gets a beard!" over and over until Mother made him sit again.

"Give my son some ale," said Da.

"Oh, he's much too young for that," Mother said.

"I say it's time." Da poured a tall mug for himself and a small one for Miles. "Take up your mug of tea, Mother," said Da. "And yours, too, Tymm and Hanna." They all raised their cups.

"To my son," said Da. "Soon to be a man!"

He plucked his fiddle from the wall. "Bring out your flute, son, and we'll play us a tune."

Miles shook his head. "Not tonight, Da."

Da replaced the fiddle, sat again and leaned forward with his elbows on his knees. Hanna stirred the fire. The cottage seemed all too silent without the evening's music, for she'd been used to Miles and her da playing most nights.

If Granda were still alive, he'd tell them all a story, whichever one they asked for but the Shriker's tale, and she'd never ask for that. She kneaded the memory of the Shriker's tale in her mind, pressing it down as she would press against rising bread dough, until it was well tucked in.

Mother patted Tymm's head. "Bedtime, little man."

Da yawned and stretched. "I'm all done in myself."

Hanna hung up the drying towel, kissed Mother and Da, and left the kitchen.

In her room she lit the candle and changed into her sleeping gown. The wool blanket felt heavy across her body; still, she shivered in her cot remembering the paddy paws that had followed Rory Sheen. And how his own dog, turned monster by the man's betrayal, had devoured him at last.

Miles had spent the last hours with Granda before he died. Had he told Miles more about the Shriker then? Were there some who heard his call, like the Falconer said? She wanted to ask Miles, but he'd gone strangely silent since the wolf attacked them on the byway. She knew it wasn't his fault, only that he was late to fetch her, but she hadn't been able to convince him of that. If she went to him with her questions now, he wouldn't speak with her, she knew that, too. So she pulled the blanket up to her chin, closed her eyes, and tried to sleep.

Over the next few nights, as the moon waxed from gibbous to full, Hanna began to notice a far-off sound. *The wolves are calling in the woods,* she thought. *They're howling at the moon, and that is all.* She did not go in search of the Falconer, as she'd been told, but kept the sound secret. It was only a wolf pack, after all.

Night on night she felt the call come louder. And soon there was another reason she kept the calling secret. There was music in the howl. A sad song that fingered down her throat, moving toward her heart. Soon it was the beauty of the song that made her keep it to herself, for she didn't want the tune to leave her.

As the moon swelled to fullness in the sky, the nocturnal song grew louder, deeper, richer, laying an enchantment on her. At last she fell under its magic spell. The song drew her from her bed. She slid outside her window and wandered through the garden gate.

Wrapped only in her sleeping gown, Hanna left the cottage for the trees.

THE DEEPS

THE DEEPS

And his moon call is a spell song
to those who come to die in his jaws.

—THE LEGEND OF THE SHRIKER

MILES COULDN'T FIND HIS SLEEP AND LEFT HIS COT TO pace the hall. Seeing Hanna's door open, he stepped inside, and his breath caught in his throat. Gone! How had she left without his hearing? How long had she been gone? No time to run back to his room, he slipped through Hanna's window. Hanna's dreamwalks rarely took her far before she woke. Never farther than the garden or the well. He was sure to find her. Still, he cursed himself for letting her get out, especially now.

Miles searched the garden. He'd learned not to startle her awake, but just guide her home. The one time he'd tried to wake her, she'd howled and wept into her

123

hands. He'd held her while she shook. She wouldn't tell him what she'd seen in her dreamwalk that night, more than to say, "The unicorn. The beautiful . . ." She choked and cried out. "Don't kill her!"

It had taken him all night to calm her down again. After that he'd never tried to awaken Hanna from her dreamwalks. His sister came awake peacefully enough when she did so on her own.

Miles checked the fence and the sheepfold. Not there. He hurried to the barn and looked in every stall. Gib flicked his tail and whinnied. Miles ran outside and circled the cottage. Not at the well, either. Now he was stumbling through the long grass toward Granda's grave on the high hill. He didn't shout her name, for in her dream she wouldn't hear his call, but he looked for some sign of her, anything to tell him where she'd gone.

Ten minutes later he was racing for the forest's edge. Not Shalem Wood. She couldn't have gone in there! He plunged into the trees, found a path. Kept running.

His feet pounded the forest floor, he heard his breath, his heart thundering in his ears. But the woods were strangely quiet. Stars spread out above and glittered cold silver over the trees.

He took the right-hand path. One he'd traveled with the Falconer only weeks before when they'd gone herbing. It was then he saw a flash of movement half a mile ahead. Hanna! It must be! What kind of dream would take the girl so far from home? Miles sped past white-barked elms and wizened oaks.

In the moonlight Hanna's sleeping gown was a pale silver color, her movements flowing as a leaf riding downriver. She traveled with a sureness of direction beyond the ken of a dreamwalker.

On she went, and her steps were gathering speed, but he should catch up to her soon. She changed direction suddenly and disappeared through the bracken. He couldn't lose her now!

Miles raced uphill and dived through the undergrowth, his sleeve catching on the brambles. Had she gone in here?

"Hanna!"

The name echoed through the wood. No answer from his sister, who was still lost in her dream.

Shadows moved, growing large, then small, as the moon went in and out behind the clouds. Leaves stirred in the maple trees, like so many small hands in warning.

And as he entered a cool, dank place in the wood, a rotten smell outran the wind. Miles's pulse quickened. The smell meant danger. He had to find her. Wake her up this time. Crying fit or no.

He must have left the trail at the wrong place. Fighting his way back through the brambles, he found the trail again. Ran farther up. A flash of white on his left. There!

"Stop," he called. Rushing to her from behind, he grabbed Hanna's arms. "Come away now!"

Hanna broke free and ran toward the towering pines. A swirling sound grew from somewhere near the giant boulder in the center of the deeps. A shadow rose from the forest floor. First came the giant head, then the broad shoulders and the long, furry back. The shadow grew darker, broader, until it formed a monstrous dog, bigger than a wild bear. He fixed his coal-bright eyes on Hanna. With his head raised, the black beast was six feet tall, if not seven, standing on all fours.

Miles saw all this in the time it took to heave a shudder, and he knew at the same moment he was looking at the Shriker.

Hanna held fast to the spot as the beast towered

over her. She seemed enspelled by his glowing eyes, for she did not move legs, nor feet, nor arms, nor mouth to free a scream.

Miles wanted to cry, "Run!" But the Shriker hadn't yet seen him. A weapon! He needed a weapon! In his haste to follow Hanna he hadn't brought his bow or knife, and he cursed himself for it. He must fight the thing, but with what? His bare hands?

A growl deep and low as the earth itself poured from the Shriker's throat. Miles's knees fairly went out from under him as the dog bared his fangs and narrowed his glowing eyes at Hanna.

Miles glanced about for something to fight him with. Anything. The pine to his right whispered in the wind, and he looked up. He'd attack the beast from above. He climbed up the ancient tree and scooted out onto a sturdy limb near the top. There he broke off a slender branch. He'd land on the Shriker's neck and thrust it deep into the beast's eye. Miles gazed down, stick in hand. Trembling.

On the ground below, the monster's head swayed back and forth over Hanna. He snarled and opened his jaws.

In a flash Miles leaped off the branch.

The beast moved as he plummeted down, and Miles saw that he'd leaped too far. Within a split second he'd miss the monster's back and be smashed to pieces on the boulder. Miles dropped the stick, clamped his jaw, spread his arms, and held a picture in his mind.

Aetwan.

Falcon.

Giant falcon.

Open.

Breathe.

There was a sudden prickling in his arms and a spreading of his flesh flat against the air. His arms lengthened, legs shortened, eyes sharpened. At the moment of change he swerved away, just inches from the boulder, and shot upward on giant falcon wings.

Miles swooped down low. With a searing cry he tore off a piece of the monster's ear. The Shriker howled, his jaws wide as a crack in the earth. He leaped up, clawing the air wildly, but Miles flew just above his reach. Pumping his broad wings, he circled the treetops, then dived again, ready for the kill.

Suddenly, down below, the Shriker shape-shifted,

his thick fur lengthening to feathers, his forelegs sprouting into giant wings. Miles watched with fear and wonder as the beast changed shape. He tore away from the earth with a strange ripping sound. Then he flung himself into flight, his deep growl rising to a falcon's cry.

Miles darted over the pines as the Shriker pumped behind. Turning suddenly about, he flew at his enemy. Crashing into the beast, he clawed his feathered chest with his sharp talons. The Shriker clawed him back, but Miles pumped his wings to stay in place long enough to gash the creature's left eye.

With a wide-beaked scream the enemy flew higher. He circled once, then threw his full weight at Miles, ripping off part of his wing.

Pain flooded Miles's body as huge, bloody feathers twirled to the forest floor. He struggled desperately to free himself, but the deadly talons were embedded in his flesh. With mighty screams, both creatures hurtled to the earth.

FALLING

*"I name you Shriker.
Shape-Shifter. Mighty Hunter."*

—THE LEGEND OF THE SHRIKER

HANNA STOOD BACK, SUCKING IN SMALL, FEARFUL BREATHS as she stared at the giant falcon sprawled on the moonlit ground. She'd seen Miles fall from the tree. Watched his body elongate, his arms growing into wings as he changed from boy to bird. It was this startling change that had finally torn her from her trance and woken her to the hideous beast swaying overhead.

The scream that was lodged inside her throat had escaped at last. She fled her attacker, then whirled round just in time to see the Shriker's transformation—quick as a shifting shadow—from monstrous dog to giant bird as he took off after Miles.

Bloody feathers fell, and the screeching was so loud she covered her ears. "Miles!" she cried. "He'll kill you! Come out of the falcon's form!" But Miles did not change back.

Less than ten feet away from her now a wounded falcon lay bleeding, but which one? How could she be sure in its present form if this wounded thing was brother or beast? Uncertain and shivering, she stood apart, held in place by fear.

In the woods not far away a misshapen shadow gathered into itself. It limped through the bracken, dark to darkness moving. Under the cover of night it vanished into the deeps. A smell of death and decay went with it, and a bitter hunger clung to its insides.

Night clouds swept across the sky, and the stars appeared as small and bright as scattered coins on the ocean floor. A gust of fresh wind filled the woods. Slowly the form beside the boulder changed, talons to feet, wings to arms, body to boy. And Hanna saw the familiar face of her own brother.

"Miles!" She ran and knelt beside him.

"I drew his blood," said Miles, smiling.

"As he drew yours." She tore the hem of her sleeping

gown, wrapped it around his bloody arm from shoulder to elbow, and tied it in place. The wound was deep, and blood seeped through the makeshift bandage. "You need help," said Hanna, suddenly afraid for him. "We must get home."

Miles reached up with his good arm. "Help me up."

She drew him slowly to his feet. And together they left the deeps.

They traveled for close to an hour, and still she wandered on unfamiliar ground. She knew Miles could find his way out of Shalem Wood anytime he was well and strong, but he was too weak to show her the way out now. Unsteady and silent, he walked with his head drooped. He seemed unaware of where they were and could barely lift his feet. She pressed her hand against his bloody bandage and guided him along.

Hanna found a trail at last and took it, hoping to find help, but the trail ended in a glade. She held Miles up, panting, trying to gather her strength. She must go on, for he was losing too much blood; even now she felt the sticky fluid on her hand where she pressed it against his shoulder.

Across the glade a knoll rose up with an ancient

cedar tree atop. Its broad trunk covered nearly the whole hill. Peering through the dark, she saw what looked to be an ivy-covered door set into the base of the hill. She dragged Miles up to it, wanting to knock, yet fearing what may be on the other side. Before she could decide what to do, the door swung open of its own accord and showed a blazing fire at the hearth within. Granda had told her trolls from Oth sometimes crept into Shalem Wood. Some were said to claim hollow hills or hermits' houses for shelter. Fearing dark magic, Hanna was about to turn from the dwelling, but Miles tore away from her, staggered into the room, and fell facedown upon the floor.

The Falconer stepped out, it seemed from the very wall, and hovered over Miles. So this was where Miles's teacher lived. Hanna caught a startled breath, then cried, "Help him. Can you, please?"

"We'll lay him over there," said the Falconer. Together they lifted Miles to the pallet against the far wall and covered him with a rough blanket. Hanna saw that the walls themselves were nothing but dirt and stone, and the place where the Falconer hung his cloak was a simple jutting root.

"It's his arm," said Hanna.

"Ah, it's more than that," said the Falconer, unwrapping the bloody rag. "You'll bring me a bowl of warm water from the pot, and the clean cloth on the table." Hanna did as she was told. The Falconer rubbed a spiky leaf between his hands, then carefully bathed Miles's arm. She bit her lip as the glowing firelight revealed how deep the wounds were. The Shriker's talons had cut three gashes from shoulder to elbow. All in a straight line, like furrows in the soil. Halfway down Miles's arm a bit of white bone showed through. Her stomach tightened at the sight.

Fearing she might be sick, Hanna turned her back, but the Falconer pressed the washing leaf to her, saying, "Wipe your hands with this." She scrubbed her hands with the rough leaf, which felt like moist sand on her palms and smelled like winterleaf. When she looked back at the pallet, the Falconer was rinsing his cloth in the water bowl. The water had gone from pink to red. He cleaned the wound again. Miles moaned as the old man worked.

"You're hurting him."

The Falconer paid her no mind at all. Laying the cloth aside, he left the room and returned with a tincture bottle. ORASIAN, the label said. He measured out a bright orange spoonful and gave it to Miles. Next he took a piece of moldy bread from the cupboard, scraped the mold onto a dry cloth, and brought it to the cot.

"What are you doing?" asked Hanna in alarm.

"I'll be protecting the wound against after-ill if you move aside."

"With moldy bread?"

"Ah, and there may not be enough, at that."

"You'll poison him," cried Hanna.

"He's already poisoned, if I know the claw that tore the boy. Now, you'll hold his arm for me while I apply it if you're wanting to keep your brother."

"Promise you'll heal him."

The Falconer's look softened. "There's none can promise that, Hanna. But I can try."

Against the rough covers Miles's face had gone gray, and his features had the same lost look as Granda's had before he died. Hanna felt suddenly more afraid than ever. And she quickly did what she was told.

The Falconer applied the green powder to the edges of the wound. "Now," he said, "press the wound together, so."

She held the skin together while the healer plucked leaves from a bundle hanging from his ceiling. *Heal him, heal him,* she thought as the Falconer moved about slowly and deliberately. *You're a leafer and you can.* But she knew too that the wounds were of another kind altogether, and herbs might not be enough.

The healer softened long green leaves with steam from his boiling kettle, then cooled them in the air. "Stitch leaves," he said. "Hold his arm steady while I lay them on the wounds, and keep a good grip on his arm until they dry. The stitch leaves will knit the wounds together better than any sutures could."

Hanna held Miles's arm. She watched his face, heard his shallow breathing. *It's my fault he's hurt so,* she thought, and with the thought tears came. She drew her head back a little so they wouldn't fall on Miles or on the Falconer's hands as he worked.

When the stitch leaves were dry, the leafer wrapped the wounded arm in pale cloth, shoulder to elbow, to wrist. Hanna stepped back, watching, waiting. The Falconer spoke quiet words over her brother in the Othic tongue. She heard the name of the Maker, eOwey, and the word *abathan,* "peace." So she thought he must be saying a kind of prayer, though she couldn't understand the other words or why he paused between the saying of each line to lift his hands to the four directions. All was new to her. The leafer had come to tend Granda, and he and Old Gurty had brought herbs to Mother when her throat pained her, but Hanna had never watched them at their work.

Last the Falconer leaned over and blew a long breath at Miles's heart, as if to liven the coals in a fire. In the blowing was a sound, too deep and too rich to come from a single voice. The breath sound was like the chants Brother Adolpho led in the worship hall of the kirk, where many voices sang the Konor-duvan, the making chant, which held both the making and receiving in it. But the Falconer's call was other than this, and she suddenly knew what she was hearing. The sound the Falconer brought forth was Miles's keth-kara. He was giving Miles his pure self-sound. The song eOwey had sung at Miles's beginning.

Hanna knew that a holy one might pass on a keth-kara at a time of blessing. She'd seen Brother Adolpho sing a keth-kara in a coming-of-age ceremony at the kirk once or twice, but she didn't know the Falconer was trained in such mysteries. Hanna thought this all in a moment, but her wonderings vanished when she saw Miles's face begin to change.

First a rosey color came to his lips and cheeks, then his eyelids twitched as if he was dreaming. Hanna settled into the low sound the Falconer was calling. Miles's keth-kara was like an underground river finding its way to the surface, then rushing clear over the land. And it was like a low wind that swept across the dales in winter, swirling snow flurries up into the trees. And it was like nothing at all she'd ever heard. But it was beautiful.

At last Miles turned his head and his eyes fluttered open. "Ervay," he whispered.

The Falconer nodded to him and then to Hanna. "He'll live," he said. He turned, stiffly, seeming very old indeed now. The rushlight on the table shone across his face and lit the beads of sweat yellow-bright above his brows. Crossing to the alcove, he reached for his Y-shaped flute and began to play the slender silver ervay. Hanna fell back in the bent-willow chair, feeling now some hope, and with that hope a tiredness from the strange and hard encounters of the night. Her legs ached and her arms, and her head felt heavy.

This was the first time she'd ever heard the ervay. She knew at once why Miles loved it so and why he longed to play it himself, for it was indeed magic. Her breath grew shallow as the Falconer fingered the double pipes, sending both tune and harmony into the air. A sound like birds calling from tree to tree, or small waves rolling up to shore. So it was forest and sea both in one song. She watched Miles on his pallet, a look of peace and pleasure on his face as he listened. After another song Miles closed his eyes and drifted into untroubled sleep.

The Falconer polished the ervay and hung it back on the wall above his books. It was very quiet inside his house now with Miles asleep, and the falcon on his perch sleeping also. The old man took the blackened kettle from its iron hook and poured a cup of thick brown liquid. "Thool?" he asked.

Hanna wiped her eyes with her dirty sleeve and nodded gratefully. The thick drink would warm her dry throat. As she drank the sweet, hot thool, the Falconer sat before the fire.

The peace she'd felt a moment before deserted her now as she looked at the tilt of the old man's head.

He was waiting to hear why they were out so late in Shalem Wood and how Miles came to be wounded. She swallowed, put down the mug, and pressed her lips together. How could she form words around what happened in the deeps? It had begun like a bad dream-walk, but this time the monster was real, real enough to attack Miles and nearly kill him. Then Miles changed into a falcon. He'd actually changed shape in midair. She blinked at the strange memory. It couldn't be so, yet it was so. Where could Miles have gotten such a power?

The Falconer took out his tinderbox and lit his pipe. Could she trust the old man with this strange tale? He'd helped Miles with his wound, and he seemed trustworthy enough, but how could she explain to him, explain to anyone, what she'd seen?

She squinted at the blazing fire and tried to calm herself.

"You should have come before now," said the Falconer.

Hanna started. "I couldn't come," she sputtered. It was only a half-truth. She'd stayed away on purpose, for she was unsettled by the Falconer's warning that day near the graveyard and wary of Shalem Wood even in the daylight hours since Polly's death. "I brought Miles here," she added, though she didn't say she'd only happened upon his dwelling.

The old man looked across the room at Miles. "A clever boy," he said. "And dangerous."

"Miles is not dangerous!"

"Power is," said the Falconer. He leaned back and puffed his pipe. Smoke rose in a thin gray tree above his head.

Hanna stared at the Falconer's golden eyes, then looked away. "Do you know what happened in the woods?" she whispered.

"I was not there, but I have other ways of seeing."

Aetwan stirred on his post, stretched out his neck, then settled again. The Falconer leaned forward. "There are powers at work here and mysteries beyond our knowing. You're in a deal of danger. One look at your brother tells me that." He rapped his pipe against the wood. *Crack, crack.* "I'll be of aid if I can. But I'll need to know all of it, and from the beginning."

Hanna tore at her nail, an old habit she was finding hard to break. "I don't know where it begins," she said.

"Not for myself and not for Miles. How can I tell you what I don't know myself?"

Her answer came with such force of emotion that Miles awoke with a start and sat up. "Hanna!"

She leaped from her chair and rushed over to him. Miles gave her a warning look that said, *Don't tell.* He brought his legs over the side of the pallet. "We have to leave," he said through gritted teeth.

The Falconer shook his head. "You're weak and should stay abed longer." But Miles was already standing, with his hand against the table for support. "We should go now, before Mother and Da find us missing."

Hanna wavered between them. Feeling the strength washing from one to the other like waves caught in the tide pools. She wanted to stay and find the help the Falconer was offering. But more than that she wanted to go with Miles—leave the underground dwelling and the dark dream of this night behind.

Seeing that they were clear on going, the Falconer took hold of his walking stick.

"It's nearly daylight," Miles said, glancing out the window. "We'll find our own way home."

Hanna lifted the latch, opened the door, and

turned for one last look. "Thank you for your kind help," she said.

The Falconer sat to face the fire again. "Aetwan will accompany you," he said with a backward wave of his hand. And before they could protest, Aetwan flapped his wings and flew into the predawn forest.

Miles stepped outside, gripping his injured arm. The door closed with a *click*, and they started for home.

The sky above was the deepest blue, and the stars were bright against it. Soon the sun would rise above the ocean. They walked through the damp woods, pungent with evergreens and the dusky smell of earth. Just beyond the babbling brook Aetwan landed on a branch above the trail and folded his wings. Hanna was about to step beneath him when the bird gave a sharp cry. She stopped short and looked up. Aetwan cocked his head and peered at Miles.

"Change thrice and you free dark power," cried Aetwan.

Hanna jumped back, surprised. Miles stood, mouth agape, his dark eyes shining.

"Come on," croaked Miles. He took Hanna's hand and pulled her under the branch.

Aetwan squawked again, "Change thrice and you free dark power."

"Falcons can't speak," said Hanna, though of course Aetwan just had. The words "dark power" still echoed in her ears.

Miles tugged her down the trail, still weak from his battle, but strong enough to know his own mind. On they went under the forest canopy, with fear behind them and home before them, and they did not look back.

TRUTH TELLING

TRUTH TELLING

Bite the tender tips of bitter grass,
and you cannot tell a lie.

—*Entor's Herbal*

Mother left Miles on his cot, shut the door, and led Hanna to the kitchen. Taking her seat in the firelight, Hanna leaned up to the table with folded hands.

Da scooted his chair up beside her. "Tell us what happened, daughter."

"I . . . I went into the woods," she said. Her tongue felt thick in her mouth. "There was a song I was following."

"What sort of song?" asked Mother.

"I don't rightly know. A calling song. I followed it, and Miles must have come after me."

Mother dropped a handful of chamomile into the

kettle, stirring the dried flowers in the boiling water until the room filled with the smell. Chamomile was her cure-all, and she was making plenty of it now for Miles. Hanna leaned against the edge of the table, feeling the pressure in her ribs. It would be hard to tell the next part. Mother hated any mention of the Shriker. She said she didn't believe in the beast, but she'd lived under the weight of the Shriker's curse all her life. Any word at all about him was sure to upset her.

Hanna set her jaw. Pulling out the words would be like hauling stones from the earth, but she tried well enough. "The next thing I knew, the Sh . . ." She bit her lip and looked down at the floor.

"Go on, Hanna," said Da, patting her hand.

His touch gave her courage. She wanted to tell. Had to tell, the darkness of the beast was still so heavy on her. "The Shriker was swaying over me."

Mother spun round. "The Shriker," she gasped. "The beast's not real. We've told you that and told you!"

"A *wolf*, you mean," corrected Da, his brows tilting.

"Aye. A wolf," said Mother. "I knew it. It must be the very same one who killed poor Polly and then attacked young Mic."

Hanna started. "Not a wolf. The Shriker. It's true! And Miles will say the same when he's well enough. It was he who changed himself into a giant falcon to fight the monster."

Da looked at Hanna with disbelief, then he let out a hearty laugh. "Miles changed himself into a falcon?"

Mother crossed the room. "Oh, my poor Hanna," she cooed. "What terrible dreams you have." She shook the honey spoon at Da. "It's all those stories Granda used to tell her. My father filled the poor child's head with it all."

"No," cried Hanna. "It's nothing to do with Granda's stories. And I'm not a child. I'm thirteen now, and I know what I saw!" Hanna sucked in a breath. She'd never spoken to her mother that way before, but to have all the fears she'd faced last night dismissed as a dream was too much to bear.

"Please," she said. "There's more. I . . ." She sat on her trembling hands, then plunged into the rest of her story. "After Miles changed into a falcon, the Shriker leaped up and grew wings too, so there were two giant falcons fighting in midair. When the battle was over, Miles fell to the ground and changed back into himself again, and I took him to the Falconer's so he could dress the wound."

"No more of that, Hanna!" Mother's eyes were wild: Fear or anger, Hanna could not tell which. Mother leaned over and pressed her hands against the table as if she were pushing down the words Hanna had just said. "Don't breathe a word of that story," she whispered. "Not to another soul. Not with your mismatched eyes and all. Or the townsfolk will think you're a . . ." Her lip trembled.

"Now, Mother, don't go on about that," said Da.

Hanna shivered as if her chair were ice, but Mother *would* go on.

Mother straightened up standing behind Hanna's chair. She looked at Da. "The townsfolk hadn't taunted us in years, Keith, and we had a right proper family, but when the midwife died the night our girl was born, and when they saw the child themselves, saw that she was . . . different . . ."

Mother began to weep. Hanna shook below her as if her mother had released a storm. She wanted to speak, but the words caught in her throat. *Ice,* she thought, *I'm covered in ice.* Her teeth began to chatter.

Da stood, then stepped between them. "Now look how you're upsetting our girl, Mother!"

Mother wept all the louder. But Da took her shoulders in his hands, and none too gently. "Don't go blaming Hanna for the way she was born or for the townsfolk's backward thinking. The color of her eyes means nothing at all, no more than the Shriker's tale. It's all the old legends that haunt our isle and keep us down. You know that."

"I know," said Mother. "I know." Her words saying one thing, and her tears another. Hanna wanted to believe the words, but the tears and the years of resentment behind them were stronger. They were only salt water, but cutting all the same. Suddenly Hanna felt very alone. She longed to go back to the Falconer's. He'd *asked* her to tell him what happened. He'd believe her story, she was sure.

Da let go of Mother's shoulders and patted her back. "Well now," he said, "our girl had a bad dream, and that's all."

"Aye," whispered Mother. She wiped her eyes with her apron.

"If the tea's ready, pour some for me and for your daughter."

"I'll just be dripping in some honey," said Mother with a sniff.

Da touched Hanna's cheek with his forefinger, trying to draw her gaze upward, but she kept her eyes on the clean swept floor, the table legs, anything but her da's face. Mother filled his cup, then Hanna's, as Da sat down again.

"It was good you woke up from your dream to help your brother, Hanna."

"It was," said Miles, stepping through the kitchen doorway.

Mother turned, splashing tea upon the floor. "Son. You should be abed."

Miles cradled his hurt arm and leaned against the doorsill. "I'll be all right."

"Hanna was just telling us her dreamwalk," said Da.

Hanna looked at Miles's pale face. She wasn't sure how long he'd been listening to them from the doorway. "I told them what we saw in the deeps," she said. "Tell them, Miles." It was a plea wrapped in a command. She needed his support more than ever. Hanna waited, knotting her fingers together over her lap as if to tie something in place.

"I saw Hanna was missing, and I went after her.

She'd gone a long way this time before I caught up with her, far into the wood."

"And when did the wolf come after you?" asked Da.

"We were in the darkest part of the forest when we were attacked."

Hanna looked at Miles through a blur of unshed tears. He would tell them now and they'd believe her story. Miles tugged on his bandage, his face still gray with pain. *Tell them*, thought Hanna. *Tell them true.* He gazed back at her, eyes fixed.

"Do you think it was the same wolf that broke Mic's arm, son?" asked Mother.

"What?" said Miles in a startled voice. "How would I know? I didn't see Mic's attack. I was up the road and all." He sighed and rubbed the stubble on his neck.

"To my mind it must be the same wolf," said Da.

"But it wasn't a wolf," cried Hanna. "A huge, wild dog! A beast . . . it was the Shriker!"

"Hush, now, with your ramblings, Hanna," said Mother. "You'll be upsetting your brother all the more, and he's still in pain."

The room seemed to swirl about her. Hanna leaned

against the table and pressed her feet to the floor.

"It was a wolf, Hanna," said Miles. His head was tipped as if he felt sorry to tell her, but his eyes were hard.

"I wasn't dreaming," cried Hanna. "You fought the Shriker! You know it's true!"

Da got up and went to the door.

"Where are you off to?" asked Mother.

"The Shriker's legend has terrorized the villagers long enough. It's a *real* wolf we're after, and he's a man killer. First Polly Downs, then Mic, now he's gone after Miles and Hanna." He took his cloak from the sill thorn hook. "This lone wolf has to be destroyed before he attacks again."

Da slipped on his cloak, the dark brown taking in the window light. "Can you tell me where you were, son?"

"The woods were dark." Miles tilted his brows in thought. "There was a large boulder there."

Hanna set her jaw. So, he recalled the boulder well enough!

"Aye, well there are boulders everywhere on Mount Shalem," sighed Da. "I'll take the cart to Brim and fetch some men. Mic's da will want to kill the wolf, for one, and I've no doubt there'll be a few others brave enough to come." He pulled on his boots. "The Falconer will want to help us track him too, I'm bound."

"No," said Miles, suddenly stepping to the table. "The leafer won't be home, Da. I'm sure this is the day he crosses over to Tyr Isle to tend the sick there."

Da donned his hat and opened the door. "Well, I may be able to catch him down at the docks."

"Come, son," said Mother, reaching out her hand. "Let me put you back to bed." Two shadows passed along the wall as Mother guided Miles from the room.

Alone in the kitchen, the low fire sparking red as old blood in the woodstove, Hanna put her head in her hands. She pressed the heels of her palms into her eyes and felt their coolness against her lids. A sob climbed up her throat. She set it free. Another followed. Miles had lied. He'd lied.

She breathed in and out, trying to quell her anger. At last she leaped up and headed for Miles's room. She'd make him tell the truth before Da left to gather the hunters.

Down the hall Miles lay in bed, his eyes to the window.

"Why did you do that?" cried Hanna.

"Do what?"

"You know what, you liar!" She started for his bed, but Mother swept through the door.

"Hanna, leave your brother be!" she shouted. "He's hurt and he needs his rest. Go on with you!"

Hanna ran to her room, threw on her cloak, and raced outside. Da was hitching Gib to the cart. She worked to stop her trembling, sniffed, and wiped her eyes with the back of her hand. "Will you take me with you?"

"Why ever for?"

"I want to go." Hanna looked at her da, saying this and no more, for she couldn't tell him she needed to see the Falconer. Da climbed into the cart. "Now, Hanna, a young miss isn't wanted on a wolf hunt."

He'd said "young miss," not "child." It might be he'd heard that part of what she'd said in the kitchen. She wished he'd believed the rest, too, but he was a man of the real world, and he'd never believe in the Old Ways.

"I just want to come to Brim. You can bring me back here before you start the hunt."

Da rubbed his neck and gazed up at the clouds. "I will be passing back this way," he admitted. Then with a shrug, "All right, Hanna. But tell your mother you'll be coming along."

Five minutes later Hanna returned with the market basket. She climbed up the cart steps and settled herself on the high seat next to Da. Da jiggled the reins, and Gib started down the dirt track. "What's the basket for?"

"Mother wants some salt for the baking and tamalla herb to help Miles sleep off the pain." She settled the basket in her lap. "I'll get what herbs I can at Gurty's stall."

Gib rounded a bend, and the cart bounced up and down on the rutted road. Hanna wiggled on the hard seat. Her legs and arms were still sore from helping Miles hobble through the woods hour after hour last night.

From her high perch she watched the meadow grass swaying in the morning wind. Mother and Da had called it all a dreamwalk. But it hadn't been a dream. She was sure. Still, why had Miles sided with them? Miles's lie stung as much as Mother's words. *We had a right proper family, but when the midwife died the night our girl was born, and*

when they saw the child themselves . . . saw the child themselves . . .
The words spun round and round in her head in time
with the cartwheels below. She would never belong,
with her mismatched eyes and her strange dreamwalks.
Never grow up and marry and have a family of her own.
She wanted that as much as any girl.

"Your brother was brave to fight the wolf," said Da.

"What? Oh," she said. "Aye, he's brave." She managed to say that, but nothing more, the words "He lied!"
waiting to leap off her tongue.

Hanna ran her hand along the mending stitches in
her skirt: only the smallest of stitches now where the tear
had been. She felt alone, even sitting close to Da, and as
they neared the town, she hoped it wasn't too late to find
the Falconer.

Down by the docks Old Sim lowered the net he
was mending. "Oh, well now, you've missed the leafer.
He just took Skep's boat. If you look out yonder," he
said, pointing his large-knuckled hand out to sea, "you
can see him yet."

Hanna stood beside her da and gazed beyond the
docks to the swelling water. A small boat was sailing
toward the little offshore island, and the day was clear

enough to see the Falconer sitting tall and gray-caped in the stern.

"He should be back tonight," said Sim. "If there aren't too many gone down with a fever and such on Tyr."

Da gave a quick nod. "Thank you kindly." He patted Hanna's back. "You buy what Mother needs at the stalls, and we'll meet back here, daughter." He turned stiffly and headed up the road for Mic's cottage.

Up at the market Gurty had but a single bundle of tamalla, and the price was very dear. "That'll be three drena coins," she said, and she wouldn't bargain lower. The bag of salt sold for much less, thank goodness, and Hanna was back down at the shore long before her da arrived.

Slipping off her boots, she crossed the wet sand and bent to retrieve a clamshell and a moon shell, both broken. A half treasure, Granda used to call them, but Hanna gathered even broken shells sometimes.

A rushing wave brought seaweed to her feet. The long strands tickled her bare legs, wrapping them in wet green ribbon. She shivered and danced about to free her feet, running from the foamy wave, but a round shape tangled in the green made her turn and look again.

Another wave came, stole the seaweed and the stone. It was a stone, wasn't it? Hanna dropped her shells and ran closer. The wave receded, and just as the stone was rolling away, she swept it from the shallows and held it in her open palm.

Wet foam hissed softly along the sand. Water washed about her bare legs, rooting her feet deeper in the sand, but she stood still, looking at her treasure. The stone was egg shaped, a blue gray color, and as translucent as morning mist. She turned it over. A small, jagged line shone bright white against its side, like captured lightning.

The wave drew back like a breath. Hanna held the stone up to the sunlight. Granda had once said the Sylth Queen favored sapphires above all other jewels, and hearing that as a small child, she'd looked for blue stones herself. Up on the mountain and down at the shore. She was an island girl and not a Sylth Queen, after all, but an island girl could find a stone and see the beauty in it. Granda had taught her that.

The wet stone began to dry in the wind, but it was still a soft, shining blue. Hanna drew her feet from the sucking sand where the waves had buried them, and headed along the beach. The stone might be a piece of luck, and she sorely needed luck right now. She could imagine it was a kind of jewel, given to her freely by the sea, one for the holding and not for the wearing.

Cupping the smooth beach stone to her side, Hanna looked out over the water. Tyr Island was only a mile from shore, and she could make out a few fishermen's cottages from where she stood. She wondered which cottage the Falconer was in and whom he was tending now. How strange that only days before she'd feared the old man so. Was it the gentle way he'd tended Miles's wound that had changed her mind toward him? The music he'd played on his silver ervay, or the way he'd poured her thool and bid her drink before he'd bothered to fill his own cup?

Now she was seeking him as she never thought she'd do. Wanting the look that came to his weathered face when he was thoughtful, as he had been last night. It might be the sick on Tyr Isle needed healing, but it was hard to believe that anyone in all of Noor needed the Falconer more than she did today.

The salt wind played across her face as she rolled the stone around in her hand. The Falconer had said there were powers at work—that they were in a deal of danger. Miles's teacher wouldn't have said that if it had all been just a dream. And he'd promised he would help her if she told him everything. Now here she was ready to tell. Wanting to tell, and he was gone.

THE ARGUMENT

THE ARGUMENT

When the Darro and his ghost pack came for Rory, he and his dog gave them great chase.

—THE LEGEND OF THE SHRIKER

MILES RAISED HIS HATCHET AND CHOPPED OFF THE SMALL branch from the fallen tree. Beside him Hanna stripped the greenery from the slender branches and loaded the kindling into the wheelbarrow. Miles knew well enough why Da had sent them to gather kindling this morning, for Da thought work was the answer to all trouble. The past three weeks he and Hanna had passed from stony silence to bickering to angry silence again. They'd waged a secret war between them, or so they thought. It seemed Da, at least, had noticed.

"You'll come back with a great load of kindling and more kindness between you," Da had said.

Miles straightened up and looked across the broad meadow. His bones ached from the strange transformation he'd undergone. And the scab down his right arm still hurt where it did not itch and itched where it did not hurt. He'd had to chop the wood left-handed, which made the chore all the harder.

Hanna laid more kindling in the barrow. "Da was right to send us out," she said. "It's time we talked."

"What about?" said Miles, though he knew, of course. Still, he sought to show no sign of worry. Hanna must believe it had been a dreamwalk on the full-moon night three weeks ago and nothing more. She must think that for her safety and for his.

Hanna crossed her arms. "I saw it, Miles. That night in Shalem Wood. The . . ." She shivered.

"The what?" he challenged.

"You know." She looked at him. Her blue eye was the same color as the patch of sky he'd seen above the clouded mountain peak when they set out this morning, and it looked just as troubled.

Miles turned back to his work. He chopped another branch from the fallen pine. He didn't want to lie to her, but if he admitted to seeing the Shriker—more than that, if he admitted to her or anyone else that he'd shape-shifted . . .

He recalled the fiery look in the Sylth Queen's eyes when she made him promise to keep his power secret. The hatchet slipped in his sweaty hand. He gripped it harder. Granda once told a tale about a wicked boy who stole a jewel from the Sylth Queen's hair. Queen Shaleedyn turned the thief into a spider. And now Miles remembered that there had been a spider weaving her dark tresses that night in the deeps. He tensed thinking of it. Then, of course, there was Enoch.

No, he wouldn't agree with Hanna. And it wasn't only to protect himself, though that was a part of it. He couldn't risk the queen's anger, nor risk her taking his power from him, which would be the very least she'd do. He needed his shape-shifting gift to keep Hanna from the Shriker. He'd promised Granda he'd protect her.

Hanna was still frowning at him.

"I told you, you were dreamwalking," he insisted.

She shook her head.

He pretended not to see. He'd thought to find a spell strong enough to overcome the Shriker on Othlore, but the Sylth Queen had given him power enough to do it here, and soon. Miles wrested the branch from the thick trunk and broke it across his knee. *Crack!*

Kill the beast.

Break the curse.

He had the power to do it all now through his shape-shifting skill, if he could keep his secret. If no one interfered with him.

"Miles," said Hanna. "I know what I saw."

Miles tossed the broken branch at her feet. "Chop off the greenery there," he said. Hanna didn't budge. "Listen, Hanna. I told you before. I found you in the forest and saved you from the wolf and—"

Hanna lunged forward and pushed him on the chest. "Don't!" she cried. "Don't lie about it anymore! I saw you leap from the high branch, so I thought you'd die, but you didn't. You . . . flew."

Miles sucked in a startled breath and held it.

"You changed. Your body changed. I saw it happen. And you saved me from the Shriker." Hanna looked up at him not so much with anger now as wonder. He'd seen that look before when she'd knelt before the altar in the kirk. It gave him a strange, tingling feeling to be so admired. But he saw fear in her eyes as well, and he didn't like that so much.

High above a golden blade of sunlight pierced the clouds. Hanna was still looking at him, waiting for a word. "It's true," she insisted. "All of what I saw in the deeps. Isn't it?"

A drop of sweat slid down Miles's forehead. He wiped it away with his sleeve. He couldn't go on fooling her. What now? "We've nearly gathered enough kindling," he said. "Strip another two or three branches, and we'll be done."

He started on another branch. He'd have to make her promise to keep his power secret too. He would contain the knowledge of it so the queen wouldn't find out he'd let another see his power. But how to make her promise?

Hanna came up beside him and crossed her arms. "Why did you say it was a wolf attacked me?" she demanded. "Why didn't you tell Mother and Da the truth?"

"What would be the use of that? They don't believe in the Shriker. They never have."

"They didn't believe me when I told them, but they might have believed you!"

"Would they?"

Hanna paced back and forth through the grass awhile, thinking. Yellow warblers flew out of the gorse bush behind the oak tree. At last she shook her head. "It's true," she admitted. "They wouldn't have believed you, either, they'd have said it was the fever on you from your wounds that made you talk so."

She picked up her hatchet, stripped her branch. They worked in silence awhile. When the wheelbarrow was half full, she asked, "On the morning we came back. Did you hear what Mother said?"

"About it all being a story, and it was Granda's tales that made you dreamwalk and all?"

"Aye, that, but also . . ." Hanna wiped her brow with the back of her hand, leaving a streak of mud on her forehead. "That the family was all right, that people were forgetting the Shriker's curse, until I was born."

"No," said Miles. "She didn't say that. Only that the townsfolk were afeard after that dark-moon time because the midwife and her man were killed."

"And because I was different. She said so."

Miles shrugged. "If people talk about your eyes, they shouldn't bother. It doesn't mean a thing."

"It does to me. Do you think I heard the Shriker's call because of . . . my eyes?"

Miles thought a moment. "I can't say, Hanna. It may just be because you're a Sheen, and it's Sheens he hates most of all."

"If that's so, why didn't he call you?"

Miles didn't answer. He was stumbling over the question himself. But he managed to say, "Granda said he calls some. He never said why."

"Granda said that?"

"Aye, just before he died."

"You should have told me he said that!"

"You never asked!"

Hanna sniffed and turned away. He thought she might be fighting tears, but when she turned back round, he saw she had a fierce look.

"Listen, Hanna," he said, "Granda was sure the beast called to Polly Downs. Why else would she have gone to the woods on a dark-moon night? I'm sure the girl knew the legend as well as anyone on the isle. And think, Hanna, Polly's eyes were brown. Both brown. So you shouldn't be going on about your eyes the way you do."

Hanna broke a small branch across her knee. "I

should leave here," she said. "I'm the one putting you all in danger."

"Take no thought of that, Hanna. I'll protect you."

"How do you plan to do that?"

"I have my ways," he said proudly.

After loading the last of the kindling, Miles pushed the wheelbarrow across the meadow. He'd never heard of anyone battling the Shriker and coming out alive. Miles's chest swelled with the thought. *I'm the first. The very first.*

At a turn in the road he glanced down to Brim village far below. From so high up mountain he should not have been able to see the villagers walking from shop to shop. But his eyes were keen as a falcon's, and his vision was sharp enough to pick out the shop where he always stopped to buy twine for Da.

Miles blinked, still wondering at this new power. He still had a patch of fur on his neck from his first wolf change. Would these sharp falcon eyes last for good and all?

"Did you see the baker go inside just now?"

"What?" said Hanna. "From this far away? I can only see the rooftops, and they're small as nutshells."

It was true enough, and an ordinary boy wouldn't

have seen more than that himself. He licked his lips, tasting the pleasure of it. They started up the road again, the barrow rumbling under its weight of wood.

"That night when you changed," said Hanna. "How did you learn the magic to do that?"

The back of his neck pricked. "I told you before that I had skills in magic."

"Aye, but the power to change your form like that. How did you learn to—"

"A meer does not give away his secrets."

"But you're not a meer!"

"Not yet, but I've been studying magic, and I will be someday."

Miles stopped before a broad brown puddle. "You know I've wanted to go to Othlore. You've known that secret always. I've never kept it from you."

"Aye."

He kicked a pebble into the puddle and watched the ripples growing outward as it sank. He had to make her promise now. "What you saw in the deeps must stay a secret, Hanna. You're not to tell anyone what you saw me do."

Hanna tilted her brows, unconvinced.

Now it had come. The thing he'd feared to ask and *had* to ask. "After," he said. "After what happened. You took me to the Falconer?" It came out more as a question because he only half remembered that part of the night.

"I found the ivy-covered door," she said. "And you stumbled in."

He didn't want to ask more, but he had to know. "Did you talk with my teacher while I slept on the pallet?"

She paused to look down at the puddle, then lifted her eyes to him. "Aye. A little."

Miles's heart beat wildly. His parents did not believe, so his secret was safe with them. But if Hanna knew about his sylth gift and the Falconer knew as well, his second promise to the Sylth Queen would be broken.

"So you told him what happened in the deeps while I was sleeping." His voice shook. "And you told him *everything*. Didn't you!"

He saw her flinch. He'd flung the words at her the way Mother flung the wet washing against the rocks.

"I didn't!" she snapped. "He said he would help me if I told him all, but you awoke and we left right away."

She toed a pebble on the muddy road. "The Falconer knew we were in danger. He said so himself."

Miles took in the news, relief flooding through him in a sudden, cool wave. "Ah, well, he saw my arm and all."

"It was more than that."

Gray black clouds raced overhead, casting shadows over the gorse bushes and the holy thistle that grew along the road. The Falconer had meer powers. He *could* help them as no other man could. But Miles couldn't turn to his teacher. Not after going against him and stealing the spell from his book. Miles felt a sudden ache in his chest. If he could find the courage to go to the Falconer now . . .

No, he thought, and shut the feeling out. He'd left the meer behind the day he stole the spell, and he couldn't turn back for help. There was too much at stake. He had to keep his power.

Hanna peered at Miles's wavering reflection in the brown puddle. "When we left the Falconer's . . . Aetwan's warning. 'Change thrice and you free dark power.' I think it's something to do with your changing shape that night. I'm right, aren't I?"

Miles didn't move. Didn't answer.

"You should not change again. Not ever." Hanna was nodding at him as if they'd both already agreed on it.

His shoulders tightened. Didn't she know how much she needed his protection? "I'll change only if I have to. To rescue you from the beast."

"No," she said, her eyes darting this way and that. "There's some danger here. Some power we don't understand. You must never change again. Promise you won't."

He took Hanna's shoulders, gripping her cloak hard and fast, so he could feel her bones beneath. "How can I promise that? If the Shriker comes after you, do you want me to stand by and do nothing?"

She looked stricken, but he gripped her tighter. "Should I let him kill you, Hanna? Should I let him *devour* you the way he devoured Polly?"

"Stop it! Let me go!" Hanna tore herself away and leaped back, breathing hard. "You won't have to change again," she said. "If I resist the Shriker's call."

Miles crossed his arms. "Can you resist it?"

"I can if you tie me down."

He gripped the wheelbarrow and started walking again. "I won't do that."

Hanna raced up beside him. "Why not?"

"It's a stupid idea."

"No more stupid than any of yours."

"You'd have me tie you down after what happened with the village boys?" said Miles.

Hanna winced at the memory. He knew she still crossed the road whenever she came near the oak tree. "It's not like that at all," said Hanna. "The town boys bound me to the oak to shame me. You would tie me to my cot to save me. To keep me clear of the Shriker's call so I wouldn't be drawn into the woods."

"I don't like it."

"I've thought and thought," said Hanna. "And it's the best I can come up with. The moon will be full again in another week."

The road grew steeper. Miles grunted as he pushed the barrow. "And if Mother and Da should find you tied to your cot?"

"They wouldn't. They don't come in once I'm bedded down. And they're asleep early themselves, what with having to get up before dawn each day." Hanna looked up at the sky. "I don't know if the call will come. But if you tie me to the cot each night, I'll be safe." She turned to him. "Do you think you can do what I'm asking?"

Miles squinted back. "I'll think about it, Hanna."

"Miles?" she pleaded.

"All right!" he shouted. "I'll do it if you promise me one thing."

"What's that?"

"Promise me you'll keep my power to shape-shift a secret."

"I already told Mother and Da."

"Aye, and where did that get you?"

Hanna looked down and picked at her cloak. "I don't like it."

"And I don't like the idea of tying you down, so we're even."

She lifted her chin. He looked into her round face and saw the determination there. "Swear, then?" she said.

"Swear."

They hooked their smallest fingers and gave a tug to seal the swear. Something they hadn't done since they were young children. But never had it meant more than it did now.

THE TIES THAT BIND

THE TIES THAT BIND

Ezryeah built a shelter of bronze-wood and housed his family in it. Still the destroying winds came against them.

—*The Book of eOwey*

Miles kept his promise, and as the moon grew full, he tied Hanna to her cot each night, binding her arms as they'd agreed, so she could not roll to her side, nor raise her hands to cover her ears.

"Are they tight?" she'd whisper every night.

"Tight," he'd say back. He seemed ashamed to tie her down, so she tried always to say a good word before he left. "Thank you, brother," she whispered. Still, the trouble lined his face.

Each night Hanna lay stone still beneath the cords. The moon's bright face unveiled, spreading a soft light through the woods. As the shadows grew, Hanna began to hear a far-off cry. The call was soft at first, almost dreamlike. And shutting eyes and mind to it, she slept well enough. But night on night she grew more restless as the cry increased. How strong the feeling was that rose up in her breast. She tried to struggle against it, but the call began to pull her.

As the nights darkened and the moon ripened, the baying sound from Shalem Wood grew richer, deeper. It filled her with enchantment. *It's so beautiful,* she thought. There was no one there to warn her that she was falling under a spell. Only her empty room, her moonlit window. She trembled on her cot. The howl sounded a strange music within her. A knowing that she must go to the caller. Her blood rushed with the sound, like the singing of dark rivers flowing down her chest, her arms, her legs, and all the rivers looking, looking to spill into the sea.

At last she fell under the spell. Beneath her starlit window she pressed against the ropes, the enchantment giving her the strength to break her brother's bonds.

FOLLOWING

FOLLOWING

Follow where the blind are leading.

—Song of the Sylth Queen

Miles awoke with a start, as if someone had pinched him, yet the room was dark and still enough to hear his own breathing. He turned his head on his pillow and looked out the window. The sky was scattered with stars, like bright seeds flung by a planter. And the treetops at the edge of the forest were dusted with light.

He thought of Hanna in her room. Tonight she'd watched him tying the double knots, her pale eyes shining in the rushlight. "If this should fail," she said. "If anything should happen. Promise me you won't shift again. Promise you'll take your bow instead."

"I'll take my bow." He said that to her earnestly,

though he didn't promise the other. Still, she seemed to lighten. A smile crossed her face. "I feel like a sheep who must be tethered to a post."

"You're much smarter than a sheep," he said, and they both laughed, quietly so as not to wake Mother and Da.

"Are they tight?" she asked when he was done.

"As tight as I can make them."

"Good, then," she whispered, and he left the room blushing.

He thought of going to her now to see how she was faring. Maybe he shouldn't awaken her, but he was already out of bed. Quietly he padded down the narrow hall.

Stepping into her shadowy room, he clamped his jaw to stifle a cry. Her cot was empty! The blanket strewn across the floor, his clever knots ripped apart! The bonds he'd tied were broken as if gnawed. Miles rushed back to his room, threw on his boots and cloak, grabbed his bow, slid the window open, and leaped out. He slung the bow and quiver over his shoulder and raced over the rolling hills, his cloak swimming fishlike through the air.

He'd been stupid to think mere rope could keep the Shriker from his prey. He wouldn't let Hanna end up like Polly!

The deeps! He had to find the deeps! He'd never seen it by day, though he'd explored all of Shalem Wood through the years, alone and with the Falconer.

There was a great boulder in the deeps, he remembered that, but many large stones were scattered through the woodlands. In ancient times stones as big as cottages had rolled down the mountain slope. Where, then? Where? He ran in a panic, as a rabbit runs from wolves. Ran as stupidly as sheep run from thunder, his boots thumping on the forest floor.

Breathless, sweating, he raced. Moonlight awash around him spread satin through the trees, lighting no particular path. *Remember the trail you took to the sylth dance! Remember the night you followed Hanna!* But he couldn't remember. The first time he'd had the lit path to guide him, and the second he'd followed Hanna, her white gown glowing through the woods like a beacon.

Where, then? Oh, eOwey let me remember before he attacks her!

He turned left, his quiver slapping against his back

as he ran. He had only his bow and arrows this time. His knife was still at home, tucked away on the high shelf. He cursed himself again for agreeing to tie up Hanna. This wasn't a game!

Miles stopped suddenly at a familiar place and dived between the fir trees. There in the still night woods he uprooted the scald-tongue he'd found once with the Falconer. He'd promised Hanna he wouldn't shape-shift. He leaned against a tree for one breath, two, gulping cool night air like a thirsty man.

Change thrice and you free dark power. He knew there was something to Aetwan's warning. He'd shape-shifted twice already, so he must take the beast down another way if he could. A poisoned arrow might help him save her. Scald-tongue in hand, he started off again. Think. He must think. The deeps were in the very heart of the woods. The place of tallest trees and darkest shadow. What had Queen Shaleedyn said?

> Where the deaf are storytelling,
> Where the silent bells are knelling,
> Take the road that splits asunder,
> Nor left, nor right, but travel under.

He would close his eyes and feel the air as a swimmer feels his way through a pond; the cooler the water, the deeper the pond, and the coolest place revealed the very center.

He turned right, taking the way he felt to be most likely, and walked down the path. *Let me feel it.* Yes, here the air cooled, yet no leaves stirred, so it wasn't a trick of wind. Down the trail the coolness deepened. Farther in and farther, as a man heading for deep water with no fear of drowning. He quickened his pace, running deeper and deeper until he heard the low growl.

Take the road that splits asunder,
Nor left, nor right, but travel under.

—Song of the Sylth Queen

Miles plunged into the deeps, but he hadn't come fast enough. Ahead of him Hanna dangled from the beast's jaws.

"No!" he screamed.

The Shriker raised his head higher. His deep black form was like night doubled over on itself; his eyes shone red. Miles pulled an arrow from his quiver, wet the tip with scald-tongue, and aimed his poisoned arrow at the darkest place on the Shriker's chest. He would pierce him in the heart, if the beast had one.

Now! Miles shot. The Shriker leaned left. The arrow whizzed past his thick foreleg and dropped to the damp earth behind. Two coal red eyes fixed on Miles. The beast dropped Hanna's body on the forest floor, lifted his muzzle, and howled.

The sound of the Shriker's rage seemed to split Miles's skull, but Miles matched it with his own.

The transformation was so fast this time it filled him with internal lightning. One second he was a cowering boy; the next, he leaped up, blazing, his flesh melting in transforming fire from skin to fur, teeth to fangs, hands to paws. His muscles rippled with power. His roar cut through the night. He was mountain lion.

Miles flung himself at the monster. Tearing into him with razor claws, he bit the creature's neck.

The Shriker ran in tight circles, yelping with pain. Miles clenched his jaws tighter, holding the creature's throat a moment longer before the beast finally shook him off. Tumbling backward, he hit his head on a log. Leaping up again, reeling, snarling, he lunged for the Shriker, but the beast hurled himself at Miles and dug his teeth into his flesh.

The tearing pain in Miles's side strengthened his rage. He fought with all his might. Clawing. Snarling. Biting. But the Shriker was bigger and stronger. He shook Miles back and forth, hard and fast, till his body screamed with pain. Miles managed to drag a claw down the Shriker's throat. But he couldn't free himself from his powerful jaws, and he was losing strength. He felt his body going limp. Dark sky sped overhead and the ground blackened beneath. All was going dark. Suddenly the smell of blood shocked him to his senses. He couldn't die now, or Hanna would be next! He strained his mind to push beyond the mountain lion's shape into something larger, more powerful.

With a sharp intake of a breath, stealing dark from night, he felt his flesh broaden into the thick, menacing shape of his enemy. With a snarl he escaped the monster's hold and bared his fangs. They were eye to eye now. Burning coals to burning coals.

No longer mountain lion.

He was Shriker.

GLISTEN
GLISTEN

*They saw in that last starlight
what night had taken from them.*

—*The Book of eOwey*

Sounds of battle filled Hanna's ears. Barking, snarling, snapping.

The ground shook. Dirt, leaves, sticks, and fur flew in all directions. Hanna clutched her bloody side and rolled against the cool base of a tree, where she lay coughing and panting. Ten feet away the beasts still battled.

The pain in her side dizzied her. She clutched her wounds and bit her lip hard. She couldn't give in to it. Not now. Not yet. She had to help Miles. If only she could see him clearly. She tried to stand and fell again. *Move! You have to move!*

A loud crack sounded above and to her left as the

rivals charged each other and crashed into a pine tree. Branches rained down around her. She covered her head to shield herself from the falling limbs. One struck her shoulder, and she let out a grunt.

Under a nearby fern she spotted the outline of her brother's bow. She inched painfully toward it, clenching her teeth against the cries from her rebellious body. She pulled the abandoned weapon to her and reached for the quiver. There were two arrows left inside. Drawing back again, she leaned against the pine trunk and pressed herself to a stand.

Pain shot down her side, but she remained on her feet and loaded the bow, squinting through moonlight to get a fix on the Shriker. There he was. And there. She moved the arrow this way and that, gasping in cold panic as she did so. She'd seen Miles change into a mountain lion when he first attacked, but not this! Never this!

The two Shrikers rolled away from her and crashed against the boulder. One leaped on top, snarling. The other yowled and scratched his enemy's torso, his paws churning as if in a race. The beast on top whipped his tail back and forth and bared his fangs.

Hanna aimed her arrow first at one, then at the

other. She screamed with frustration. Which one should she kill? The beast on top was about to tear the other's throat. If Miles was below, there was no time. She had to shoot now and save his life. She aimed at the Shriker's belly. He whipped his head round suddenly, his red eyes wild.

"Miles!" she screamed. "Are you Miles?"

The beast bayed. Was it anger or a warning? The arrow slipped in her sweating hand. She bent to retrieve it. In that lost moment the Shriker on the ground struggled hard against his captor and flipped him over. They scrambled again, snarling and tumbling into the undergrowth. Hanna leaned against the tree and pulled the bowstring taut, her eyes tearing against the strain as she peered down the shaft.

A loud screech came from overhead. Aetwan swooped down, grabbed Hanna's arrow in his talons, and flew skyward with it. Hanna stumbled forward. Just then the Falconer rushed up and caught her in his arms. "Which one is Miles?" he cried.

"That one!" Hanna pointed to the one in chase. "No . . . it might be . . . I can't tell!"

"By all that's sacred!" shouted the Falconer. "He

should never have taken this shape!" He reached into his shoulder bag and pulled out a pouch. Releasing the leather ties, he took out a handful of silvery powder, ran forward, and tossed it to the night air. Each grain glowed, spreading silver light through the deeps.

The undersides of the evergreens lit up, as did the Falconer and, not far from him, the beasts. In that moment of light Hanna could see Miles's struggling body clothed inside the Shriker's form.

"Come out, Miles!" shouted the Falconer. "I call you by name. Return to us, Miles Ferrell!"

"Miles!" shouted Hanna. "Listen to him. Come out!" In the glow she saw her brother's shape inside the beast, as if he'd thrown a heavy bear rug over his body. His boyish arms extending to furry legs and giant paws. His mouth open and screaming as his outer form shaped it to a Shriker's howl.

Miles kept on fighting. From a branch above Aetwan shrieked and dived into the fray, flapping his wings and pulling Miles's shoulders with his talons as if to lift the beast from his back like an enormous fur coat. The Falconer drew his bow, but the beasts were too entangled for him to take a clear shot.

Powder fell on the Shriker's back, bright as stars on the darkest of nights. The monster yelped as though the shining grains had scorched him. In the momentary brightness Hanna saw the barest outline of a dog, clawing as if trapped inside the monster. Then in a flash the dog was gone as the rivals tumbled past the great boulder.

"Now, Miles!" screamed the Falconer, taking aim again. "Leave the Shriker's form and come back to us!" Aetwan pulled up on Miles's furry back. Bright powder illuminated the Falconer's gray cape as he ran past the boulder. Hanna gripped her side and struggled forward.

Just beyond the boulder Hanna saw a hole appearing. Opening, opening like a dark, yawning mouth that even the powder could not light.

"The passage!" shouted the Falconer.

Hanna trembled as the passage grew wider and wider, like a great tear in a cloth, only the cloth was the night itself.

"Keep clear of it!" warned the Falconer. "Change back now, Miles, before it's too late!"

"What is it?" called Hanna. "What's happening?"

The Falconer had nearly reached the fighting beasts

when the Shrikers tumbled over and over straight into the opening.

"Come back!" screamed the Falconer. *"Eldessur! Kimbardaa! Kimbardaa!"* He called in the Othic tongue, sounds Hanna couldn't understand. But it was already too late.

The mouth suddenly closed. The dark hole disappeared.

Silence followed. A quiet so deep that Hanna moaned. Nothing moved now but the falling powder, which hit the ground in a gentle whisper and went out.

*The women took their torn garments up the hill
and hung them on the trees. "Peace," they called,
and "Peace" again, but there was no peace.*

—THE BOOK OF EOWEY

Hanna awakened in the Falconer's earthen hut.
She was alone. A low fire burned in the hearth. She half
remembered being carried through the woods, waking
once to swallow something so bitter her teeth went dry.
She breathed against the tight bandages the Falconer had
used to bind her wounds, and felt a shock of pain when
her ribs expanded.

Tears formed in the corners of her eyes and slid
down her cheeks. The pain in her side made it easy to cry,
but the tears were for Miles.

Near the back wall she saw Aetwan resting, eyes
closed, on his perch. Flecks of dried blood were spattered

across his gray-feathered chest. She pictured him swooping down to take the arrow from her. How had he known she was aiming at the wrong beast? She wiped her damp cheek with the back of her hand. "Where is the Falconer?"

"Gone," said Aetwan, eyes still closed.

His answer startled her. It was hard to get used to the falcon speaking.

Pressing her hand against her side, she sat up gingerly. How long had she slept? Across the room the curtain was drawn, so she couldn't tell if it was day or night outside, and if it was night, whether it was the same night Miles had fought the Shriker. She'd have to lift the curtain to see out, and crossing the room would be painful. "When will the Falconer be back?"

"In time." Aetwan opened his eyes and let out a steely cry to caution her against any more questions.

"Sorry," said Hanna.

The falcon rustled on his post, his shoulders lifting in something like a shrug. He emitted one more word. "Eat."

There was a loaf of bread, a bowl, and a mug on the round table. Walking to the chair would hurt, but she was hungry and thirsty, so she swung her feet over the side of the pallet and gingerly crossed the floor to the simple meal.

The loaf tore easily in her hands, and the smell of baked bread filled the room. The Falconer had surely gone after Da. Da was an excellent tracker, and the Falconer knew magic. Together they would hunt for Miles and bring him home. The thought gave her strength more than the food, and she drank down the water in the heavy mug like hope itself.

Suddenly the door burst open and Mother came in. "Hanna," she cried. "My girl! My very own girl!" As Mother flung her basket on the floor, Aetwan screeched and flew outside.

"Oh, look at what the wolf did!"

"It wasn't a wolf," said Hanna.

Mother knelt by Hanna's chair. "Your da will kill him!" she said through tears. "I promise that." She put her arms around Hanna. The hug hurt, but Hanna didn't want her to let go.

STALKING

One from two and strange combining
With the other intertwining

—SONG OF THE SYLTH QUEEN

A SEARING PAIN RAN DOWN MILES'S RIGHT FLANK AS HE crept along the passage. He wanted to lie down, change back into himself, but he couldn't rest, couldn't risk changing back while Hanna was still in danger. He needed all his animal strength to kill the Shriker before the beast attacked again.

Water dripped from the roof, chilled his back and plopped in shallow puddles around his paws. He listened for other sounds. The pull of breath into lungs. The scrape of claw on stone. Only his own panting and halting movements met his ears.

He ran his tongue along the gap in his mouth. One

of his fangs was missing. Had he lost it in the battle? The Shriker's blood was still on his tongue, and the taste sickened him. In the deeps of Shalem Wood he'd seen the beast's flesh hanging from his side. The smell of his wounds was still fresh. He followed the scent. Thirst for revenge dulled his pain and drove him on. He would tear the beast apart for hurting Hanna! Let the carcass lay unburied so the carrion birds could feast on it!

The circle of dim light ahead grew larger. It must be from starlight or moonlight filling the deeps. Torn as he was, he would make it down the long passage and kill the enemy. Then he'd shake the weight of this beast form off like foul armor, though he couldn't shake off the wounds. The shape-shifter brought his wounds with him. This had happened before when . . . He stopped a moment and shook his heavy head. He couldn't remember when.

Miles's side throbbed with pain as he limped forward.

Don't lie down. Don't give in. Move. Walk. Stalk the beast.

At last Miles reached the opening. There he paused and sniffed the air. The forest was rich with odors, but there was no sign of the beast. No sign of Hanna or the Falconer, either, but then, this didn't look like the deeps. There wasn't any boulder here, and the pine trees were enormous. A thousand-year-old forest, he thought, though he didn't understand how this could be. Wasn't he on Mount Shalem?

Thick, wet ferns brushed up against his legs as he circled the giant trees. Peering through pale moonlight, he listened to the branches creaking in the wind. He must have come out the wrong end of the passage.

He would retrace his steps. Even now the Shriker might be after Hanna. The Falconer, with all his magic, might not have the power to kill the beast. He would go. He would fight.

Miles turned to reenter the passage, and let out a frightened yelp.

The passage was gone.

TWO MAPS

TWO MAPS

The Otherworld is as far away as your doubts and as close as your own heart. Do you believe in it, child?

—GRANDA SHEEN

OVER THE NEXT FIVE DAYS THE SEARCH PARTY SCOURED Shalem Wood behind packs of sniffing dogs. Hanna came as soon as she was well enough, though the pain in her side slowed her down. Most of the village folk stayed clear of the search. The boy had Sheen blood, after all. But a few outsiders, like the Avwon family, left their fishing boats to climb up mountain. And Mic's da abandoned his fields to join in, the memory of his son's broken arm still fresh enough to drive him to the hills. The farmer looked for Miles, too, but Hanna knew it was the wolf Mic's da was set on finding.

They broke off in small teams, some with Da, some

with Brother Adolpho, and others with Gurty. Hanna was on the search with Gurty, for Mother and Da put great stock in Gurty's tracking skills. Ten years back she'd found the weaver's son, Pyter, when he'd been lost eight days in the woods. Gurty brought him down mountain alive, though torn and hungry, when everyone had long since counted him for dead.

When night came, the search parties walked with torches lit, seeking Miles over the green hillocks, shouting his name along Senowey River. Still there was no sign.

After another long day without turning up so much as a footprint, Hanna left Gurty at her cottage and wended her way back down the trail toward home.

The forest was dusk blue, and robins rustled in the cedars. In the place where the path split Hanna took the less used trail. Her legs and feet were sore, and her bandaged side still ached. But her mind was full of questions only the Falconer could answer. He'd been there the night of Miles's disappearance, and she hadn't yet found a way to speak with him alone.

A single knock made the ivy-covered door swing open. "Ah, you've come," said the Falconer. He stood aside for her to enter, a threaded needle hanging from his shirt. It surprised her that she'd caught him mending, but she was less surprised that he'd been expecting her. If the old man was a seer, he might have hidden powers he could wield to find her brother.

Aetwan was perched in the corner. He cocked his head and shot her a piercing look as the Falconer latched the door.

"You've taken on some danger to travel Shalem Wood alone," said the Falconer.

"It's not yet dark," she said, "and I was in company with Gurty until just now."

"Well, warm yourself, then." The Falconer motioned to a bent-willow chair by the fire. "It won't be long before nightfall."

As he poured her a cup of steaming thool, she eyed the row of leather-bound books on the high shelf, keeping her back to Aetwan, whose fierce look unsettled her. The mug was brimful, and the first sweet sip helped to loosen her tongue. "I never thanked you for the healing herbs you gave me the night . . ." The words gave out on her. She didn't want just then to go on about what happened in the deeps, only to thank him.

"It's a leafer's job to heal the sick," he said modestly.

Hanna watched him cross the room, his stocking feet soundless on the floor. Her chest rose against the weight of worry. She hadn't come to thank him, but for her brother's sake. And the urgency of that pressed hard against her, even as the night was falling in the woods outside. "It's been so long since Miles disappeared," she said.

"Aye, six days gone, and it's very hard on us all." The willow chair creaked as the Falconer sat down. He pulled out his tinderbox, struck the stone, and lit his pipe. The smell of smoke mingled with the scent of thool. He was waiting for the rest of what she'd come to say.

She took a breath and put down her mug. "I've seen you going off alone with Aetwan each day. Why haven't you stayed with Da and the rest of us?"

The Falconer crossed his legs, the hole in his sock revealing his rough, old heel. Was it his sock he'd been planning to mend?

"Tell me, Hanna. What attacked you that night?" The question startled her. It did not touch on what she'd asked, and she worked to calm her heart as he waited for her answer.

"It was . . ." She swallowed the next word down, and

it made a burning in her throat. She would say it to him. He couldn't help her if she didn't. It was time to say the name. "It was . . . the Shriker."

"Not a wolf, then, as your mother and da believe?"

"Not a wolf! Never a wolf!"

"So your parents search for one thing, and I another. Do you see?"

She tugged a lock of hair and watched him blow a smoke ring up to the dirt ceiling. It disappeared behind the herb bundles dangling from the twisted roots.

"Let me come with you."

"I may when you are stronger."

"I'm strong!" The words came hard and fast, and she blushed at the pronouncement.

But the Falconer surprised her with a smile. "You may just help me in the search," he said. "I could do with another pair of eyes. But there are some things you'll need to know." He stood and put his hands out to the fire.

Hanna heard Aetwan flap his wings once and twice. "Trouble," he said.

"I know my own mind, Aetwan," said the Falconer, his back still to Hanna and the falcon. He was so tall that his head nearly reached the roots entwined in the ceiling. In his brown shirt and wool breeches he could have been an ordinary old man like her own granda, but even so poorly dressed there was a kingliness about him. The thick hair that flowed down his back looked like a silver stream in the firelight. She felt a reverence for him now that she no longer feared him.

The Falconer turned and held his palms out to her as he had done to the hearth. Aetwan flapped his wings and let out a shrill cry. In the center of the Falconer's left palm was a mark. A blue lit circle with an ancient Othic symbol inside. The symbol looked at once like a letter and like a winged bird, tipped and soaring within the blue circle.

The Falconer did not speak. Nor did Hanna, but she knew the blue palm sign meant he was a meer, and she felt the thrill of seeing it.

All her thoughts about the Falconer, the strangeness and the wonder of him, fell into place then. The firelight danced behind him, sending a golden glow about his head and shoulders. As his palms cooled, the mark slowly faded. She was suddenly uncertain what to do. Should she bow or . . . She got down on one knee before the meer.

"There's no need for that, Hanna." He lifted her to her chair again and said, "I'm just a man like any other."

She settled back against the bent willow as he went on.

"You asked me where I search. You know now by the palm sign what I am." He shook his head. "Your brother knows I am a meer, as does Brother Adolpho, and your granda knew. But few folk on Enness know it, though I've lived here fifty-odd years. Meers are under the High King's authority now, but some still talk of the days before the great plague when we were outlaws, and many still fear us for our magic." He sat beside Hanna. "I thought it better when I came here to your isle to appear as a leafer and musician. The townsfolk welcome a leafer whenever there's sickness about.

"But as to where I'm wandering each day with Aetwan . . ." The Falconer looked at the door as if he could see the cascading hills beyond it, though it was closed tight. "I search for the passage to Oth," he said. "There are some places still in Noor where the way between worlds opens. Mount Shalem is such a place. It's why I came here."

"But where is Oth? Granda used to say it was all around us, but most are blind to it."

"The man was right about that."

Hanna frowned, uncertain.

"Think on it this way," he said, sweeping out his arm. "There are two worlds, as close as close. One we can see, and one invisible. Yet both are here."

Hanna thought on Granda's tale. "Does the Shriker live in Oth, then?"

"Aye, in its shadow part. The legend tells of how the Darro cursed the dog and made the beast. But few know about what happened after. Didn't you ever ask your granda where the Shriker hid out for more than two hundred years before he was seen again in Shalem Wood?"

Hanna shook her head. No, she hadn't asked that; she'd never pressed Granda to tell her more about the Shriker. She regretted that now.

"Well," said the Falconer, "the Darro knew the Shriker couldn't be a part of his ghost pack, nor was the creature rightly of this world, being magical and a shape-shifter, so he took him to a place in Oth called Attenlore. Attenlore's a grand place, full of bright magic. But even then there was a shadow realm. Uthor Vale, it was called. It was the place where the sylth kings and queens of old sent those they'd banished. Uthor was a small, dark vale in those days. But it's grown broader and darker since the Darro left the Shriker there."

Hanna swished the thool in her mug, the brown and cream clouding together. "Was it the Shriker made Uthor grow larger?"

"He may have," said the Falconer, "or it may be the more creatures the sylth sovereigns banished over the years, the larger the realm became. I've never been sure which."

Hanna's gaze fell into the darkness of her cup as she saw once again the black hole that had opened suddenly on the night the Shriker attacked. In her mind's eye she envisioned two beasts rolling into it, the passage closing like a giant's mouth.

"The passage to Oth is in the deeps!" she said suddenly.

"Aye, well, on that night it was there." The Falconer stepped into the alcove and returned with *The Way Between Worlds*. "The way from one world to another is seen most often at the full moon," he said. "But it's not always in the same place. The passage moves about."

Putting the tome on the table, he sat down and opened the section near the end of the book, a place of many maps. Hanna spied a map of Noor, like the great world map Old Sim had once shown her. Though his was a sailor's map, and he'd marked all the seaports he'd sailed to as a young man. On the opposite page was a rice paper map that had the words "Oth Map" at the top. But she didn't have time to view that before the Falconer turned past it to a page that read "Noor Map: Enness Isle."

Hanna filled her eyes with all the familiar village names skirting the shoreline. There was Brim, Gladsonne, Oshenwold, and the harbor of Abbaseth, on the far side of the island, near the high cliffs of Jory. Her own island on the page was strange and familiar at the same time, for she'd never seen it drawn out. Mount Shalem rose in the very middle of the island. On the southwestern side of the mountain was Grenore Valley. Deep and wide, it was, and no one lived there. A wild place the mapmaker had painted all red and gold with autumn trees and dry spell grass.

Hanna touched the peak of Mount Shalem and traced the familiar green of Shalem Wood, encircling it from the high cliff to rolling hills to sea. Then, lifting her hand again, she touched Senowey Falls and traced Senowey River, beginning at the waterfall, all the way down to Brim Harbor, where it flowed into the bay.

"Now," said the Falconer, laying the rice paper map

from the opposite page over the top. The landscape on the rice paper map mirrored Enness, and the mountain bore the same name, but other places were oddly named. The transparent page read "Oth Map: Attenlore Isle."

"Attenlore," whispered Hanna. Again she put her finger on the mountain's peak and traced it down the far side to the dark valley between two steep ravines. Grenore Valley in her world was Uthor Vale on this map, and it was all shadowed in, as if drawn with charcoal.

The Falconer nodded at the place she was touching. "If Miles is tracking the Shriker, the beast will lead him through Attenlore to Uthor Vale."

Hanna lifted her finger and found a bit of dark chalk on it. It must have been a very old map to come off on her skin so. She blushed and slipped her hand in her pocket to wipe the color off before the Falconer noticed.

The meer went on. "Uthor is the Shriker's home, after all. So he will go back. He's not one to bear the world of light for long."

"But if Miles is there, then why have you let us all search for him day on day in Shalem Wood?"

The Falconer gently closed the book and placed his

hand atop the leather. "Miles may return at any time. And if he does, it will be somewhere on this mountain."

"He may be close by, then," said Hanna. "He may be hurt and we can't reach him!" She stood up suddenly. "If you knew about this passage, you could have stopped it up years ago. Then Miles wouldn't have been lost!" She'd shouted at him, but suddenly she didn't care. She pulled her torn nail hard until it stung.

"I was sent to guard the passage, Hanna. Not to close it."

He looked into the fire, and his eyes were bright with it. "In our world and the other, where there's light there's shadow."

"But if you could keep the Shriker from our world?"

"Would you want the sylth folk to be shut away from our world forever because of him? Would you have me tear the deyas from the hearts of all the trees in Shalem Wood and keep all magic from the world?"

Hanna slumped back in her chair. She'd wanted to blame the Falconer for everything. Or if not blame him, find him to be so powerful that he could rescue Miles, here, now, tonight. "I want Miles back," she admitted. It was all she wanted. She'd hardly been able to eat or sleep since he disappeared six nights ago. Now that the words were out, tears rolled down her cheeks. She tried to stop them, but her face and lips were already wet.

The Falconer held her, and she cried into his wool shirt. The shirt smelled of winterleaf, and under that a woodland scent like Granda's used to have, and that made her cry all the more. He patted her shoulder in quiet rhythm until her sobbing ceased. She sat back, and the old man looked into her eyes. "I've set my mind on finding him, Hanna. You should know this. I've walked by day and night as well. I miss the boy, and there isn't much time."

The Falconer held out his hand to her. Palm upward, as if the words he was about to say had a weight and she might need his help to carry them. "Your brother is in danger as much from himself as from the beast."

"How is that?" whispered Hanna.

"If Miles stays in the beast form beyond the next full moon, he may not be able to change back."

"Why?"

"It is an old law of shape-shifting. One cannot stay in another form from full moon to full moon without the risk of being trapped inside the shift. A meer is trained to know this danger, but Miles wasn't schooled in magic. He wasn't ready to receive such a gift."

"Who gave it to him, then?"

The meer frowned. "I can only guess at that. There are few who would have such power. Few indeed." He fell into silence.

Hanna stood up and paced before the fire. "Miles may have changed back already. He may be a boy again."

"We can hope this is so, but we cannot know for sure."

She turned her back, envisioning the beast's massive, dark body, his pointed ears and coal-bright eyes. She shuddered. "Miles wouldn't choose to stay in the Shriker's form for long."

"He'd want to stay strong to pursue his enemy."

Hanna licked her lip, tasting the saltiness left from the tears. The Falconer was right. Miles would never let himself be weaker than his enemy. He'd always prided himself on his fitness for a fight. He'd come home from Brim with a bloody lip as often as not, and that for only a slight—someone calling him "dirty Sheen," or a boy like Mic or Cully tossing a dirt clod at him.

She looked at the Falconer's broad shoulders, thinned with age, but still strong. "What are we to do?"

"For now you'd best take your rest. I'll look more tonight after I take you home." He stood and tugged his cloak from the hook. "Come," he said. "Night has fallen. You don't want to keep your mother and da waiting."

The partial moon shed little light on Shalem Wood, but the stars glowed crisp above the trees, and the Falconer, who was used to the ways of the wild, led Hanna home without the need of candle or rushlight.

TORN CLOAK

TORN CLOAK

*Eelan saw the lake shimmering in the air,
but it was only sunlight, and the people's
thirst increased.*

—THE BOOK OF EOWEY

THREE MORE DAYS PASSED WITHOUT ANY SIGN OF MILES, and the helpers dwindled to just a few. No one came to Mother and Da to say Miles was lost for good. Nor did Brother Adolpho suggest they hold a Crossing Over for him. Still, the silence people paid the family was eloquent enough.

The few village folk who'd left field or fishing boat to help them search went back to their daily tasks and left the Ferrells to walk the woods with the Falconer, Brother Adolpho, Taunier, the woodsman Hewn, and Old Gurty. So there were only eight of them left, nine including Tymm, who was too young to be of any real help.

At midday the search party met at Fisherman's Pole, a jagged rock outcropping halfway up Mount Shalem that gave all a fine view of forest and meadow below.

"Where's Hewn?" asked Da.

Gurty clucked and looked down the hill. "The woodsman is never one to be on time." They sat down and started their meal, sharing news of their search among themselves.

In the small circle of seekers Taunier was the first to share his news. He tilted his head so his dark-skinned face and black hair shone in the sunlight as he spoke. Hanna's heart beat faster. She couldn't help admiring him, though she tried not to show it. As Taunier tore his bread, he told about the trail of broken branches he'd followed, which led to the slain body of a deer, wolves' work from the looks of it. There was little left of the carcass and no sign of Miles.

Hanna's mother whimpered as he said this, and Hanna squeezed her hand. The word "wolves" still came hard to Mother's ears.

The rest shared details of their search. There was nothing new. Hanna ate without tasting her food, the hope of finding Miles she'd felt the week before slowly fading. Across from her Brother Adolpho whispered to the Falconer, who nodded thoughtfully. The square-shouldered, brown-robed Brother and the tall, slender meer were altogether different and the same, like earth and tree come together.

The wind strengthened. The air faintly smelled of seaweed and fish that secreted Turnbow Bay. Da stood leaning against his shepherd's crook. Throughout the meal he hadn't bothered to look at the others, but kept his eyes moving uphill and down, scanning rock, river, and tree line, looking everywhere for his firstborn. Hanna followed the line of his gaze and spied the woodsman Hewn hobbling up the hill with his black bear hound, Kip, trotting alongside.

He stopped halfway up to shout, "Found something!" then hunched over and coughed from having to call so loudly. They came down through the long grass and gathered round the old man. Kip licked Hanna's elbow. She shuddered and pulled away from him. A good dog, she knew. But Kip was so like the Shriker, with his broad-set shoulders, his long black fur, and his strong jaw. *It's only a dog*, she thought. *The Shriker's three times his size at least.* She set her jaw and made herself give the bear hound a pat. Kip panted happily and wagged his bushy tail.

"It's this," said Hewn, drawing a torn piece of dark green cloth from his leather waist bag.

"A piece of Miles's cloak!" cried Mother. "It must be! I'd know the color anywhere!" She took the cloth and rubbed it across her cheek.

"Where did you find it, man?" demanded Da.

Taunier held up a grimy hand. "Wait." He drew a cloak from his weathered pack and lifted the corner for all to see. The green cloth matched the ragged hole in Taunier's garment. "I tore my cloak somewhere in the woods this morning," he said. He folded the torn piece inside his cloak and placed them in his pack.

Mother moaned. All else were silent, but it was a sound any one of them could have made.

Da turned his back on Taunier as if he'd cheated them in some way. Hanna felt a pang. Taunier had been so helpful, so willing to search for Miles when the rest of the villagers had abandoned their family.

"I have to go back to the blacksmith's," said Taunier suddenly.

"It's not your fault," said Hanna. "It's only that we thought—"

"I'm expected to work the forge." Taunier set his jaw

and started down the hill. He did not promise to come back on the morrow as he had before.

"Call out to him, man," said Brother Adolpho, "and tell the boy good-bye." But Da stared at his flock and could not speak to Taunier. There'd been a moment of hope. The only moment they'd had since Miles disappeared. Now it had passed, and Da's back was stiff with its passing.

Hewn elbowed Gurty. "Will you come search with us?" he asked.

Gurty stood stony faced, as if she hadn't heard him. A gust of wind blew her gray hair straight back from her brow. The corner of her yellow shawl fluttered out behind her. "Garth Lake," she said.

"Ah, well," said Hewn, feeding a bit of his bread to Kip. "Have it your way, old woman."

The Falconer sent Aetwan flying and stepped up beside Gurty. "I'll walk with you," he said. "It's the way I'm taking."

Hanna didn't wonder why he'd look to her. She'd found Pyter, after all. "I'll go with you too," she said.

Mother crossed her arms and frowned. "You're to come home before dark," she said, and Hanna agreed.

They stood in a circle before leaving, and Brother Adolpho offered up a simple prayer. "eOwey open our eyes to find the boy Miles, who has lost his way."

Then they all parted and trailed in three directions through the blowing grass.

HUNTING

HUNTING

*Kwium lost his way and slept
in the hollow of a tree.*

—*THE BOOK OF EOWEY*

D EEP IN THE WOODS OF ATTENLORE, MILES HID INSIDE
a hollow log, waiting to regain his strength. He awoke
nightly to lick his wounds, to creep out and hunt small
game, to drink, but always he returned before dawn—the
sun of Attenlore being too bright for his hound's eyes.

Many times when he first awoke and felt the chill
of loneliness, he longed to change back into a boy again.
He'd imagine hands. Arms. A human face: *his* human
face. He'd work on the image until his head pounded.
Then a strange beast scent would waft through the air,
filling him with fear, or a noise outside his shelter would
startle him. Head lifted, ears cocked, he'd wait until the

scent changed or the noise passed: all thoughts of shape-shifting back into a weaponless boy chased away again by his fear. And so he did not turn. He kept his thick hide, his fangs and claws. They were his only protection against the one who hunted him.

Days and nights fled by. The boy dreamed inside the beast, the coursing of sun and stars all the same to him in his dwelling.

Late one afternoon beetles scratched inside the rotting wood. It was beyond human hearing, but Miles's sharp hound's ears caught even the smallest sounds. He raised his great head in the dark log and ran his tongue along his teeth, feeling the gap where his fang should have been. He was hungry. He must eat. It was daylight and he should wait, but he'd killed only rabbits, stoats, and other small game in his nightly hunts, and his belly wanted more.

Miles crept through the rotting log. At the opening he paused and blinked. How the light stung his eyes here! He shut his eyes and sniffed the air. The stench of his injured hide filled his nostrils. He sniffed beyond the odor, testing the air for the scent of other beasts, of the *one* beast who wanted him dead.

Layer on layer of odors entered his brain. The smell of damp woods filled him. Birds in the copse nearby had a dusty smell. Flowers, a radiant scent—like smelling light. He marveled at it: the world of hearing, of taste, of smell, opening anew to him. Compared with this, his boyhood ears had been stuffed with cotton. His tongue, swaddled. His nostrils, corked like bottles.

Miles pushed his way outside. Bits of wood came away on his back as he left the log. He narrowed his eyes against the light falling through the branches and wove stiff legged toward the gurgling sound of a forest rill. At the stream he lowered his heavy head and drank.

Thirst eased as he lapped the cool water with his curled tongue. Now his stomach rumbled louder. He was weak with hunger. Before he could track the Shriker, he would have to kill and eat larger prey.

Padding across the streambed, he squinted against the bright sky and peered at the blowing grass.

A sweet smell filled his lungs, but the flowers bobbing in the wind were stripped of color. All had gray blooms, or black or white. Even the wild roses on the edge of the lea were dark gray. He blinked, confused. *I've slept too many days inside the log,* he thought, *and my eyes aren't used to daylight.*

Skirting the meadow, he hid behind a wild bramble upwind of the stream. From this shady spot he could spy on the animals that would come to drink. He'd hunted in Shalem Wood many a time with a bow slung over his shoulder. And he'd returned with game for Mother's stew pot. He had no bow this time, he had no knife, but he didn't need them. He was the weapon.

Sunlight fell across the standing stone in the midst of the meadow. Miles looked closer. It was a stone, wasn't it? Or was it an ancient tree whose branches were broken? It had three thick spires coming out the top, like broad fingers reaching for the sky.

Beyond the stone tree (he decided to call it that, whatever it might be) water spilled between the rocks, calling the thirsty to the stream. Miles crouched behind the bush and waited. His wounds were healing, and all he needed now was food.

A flash of white in the corner of his eye gave him hope. His first victim, and it was something large! He licked his muzzle. A white horse emerged from the woods to drink at the stream. The horse stamped and swished its long tail in motion with the breeze.

Miles rose to get a better look. Just then the horse

lifted its head, and he saw the shining horn. A unicorn. A female, he was sure. Proud and more beautiful than any creature he'd ever seen. Ah, if Hanna could see her! How many times she'd dreamed of it. Though in her dreamwalk the unicorn was hunted down by wild beasts, and she'd awaken, screaming. Well, this unicorn was safe enough. He wouldn't attack her for her meat. He'd let her drift back into the woods.

Miles's stomach growled. He wanted her to finish her drink soon so other creatures would come to the water's edge. Those he could kill and eat. Drool dripped from his mouth and splashed onto his paws.

The unicorn tilted her head and stiffened, sensing his presence, or so he thought, but then Miles heard something too. A rustling sound in the woods off to his right. He cocked his ears. The unicorn lifted her head and tensed.

Suddenly the Shriker burst from the forest and charged. The air around him darkened as he chased the strip of light across the lea. Miles ducked behind the bush.

At the edge of the meadow the unicorn wheeled round and raced toward the stone tree, her hooves digging up the soil, sending clumps out behind as she gathered speed. *Run!* thought Miles, as if his thoughts could press her on. He wanted to run himself. But he was too weak to fight the Shriker now. He needed meat first, and lots of it.

Across the meadow a fox dived into the underbrush. The Shriker took no notice of him. He was after bigger game.

Miles's heart pounded in time with the unicorn's galloping hooves. In his mind he heard Hanna's screams. *No! Don't kill her! Don't!* His legs trembled as he watched the Shriker plow into the unicorn's side, sink his teeth into her flesh, tear a long gash down her neck. Hanna's dream! It wouldn't end this way! He wouldn't let it end this way!

Bolting from his hiding place, Miles bounded for the Shriker and knocked him to the ground. The unicorn stumbled toward the stream, too hurt to run.

The enemies fought as they had before, barking, snarling, circling. They rolled through the grass, tearing fur and flesh. The Shriker bared his teeth and bit again. Pain knifed through Miles's leg. He howled and fell onto his side. A bloody strip of hide dangled from his left foreleg. He lifted his head in the waving grass. Tried to rise. Fell.

The Shriker bounded across the lea again and knocked the unicorn down. The unicorn flailed under the monster's weight. The monster bared his bloody teeth as he went in for the kill.

No! Miles rose one last time and charged. He hit the Shriker broadside, and they rolled along the ground, tumbling into the stone tree. The Shriker threw his full weight at Miles and wedged him against the stone trunk. Miles kicked and kicked, but the beast was stronger. With his last bit of strength Miles lunged forward, snapping his jaws shut. Wrenching his head back, he tore open the beast's old neck wound.

Fresh blood spilled down the Shriker's chest. He howled, fell back, then turned and ran into the woods. Miles collapsed.

The sun lowered behind the high hills. Miles ran his tongue along the gash in his side and bathed his foreleg where a strip of skin hung down along the bone. New wounds, but his old wounds had not torn open again. He had been lucky this time.

A cool breeze passed through the meadow. Grass whispered about his head. The day dimmed to dusk. He didn't have to squint now. Miles stood, weakened from his long battle, ravenous with hunger. Across the field he saw the white form in the grass.

He padded over to the unicorn. Such a beautiful creature. Even in death her legs were partly bent as if she were running. He shuddered. Hanna's dream. It had all happened just as she'd seen it, but he never thought he would be one of the dark beasts in chase.

He nuzzled the unicorn's side where the Shriker had feasted on her flesh. The smell of her sweet meat filled his nose. His belly tightened. His head grew light. She was already dead and he was hungry. So hungry. The boy fought against his hunger, but the beast drooled over the meat.

Miles turned his head this way and that. No one would see him eat. His body cried out for the food. He bowed his head and trembled as he sniffed the unicorn's neck.

*The trees seemed as old as Noor itself,
standing burned and broken in the
midst of the lake.*

—*THE WAY BETWEEN WORLDS*

AFTER AN ARDUOUS HIKE HANNA, THE FALCONER, AND Gurty reached the mountain lake and stood together looking down at the water.

"It's a ghostly place," said Gurty. Hanna felt the same, for mist was blowing across the lake, a common sight in the morning, but it was a rare thing to see so late in the day. It seemed as if the lake itself was forming its own clouds, which rolled thick and white and fingered through the woods.

Through the mist Hanna could see three tall, leafless trees on a tiny isle in the midst of the lake. All were blackened, as if they'd burned in some long ago fire. They stood like three giant sentries who had died on their feet and never lain down to be buried.

Crickets sang a summer song in the grass below, but the lake had the look of winter to it. A chill air blew across its hidden surface. "Why did we come here?" asked Hanna.

"Do you hear them?" asked Gurty.

"Aye," said the Falconer.

Hanna thought Gurty was talking of the crickets but saw that the old woman was looking at the burned giants.

"Attenlore," whispered Gurty.

"Aye, child," said the Falconer.

Hanna frowned. He'd called Gurty "child." What could the Falconer have meant by that? To Hanna's left Gurty trembled and her green eyes shone.

Then Hanna heard a sound like no other. It began softly, but soon it was growing. A hum that was a moan. A song that was a cry. A howl that was a lullaby. And through the mist, long, dead branches moving.

"Old Men of Mount Shalem," said the Falconer, "will you give us passage?"

Mist thickened as if heavy curtains were being drawn against them. The giant trees disappeared, their voices growing, then silencing to rise again like waves across the shore.

"Follow where the blind are leading,
Listen where the mute are keening,
Where the deaf are storytelling,
Where the silent bells are knelling,
Where the river's blood is streaming
And wild animals are dreaming.
Things are never what they seem,
Find the lost inside the dream."

All this Hanna heard as the voices crossed over the misty water. And the words seemed to come from above and below, behind and before, as if she were in the middle of the lake. Staff in hand, the Falconer went down the hill, and Gurty followed with Hanna. They walked along the shore where bush met rock met water, and the Falconer stopped at a small stream.

Red brown rocks lay in the tumbling brook. They looked to Hanna like small beating hearts in the streambed. Near them the stream merged with Garth Lake, and so the Falconer stood "where the river's blood is streaming," as the chant had said.

He turned and faced the blackened trees, now silent on the island. Raising his foot over the water's edge, he stepped out onto the lake. Hanna expected to see his boot go underwater, but it rested on the surface. He took another step and another. The mist arched over him like a great gray hood, and a pale, cream-colored light shone through the opening.

Gurty followed the Falconer onto the lake.

Hanna could not tell how they were crossing the water until she herself put out her foot and found that her boot rested on a walking stone just breaking the surface of the lake.

Not far ahead the Falconer and Gurty stepped first one way and then the other, the gray passage opening before them as they went on. Hanna trailed behind, pausing after each step. Mist swirled around her boots, and try as she might, she couldn't see the walking stones the Falconer had used to cross the water.

The more Hanna faltered, the greater the distance grew between her and the others. She put out her foot.

Seeing no stone ahead to place it on, she drew back and waited. "I can't find the way," called Hanna.

"You're in the way," said Gurty. She and the Falconer were off to the right now and heading for the burned giants.

Standing on her wet stone, Hanna watched their outlines blend into the mist until they vanished. She could still see the giants' coal black forms, their thick arms bent, their twig fingers outstretched in greeting or in warning. All the tops of the burned trees were sharply broken, as if each wore a blackened crown.

Silence covered Garth Lake, and Hanna grew afraid. "Gurty?"

No answer.

"Where are you? I can't see you."

Hanna's pulse quickened. Her hands grew cold. Should she go after them or run down mountain and get help? What was the right way? She turned toward the shore and scanned the surface. The stones she'd taken here lay under the whirling mist. Trying a step, she pulled back suddenly when her boot sank into the cold water. Both feet on the stone again, she felt the chill as water seeped through the leather and soaked her foot.

Facing the giant trees again, she saw what looked like misty animal shapes running across the lake's glassy surface. Clouds of sheep, and gray white horses, a unicorn among them; then came smaller shapes, flying above like birds. "And wild animals are dreaming." A second sign that this was the passage the Falconer had asked for. She put out her damp foot, touched the surface straight ahead, sank, moved her foot to the right, and found a walking stone.

Things are never what they seem, she reminded herself.

A moment later, when the gale struck, she entered into the truth of those words.

WILD ESPER

*Wild Esper is a wind woman,
and she can ride an angry storm
as well as a playful breeze.*

—GRANDA SHEEN

THE WIND SWEPT HANNA OFF HER FEET AND BLEW HER
across the surface of the lake. She flailed against it, but
the more she fought, the stronger the gust became. Higher
and higher she flew over Garth Lake and into the line
of maples and copper beeches edging Shalem Wood.
Tumbling and twirling in the air, she thrust out her
hand like one drowning and grabbed a maple branch.
Hanna gripped the bough beside the fluttering leaves,
her body blowing sideways like a scarf.

The gale rose higher, singing in a thousand voices.
Still she gripped the branch tight. The maple tree
bent low, until it seemed the trunk would split in two.

Branches wrapped around Hanna like motherly arms as she held on.

A sudden forceful blast ripped the maple out by its roots, a thundering sound filled Hanna's ears as the tree came free, then both were sucked into the center of the storm.

Round and round they swirled over Shalem Wood, down the mountainside, and far over the sea. The island grew smaller as Hanna blew away from the land.

"Let go of the tree," called a voice. "She'll slow the journey."

"Who is talking?" shouted Hanna.

"Who is talking?" the voice sang back. It was a woman's voice, deep and clear and rich. Hanna looked up through the blowing branches and saw only shades of blue above her at first, but tipping her head farther back, she began to make out the giant face of Wild Esper, the great wind woman, who could change her form to match all weathers—a child on breezy mornings, a woman in chill wind, a hag in winter storm—but she was a woman now, her body long and flowing as a mountain river, her face crystal blue as winter water, her long, silk-spun hair mingling with the tumbled mist.

"Where are you blowing me?"

"Let go and you will know." Wild Esper looked ahead, her eyes burning bright as stars.

Hanna gazed down at the sea far below. "Promise you won't drop me."

"I'll hold you up," promised Wild Esper.

She felt the wind woman's power all around her, more than enough to bear her up. The maple wasn't helping her anymore. At last Hanna loosened her grip. The tree swirled downward and fell into the white-capped ocean. She watched the maple floating on the sea. How small it looked bobbing on the waves below.

With the letting go Hanna felt the wind soften and grow warm all around her. "Ah," sighed Wild Esper, "now we can blow through." The wind woman lifted Hanna higher still. Hanna put her arms out, birdlike, and let herself fly.

"Will you take me to Attenlore?"

"To Attenlore," sang Wild Esper.

Hanna reached up and tried to touch the wind woman's hand, but hers only slid through the enormous fingers, Wild Esper's skin all rushing wind.

They crossed the sky, soaring above the island; the

houses in Brim below looked small as snail shells, the trees as slender as grass. They gusted down lower still, clearing the line of cedars, pines, and oaks, then crossed over a silvery thread that showed itself to be a stream.

We're over Enness still, thought Hanna, *when will we get to Attenlore?* Then she remembered the rice paper map and how the two worlds touched and mirrored each other. How would she know when she crossed over into Oth?

Wild Esper rushed above the brook, blowing Hanna this way and that as the water wove around rocks and cut its way down mountain. Farther up the slope the stream widened as it ran through a meadow. One half of the meadow was green, and the other was darkened by cloud shadow.

Wild Esper gusted to the sunlit side. A foot above the ground the wind woman let go her hold. Hanna tumbled down into the soft grass and lay on her back, sucking in deep breaths. Above the field Wild Esper swept higher and higher into a thin swirl of clouds and slowly vanished.

Sweet-smelling grass bobbed all around Hanna, and she spread out her arms. Her body tingled as if she were still falling, and her head swirled. She lay with her hands outstretched, flattening her palms against the ground, for a long while until the spinning ceased. At last she took a deep breath and sat up. How thick the grass blades were, and how tall. She rubbed the feeling back into her arms and legs, stood up, and looked about.

By sight and smell and sound, this was Attenlore. She was sure of it without knowing just why. It seemed much like Enness, but brighter, more wakeful. The air about her glowed as if it were filled with glisten powder. And everything was humming with life.

Hanna turned about. She was here to find Miles, but before she could start searching, before she could do anything at all, she had to run. The beauty here filled her chest full to bursting, and if she didn't run, she'd have to shout or whoop or sing! So she raced through the glorious meadow. "Oh, beautiful," she cried. And in that moment she felt as if eOwey had brought her straight into the afterlife of Eyeshala.

Hanna ran from one end of the meadow to the other. "Find the lost inside the dream," the call had said. Now here she was in Attenlore. She'd feared to come and longed to come, but what was there to fear? She'd been afraid for nothing. Such a place. She could search for Miles and happily. He wouldn't want to stay inside the beast form here.

First she had to look for the Falconer and Gurty. Both should be here, but there was no sign of them in the meadow. Hanna rinsed her face in the stream, took a deep drink, and stood again, water dripping from her fingertips.

She peered across the stream at the far side of the meadow, which was still in shadow, and saw what she'd taken at first to be an ancient oak tree, standing tall, broad, and leafless, and extending into three spires at the top. But she saw now through the blue-dark air that it might be a standing stone instead. It wasn't brown like the boundary stones raised by the first folk of Enness Isle a thousand years ago, but a grayish white color like that of cresting waves or ash. In the midst of the shrouded field the stone's three spires, crowned in sun, were the only brightness glimmering on that side of the meadow.

Hanna had a strange sense that she'd seen the stone before. Not once, but many times. But where could she have seen it? She'd never been to Attenlore before. The surrounding grass was so dim she was sure she'd have a better view of the stone tree once the clouds parted. But when she glanced up to find the shielding cloud casting its broad shadow on the ground, she saw only clear sky, blue as her mother's eyes in the very center, and blushing orange along the mountainside, where the sun was sliding down. There was nothing overhead to make the far side of the meadow dark.

Coldness crept over her, as if the shadow was moving slowly toward her. Uthor Vale didn't reach out this far on the Oth map she'd seen in the Falconer's book. How could such a shadow be here in this lovely meadow?

Water babbled near her feet, birds sang in the nearby wood, and she could hear the rustling sounds of small animals in the greenery, but there was no sign of the Falconer or Gurty to calm her sudden fear. No prints or broken branches to show their comings and goings. Why hadn't they waited for her? Why had they left her alone?

Hanna wiped her hands on her skirt. A thrumming sound came from somewhere behind her. It was loud and sweet. She wanted to look around, but she feared turning her back on the shadow. Lifting her foot and drawing it behind, she carefully walked backward into the meadow, which still felt safe, drenched in the warmth and the colors of the setting sun. Step by step she drew away from the stream, all the while keeping her eyes fixed on the blue-dark air across the water and on the stone tree.

The thrumming sound grew and grew. It swelled in the air like the insistent flight of hummingbirds. Too curious to wait any longer, she turned and looked up. The air was sparkling with swirling lights. Hanna blinked as the lights flew closer. What . . . what were they?

Sparks flitted this way and that. One stray light dipped down near enough to view, and Hanna saw his tiny face. Woodland sprites! Hundreds of them! Hanna held her breath as they circled over her. Suddenly the sprites swooped down, and she felt a tickling all over as they lifted her from the ground. "Wait," she called. "I have friends to meet here. We're looking . . . ," she panted. "Have you seen my brother?"

No answer. Only the music of their wings as Hanna was borne up over the green-tipped trees skirting the mountainside. They followed the wending stream below until it spilled into a broader river. High above them

Senowey Falls crashed down the mountainside, but farther down, where the rocks were steep, the river fell again in smaller falls, spreading into pools that gathered golden, then rushed white again down mountain, like an ever-flowing stairway.

The sprites flew her over the largest river pool of all. In the middle was a small island. Over the tiny isle the sprites hovered just long enough for Hanna to take in some of what lay below. A castle, or something like it, rose up in the center of the isle. Its shining walls seemed to be made of the very water and mist from the stair-step falls that spilled into the pool.

Granda had told her of glimmer kingdoms, castles all of wind, mist, or stilled water, which could appear or disappear in the blinking of an eye. She'd imagined the sylth palaces, but what lay below was more beautiful and strange than she'd thought of in her own mind.

The glimmer castle was surrounded by trees, which edged the small island. The castle was quite large, but it had no roof at all atop. In the high end of the wide room the Sylth Queen sat on her flowered throne, sur-rounded by her attendants, swathed in golden cloth and green. A crowd of sylths and sprites were gathered on the stone floor before her. Some holding flowers. Some with streaming banners.

"Oh, look," cried Hanna. The sylth folk had parted long enough for her to see the Falconer and Gurty seated below the queen's dais. She took all of this in within a moment's time, her heart beating to the thrumming of the sprites' wings.

The sprites set Hanna on a stone seat between the Falconer and Gurty. "Oh, isn't it lovely!" she said, looking first to Gurty, then to the Falconer. Neither answered her but sat still as still, their eyes fixed on the queen. Hanna had spoken out of turn while everyone awaited the queen's first word, and she blushed, smoothed out her troubled hair, folded her hands, and looked up.

The queen's face shimmered as bright as the rippling water. Her black hair was adorned with woven strands as delicate as spiderwebs. A giant monarch butterfly rested on her shoulder, its orange and black wings outspread.

Hanna was watching how the queen's gown changed from blue to purple to green in the sunlight, when her view was suddenly blocked by a sylth knight who stepped before the throne and bowed.

"Is this all?" asked the queen.

"It's all of them, Queen Shaleedyn."

"And you found her in the meadow?"

"In the very place."

"And the Oak King?"

"He is all in shadow now."

The queen dismissed the knight and looked down at the Falconer.

"*Braughnoick*," she said.

Hanna started, for *braughnoick* meant "old man" in the Othic tongue, and the word was often used unkindly. Still, the Falconer stood and said, "Aye, Queen," in a most respectful manner.

"You are strangers here in Attenlore," she said, her voice cold and clear. "I see that one of you is sqyth-born."

Hanna didn't know what sqyth-born meant, but the words made her suddenly uneasy. The queen looked down at her with piercing violet eyes. She had more to say, and the sound of the falls behind gave company and depth to her speech. "We have felt your coming to our world," she said, "and we have prepared a showing for you."

The Falconer bowed his head. "Thank you, Queen Shaleedyn. You may wish to know that we have crossed into Attenlore on a quest to find—"

"Be seated now," she said abruptly. Her pet monarch fluttered its wings. The Falconer sat again.

Hanna leaned in close to his ear. "When will you ask her about Miles?" she whispered.

The Falconer gave her a warning look. "We must abide by the queen's wishes. But don't worry, Hanna. I'll find a way to speak of him soon."

Sprites flew up and made bright patterns in the air above the throne. A showing could mean music or dance or any kind of sport. Hanna's body trembled with expectation. The queen's musicians stepped out from the crowd and began to play. Soon Gurty's head fell to her chest and she began to snore. *How can she fall asleep at a sylth gathering?* thought Hanna, but as she waited in her chair, she found her hands and feet growing heavy. She yawned. A delightful, tingling feeling ran up and down her body, and her eyelids drooped.

The banging of a drum awoke Hanna some time later, and she blinked in the pale light. While she was asleep, the sylth music had changed to a low, crooning song and the day had dimmed to dusk. Light orbs of orange, yellow, red, and blue hung in the air above, spreading a soft light below. The instruments sang a sad tune much like the graveside dirges that were played at a Crossing Over. All around the stone chairs a line of the sylth guard in glassy armor stood at full attention. Hanna ran her eye down the row, saw the bows and spears. When had they come and why so well armed?

She wanted to ask the queen but found she couldn't speak. Two slender threads across her mouth were silencing her. On either side of her Gurty and the Falconer had just discovered the same thing. Tiny spiders crawled over them. While they slept, the spiders had spun webs about them. The silken threads were woven tightly around their bodies from head to foot. She'd felt a tickling sensation a moment before she fell asleep, but she'd ignored it.

The webs were so nearly invisible she could not believe they had any power to keep her still. Yet when she tried to bring her hands up from her lap, she found the silken threads to be impossibly strong.

Queen Shaleedyn smiled. "You do not need to struggle," she said. "The spell webs will hold."

Hanna's heart raced. What sort of trick was this?

"You are strangers here, as I said before, and we knew your human smell as you entered our realm. We heard your heavy footfall in our woods. And it did not take you long to break the law."

Hanna wanted to scream, "What law?" but her lips were bound tight. Beside her Gurty moaned inside her gossamer webs, and to her left the Falconer was struggling to speak.

FRITT THE SPY

Where the river's blood is streaming
And wild animals are dreaming.
—THE OLD MEN OF MOUNT SHALEM

THE DRUM SOUNDED AGAIN, AND HIGH ABOVE THE GLIMMER walls a score of sylths flew, bearing up a large, dark cloth. They lowered their burden to the stony ground before the captives, then tossed flowers on the dead unicorn that lay atop the cloth. Lilies and wild irises fell across the body, but beneath the heavily scented blooms the bloody gash in its throat could still be seen.

Tears streamed down Hanna's cheeks. Here was the unicorn from her dreamwalks. She'd seen her again and again, running from two large beasts, though she could never make out the look of them. And in that moment she remembered where she'd seen the stone tree before. In

246

her dream the unicorn had run past the three-spired tree.

"Here," said Queen Shaleedyn. "Look long at the work you've done." Her violet eyes seemed larger now and cold as the coming night. She raised her proud chin. "Surely in your world as in ours the unicorn is a magical beast and above the hunter's rights to slay for meat!" Her voice picked up strength, as a gale does rising early in the first hours of a storm. "Yet you come to Attenlore and kill my beloved steed, Neurreal! She was free to wander as she willed but loyal to me always. Whenever I wanted to ride, I needed only speak her name, and she would come." Shaleedyn's lip trembled. Again, and more softly, the queen added, "She'd cross all Oth to come."

Both Hanna and Gurty were trying to protest through clamped jaws, and the Falconer struggled against the webbing that held him fast to his seat.

Queen Shaleedyn came to a slow stand on her platform above the crowd. Her monarch took sudden flight. *"Hessha elandra,"* she whispered, stirring her finger in the air. As she stirred, the sound of rushing wind overcame the music. The queen's hair and gown began to blow in the wind of her own making. *"Elandra!"* she said again. The sylth folk moaned and cowered, their banners whipping in Shaleedyn's gale. The cold wind she was stirring rose high and higher, and the trees outside the glistening wall began to sway.

"The law demands payment for this death," said Shaleedyn over the keening. "If your human world is peopled by half-awakes who have forgotten the ancient laws, then know that our world is not. We the folk of Attenlore live and die by the law of the Old Magic."

By some power Hanna could not imagine, the Falconer finally struggled to a stand and spoke through his spell webs. "Queen Shaleedyn. This murder is evil to our eyes as well. We did not do this!" His long hair blew back in her storm; still he stood in her great wind. Hanna watched him try to raise his hand, but he could not break the webbing around his arm.

"Queen Shaleedyn," he cried. "We, too, honor the Old Magic!"

The queen stopped stirring her finger, and the wind began to die down. The trees outside the glimmer walls settled to a murmur, and the banners ceased their fluttering. "*Braughnoick*, I see you have some power, but there is the smell of your world on this killing, and you three are the strangers here."

Hanna looked up at the Falconer, whose gray head was bowed. The sylths lining up on each side whispered one to another, but she couldn't hear what they were saying. Then a loud commotion made the sylths at her right draw far apart.

"Who comes to disturb my court?" asked the queen.

A fox, flanked by more sylth guards, trotted up beside Hanna.

"I have news," said the fox.

"Your news can wait," said the queen. The sylth guards turned about, but the fox kept his footing.

"Your majesty will want to hear this," said the fox.

Queen Shaleedyn flared up like a candle flame; a sudden ring of purple fire surrounded her, and the roses around her throne shone in the brilliant light. The fox threw himself to the ground and covered his eyes with his paws. Hanna looked aside as far as the webbing would allow. But the Falconer faced the fire straight on and did not avert his gaze.

"I know what happened to Neurreal," the fox said, his eyes still covered.

"We know this, Epitt," said the queen. The purple flames about her head cooled and died down.

The fox lifted his head just enough to see the body laid out on the ground at the far end of the courtyard. "I saw the killing done," he said.

"Rise, Epitt," said the queen. "And look about."

The fox did so.

"You are too late with your news, fox. We have already caught the trespassers from the human world."

Epitt's lip curled to a snarl. "Ah," he said, "I sniffed these human folk out myself today. Your guards have caught these trespassers," said Epitt. "But I saw the ones who broke the law."

Shaleedyn fingered the sapphires at her neck. "Tell us what you saw."

Epitt bowed his red head, then raised it again. "The Shriker," he said.

The name sped through the air like a thick shadow. Orb lights dimmed in its wake and some went out altogether. Hanna heard scrambling sounds as the sprites hastened to relight the orbs. Red lights and blue and yellow warmed one by one, and when enough light had returned, Epitt continued. "There were two of them, Queen Shaleedyn. They attacked Neurreal and tore her throat. Then they fought over who would eat the kill."

The courtyard fell silent with the news. No one moved. Only the orbs flickered, as if fighting to remain lit. At last the queen spoke with a voice like breaking ice. "There is only one beast by that name, Epitt. The one so named by the Darro three hundred years ago. There cannot be two."

"This I know, Your Highness," said Epitt. "But that is what I saw."

Hanna's terror grew. This was worse than being accused of killing the unicorn herself. At least before she'd known that it was a mistake and there was some hope of proving their innocence to the queen. But Epitt's news hit her like pelting stones. Miles still wore the body of the Shriker. Worse, the fox had seen him and the Shriker kill the unicorn. It couldn't be true, but there had been two beasts in chase in her dreamwalk, and two who fought over the unicorn. Her body shook as she saw them now clearly in her mind. Great, dark monsters. Bearlike, but wild dogs both.

"We know something of this, Queen Shaleedyn," said the Falconer. "If I may speak."

The queen nodded, but her brow narrowed with displeasure. The Falconer raised his arm, breaking through the silken webs. In the quavering light he held his left hand out to a burning orb until the Othic symbol on his palm shone blue. Hanna watched it appear as she had the night he'd first shown her the sign.

"So, you are a meer," said the queen. She tilted her head and studied him with her violet eyes. "Tell us the truth, then, Falconer."

He bowed his head to her, for she'd looked more closely at him and discerned his name.

"I will tell you what truth I know." The Falconer put his hand on Hanna's shoulder. "This is Hanna. She was entranced in our world and called to be the Shriker's prey."

Queen Shaleedyn leaned forward. "How is it she still lives?"

"It is by some great magic she was spared, though I do not know its origin," said the Falconer.

"Tell me, what spell was used?" ordered the queen.

"No spell," said the Falconer, "but the shape-shifter's art."

A sigh rippled through the crowd, up and down the great hall.

"Be gone!" said the queen. And suddenly musicians,

dancers, and other sylth folk disappeared. Only a small group remained before the queen under the burning orbs: Hanna and Gurty in their chairs, the Falconer standing tall, and across from him, the sylth guard. Epitt the fox had vanished with the rest.

Queen Shaleedyn looked down at Hanna. "This girl has a brother," she said.

"Aye, Queen."

"So it happens again," said the queen. Her eyes seemed far away when she said this, as if she was looking somewhere in the past.

So it happens again? thought Hanna. *What did she mean by that?*

The queen seemed to awaken from her daze. She waved her hand at Hanna and Gurty, and the webbing broke apart. Hanna brushed the silken threads from her face and front.

"There was a boy who gave us pleasure with his flute," said Queen Shaleedyn. "Ah, such music." She adjusted her shimmering gown, then frowned at the Falconer. "A gift was given."

"Ah," said the Falconer. "A sylth gift."

"The wind chose it," corrected the queen.

Hanna looked up at her. Did she mean Wild Esper? Why would a wind spirit give Miles that kind of power?

The Falconer bowed his head a moment, then raised it again. "The wind," he said thoughtfully. "These are great powers indeed and as old as the oldest magic."

Queen Shaleedyn leaned forward. The glimmer wall behind broadened her reflection, so there seemed to be two of her, one human size and one giant size. "The law was broken, and we shall deal out just punishment here in Attenlore. The Shriker's laid claim to my lands long enough. He's crossed the walls and forced the boundaries farther out." She made a sweeping motion with her arm as she said this. "The more he hunts, the larger Uthor grows. Now he and this shifter have killed my Neurreal. This murder was crime enough, but to poison the meadow where the Oak King Brodureth stands—to blight the place where we go to honor Deya's Eve!" Her voice was growing louder with each word. "The Oak King of old, though he is stone now, is father to many in the wood. The Shriker's kill fouled his meadow, and now King Brodureth stands in constant shadow. What punishment is cruel enough ever to pay for that?" She was at a full stand now on the dais, towering over them. "This is our trouble, Falconer! Not yours. Your kind have done enough."

"But it *is* our trouble," cried Hanna, leaping from her seat. "Miles is my brother!"

"Banished!" called the queen. She raised her hand and said, "The door closes now!"

Suddenly the bright orbs, the glimmer walls, and the sylth guard disappeared like snuffed-out candles. Hanna felt herself wrenched up and tossed skyward.

Blackness everywhere. She screamed and flailed. Nothing to see. Nothing to hang on to. Then she was falling down and down and down.

At last she landed with a splash and sank deep under cold water. Frantic for air, she swam upward and broke the surface, choking. She was treading water in the middle of Garth Lake. "What?" she cried. "What's happened?"

Gurty splashed down beside her, let out a startled scream, and went under. Hanna dived for her, clenching her jaw against the cold. She swam as best she could with clothes and shoes still on.

Catching Gurty's arm, she pulled her to the surface. Sputtering and taking in breath after breath, they clung to each other. Then the Falconer swam up, took Gurty's other arm, and helped Hanna pull the old woman back to shore.

PREY

PREY

The taste of victory was on their lips and blood was in their mouths.

—*The Book of eOwey*

MILES FELT VICTORIOUS NOW AS HE CROUCHED IN THE windy forest gorging on the stag. The deer had charged him and tried to gore him with his antlers, but Miles had won out in the end. He paused and shook his head against the annoying flies. Then changed position over his prey.

A boy would never have been able to slay the deer with his bare hands or spill its life's blood with his small teeth. Pride surged through him as he tore the deer's flesh and chewed the strong-tasting meat. His nostrils filled with the smell of fresh kill, and he reveled in its flavor. He was king of beasts here. He felt the muscles in his broad shoulders ripple with newfound power.

The breeze picked up and blew against his side. He leaned into it as he ate. So windy here, and he hadn't been able to escape it. It almost seemed as if the wind had chased him across the meadow and pushed him farther into the woods. Strange thought.

He paused and lifted his nostrils to it. A sharp, clean smell of grass and evergreens. Lavender grew nearby, he could smell that, and the tang in the air told him that sage grew somewhere in these woods where sunlight penetrated the canopy.

He tore another piece of meat and chewed, feeling his life and strength returning as he ate. He was a beast on the prowl, and now that his belly was full of meat, he would have the power to overcome his enemy.

Kill the beast.

Break the curse.

He chewed in rhythm to the chant. How they would welcome him home when this victory was won! He'd be the hero of Enness Isle. A hero across all of Noor. They'd recount his battle in the history books. Miles the beast slayer!

He tasted victory even as he ran his tongue along his muzzle, cleaning off the blood.

THE QUEEN'S SECRET

So it happens again.

—THE SYLTH QUEEN

HANNA RETURNED HOME DRENCHED AND FREEZING FROM Garth Lake.

"You're wet as a fish!" Mother scolded. But when she saw Hanna was shaking, she soon had her warm and wrapped and by the fire. It was no good at all telling Mother and Da she'd been to Attenlore and back, so she kept that to herself, saying only that she'd fallen in the lake and the Falconer had rescued her. True enough, for she'd started to sink as she tried to help Gurty, and it was the meer who'd brought them all to shore.

Over the next week Mother and Da searched the woods with Brother Adolpho. And while Gurty was called away to tend the sick on Tyr Isle, Hanna went looking with the Falconer. They returned to Garth Lake many a time, searching for a way back to Attenlore, but the Old Men of Mount Shalem no longer spoke out magic. Standing tall and black in the midst of the lake, they seemed nothing more than burned trees now, and broken.

Summer was coming to an end. The first of the autumn storms blew in from the sea. The Falconer coughed and shivered as they sheltered under a tall cedar, waiting for the storm to pass. He'd taken cold from the drenching in Garth Lake the week before, but today his cough seemed rougher. Hanna thought to say he should be abed, but the man was a leafer. He must know his own needs. There were but thirteen more days until the next full moon. If they couldn't find Miles and help him to change back to himself in time . . . The thought came with an ache in the stomach and a clenching in the throat. She needed the Falconer here. Brushing her wet bangs back, she watched the water dripping from the end of his long nose.

"We've looked and looked for the passage," said Hanna. "Why can't we find it?"

The Falconer peered through the branches. "There are few places left that open to Oth. But new entryways appear from time to time, so a meer must be vigilant and look for the signs." The old man turned to Hanna. "These signs are not seen with the eye alone. The seeker must look with the eye of the heart."

"How can you see with the heart?"

"It's something no one can teach you, Hanna."

Hanna leaned against the rough trunk and gathered her courage. She had to ask. "What if the passage here in Shalem Wood is closed now? What if it will never open again?" She trembled, waiting for his answer.

The Falconer cleared his throat. "Don't be giving up so soon, Hanna. Mount Shalem is a hallowed place of old. It was once a part of the Dragon Lands." He sniffed and wiped his nose. "The passage may be hard to find, but it is here. Of any place it must be here, where so many ancient guardians dwell."

Hanna imagined dragons on Mount Shalem before men ever came to settle here. It wasn't hard to picture great blue taberrells soaring overhead alongside golden terrows, even on this stormy day. The sound of wings flapped overhead as Aetwan flew above the rain-drenched trees; the sight of him brought her back to the island here and now. The Falconer had said there were ancient guardians here. Not dragons. It couldn't be. "Who are they?" she asked.

He didn't answer her right off, but patted the giant cedar trunk as one would pat a noble horse after a long ride. "These trees are very old and wise," he said. "And their roots go deep and deep. The oldest ones live close to a thousand years, and they hold world and world together."

"Like bridges?"

"Aye, a bit like that."

Hanna liked that. She smelled the rich, wet air, full of woodland scents, and heard the knocking of a wood-pecker somewhere above, working in the rain. "But there are woodlands all over Noor."

The Falconer sneezed and wiped his nose. "True enough," he said. "But many people have moved into the forests. Here the woods are left alone. Fear of the Shriker has kept people out."

The thought was like a stone to window glass as it broke within her mind, but it was true and Hanna knew it. Only the shepherds, goatherds, and leafers like the Falconer and Gurty lived in Shalem Wood or near it. She wondered that such an evil thing as the Shriker could bring some goodness to the world, but there it was. Shalem Wood was a wild place, an entry to the Otherworld, and the Shriker's legend had helped to make it so.

The rain ceased. Pearl white sunlight fell through the branches, warming the woods all around them. They started up the path again.

"I've been wanting to thank you," said Hanna.

"What for?"

"You stood up to Queen Shaleedyn. You said Miles didn't kill her unicorn." She swallowed once. "I'm sure he'd never do that, even if he was still caught inside the beast form." She *was* sure, almost completely sure, but she needed the Falconer to say so too.

"Well, the boy needed defending." He didn't say more than that.

They crossed into the meadow and walked along the ridge where the boulders leaned like giants' heads, looking down the mountainside. "Granda told us there was always more than one victim in the dark-moon years, but only Polly died this time since the Shriker's return, and that's because of Miles."

"It's true your brother's stopped him from attacking at each full moon. He saved you and any others the Shriker may have hunted down those nights. No one has ever done that before."

The meer's words sent a thrill down the backs of Hanna's arms. Miles had taken far too many risks, but he'd also been brave, and he'd kept the Shriker from his kill at every full moon; so far he'd fought him off.

They stepped past thorny gorse bushes. The Falconer coughed, then took out a cloth and wiped his nose. "It's good you and Gurty haven't taken ill from the drenching in Garth Lake."

"Aye," said Hanna. "And you have to get well soon." She said this out of love for him, but there was a desperateness below the words. He was the only one on Enness Isle who had the power to help her find Miles.

"Gurty can help you search," said the Falconer, as if he'd heard her thought.

Hanna's pace faltered. "She's no help at all!"

"Don't be unkind, Hanna, she may be of help in time."

"I don't have time! You said so yourself. We have only thirteen days to go. Gurty can't help me find Miles the way you can. She doesn't have any real power."

"And you do?"

Hanna felt heat rising up her neck. She didn't answer or look up at the meer's face.

"It was Gurty took us to Garth Lake, if you remember. She's a seer in her own way, Hanna, and she may play her part yet."

The Falconer tapped a boulder with his staff, and a bit of moss fell off. "There's much that's still a mystery," he said. "It's not known how the Shriker found a way to break through the queen's boundary in Uthor. If we knew that, we'd be closer now to finding him, I think, and to find him is to find your brother Miles."

Hanna rubbed her arms under her damp cloak as she walked along. She felt chilled even in the sunlit meadow. There was something Queen Shaleedyn had said that still puzzled her. "I was wondering," she said. "Do you remember what the queen said just before she banished us?"

The Falconer stopped and looked at her, waiting.

"She was telling us how she gave Miles his power— a gift, she called it." Hanna frowned, remembering. "Then she said, 'So it happens again.'"

"Ah, you caught that too."

"So," said Hanna, "she gave someone else a gift, I'm thinking, and it all went wrong, the way it has with Miles and . . ." She stopped herself. She'd had an idea forming in her mind but was afraid to say it. What if she was wrong?

The Falconer's brows were tilted. He was still waiting. She had to go on. "Do you know about the tree?" The word "tree" came out in a whisper, and it left her lip trembling in its wake.

The meer tipped his head, a ray of sunlight falling on his wet hair. "The Enoch Tree, you mean." It wasn't a question. He gazed at her intently but not unkindly.

"Granda said his brother was chosen to be trained up as a meer. I was thinking the queen might have given him the gift for magic, but that it went wrong. Granda said Enoch was sent home from Othlore for some reason, but he didn't know what happened there."

"Enoch stole an ancient text." The Falconer's voice was biting. "A book filled with secrets of Oth. And one that told of the beginning time when Noor and Oth were one. Enoch was hungry to learn spells and impatient to gain power."

He took a breath, coughed, and tried to calm

himself again. "I was teaching on Othlore back then. And if Enoch had come forward and turned the book in once we discovered the loss . . . but he tried to cover his tracks. The boy burned it."

"The only copy?"

The Falconer nodded. "Only the High Meer was to read from the text, such was the power hidden in its pages."

Hanna felt a wave of shame for her family. She didn't want to hear more, but she needed to know all for Miles's sake. "Then he did something else once he returned home," she whispered, "something so terrible the Sylth Queen imprisoned him in the oak tree." She stopped on the path. "What did he . . . do you know what evil thing he did?"

"The queen knows that. I do not. But he was imprisoned fifty years ago."

"Around the time the Shriker came back to Shalem Wood?"

"Aye. I've long suspected Enoch had something to do with that, but I had no way of knowing it for sure. The queen's words gave us more light to see by."

Hanna tugged a leaf from the aspen tree. Turned it

over in her hand. The Sylth Queen, the Shriker, Enoch. All had come together on the high cliff. Yet none but those three knew the how or why of it. And if a clue to finding Miles was held within the Enoch Tree, the man inside could not speak the way, for though his mouth was open in a scream, it had stayed silent these fifty years.

CAPTIVE

CAPTIVE

Breal of Kelleneur built a worthy vessel and sailed across the Ebring Sea in pursuit of the great serpent Wratheren.

—THE EPIC OF BREAL

"LISTEN," SAID THE FALCONER. MILES STOOD WITH HIM on a platform. Darkness all around, but his teacher's face shone lamplike in the gloom. In the distance a spinney bird sang, a clear-bright tune that rose and fell, and with the song Miles began to see, as if curtains were parting. He was on a stage in the middle of a great, round amphitheater, with long stone stairways coming out from the center like spokes in a wheel. Thousands of people filled the seats. And on his right the High King of Angalore sat in a favored spot, the king in red velvet robes, his wife in blue.

"Now play," whispered the Falconer. Miles should

have felt a rush of fear, but his heart was light, so light it seemed the stage was floating upward. He raised his flute and blinked. When had his teacher handed him his own silver ervay? It was a high honor indeed to be gifted with an ervay, and such an instrument was passed on only to a worthy musician. A warm pleasure filled him. He turned to thank the Falconer, but the meer had vanished, only a pale light remaining in his place.

Miles's feet lifted off the stage, the air pierced with golden light as he played the silver flute. Joy spread outward from the song, to king and queen, to the people in the seats. As the melody changed, he saw the joy change colors: daylight blue, sea green, then red rose petals falling through the air. He would never leave this moment. He'd stay here forever. . . .

A strange voice awakened him. Miles sighed and lifted his groggy head. He blinked his heavy lids. Such a dream! He wanted to lie down and go back inside the song—to see the king smile, watch the queen nod in time to his music. He tried to move his fingers. No, they were paws now, not suited to play the flute at all. Paws. Strong, heavy weapons. He felt a sudden sadness. He should turn back into a boy again. He'd kept himself long enough inside the beast. A sudden sound nearby made him start. He was not alone.

Open wide now, his eyes slowly adjusted to a dim light, and the clearer the picture became, the more his horror grew. No wonder he hadn't been able to move. His paws were bound up front and back. He was trapped in some rolling cage.

He peered through the bars at the two disheveled beings at the low fire. Sylths in ragged cloaks and patched breeches.

"We're sure to get well paid," said the sylth in green.

The other rubbed his chin. "Aye, we will."

How could he have gotten here? He sniffed at the sharp pains in his side and found three arrow wounds. They'd shot him and put him to sleep with a potion. Tamalla, by the smell of it.

"She'll restore our wings."

The brown-cloaked sylth shook his head. "No, never that. Our wings are gone for good, Reyn, but she may let us live in Attenlore again."

"Ah, well, Perth, I'd do anything to be free of the stink of Uthor Vale."

Miles began to chew through the cords around his forepaws.

By the fire Reyn lifted his cup. "We owe the beast something for setting us free."

"He didn't! He only broke through the queen's wind wall and made a way for us to escape from Uthor."

"Us and others, I'm thinking."

Miles cocked his ears. Wind wall? He hadn't heard of such a thing before, but it was clear the Sylth Queen had tried to contain the Shriker, and still he'd broken free.

Perth poked the fire with his stick. "I say we don't owe the Shriker anything. He escaped to please himself!"

"And now we're pleasing ourselves," laughed Reyn. He tossed more kindling into the fire.

Perth raised his cup. "Aye. No more skullen snakes hanging from the trees!"

"No more gullmuth beast hunting after us!"

"No more trolls anxious to dig our graves!"

"Hear, hear, I say to all that!"

Front paws free, Miles began gnawing the ropes around his back legs. He was groggy, so even this was hard work. His mouth was numb, and he couldn't feel the rope on his tongue, but he chewed.

"The loot will do us good. And she'll give us plenty for this monster. Three hundred years he's savaged Attenlore, and as for his latest kill . . ." Reyn's next words were a whisper. Miles heard the sound but couldn't make out what he was saying under his breath.

"Ah," sighed Perth. "You almost feel sorry for a beast who's coming up against the queen's justice."

Miles's ears pricked. So, he'd been captured for a reward! Why? What had he done? He'd misused the gift she'd given at first, and attacked Mic on the road, but that was long ago now. Since that night he'd shapeshifted for good reason. Shaleedyn wouldn't blame him for fighting the Shriker to protect his sister. His head felt stuffed with cotton wool. He was dizzy, and his body felt heavy. With some effort he put out his right foreleg and tried to stand, but the tamalla still pulsed through his veins, and his paw slipped awkwardly on the floorboards.

"He deserves whatever Queen Shaleedyn dishes out for killing her unicorn," said Reyn.

Miles started. He tried to call out, "I didn't kill her!" but his words came out as a growl.

"Look sharp!" Perth leaped to a stand. "The beast's

awake!" There was a loud cracking noise as Reyn approached the cage with a whip. "Keep down, monster!"

Miles felt the stinging whip on his right flank. Leaping up with sudden fury, he turned about. The dizziness hit him square on. His head pounded as if he'd crashed into a stone wall.

He collapsed again into blackness.

LEAVING

LEAVING

*eOwey open our eyes to find
the boy Miles who has lost his way.*

—BROTHER ADOLPHO

THE FALCONER SAT BY THE FIRE WRAPPED IN HIS THICK green blanket. His cold had worsened but he would not yet go to bed. "There are things you'll need to know," he'd said as Hanna hung the kettle over the flames. He turned the page and read a passage from *The Way Between Worlds* aloud in a scratchy voice as Hanna brewed slippery elm tea. There were only nine days until the next full moon. *Listen,* she told herself, *the book will help.*

The old man read, "'Whether a meer's kith be found in the elements of earth, air, fire, water, or ether, a meer is to befriend the natural world.'"

Hanna found the book confusing. She felt she'd

275

understood the part he'd read about befriending the natural world, for she loved her island home and had a special heart for the trees, but the other section . . . "How does a meer find a kith in the elements?"

"Tell me how you came to be in Attenlore, Hanna."

"I fell. Then I . . ." She gave a crooked smile. "I flew."

A twinkle shone in the old man's eyes. "You grew wings, then?"

"No." She laughed. "I was taken up by Wild Esper."

"So you have a sky kith."

Hanna wiggled her toes inside her boots, remembering the strange and sudden joy she'd felt when Wild Esper blew her upward. The chill rush of flight as the gusts lifted her over Mount Shalem. But the wind woman hadn't seemed friendly, only wild and strong beyond imagining.

"You may find such help between the worlds again," said the Falconer. "Be vigilant and look for the signs." It was a line right from the book, and he was saying it to her as if she were a meer.

"But I'm not . . ." She turned away, confused. The tea was ready, and she poured him a cup. "Why don't you read a page that tells us how to get back in?"

He coughed a hacking cough until his eyes watered. Hanna drew closer. Should she pound his back the way she pounded Mother's when the coughing shook her so?

The Falconer blinked his watery eyes and closed the book. "Well," he said, "the map's there, as you've seen before. But the way to Attenlore"—he ran his hand along the leather spine—"that knowledge is beyond the pages of a book."

"Then, why read from it at all?" Hanna bit the inside of her cheek. She hadn't meant to raise her voice.

The Falconer tilted his bushy brows. "This book may not tell you *where* to look, but *how* to look."

Hanna stared out the window and saw two black-winged kravel birds sheltering in the wet trees. What did he mean by *how* to look?

Steam rose from the Falconer's mug, parting in a gray tide as it met his face. He blew on the surface and drank slowly. There was a grayness to his skin Hanna didn't like the look of. "You need to drink it all to get well," she said.

"Sit beside me, Hanna." He patted the bent-willow chair, and Hanna sat. Aetwan's feathers ruffled as if a wind were blowing past his perch, but all else in the little room was still.

The Falconer took a labored breath. His golden eyes shone as if they, too, brought light to the darkened room. The slippery elm might ease his throat, but it wouldn't touch a fever. She was sure he was feverish, though she was too shy to feel his brow.

"Hanna," he said softly. "There may be good reason why Wild Esper helped you cross between worlds, whether she's your kith or no. The wind woman was sorely hurt by the Shriker."

"How can a beast harm a wind spirit?"

"You can hurt someone well enough by harming someone they love." The Falconer had the same look on his face that Granda used to have when he was about to tell a tale. But she was in no mood for a story just now; she had Miles to think of, and she had the old man's health to worry about. If she had a leafer's skills, she could make him well—now, today—and they could search. Hanna felt as useless as a wet candle and angry with herself. "What you're about to tell me," she said, "will it help us find Miles?"

"A little more knowledge weighs nothing at all, so you won't find it a burden."

Hanna didn't understand his answer, but he seemed

determined to go on. He'd never led her astray, so she settled into the rough-hewn chair to listen.

"I came to Enness years ago with a magical creature. A golden terrow dragon hatched from an egg I'd found on Othlore."

Hanna's mouth made a little O of wonder. She'd heard of terrows before and the meers of Othlore who rode them skyward, but it was an old tale.

"I named the terrow Furleon, which means 'fire keeper' in Kumarian. He was mine for the raising, his mother having died before he hatched. Meers who raise terrows from hatchlings are meant to be their guardians," said the Falconer, "but Furleon had a love beyond that of men, for even a meer is held to the soil. So we are bound to the earth, but a terrow is not.

"Here on the isle he met Wild Esper. The wind spirit played with Furleon day to day as a girl will play with a young pup." The Falconer stopped, and his eyes had a faraway look.

Hanna brought the tale back with a question. "Did you give her the terrow?"

The Falconer coughed. "I would never have done that." He looked across the room at his falcon. Aetwan tipped his head and peered back. "Creatures of the air have their own hearts to give." He spread his fingers wide and winglike, though his hands stayed in his lap. "Furleon gave his heart to Esper. So I released him."

He smiled to himself, his eyes seeing beyond the walls of his small house to something in the past. "That was more than forty years ago, but I can still see them. They were happy playmates, and he flew with her in breezes and in storms. There are few who could ever do that," he said with pride. "He'd be flying with her still if the Shriker hadn't downed him."

Hanna didn't have to ask how the Shriker had done that, for she'd seen the beast shape-shift into a giant falcon that first night in Shalem Wood. "Why didn't the wind woman fight back?"

"It was dark that night with the moon eclipsed, as it always is when he first shows himself in our world. The wind woman fought all she could, but once the Shriker had Furleon, he shifted back into himself again, and Esper can do little to a land creature huddled in the deeps of a cave. So the Shriker killed the golden dragon, Esper's and mine, and—"

"Don't say more," said Hanna. "Please." She saw it

all well enough in her mind to know the Shriker ate the terrow, and she didn't want to hear the Falconer say it. Now he was coughing again. She leaped up, poured the last bit of tea into his cup, and slipped it into his hands. He nodded, took a slow breath, and drank.

Hanna gazed up at the dried herb bundles hanging from the ceiling. "The slippery elm isn't enough," she said. "Tell me what else you need to make you well, and I'll brew it."

"The herbs I need aren't here."

"Then, tell me where to find them," insisted Hanna. "You must get well right away. I need your help to find Miles."

The Falconer wiped his nose and folded his kerchief. "You will have to search without me."

"I can't!"

He gave her a questioning look, as if she'd just told a lie, but she met his gaze. "It's true," she said. "Wild Esper rides the wind whichever way she pleases. And I can't even see her most times."

"Aye, wind spirits cloak themselves and are rarely seen by humankind."

"I don't have the power to call her to me," said

Hanna. "And even if she does come and take me to Attenlore, I don't know how to find Miles once I get there." She was suddenly trembling, and she worked to control herself, but the trembling only grew worse. "I'm not wise like you."

"No," said the Falconer. "You're wise like Hanna." He touched her shoulder. A light touch, like a breeze she could barely feel, but with that touch her trembling ceased. "This has always been your story," he said. "Yours and Miles's. I was only here to come along with you for a time."

"But . . . I don't understand."

"Remember the day at the kirk when I said you would come to me when you heard the Shriker's call?"

"Aye."

"And you came."

She nodded.

"Well," said the Falconer, "I cannot see far, but I saw that." He closed his eyes. "Now I see a little more. You will seek your brother in the Otherworld. For the boy who is bound must be freed by your hand."

Hanna looked down at her hands. They were so small compared with the Falconer's, and she had no sign of power on her palm. How could she do this alone?

"Why won't you come with me?"

The Falconer tipped his head. "I'm old, and the time has come for me to move on."

"Move on to where? If you have the strength to go somewhere, you can come with me."

He ignored her plea. "I have to go soon," he said. "But I'll speak to your father first. Will you go fetch him for me?"

"Aye," said Hanna. "But tell me where you're going."

"All of us are on the way to where I'm going, Hanna. I won't be alone, and neither will you."

Hanna suddenly knew what he meant by "where I'm going," and she couldn't bear to let him see her weep, so she leaped up, tore her cloak from the root hook, and swept out the door.

The rain had ceased, and the day had turned cold and bright; red-orange leaves glowed like torches in the maple trees. And the birch trees were golden. Under their blowing boughs Hanna sped up her pace. She would send Da to the Falconer as he had asked her to, then she would go to Gurty's cottage. The woods woman had been little help in finding Miles, but both she and the

Falconer were healers. If the Falconer was too sick to find the herbs he needed to cure himself, Gurty would have to do it.

The green bracken made a soft swishing noise against her skirts as she flew past. Blue jays flitted from tree to tree. The woods were alive with light and color, but she didn't take much notice. Beauty cannot pass through fear, nor can it pass through anger, and she was both—afraid for the Falconer, and angry with herself for not going to Gurty sooner.

HAG WIND

HAG WIND

The sea serpent Wratheren left the Ebring Sea and winged his way to the moon.

—THE EPIC OF BREAL

ROUGH-HEWN CARTWHEELS BUMPED ALONG THE RUTS, catching on tree roots as Reyn and Perth pulled the rolling cage toward their goal. Miles paced and groaned, trying once again to shape his mouth to human speech. He tried the words "Stop" and "I'm innocent," but they came out as low growls. If only he could tell them. He didn't kill the unicorn. Didn't even eat her flesh after she was dead, though he was starving and needed the food. He'd left her body in the meadow and gone off hunting other game.

For two days and nights he'd tried again and again to plead his case before his sylth captors, but all his words were garbled, and they only ended up whipping him when he growled.

At night, while his jailors slept, he'd tried to shape-shift and make his escape. With a human arm he could reach through the narrow bars, with human hand unlock the gate. But his muscular forelegs would not lengthen into slender, hairless arms. His paws would not finger into hands, and the more he tried to change without success, the more frightened he became.

He was sure the tamalla they'd shot him with had made his tongue too thick and clumsy for any kind of clear speech. Was it also preventing him from shape-shifting? That had to be it. He held on to that reason, though a darker, unspoken fear lay below that.

It was midday now in the dense forest, and even with the sheltering trees a strong wind was blowing in from the north. Miles paced inside his cage. With every step taken toward the Sylth Queen's throne, the danger grew. If he could not return to himself, Queen Shaleedyn would not recognize him. She and all the sylth folk would call him Shriker. And from what he'd gleaned from his captors' chatter, the queen had a terrible punishment in store for him.

Reyn and Perth tugged on the long pole handles. Another gust blew past as they struggled to pull the cart along. The jail cart swayed to one side. A cartwheel sank into a rut.

"Pull harder!" called Reyn.

"I've been pulling more than my share!"

"And I say I've done more pulling than you!"

"You never change!" shouted Perth. "When we dug the gullmuth pit, it was just the same. I slaved in the rocks and dirt while you looked on."

"It was I who did the digging!" protested Reyn. "And I put the stakes at the bottom to slay the monster!"

"But was he slain? Never at all! You refused to help me finish covering the pit from view!"

The wind increased, and both shouted at once, "Hold on!" But Perth could not keep his grip and dropped his pole to the ground.

"Leave me to it," shouted Reyn, "if you're too weak to pull your weight!"

Perth reached for his bow. "And let you take all the gold?"

Now Reyn dropped his pole and drew his knife. "What will it be, then?" He leaned into the heavy wind, trying to wave his weapon, but the gale pushed him back. The cart tipped, and Miles slid to one side.

"Watch out!" shouted Perth. "It's going to blow over!" He tried to run at the cart but was suddenly swept off his feet and thrown against a tree trunk. There was a loud cracking noise as a branch broke and swirled down to the path. Perth slid to the ground, and Reyn turned toward the jail cart, trying with all his strength to fight the oncoming storm.

Another crack, loud enough to split Miles's ears this time, and a giant pine came crashing down between the sylths and the jail cart. Miles pressed himself against the back end of the cart and howled. One foot closer and the tree would have crushed him!

"Away!" screamed Perth. The sylths ran before the blowing wind.

"Quick!" shouted Reyn. "Find a hole to hide in!" Torn branches swirled behind Reyn and Perth, striking them both on the head and back as they fled screaming down the trail.

More trees tumbled down before the jail cart. Miles rammed against the bars, desperately trying to break free. The cart rolled backward. A screaming gust lifted the cart and spun it around and around in the air. Miles tumbled against the bars on the other side, straining to come to a stand, but the wind held him fast.

As the cage flew over the wild wood, oaks and elms torn up by their roots spun past. Miles pressed his muzzle between the bars and saw a young stag blow by, his horns caught in a spinning branch. Higher and higher he went. Up into the clouds as the howling wind sang all around him. Miles strained to see more through the bars. Was there a wind spirit above? Noorushh or Wild Esper? He couldn't see a face overhead, nor any kind of shape. Only blue.

Using all his power, he tried to pull himself away from the bars, but his raw animal strength meant nothing to the storm. He trembled. Fell against the side again. He could ride this storm, even fly against it if he shape-shifted. He must change fast, before the cage fell.

Miles imagined a falcon's sleek, feather-covered body slipping through the bars, his broad wings pumping high and higher above the storm. He'd shape-shifted into that form before. Changed quickly enough to break his fall that night in the deeps. He could do it now.

Spreading his forelegs out long, as if they were

wings, he saw it all and clearly. Willed it with every fiber in his body. But he did not change.

If the cage should fall from this great height . . . if he couldn't get out . . .

Miles roared. The cart rattled. But the keening wind was louder. It stripped the sky, tore him from the sunlit lands of Attenlore, and swept him westward to the shadow vale.

The cart spun down over the dark valley and crashed into a tree. Miles tumbled through the branches and landed in the blue-dark snow.

Bashed and bruised from the fall, he raised his head and looked at the broken jail cart. High in the branches above, the wheels still spun.

The valley had him. Uthor. Uthor. Uthor.

THE CROSSING OVER

THE CROSSING OVER

*Ezryeah sought the teacher
who lived across the river.*

—*The Book of eOwey*

After breakfast Hanna planned to visit the Falconer and see how he was faring with Gurty's healing herbs. The night before, she'd left the old woman wagging her gnarled finger over the Falconer as he lay upon his cot. She smiled to herself at the memory. Gurty, so small, leaning over a tall tree of a man to scold him back to health. When his fevered cough was cured, they'd seek the passage back to Attenlore and rescue Miles. Soon. It must be soon.

She was rinsing out her bowl when there was a knock at the door. There stood Gurty in her damp red head scarf. Hanna read her down-turned lip and puffy eyes and saw the meaning there. "I brought you to him too late," she cried, burying her face in Gurty's rain-drenched shawl.

"Hush, pet," said Gurty. "He was long past any cure I could give him from the start."

They wept and held each other in the open doorway, shaking like windblown saplings.

Many a villager came to the Crossing Over: townsfolk from Brim and Gladsonne. Others sailed over from Tyr Isle, and some folk journeyed from as far as Abbaseth. It surprised Hanna to see so many gathered on the hill, when the Falconer had been a lone mountain dweller, but before the service she heard one villager after another telling tales of how the good man had come to their sickbed with herbs and tinctures. And how he'd medicined them day on day until they were well enough to step back into their lives.

They laid the Falconer near Granda's grave in the shadow of the giant oak tree. It was a good place to be buried, halfway between the mountain's peak and the sea, with a view to both.

Brother Adolpho was reading from *The Book of eOwey*.

He came to the last line: "'And our blessings on the traveler.'"

"Our blessings on the traveler," said all who stood about the grave.

Repeating these words with the others, Hanna looked up and spied two more people at the gathering. Both were strangers to Enness Isle. The two stood apart from the crowd. One was a tall, black-skinned man. His face did not look old, but his long, curly hair, worn in a single braid down one side, was starry white. The other, a round-faced woman, was nearly as tall as the man, and her eyes were deep blue. If the man were the night sky, then she would be the blue of the day, both in her eyes and all around her face where her azure-colored hood covered her head. When the woman pulled it back, Hanna saw a slender gray streak cascading down her light brown hair like a silvery waterfall.

The strength of the strangers' presence and their quiet manner made Hanna think they must be meers, though how they'd heard of the Falconer's death in some faraway place and managed to sail here so soon after was a mystery.

After the final song Hanna lay a gathering of

poppies and lavender on the Falconer's grave. She stood again and brushed the dirt from her knees, then stepped beside her mother. She thought to take her hand, but her green-stained fingers were still wet from the poppy stems. "Miles would have liked to play 'Good Friends Parting' to honor the Falconer today." Mother nodded, but she would not look at Hanna. To her mother and her da Miles had become a silence and a longing.

Some of the crowd began to leave. Hanna stepped around the broad oak tree, lifting hand to brow to shield the westering sun from her eyes. It was up to her to find Miles now. She trembled at the thought of venturing to Attenlore alone.

The sun glanced across the sheer cliffs. And the smallest of shadows glided over the rocks, but Hanna was too lost in thought to notice. She didn't hear the high-pitched cry or see the circling above. Indeed, she didn't know what made the crowd draw back, jaws dropped, eyes wide, until Aetwan swooped down and landed on her arm.

There is water in the world.
Good and clean and sweet.
But a meer must seek the well within.

—THE OTHIC ART OF MEDITATION

Aт NIGHTFALL HANNA SAT BY THE FIRE WITH MOTHER mending her cloak for the next day's hike, a journey she must face alone, now the Falconer was gone. She heard footsteps outside. There was a knock at the door.

Da put down his pipe. "Come in," he said. Hanna peered around her da's broad frame to see who it might be. She drew back again when the two strangers she'd seen at the service crossed the threshold. The woman removed her blue hood, and the dark-skinned man, his gray.

Mother arose suddenly, the wool she had been carding dropping to the floor. She gripped her sharp wool comb against her middle, forcing a smile. Hanna stood beside her mother and looked to the floor, for these were strangers and they might not like her mismatched eyes.

"Good eve," said the man in a rolling voice. "I am Eason, and this is my fellow, Olean."

"I was told you would come," said Da.

Hanna looked up, surprised to hear this. Mother must have been as well, for Hanna felt her arm go tense beside her. Still, Mother remembered her duties and quickly stepped aside. "Come sit by the fire," she offered. Both came closer, but neither took a stool.

As Da went down the hall to his room, Tymm's curly blond head appeared from the loft and he crept down the ladder. He stood breathing loudly beside Hanna, tugging her shawl once, twice, before he found his tongue. "You were at the Crossing Over."

"Hush," said Hanna.

Da returned carrying a letter sealed with green wax. "I'm to ask you for a sign," he said. Eason nodded. The pair turned round and held their palms out to the fire. After a moment's time they showed their hands to the Ferrells. Othic symbols appeared on their left palms, pale blue and glowing with their own light. Hanna saw the Othic shapes were quite unlike the Falconer's. The symbol on Olean's hand curved like a triple letter *S*, which looked like flowing water. Eason's sign was shaped much like an eye, only rounder than a human eye, and there was a jagged mark cascading down the center like swift blue lightning.

"Aye," said Da, "you're meers, all right." He gave the letter to Eason. The meer opened it at once. He read down the page, then gave it to Olean, who did the same.

Had the Falconer sent for these meers to help her find Miles? That must be so. He wouldn't leave her all alone to search for Attenlore. The room seemed uncommonly hot as she waited.

The fire crackled. At last Olean looked up from the letter. "The Falconer says here that your son should be tested for an apprenticeship on Othlore."

Hanna's throat tightened. She must mean *after* they found him. Once he was safely home, then he could be tested. He'd always dreamed of going. "You'll have to be strong and help take care of Mother when I sail away," he'd warned. "But I'll come home powerful in magic." She remembered how his eyes had taken on the fire when he said that.

"Our son...is away," Mother said in a choking voice.

"Gone a month now," said Da.

"Not quite a month," added Hanna. "The moon's not yet full again, and—"

"We have to walk miles and miles every day to look for him," said Tymm. Mother slumped onto her stool and rubbed between her eyes.

Hanna stepped forward. "Will you help us find my brother?"

"We've come on behalf of Othlore," said Eason. "And there are more lands we must visit to test future apprentices."

"Miles would pass any test that you have," said Hanna. "Only stay and help us." Her voice had sharpened with the plea. Wasn't that why they'd come here? To help her cross into Attenlore? She couldn't say this in front of Mother and Da, but surely . . .

Olean touched her heart. "If we could stay, we would," she said wistfully, "but we cannot. Our ship sails on the morrow." She searched the letter once more, pursed her lips, then looked up. "The Falconer says here that your daughter's likely to have the Gift as well." She folded the letter and looked squarely at Hanna.

"We can test her, if you like," said Eason.

"What, Hanna?" Da's surprise came out in a quick laugh, and Hanna felt the sting of it.

Mother reached up and put her arm about Hanna's waist. "He couldn't have meant Hanna. She's . . ." Mother faltered, and Hanna's mind heard the unsaid words in taunting whispers. *She's a dreamwalker. A girl to hide away.*

"The Falconer only meant for you to test Miles, I'm sure," said Mother. "He's the brightest of boys. We don't abide with magic in this house. It's schooling in the healing arts he'd be wanting from you. We'll be needing another trained in healing here on Enness, now the Falconer's gone."

"Aye," said Da. "Miles would make a good leafer, for the Falconer was teaching him the way of herbs. And he plays the flute like a bird. You also have music meers at your school, I'm thinking."

"Music is fine, but it's not a needed skill like healing the sick," said Mother firmly.

Eason bowed. "I myself teach music."

"Well now," said Da. "There, Mother. Do you see?"

"A girl may be chosen as well as a boy," said Olean, bristling.

Eason put a steadying hand on her shoulder. "You

say your son has been gone nearly a month now," said Eason. "Yet the Falconer's letter was written and sealed only last week."

"You see!" Da said triumphantly to Mother. "The Falconer still believed that Miles can be found. And many said the man was a seer who could see into the future."

"Aye," said Mother, her voice warming with hope. "We'll find our boy just like they found Pyter at last!"

Olean tucked the letter into her leather bag.

"Do you need a place to bed down?" asked Da, still the kind host, though Hanna guessed his mind was more on the matter of his lost boy.

"We stay at the Falconer's," said Eason. "But our water bags are empty. Is there a well nearby?"

"Hanna will take you there."

"I will too!" said Tymm.

"No," said Mother. "Back up the ladder with you, little man."

"I'm not little," he said around a yawn.

Hanna slipped into her room to grab her cloak. "The meers are here," she whispered hurriedly. Aetwan peered down from the shelf. The shadows in the room barely moved, but it seemed as if he shrugged.

"Are you coming out to meet them?"

No answer still.

"So you'll not come out?"

He tucked his head under a wing to preen himself. "All right, then," she whispered to the dark.

Hanna led the guests down the stone steps around the back of the cottage. At the well she lowered the wooden bucket down until she heard a splash. The stars overhead were bright as chipped ice, and when she raised the bucket, she saw the starry head of the constellation Wratheren reflected on the water's dark surface. In the bucket's mirroring the moon near the starry serpent's mouth was nearly full. She broke the reflection with the dipper, and they all took a drink. Then Eason filled their water bags.

Olean pulled up her hood and peered at Hanna so intently that Hanna blushed. *She's looking at my eyes*, she thought.

"What is it you wish?" asked Olean.

Her wish? Hanna struggled to turn away, but she felt as if she were falling into Olean's steady gaze. What did the meer mean by "wish"? She'd wanted to be loved. To marry when she was grown and have children of her own. But would she ever marry, with her eyes? And if that dream could never be, could she leave Enness Isle and train up as a meer? She hadn't ever studied magic. But the Falconer had said she might have the Gift.

Standing here so close to Olean, she wondered what it would be like to learn the ways of healing and become a guardian between the worlds as the Falconer had been. "I wish . . ." She paused, waiting for the right words to settle on her tongue. No, she couldn't leave all behind to go with them, no matter how wonderful it sounded. "I need . . . to find my brother."

Olean nodded, and she did not seem disappointed. "In two months' time we sail past Enness on our homeward journey. We may anchor here again." The promise in her words settled over Hanna like brightly colored sparks. There was time and some hope that Miles would yet be chosen. And if they asked her again to come with them once Miles was found, what then?

Eason pinned his cloak against the breeze. "We see you're set apart here."

"Set apart?"

"As one who is sqyth-born," added Olean.

Hanna crossed her arms. "I've heard those words before, but I don't know what they mean."

"You have one eye to the earth and one to the sky."

Hanna blinked as she took this in. Her mismatched eyes again! But the look on the meers' faces wasn't harsh or fearful. What did it mean to have one eye to the earth and one to the sky? She tasted the thought, rocking back and forth on her heels, unsteady with the newness of it.

Olean touched her cheek. "Remember, it's a rare gift you have, daughter."

Hanna's eyes welled up and she looked away. The kindness of the remark filled such an emptiness in her she steadied herself to hold down the sob; still, it rose up her throat like a bird loosed from a cage, ready to cry out or sing.

The meers waited in silence as she stood windward awhile, letting the swift air break across her damp face. "No one has ever . . . said it was a gift before," she whispered.

"Then, the words are yours to keep," said Olean.

Hanna thought there could be no better gift than that. Finding beauty, even hope, in her mismatched eyes. Tears welled up again, but she blinked them back.

"Before the night's far gone," said Eason, looking to the path, "we'll both need our sleep. But we won't leave you without direction, Hanna."

"When you tended the Falconer in his last days, did he leave you some token?" asked Olean.

"No."

The meers looked at each other. "The letter indicated otherwise," said Eason. "You will want to ask your father about that."

"You may have found something on your own to carry with you on the search, then," said Olean.

Hanna wasn't sure what the meer meant, but without thinking, she reached into her pocket and wrapped her fingers around the egg-shaped stone she'd found on the beach the day she went to town. She'd kept it with her since she'd found it, and was sure it would displease them. It was, after all, only a stone, but she drew it out anyway and held it in the flat of her palm.

The stone seemed dull under the night sky, which darkened its natural blue gray color, but the starlight brought out the crystal crack down its side. A crack that seemed to Hanna so much like the first life signs of a little chick greedy for the outside world.

Eason raised his eyebrows, and a deep crease lined his dark forehead. Olean let out a soft sigh. "How did you come by this?"

"It came to me from the sea," said Hanna. She blushed, for the stone hadn't actually come to her, only tumbled up in a foamy wave. "I mean, I found it on the shore," she said.

"You were right the first time." Olean touched the stone. "It's warm," she said, and Eason smiled.

"What are you talking about?" asked Hanna.

"It's not for us to say," said Olean. "But take this stone on your journey, and you'll know soon enough."

Hanna slid the stone back into her pocket. She felt a sudden liking for both meers and an even stronger need for their wise reassurance, which seemed to spread outward from them like a warming fire.

"I wish you would come with me," she said.

Eason tied his water bag about his waist. "No one can make this journey for you, Hanna."

"The Falconer said the same. He also said I would not be alone."

The night wind ruffled Olean's blue hood. "Aye," she said, "and he was right."

"But I don't understand."

"A sqyth-born child has more than one kith," said Olean.

So she had more kith to help her? Hanna looked up, remembering the chill and wondrous feeling of flight as Wild Esper blew her into Attenlore, and she longed to feel that flight again. But if she had an earthly kith, she didn't know who that might be. She lowered her head, thinking to ask Olean, then felt suddenly shy. A person shouldn't have to ask who her friends are; a person should know that for herself.

Eason removed a beaded strap from about his neck. "Glisten," he said, holding out a small leather pouch. "Do you know its use?"

In her mind's eye she saw the Falconer tossing the shining powder in the deeps. Like tiny shooting stars, it had lit the woods and shown her brother's form inside the beast.

"Aye," she said, and reached for the little pouch.

*Ezryeah burned his ancestral robes
and scattered the ashes in the sea.*

—*THE BOOK OF EOWEY*

DA BROUGHT A NEW RUSHLIGHT TO HANNA'S ROOM AND placed it on her little table.

"Da?" said Hanna. "Did the Falconer leave me a token?"

Da gave a nod. "I was waiting to give it to you."

Da drew the stool beside her cot, keeping his back to Aetwan, who slept atop the corner shelf. Hanna sat up as Da pulled something from his pocket. He uncurled his fingers. The rushlight haloed his hand, and there in his open palm lay a shining silver key.

"The Falconer said you'd know what to do with it."

Hanna didn't know, but she saw the hopeful look in Da's eyes. "I'll do my best," she said.

Da handed her the key. Hanna took the gift, felt the cold of it, and wondered what door it would open for her and where the door was.

"The Falconer said I'm to let you and Gurty keep looking for Miles, and I'm not to prevent you." He was speaking in a quiet voice so as not to awaken the bird.

Hanna nodded, still thinking on the key.

"Will you keep searching, then, daughter?"

She looked up. "Aye."

"Ah," he sighed. "And I will too. And when will you give up the search?"

"Never, Da."

"That's my girl." He hugged her close, and she could smell sweat and sheep and the greenness of the mountain in his shirt. "Tomorrow I'll turn east to look in the foothills. Will you come that way with Gurty?"

Hanna shook her head, and they both looked down at the key.

"Is there anything you're not telling me, daughter?"

Hanna closed her fingers over the key. His question brought so many pictures to mind, and she watched them pass like misty breaths upon a cold window: first the Shriker, then Attenlore, then the Sylth Queen. But she could say nothing of these things to her da, a practical man who saw this world and no other, so she landed on the only truthful words she dared. "It's this, Da," she said, looking into his weathered face. "I'm sure Miles is still alive."

Da's eyes twinkled, and she saw the tears held behind their sudden brightness. "The Falconer said the same. And do you know there's not many left who still believe it? But we'll find him yet, Hanna."

The meers had said they would leave before dawn; still, Hanna felt disappointed when she opened the Falconer's door and saw the empty table and the cold hearth. There were blankets folded on the pallet, an iron cook pot on its hook, and a rushlight on the table, but in the alcove only the meditation cushion remained. The books were gone, so were the dried herbs. And there were round marks in the dust on the shelves where the tincture bottles used to be. The smell of winterleaf, which the old man had been so fond of, lingered in the air, but that was all.

The meers had taken the Falconer's books and herbs. The empty alcove sent an ache through her.

"He's gone!" she cried. She sat on his pallet and wept for the Falconer as she hadn't been able to do at the Crossing Over. "They shouldn't have taken your books," she sobbed.

"Look," said Aetwan.

"Look at what? There's nothing to see here anymore."

Head in hands, she cried. The movement of her swaying upper body made the dust motes swirl round her in the morning light. The small room blurred. Her nose ran and her throat ached. At last she wiped her puffy eyes and caught Aetwan watching her from his perch. She felt he could not understand her tears, though he must be missing his master in his own way. "All right," she said with a sniff. "I'll look." She went to the alcove and ran her hand along the empty bookshelf; a flurry of fine dust made her sneeze. She touched the Falconer's meditation cushion, heard the straw rustling under the thick red cloth. Back in the main room she whisked the pine broom from the hearth and began to sweep.

Pushing the broom beneath the pallet, she felt the bristle tips run into something hard. Hanna poked about a bit, then stooped and pulled out a long wooden chest. She pulled upon the lid. Locked, of course. Going down on one knee, she took the silver key from her pocket, fit it in the keyhole, and turned it to the right. *Click!* Hanna lifted the lid and let out a soft sigh. She was sorry right away for doubting Eason and Olean, for they hadn't taken anything at all. The chest was full of everything she'd missed.

The Falconer's books were stacked against one side of the trunk, along with his tinderbox and his many tincture bottles. Next to them were pungent-smelling dried herb bundles and a leather herbing pouch. The right side of the chest was filled with a large, gilded box, which took up half the space inside. She'd been so happy to see the contents, she hadn't noticed a small note attached to the inner lid of the chest. It read:

> The Book of eOwey *is for Miles and Hanna Ferrell. The contents of the gilded box are for Miles. The wrapped leather parcel beside it shall be taken to Attenlore and given to Miles there. All else within this chest I give to Hanna Ferrell. Remember you are loved.*

The note was signed with the single letter *F* and the Othic symbol Hanna had seen on the Falconer's palm. Hanna lifted the leather parcel meant for Miles. It was very light, a little more than one foot long and six inches wide. Here was a thing she was to bring to Attenlore. She resisted the temptation to open it and slid it carefully into her pack. Next she took up a tincture bottle and read the label in a spill of sunlight from the window. Orasian. The bright orange medicine the Falconer had given Miles the first night they stumbled through his door. Hanna wanted to read about all the tincture bottles in *Entor's Herbal* and learn more of the dried herbs in the pouches. But that wouldn't help her find Miles, so she replaced the bottle and brought *The Way Between Worlds* to the table.

The heavy book had a musty odor tinged with pine. She ran her fingers across the gold embossed letters, then gripped the corner of the text and closed her eyes. "Help me find the passage into Attenlore," she whispered. Whether it was a wish or a prayer did not matter to her, only that she must believe *The Way Between Worlds* held secrets that would help her find Miles.

She lifted the thick cover and was surprised to see that it was a handwritten volume. She'd seen only the maps before this and had been too busy brewing tea to notice the print on the other pages. The letters were slender and slanted a little to the left, and many of the pages had drawings of plants and animals in the margins.

Hanna traced the green vines that crept up the left side of chapter one, then quickly paged through the book looking for clues on Attenlore. If only she could uncover a spell that would help her find the passage. There were only five days left before the next full moon. The book had to tell her something.

The passage the Falconer had read on their last day together was near the end of the book. She turned to that portion, fingering down page after page until she read the word "Hanna." Starting at the word, she turned to look at Aetwan. He tipped his head to the side and returned her stare.

"My name is here," she said. "What does it mean?"

"Read," said Aetwan matter-of-factly.

Hanna trembled as she began to read the script. In page after page her own story grew before her eyes. All of it was there, and it was in the same slender lettering as the rest of the book. So this wasn't a copy of some ancient magical text, but the Falconer's own work. She

read on until she came to the words at the bottom of
page 411.

*There is work yet to do with the Shriker. I had thought
to finish this work before my death, but it is Hanna and
Miles's story now. There are many pages left in this book
to complete, and so I give my quill to Hanna.*

Hanna turned to the next page, which was blank
but for a drawing of a gnarled tree branch along the
margin and a single unfinished line atop.

Hanna went to the Enoch Tree and essha . . .

She rubbed her forehead. She was to climb to the
high cliff and seek the tree. But what did "essha" mean?
The cream-colored page lay stark beneath the Falconer's
lettering. Hanna peered back inside the chest. In the
corner, with the tincture bottles, she spied the Falconer's
ink bottle. The tip of his feather quill poked out from
beneath Miles's gilded box. She pulled the quill from its
hiding place and ran the feather along her cheek.

The book was hers to finish—and the quest.

THE WIND WALL

THE WIND WALL

There are powers at work here and mysteries beyond our knowing.

—*THE FALCONER*

SOMEONE WANTED HIM HERE. ENOUGH TO KEEP HIM alive. Enough to hold him captive here in Uthor Vale, where all was covered in shadow, even in the day. Miles's shoulder was still bruised from his fall after the jail cart hit the oak tree, though the crash had happened a while ago. How many days? He wasn't sure. Time was masked here in Uthor. Dim days succumbed to darker nights, with no division between the two.

He didn't want to have to fight the Shriker here. He wanted to choose his place of battle. Uthor Vale filled him with a constant sense of dread and drained him of his power. There was too much darkness here, too many strange beasts, like the giant gullmuth roaming through the woods. He shuddered, remembering the last time he'd nearly run into the gullmuth—a hideous, hairy mammoth with a great, birdlike head; he'd slipped into a cave just in time. The gullmuth was a monstrous killer. The great beast frightened him even in his Shriker's form.

The shadow realm was the *wrong* place to fight his enemy. The Shriker had lived here long and knew every inch of ground. Much better to lure the cur to a high cliff in Attenlore, pounce on him full force, and watch him plummet to his death. Miles snarled under his breath—that would finish him.

A dull ache flowed down his leg as he limped up the steep-walled valley. He would win out this time—break past the wall of wind at the valley's edge and free himself from Uthor.

The branches thickened here. Plenty of places for skullen snakes to hide. Miles padded stealthily through the snow so as not to disturb them. Near the top of the valley he stopped and peered out. Attenlore! Rolling hills softened with snow. Only a few more steps and he'd be free. Miles licked his muzzle, tasting the sweetness of the thought.

"I'm ready," he said.

His words were no longer growls. Once the tamalla had worn off, he'd found a way to master speech in the Shriker's form. He could speak now in a husky voice that was both powerful and deep.

Miles broke past the tree line and met the Sylth Queen's wind wall full force. None but the Shriker, and the few that dared to follow in his wake, had ever broken through this wall, but he was strong. He would break through. Paws firm, head down, he leaned into it. The stinging wind blew his fur straight back. He took one step, two. It was like pushing against an ocean wave. The harder he pressed, the harder it pressed back.

Fighting his way past a pile of rocks, he gained two feet of ground, then faltered. He dug his paws in deeper. *Steady. Stand strong. Don't give in.*

A sudden heavy gust swept him off his feet and sent him tumbling down the hill.

He smashed against a tree and lay dazed a moment before sitting up. Shaking snow from his head, he came to a stand. The wind wall had a presence in it.

"Who are you?" he called.

"Who are you?" the voice called back.

"What do you want?"

"What do you want?"

Miles quavered with exhaustion, snow clinging to his matted fur. "Show yourself!" he howled.

"Show yourself!"

It was his voice and not his voice. The wall was keeping him in this valley full of skullen snakes, trolls, wraiths, and evil clawkeens: all the creatures that were banished from Attenlore. But he was innocent.

"I'm not a beast!" cried Miles. "Why imprison me here?"

"Why imprison me?" the voice called back.

Looking up, he saw the wind take on a sheen like water, and in the sheen the Shriker stood, challenging the wall. Was this how he saw himself or how the queen's wall saw him? He wasn't sure, but it was wrong; either way, all wrong.

"I'm not who you think I am!" he cried.

"I'm not who you think I am," the voice called back.

Miles howled, rushed the wall again. He hit it full force, drove his way in about a foot. Once more he was lifted off the ground and blown back down the hill. He was flat against the snow, the wall pressed hard against him. It held him down like a bully in a fight. At last the wind left him and blew back up the hill.

Miles lifted his head. "Why won't you let me out?"

No answer. Snow fell softly through the high branches. Flakes settled on his damp fur, chilling his spine. Miles stood up and shook the snow from his back.

Alone.

His ears rang with the silence.

His nose filled with the sour smell of his own breath.

THE CLIFF

Some said the Stone Man lived on,
though never did he move.

—"THE STONE MAN," A LEGEND OF OTH,
FROM *THE WAY BETWEEN WORLDS*

It WAS STILL MORNING WHEN HANNA STORED THE BOOK
in the trunk and left the Falconer's to follow Aetwan's
darting shadow up the steep ravine. Five days left to find
Miles before the next full moon, yet the Falconer had
sent her to the Enoch Tree. The meer would not delay
her quest, she knew. There would be a message waiting
for her on the cliff, a sign, a way to Attenlore, something
to help her find her brother.

She pushed herself to climb faster. *Essha.* She
thought on the last word in the Falconer's book as she
scaled the rocks. What did it mean? Could the word be
the beginning of a finding spell?

Essha. A sound like leaves whispering in the wind, but there were few trees up here. Hanna kept climbing. The cold morning air chilled the sweat on her face. Just below the cliff top she bent down, hands on knees, to catch her breath. It was a desolate place of gray rock mapped in green and silver lichen. Dry grass sprouted here and there in the crevices; the longer yellow blades blew sideways in the stark breeze like old men's beards. Close to the flat-topped cliff a few pine trees huddled beside a lone red-leafed maple. All the trunks leaned left from years of battling the mountain wind.

Hanna paused to tie her hooded cape before stepping up to higher ground. Aetwan cried out, circling above, but she didn't need his warning to tell her where they'd come, for now she was at the very top, facing the stunted Enoch Tree. It stood in the last possible place a tree could grow, its roots clinging to the cliff edge. Above the roots the trunk twisted round as if it were making ready to leap into the abyss.

Hanna remembered this, all of it, and she was no less frightened now than she had been the first time she saw the tree. It was hard to believe the old man enspelled in the oak was Granda's brother.

A slender pine branch dipped as Aetwan came to rest halfway along the bough. He would not land on the Enoch Tree. She knew this, for she herself could barely look at the knotted trunk and gnarled branches. She felt her knees weaken at the sight of the horror-stricken face near the top of the tree, his hollow eyes looking out across the cliff, his mouth open in a silent scream.

A gust blew against the lone tree. The branches creaked. Suddenly Hanna was filled with doubt. "Aetwan," she said, "why did the Falconer send me here?"

"Listen," said Aetwan.

She held her ground and tried to listen to the sounds on the desolate cliff. There were no birdcalls, not even the rough caw of a kravel bird up here. No animal sounds either. All she could hear was the high wind shrieking across the cliff top. The sound was so much like an angry woman's cry that she looked skyward for Wild Esper. Thin clouds flew past, but the wind woman did not show herself. Still, Hanna wondered if Esper was here. Could essha be a wind call?

Hanna leaned into the strong wind, shouting, "Take me!" She lifted her hands. "Take me to Attenlore. I'm ready!" The wind strengthened. Hanna's hooded cloak blew back. She fought to keep herself standing.

Hanna looked skyward. "Essha!" she cried. A heavy gust tore Eason's pouch from her neck. "Wait," called Hanna. "I need the glisten!" The wind twirled her round and round. Hanna fell forward, striking the granite. She'd thrown out her hands to protect her face and bit her lip in the fall. She lifted her head, the taste of blood in her mouth. The wind had taken her so easily when she was at Garth Lake. What was wrong?

"Esper?" she called. No sight of her and no answer. Only the blowing. Ahead of her Eason's leather pouch rolled across the cliff top, the beaded ties flying. The pouch flew open. Glisten powder blew into the air.

"No!" Hanna lunged for the pouch. She couldn't let it spill. She needed it to see Miles. The wind pressed against her. She crawled forward on her belly, grabbed the pouch, and looked inside. Half full. Quickly she tied the strings shut and slipped it into her pocket. She struggled to rise against the heavy gusts.

A spray of glisten powder swirled toward the precipice and landed on the roots of the Enoch Tree. The roots enlivened like a nest of vipers.

Hanna froze. *Move! Get away from it!* Taking a breath, she worked her hands and knees as she tried to crawl backward, but it was like backing into a wall. Before her, glisten powder starred the trunk, and as the twinkling lights swirled up inside the tree, the man inside began to move. His knees wavered and his torso twisted round.

Aetwan flew overhead. "Enoch!" he called. "Enoch!"

The powder rose higher up Enoch's neck, his chin, his mouth. A terrified scream tore out, cutting sharply through the air.

Hanna covered her ears. "Stop!" she cried. The scream rose in pitch. The man inside the tree doubled over. He wrapped his brown hands around his legs, pulling hard to free his feet from roots and rocks. "Stay back!" he screamed. "Get away!"

Hanna's jaw dropped. Was he afraid of her?

"I won't hurt you," she called. But her voice was lost to him. He didn't seem to see her at all. He was captive in some horrible dream, and he thrashed and wailed, struggling all the harder to free his feet from the roots.

Aetwan flew upward, then dived at the flailing branches, beating his wings wildly against the tree to keep Enoch from uprooting himself and plunging into the abyss.

"Help him!" cried Aetwan. He dug his talons into Enoch's shoulder and flapped his wings, trying to pull him back.

Hanna was afraid to move. She didn't want to help. *He's Granda's brother,* she thought, *no matter what he's done. And if he jumps, he'll die.* Suddenly she lunged forward and grabbed the man's ankle. The flesh on her arms rubbed raw against the cliff rocks as Enoch dragged them both closer to the precipice. She gritted her teeth. Dug the toes of her boots into the rock. Pulled and pulled.

"Don't let him jump," screeched Aetwan.

"I'm trying!" One foot was completely free from the roots, and Enoch was nearly over the edge. "He's going to leap," cried Hanna. Suddenly the glisten powder faded, and the screaming stopped. The man's face sank back into the bark. His arms stilled inside the branches. Hanna let go her hold. Roots curled about Enoch's feet and buried them again. All went suddenly still.

Hanna sat up and wiped the dirt from her stinging hands. Her body shook, but she managed to ease along the cliff top, pull Eason's pouch from her pocket, and tuck it safely in her rucksack.

Aetwan settled in the highest branch of the solitary maple tree and began preening his feathers. Ears still ringing, Hanna tried to press herself to a stand, but her knees gave way, so she leaned back on her hands, sucking in breath.

"Is that what you wanted?" she shouted. "Was I supposed to come here and listen to *that*?" She worked to hold back angry tears, but they fell anyway.

Aetwan peered down at her and let out a loud screech, hurling it in her direction as if the sound were a stone. Abandoning the tree, he swept upward, circled once, then turned sharply and disappeared into the woods below.

Hanna licked salty-tasting blood from her lip. Whatever it was she was supposed to do here had passed her by and she'd failed. Even Aetwan had deserted her. She stumbled down the slope to the maple tree. Curling up in its shadow, she pressed her cheek against the ground, welcoming the feel of the warm earth against her face.

ESSHA, HANNALYN

Some are caught in their own anger,
as if their shadows swallowed them.
It was that way with Enoch.

—*THE WAY BETWEEN WORLDS*

Hanna awoke and touched the dried blood on her lip. She did not know how long she'd slept, but the lengthening shadows along the ground told her it had been more than an hour's time. Her muscles were sore and her eyes puffy. She sat up stiffly, turned her head, and sucked in a sudden breath.

A tall, bright figure was emerging from the maple tree. Hanna blinked, thinking it a dream, but the figure only brightened.

The tree spirit was halfway out of the tree now: a deya, long and lean as the trunk itself. She burned like a pillar of flame, her hair, body, and gown blazing now red,

327

now yellow, now gold. Freeing herself from the shivering maple, she came gracefully forward and hovered above Hanna.

"I am Shree," she said in a voice like whispering fire.

Hanna could find no words at all to give answer. She couldn't even move to nod her head.

"Do not be afraid. My flames will not consume you." The deya reached out a long golden arm and touched Hanna's head. There was a sudden tingling warmth against her scalp, but no burning there.

"You see, Hannalyn?"

"I am called Hanna," she replied in a choking voice.

"'Lyn' means 'human female,'" said Shree.

Hanna took this in, and gathering her courage, she forced herself to a stand. "How is it you know my name?"

The deya wavered in the wind. "You are the sqyth-born child."

Hanna blushed. She was still not used to the word "sqyth-born," nor what it meant to be called this. "Are you the one I was supposed to meet?"

"Before we freely speak," said Shree, "I will know which way your heart grows."

"What do you mean?"

"If your sqyth-born heart is twain between growing earth and blowing sky, how am I to put my trust in you?"

The question stung. "I've always loved the trees," said Hanna. "I would never betray you." The words fell leaden between them, for suddenly she saw herself blowing above the island, dropping the maple tree into the sea at Wild Esper's command. She looked into the deya's golden eyes and shuddered at the memory, wondering if Shree had read her thoughts.

"Truth," said Shree, and Hanna knew what she must say. "A tree was torn up in a storm," she admitted. "One that I was holding. And later . . . I dropped it in the sea."

Her heart beat wildly at the confession. A fiery root wended out of Shree's gown and wrapped about Hanna's ankle. She looked up at the deya, sweat pouring down her neck, but she did not try to break free. Instead she thought of all the trees in Shalem Wood. How she loved their green, whispering branches. How many times she'd spoken to them and told them all her secrets. They'd listened to her all the times she leaned against them crying when the villagers had been especially cruel. They'd always given her their company.

The deya's golden hair lifted and fell in the mountain breeze. Hanna waited, trembling in her grip. At last Shree gave a nod. "We gather this," she said. Slowly the root retreated into the folds of her shimmering gown.

Hanna breathed a sigh and looked down at her dirt-stained hands, wondering what to say next. "The Falconer told me to come here."

"Ah," said Shree. "A good soul, this one. His husk lies beneath Oskulath's Oak, but his spirit free-walks now."

"How do you know?"

"We have roots."

Hanna frowned. "How do your roots help you know?"

"We essha."

Hanna brightened. "What is this word 'essha'?"

"'Listen. Understand.'"

"The Falconer said I was to come here and essha. My brother, Miles, is lost in Oth and I need help. Are you the one I am to listen to?"

"There are many things to essha, Hannalyn. We

deyas have lived long where the wind speaks. And in the dark we whisper root to root. We know all the stories blowing and growing from time's beginning."

Hanna imagined the breeze passing stories through the woods from leaf to stem to bough. As she saw this in her mind's eye, her feet began to tingle, and suddenly she saw an underground world where trees spoke root to root from times long ago until now. Stories of the world from its first greening, the birds of the air, the beasts of field and forest, and the first folk of Noor.

She felt as if the deya was passing these things to her across the small patch of rocky ground between them. The dreams rose up her feet and washed through her body. The birthing days and dying days of all the souls on Enness Isle flowed through her mind like clear stream water. Then in a moment the vision passed.

Hanna tipped her head up and looked into the deya's bright face. "Do you know about all of us here?"

"We watch the lyns and the eryls on Enness."

Hanna did not have to ask what Shree meant by "eryl." She knew somehow that it meant "human male." "And you know my story," she said, "mine and Miles's?"

"Your tale is unfinished."

"Do you know why the Falconer sent me here?"

"You have come to heal Enocheryl."

"No. I don't know anything about Enoch. I've come to rescue my brother Miles."

"It is the same thing," said the deya.

Hanna frowned. "Why do you speak in riddles?"

"It is only a riddle from the topside," said the deya. "Go down to the root."

"How do I do that?"

The deya raised her arms. A crimson leaf swirled to the ground, landing beside Hanna's boot. Hanna picked it up. It was cool to the touch.

"Essha for Enocheryl." Shree's voice was softer now and almost motherly. Hanna seated herself on a flat stone, crossed her legs, and looked up at the deya's ever-changing face.

"Enocheryl grew here. Tall for an eryl. He left Enness for Othlore to gather magic there, enough to break the Shriker's curse."

Hanna took in a breath. "It was for that he went to Othlore? But . . . how do you know?"

"He shouted his dream to the wind, to the trees, and to the mountain. The wind essha and we essha. We knew why he sailed away. But he came back too soon and full of anger."

Hanna nodded. "The Falconer said he was sent home for stealing a spell book and burning it. And he was banned from the meer's isle for good and all."

"I gather that in," said Shree, her arms waving toward herself like slender branches in the wind. "This blows to us a missing part. We deyas are not free-walkers as you are, and we did not know what happened on Othlore. We saw anger. Anger is root rot to an eryl. It destroys." Her arms waved softly up and down, red and yellow gold in the sun. "Then one day love came to Enocheryl, and we thought all would be well in his story."

Hanna remembered that part of Granda's tale. A green-eyed girl who brought Enoch little cakes and cider.

"Love came. But the green-eyed lyn was like the flower that brings too many bees. She went off with another." The deya swayed a moment before speaking again.

"Enocheryl's anger grew worse after that. He'd had it in his mind so long to be a meer of great power. To hold much magic in him. First the meers had turned him away, then his da, and then the green-eyed lyn. All these turnings sent poison to his heart.

"Enocheryl did not want to be a shepherd, a lowly eryl with no magic power. Soon the bad sap in his heart went down to his feet. High up on the cliff he took his anger out on his sheepdog. He kicked him one time, two, and many more until the dog was dead." Shree swayed more, and Hanna felt the swaying in herself. She swallowed the sick feeling rising up in her throat.

"Enocheryl dropped the dog's body over the precipice to hide his evil from the people. But we deyas saw. We essha. And the dog's death cries did not go unheard."

The deya's flame reddened. Hanna closed her eyes. Heat waved from the deya, but Hanna felt her own burning. It was an awful thing to have blood kin who'd kicked a dog to death. She felt no pity for her great-uncle Enoch Sheen, only loathing.

"It happened in this place on a dark-moon night. First the killing, and then . . ." Shree bowed her head. Hanna waited tensely, remembering what Granda had said about the Shriker at the dark-moon time.

"Enocheryl lifted up his arms and cast a power spell. Othic words no eryl or lyn should speak. One he must have learned from the stolen book on Othlore. I gather that to me now that you have spoken of the book. For where else could words this old have come from?

"He cried the incantation on the cliff that night under the swallowed moon. The spell traveled far from our world to the land of Attenlore, and farther still to the shadow realm of Uthor. A summoning from dark to dark that broke the queen's wind wall and brought the Shriker forth.

"The beast broke through. The queen flew after. And we watched the Shriker's attack. He had his teeth in Enoch's side, for the man had garbled the spell, left out the word that would have cast the Shriker down into the underworld. Enocheryl would have died that night if the queen had not saved him."

"How was that?" asked Hanna.

Shree blew this way and that, a quiet hissing sound coming from her hair and gown. "The Shriker's teeth were in him when she enspelled Enocheryl, and there was much blood and much blood.

"This we know from before and this we tell you now. The Sylth Queen gave Enocheryl the gift of magic in his fourteenth year, hoping he would kill the Shriker. But he disappointed her. On Othlore he did not wait for his learning season. Instead he stole the power spell. This new piece you gave us. This was why his power failed. A stolen spell is never rightly wielded.

"For the eryl's failure to kill the Shriker, Queen Shaleedyn caught him in the oak. The Sylth Queen's punishments are swift as a night storm."

"But you said she saved his life."

"By the laws of the Old Magic, the queen can punish wrongdoing by turning a lyn or eryl into a four-legged creature, or one with wings or fins, she can cover them in stone or wood, but never can she take a life."

Hanna wrapped her cape about her, suddenly cold. The queen had imprisoned Enoch not for kicking his dog to death, but for miscasting a summoning spell that brought the Shriker back into the world. "The Shriker comes again each time there's another dark moon," said Hanna.

"We said a stolen spell is never rightly wielded. The spell Enocheryl cast renews itself when the moon is swallowed by the dark. And once the beast is free, he hunts as any beast will do."

Eyes closed, Hanna gripped her knees and rocked back and forth. She wanted to spit the story out and be rid of it. It was dark inside her head, and it was her own night she was making.

"Where have you gone, Hannalyn?"

Hanna opened her eyes. "It's a terrible story."

The deya tipped her golden head. "It is not a story, only part of one. It is not yet finished."

"I still don't see how it can help me find Miles."

"Essha, Hannalyn."

WISE ROOT

WISE ROOT

*Deyas know by root and
whispering wind where travelers
go and where they've been.*

—*The Way Between Worlds*

Hanna returned home late from her day's search,
then sat at the corner table in her room paging through
The Way Between Worlds. There was little in the book to
help her understand Shree's words. How would knowing
Enoch's tale help her find Miles? She went through the
story again and again in her mind as her cup of thool
cooled beside the book. Both Enoch and Miles were
shepherds' sons, and both wanted to learn the ways of
magic from the meers on Othlore. Had Miles wanted to
go to Othlore to learn a magic spell to break the Shriker's
curse, as Enoch had? He'd never told her that.

There was more to Enoch's tale—the dog he kicked

to death and the stolen spell. Miles had never stolen a spell, had he?

She searched the pages of the Falconer's book and found nothing more on Enoch. Shree's tale was hers to think on, and she'd have to solve it on her own.

Hanna bent over the pages. There had to be a way back into Attenlore. She turned to the Enness map, laid the Attenlore map atop, and shuddered. The shadow realm had grown. How could it have? She blinked at the dark drawing. Uthor Vale had broadened, spilling over like black oil from a bucket. The Falconer must have changed the map before he died. Hanna looked closer. The meadow near the south rim of the vale was darkened. The same flowered field where Wild Esper had left her, she was sure. For there was the three-spired Oak King standing near the stream. Even under the chalk shadow she could see the place where the queen's unicorn was slain. She quickly turned the page, heart pounding, eyes stinging.

On page 352 she found at last an opening spell. A small thing, but she'd use anything she could to help her open the way to Attenlore. She practiced the spell silently, knowing better than to say the words aloud here in her room.

The next day she stopped while searching in the wood with Gurty to say the spell.

"Open as you have before,
Let the traveler through the door.
From this opening begin,
The only way out
Is in."

Gurty cackled. "Charms, is it now?" she said. "And what will you be doing next?"

Hanna blushed and walked on.

"You'll not find a way by charms alone," said Gurty.

"Why not?"

"Wouldn't the Falconer have said the verse himself if that were all that was needed?"

Hanna thought on this and knew the old woman was right. The Falconer would have used any powers at hand to rescue Miles. They crossed into the meadow and passed a rotting cedar stump with a young tree growing up from the middle.

A cool breeze played over the poppies and wild lavender that grew here and there in bright patches. It was a beautiful place, but in her mind she saw the meadow in Attenlore. It was darkened over now if the Falconer's map was right. She thought of the border of the shadow realm, a border she must cross, and bit the inside of her cheek.

"Where have you put your mind, girl?" asked Gurty.

"With Miles."

"Ah, and that's where it should be." Gurty's face took on a thoughtful look under her gray, blowing hair. She paused, reached into her pocket, and pulled out a small blue root. "I have no real power," she admitted. "And I've been more a burden than a help to you."

"That's not true," said Hanna, but she felt a pang of guilt, for she'd been thinking just that most of the day, and she'd said the same to the Falconer. "What have you got there?"

"Wise root. It's from the azure tree—the tallest and oldest trees in Noor." She pressed it into Hanna's hand. "If you should stumble into Uthor Vale, a place a-crawl with devilish trolls, shadow wraiths, and skullen snakes," she said, waving her hands about, "this root will come in handy." Gurty brushed the dry moss from her skirt. She squinted at the pale sun, which hung like a white disk now behind the heavy clouds.

"When would I need the root?" asked Hanna.

"Well now, how would I know that?" huffed Gurty. "But when you do, crush it and spit on it to make a paste for wounds."

"Why don't you keep it with you? It's light to carry, and you know how to use it, and . . . you're coming with me, aren't you, Gurty?"

The old woman cocked her head. "I don't know which way the fire's leaning yet," she said. "And anywise, those who cause the curse must break it, and the breaking's in the blood."

"But I didn't cause the curse," she said. "It was Rory Sheen did that. And I didn't ask to be born a Sheen, or to be a dreamwalker, or to have mismatched eyes, or . . ." She gulped in a breath. No one outside the family knew that she dreamwalked. She hadn't meant to say it aloud, not any of it, but now that the words were out, she let the thought behind them pour out too, as the last bit of water will roll down in droplets when the pitcher's nearly empty. "Gurty," she whispered.

"It wasn't my witch eyes that made him call me, was it?"

"Your witch eyes, maybe, *and* you're a Sheen. Both might be reasons for the Shriker's call. But there's more here for the seeing."

Hanna stepped back, not sure she wanted to hear what the "more" was.

"I've spent years in these woods," said Gurty. "Searching for one thing and finding another. Look." She reached up to the giant cedar by the trail, tugged a branch down between them, and gave a knowing nod.

"What am I to see?"

"Why, what's there, of course." She wiggled the branch so the green needles wavered.

"A branch," said Hanna. "With smaller branches growing from it, all covered in flat green needles. But how does this answer the question about my eyes?"

"Use them for looking."

Hanna touched a twig, counted fourteen smaller twigs, all sprouting thick, flat needles. Looking closer at the one near Gurty's hand, she noted every flat needle was made of tiny leaves growing from the stem like branches from a trunk. Each one was like a little tree the size of her fingertip. She drew back a bit and saw each twig was like a tree as well; most were the length of her middle finger. The slender branches were the same, and the branch itself, which Gurty held down. From small to large, the tree shape repeated over and over.

Hanna rubbed the bumpy cedar frond between her fingers, letting the new thought grow inside her. She'd lived near Shalem Wood all her life and never noticed this. "Is what you're showing me how parts of trees are like the whole of them?"

Gurty smiled. "Aye, there's a pattern. Your eyes work fine, I'd say."

"But I wasn't asking *how* my eyes worked or *if* they worked, but what my eyes have to do with being called, or whether—"

"Who else has the Shriker attacked?"

Hanna started. The question had nothing to do with trees or leaves or the color of her eyes.

"Tell me whom you know of," said Gurty. Her voice was rough and soothing at the same time, like a gurgling stream.

Hanna thought on the victims she knew for certain. There was the midwife and her man, then Polly Downs.

The Falconer's terrow, Furleon. And there was the queen's unicorn.

Hanna told her all the names she'd thought of.

Gurty wiggled the branch. "And where's the pattern?"

"There is none," said Hanna.

The old woman let go the cedar branch, and it bounced above them in the dusky woods. Gurty sent a green-eyed look Hanna's way. "You're a Sheen by blood, so he may have called you anywise. But you have a loyal heart, and kind. Think on the others. Wasn't your midwife loyal to your mother to come up mountain on a stormy night? And her husband, so love-struck that he went after the beast all by his lonesome? Wasn't Polly loyal to Tarn? And Furleon to the wind woman? And didn't the Sylth Queen tell us Neurreal always came whenever she called her?" Gurty nodded to herself. "I've a mind to say it's love and loyalty the Shriker can't abide."

The branch above was still now, and it was Hanna trembling. She was loyal to Miles and to the Falconer, and she always would be. But Gurty had said another thing. Love.

"Who loves me?" she whispered.

"Girl," said Gurty, "if you don't know that . . ." She turned abruptly and walked into the woodland shadows. Hanna, with hands in her pockets and questions settling on her heart, followed after.

*"Your master has betrayed you.
And through his betrayal man's
best friend becomes his worst enemy."*

—THE LEGEND OF THE SHRIKER

THAT NIGHT HANNA SWEPT THE KITCHEN FLOOR AS
Mother tucked young Tymm in bed and Da read by the
fire. As she whisked the crumbs into a pile, she wondered over Gurty's words. Was there a pattern here? Did
the beast call those who were loving and loyal? If that
was true, as it seemed to be, Enoch's story didn't fit the
pattern.

It was Enoch who first brought the monster back
to Shalem Wood fifty years ago, Shree had told her that,
and it wasn't over love or loyalty, but through a summoning spell.

Hanna dumped the crumbs into the trash. The

beast would want to hunt Enoch down—take revenge on a dog killer like his own master, Rory Sheen. Aye, she could understand that well enough. Some he hunted, others he called. Miles had told her that. So he'd hunted Enoch, and others like Polly, like herself, he called.

Heading down the hall, she fetched the knapsack from her room. Why call those who were loyal? She stopped in her doorway, suddenly remembering the argument she'd had with Miles the day Granda told the Shriker's tale in the cave. Miles had insisted Rory's dog was a loyal hound to begin with. But that was before the Darro cursed the dog.

Back in the kitchen Hanna filled a bag with dried mushrooms and stuffed it in the rucksack. Would the monster try to summon her again at the next full moon? She couldn't let her fear of him get in the way. It was Miles needed saving now. And if the monster called her, she'd be all the closer to finding her lost brother.

Miles's room was dark. No rushlight there. Still, she knew where he kept his weapons. Hanna took the hunting knife down from the high shelf and hid it in her rucksack.

At dawn Hanna stopped halfway up mountain to catch her breath and eyed the rose-colored clouds before pressing on. Her heart lifted at the sight of the broad-winged falcon flying beneath the cloud spray. "Aetwan," she called, waving at him. He spiraled slowly downward and perched on a pine branch.

"You've come back to me," cried Hanna.

Aetwan cocked his head and opened his beak. A small, triangular object fell to the ground by Hanna's feet. She stooped to pick it up and turned the triangle over so the glassy side winked in the sunlight.

"A mirror," said Hanna.

"A troll glass," corrected Aetwan.

Hanna looked up. "What does it do?"

"Trolls can't look at their own likeness."

"Oh," said Hanna. "What happens if they do?"

Aetwan squawked, or laughed—Hanna couldn't tell which. "You'll see."

"You're coming with me to find Miles, aren't you?" She gazed up at him. Waiting. Hopeful.

Aetwan's neck feathers puffed out. "Can't," he squawked.

"Why not? It's your home, after all." No one had

ever told her this, but the animals and birds from Oth spoke, as Aetwan could, so she'd guessed he wasn't hatched in Noor. The falcon still hadn't answered her challenge. "I have to go and keep on searching for Miles," she said. "And there's not much time—"

"Till the full moon," interrupted Aetwan.

"Only three days," Hanna went on. "Gurty's old and slow, and she said she may not come at all, depending on which way the fire is leaning."

"You are not alone," said Aetwan.

It was what the Falconer had said, but if Aetwan left her to cross into Oth without his company . . . "If you leave me, Aetwan, I'll be very much alone."

"Look around," screeched Aetwan. It was a command as only he could give it, and she obeyed instantly, looking left and right, behind her and before her, and lastly up and down. But she saw no help at hand. "What do you mean?"

Aetwan flapped his wings impatiently. "Remember," he said.

He took off again, flying awkwardly at first, then gaining grace as he gained speed.

"Come back," called Hanna. She watched his pumping wings as he ascended at a sharp angle, his body growing smaller and smaller until he disappeared behind the clouds. "You're always leaving," she whispered, "all of you." She was staring at the clouds as if they'd swallowed not only Aetwan, but Miles, the Falconer, and Granda—taken from her everyone she'd ever truly loved. "And what have you given back?" she asked them.

Up the path in the sunlit maple grove Hanna stopped and peered through the trees. "Be vigilant and look for the signs," the Falconer had said. "These signs are not seen with the eye alone. The seeker must look with the eye of the heart." How was she to do that? Did it mean to both see and feel? She stepped under the blowing branches and took the path that breezed before her, where the leaves were trembling.

> "Such woods as these would make a stranger sleep.
> But you they will awake.
> Such winds as these would chill an enemy.
> But friend, they will warm thee."

"Who speaks?" asked Hanna. Her skirts rustled as if a tender hand were brushing against them, yet she could see no one. There was a stirring all about her, and the maple trees gave up their foliage to it. The breeze danced with red leaves and brown and yellow.

"In such hours as these a world is born."

Hanna suddenly knew the voice, and she looked about for the wind woman.

"Wild Esper," she called, turning round and round. "Where are you?"

"Where you are," Esper breezed.

"But I can't see you."

"See me."

Hundreds of leaves swirled before Hanna's feet. In a rush of colors they lifted like a great wheel before her. Light shone from the center of the turning, as if the sun were caught in the hub of the wheel. Hanna shaded her eyes against the brightness. From the center of the wheel she heard the wind woman chanting the entrance charm she'd read in the Falconer's book.

"Open as you have before,
Let the traveler through the door.
From this opening begin,
The only way out
Is in."

Hanna felt herself being sucked toward the wheel, but she dug her feet into the soft forest floor. She didn't want to go back to Attenlore without Gurty or Aetwan to accompany her. But the swirling passage, which had been as massive as the miller's grinding wheel, was closing, just as the tunnel had closed around Miles long ago in the deeps. She knew she must go now, and go alone, or not at all. Hanna gripped the bowstring across her chest. She wasn't feeling brave just now, but she loved Miles, and for that she stepped into the whirl.

Her feet went out from under her as she was sucked inside. She spun helpless, with hundreds of swirling leaves around her. Blue sky, red leaves, brown earth, evergreens, swirled into a central glow until earth and sky and head and foot were all the same. The burning at the center filled her. Heat spread over her tumbling body. She let out a scream, then fell suddenly facedown into something soft and damp and very cold.

After the eruption of Mount Eenadd
the people turned against eOwey
and made sacrifices to the mountain.

—THE BOOK OF EOWEY

AT THE EDGE OF THE FROZEN MARSH MILES STOOD BLOODY and victorious over the slain gullmuth. The monster lay beneath his paws, its broken neck twisted, its dead black eye staring upward.

Miles heaved a labored breath. It had been a long fight. He considered the gullmuth's thick, furry body, its strange, birdlike head, its bloody beak and claws. The monster was half again his size, and it should have won the battle, by all rights. But he'd knocked the beast over on its side and gone for the weak point at its slender throat.

Miles licked his torn foreleg. He'd dodged the gullmuth's beak but hadn't escaped its mighty claws.

The new gash was dangerously close to the scabs left by the Shriker's teeth.

The woods, growing up from the valley floor, seemed strangely still. Miles stepped away from the body and limped through the bloodstained snow. A handful of kravel birds flew above Uthor, black-winged against the shrouded air. He would not eat this kill. The carrion birds would have their fill of gullmuth meat when he was gone.

In the broad, open space on the valley floor Miles lifted his muzzle to the air and sounded his victory cry, "The gullmuth is dead!"

His call filled the vale, bouncing from stone wall to snowy edge. He listened, ears pricked, and when the echo of his words died away at last, a great loneliness swept into him. He stepped back, his chest empty as the vale itself.

There was no one here to witness his victory over the gullmuth. No Falconer to give him an approving nod. Nor was Da nearby to call him brave and slap him on the back. His shoulders ached for the feel of that.

He closed his eyes. He was lost now to everyone he'd once loved. Buried and forgotten here in the

Shriker's realm. Miles snarled, thirsting for revenge, a deep thirst only the Shriker's blood would quench. He'd been hiding out here. Hoping to break free of Uthor Vale to fight the beast in Attenlore. But if he could kill the gullmuth, he could slay the Shriker, too. He was tired of hiding. He'd regained his strength. Now he wanted the thing done.

"Come to me now, dog!" he howled. "By tooth and claw, I challenge you!"

The muscles on his back twitched as he looked along the tree-lined valley for a sign of the Shriker. At last he spied something moving along the edge of the frozen marsh. He gave a low growl as the leafless brambles parted, bared his teeth, expecting to meet his enemy's coal-red eyes, to hear an answering growl. But three trolls stepped out onto the snow.

The trolls were but four feet tall. They shook their heads as they looked first at the body of the gullmuth and then at Miles.

More trolls appeared. A dozen and a dozen more, all with tangled hair and ragged clothes covered in muck. They stood in a tight band, armed with knives and axes, their mossy beards blowing sideways in the breeze.

Miles narrowed his eyes and looked down his long snout at the gathering. Thirty trolls or more. He could smell the fear on them.

"The Shriker," they whispered one to another, their heads nodding up and down, and then, "He's done it. He's killed the mighty gullmuth."

Suddenly the trolls raised their axes high. "Long live the king!" they shouted all at once, and threw themselves facedown upon the snow.

ARROWS

ARROWS

Such woods as these would
make a stranger sleep.
But you they will awake.

—WILD ESPER

HANNA LIFTED HER HEAD AND TOOK A DEEP BREATH. Cold air filled her lungs. It seemed as if she'd passed from autumn to winter in a moment's time. All around her the enchanted lands were covered in snow. Standing up, she saw that she'd been taken farther up mountain this time, to the snow line by the high cliffs. She bit her lip, looking downhill where the forest of pine and maple stood still untouched by snow. The woods below seemed suddenly menacing. So many places for the sylth folk to hide and spy on a traveler from another world. Which way? She had to find Miles before the Sylth Queen discovered her and threw her out of Attenlore again.

She gazed up mountain and chose to take the harder climb, which might offer a view of both foothills and woodlands where Miles could be wandering.

Shouldering her pack, she started forth, keeping her eye out for Miles's footprints as she climbed. The day was still young, and she ventured on at a good pace, staying close to the snow-domed boulders in case she needed to hide from the sylths.

After a two-hour climb Hanna hunched over, hands on knees, to catch her breath. The peak of Mount Shalem loomed high above to her right, but straight ahead, just over the side of the high plateau, lay a deep, shaded valley. The soft breeze at her back pushed her toward the basin; still, she hesitated. The valley was in shadow, not by cloud or night's coming, but by a deeper dark that seemed to grow out of the land itself.

The Shriker had hunted far and wide, and the queen was losing her lands to him. If Uthor Vale had grown so broad in so little time, how long would it be before the dark lands swallowed all of Attenlore?

Cold fear filled her chest as she gazed down, and with the chill the knowing came; Miles was down there, and the Shriker. She locked her knees to control her trembling legs. If it was her love and her loyalty that made the Shriker single her out, here was a true test of it. Did she love Miles enough to step over the edge?

Three days left to find him. She must go now, before she lost her nerve. Adjusting the bowstring across her chest, she braced herself for the journey and left the sheltering boulders. She'd taken less than ten steps through the crunching snow when a fleck of ice blew past her cheek. Hanna thought nothing of this until another whizzed by and fell dark and slender at her feet. She peered down at the sparkling snow and toed a tiny arrow with her boot.

Whirling round, she saw the swarm of sprites, hundreds of them, flying up the mountainside toward her. She was exposed on the plateau. Hanna turned and raced across the top. More arrows shot past her head and shoulders. *Run fast! Faster!* The heavy snow slowed her pace. They'd catch her soon.

Hanna darted past another boulder, tripped, and fell facedown. Leaping up with a little scream, she ran again. Her neck stung as one arrow met its mark. She slapped it and pulled it from her flesh as she stumbled through the white powder. Another sting on the back of her hand. A third on her cheek as the arrows rained down.

She felt her cheek going numb, her neck, her hand, and she was yawning even as she ran. Tamalla-tipped arrows. They must be. No. Not again. She wouldn't let herself be caught this time. If she awoke before Queen Shaleedyn, bound in spell webs, she would be banished again and never find Miles!

Snow flurried into her yawning mouth; still, Hanna pushed herself harder, flew over the top of the plateau and down the steep incline into the heart of the shadow realm.

THE HOUND KING

THE HOUND KING

Kwium's treasure map brought him to the mouth of a tomb.

—*The Book of eOwey*

MILES MARCHED THROUGH THE TUNNEL WITH THE trolls. Deeper down and deeper down they went. The passage was almost too narrow for Miles's beast form, but he set the pace for the company. There were fifteen trolls on the march, including the tallest troll, his king's counselor, Shum.

"Faster," said Miles. His voice was gruff and powerful. It took but one word from his sharp-toothed mouth to make them speed up. He watched with satisfaction as the trolls hurried on, their short legs doing double time to keep up with his stride.

The trolls feared him and thought he was the

Shriker. He would let them keep their fear for now. He was their hero and conqueror. None had ever overthrown the mighty gullmuth, though many beasts and trolls had tried. Miles had gleaned this during his stay so far in Uthor. The gullmuth monster had always won over all his attackers, whether they'd come at him in dozens or in larger troops. His first week in Uthor Vale, Miles had seen the trolls' hero mound, the burial spot of all those slain in battle with the gullmuth, and it was a hill unto itself.

Soon after he killed the monster, Miles learned why the trolls had bowed to him, saying, "Long live the king!" For the last troll king had willed upon his death that the one who overcame the gullmuth would be crowned the next troll king. Years had passed since the decree, and many trolls had died trying to win the crown; the hero mound was proof of that.

I did it, Miles thought, still amazed at what he'd done. *I was meant to be their king.*

On his first night with the trolls Shum had con-fessed there was a storeroom where the wealth of Uthor had been hidden for years beyond remembering. It was said each king of rightful rule would have the power to find his way to the wealth. And so this walking down and down inside the wending stone mines was a test of Miles's true kingship. How he was to find the hidden vault, he didn't know, but he kept his senses sharp.

The castle guards he'd chosen to bring down marched behind him under their torchlights. The trolls were small, coming only halfway up his forelegs. They smelled of sweat and grime and something else he couldn't name, and he didn't trust a single one of them, especially Shum. But he'd already formed a plan concerning the trolls, one that would ensure the Shriker's death, so he tolerated their stench.

The tunnel took another turn. Miles's left foreleg stung as he passed a line of boulders, but he worked not to limp before the company.

At last Shum stopped at a fork in the passage and waited for his word.

Miles thought, uncertain. "This way," he said at last. They turned left and marched downward. The wealth of Uthor had been mined and forged by the trolls in their long years of exile from Attenlore. The early kings had hoarded it and kept it hidden from the outside world. Trolls were always hiding things, burying them, being earth creatures themselves, and it was right to hide treasure underground here in the vale, where thieves, murderers, and monsters roamed.

Cold splashes hit Miles's back as he walked. The kings wouldn't have kept treasure in a damp place. He must have chosen the wrong way, but how could he turn back and still pass the test?

"It's damp!" growled Miles.

Shum cringed at the sound of Miles's words. "We're far underground, sire," he said lamely. The passage turned right. Shum's torchlight sputtered as three droplets fell from the stony roof. The company passed another large boulder and Miles stopped. The trolls behind him halted, unsettled and mumbling.

"Quiet!" ordered Miles. They hushed themselves as best they could, though they still breathed heavily. Miles cocked his ears. *Drip. Drip.* From somewhere far off, the dripping sound had a musical tone. Not water on stone, but water on . . . He looked to his left. Put his ear against the boulder. Aye, it came from there. "Move this aside!" said Miles. All fifteen worked to push the rock. A few blew out their torches and used the wooden staffs for pry bars. "Heave!" they shouted. "Heave!" On the third try the boulder rolled aside. A darkness and a gleaming within, and in the torchlight held and wavering Miles saw piles and piles of coins and jewels.

"Our storeroom," said Shum proudly.

"Mine," corrected Miles.

Shum's lip trembled. He bowed to Miles. "Y-yours, sire."

Miles crouched low and worked his way through the hole, which wasn't made for so large a king as he. Mouth watering, foreleg aching, he stepped up to the pile. The coins shone and glinted, but he could not see what sort of coins they were. *My eyes,* he thought. *A hound's eyes, blind to color.* He'd missed seeing the green trees and the vibrantly colored flowers when he was in the fields of Attenlore. But here, now, as he stood before this treasure, *his* treasure, not knowing if the coins were silver or gold, if the jewels were rubies or sapphires . . . He ground his sharp teeth. "Make an accounting of it," he ordered.

Shum stepped up. "It's written our store is thirty thousand gold coins. Nine hundred and seven gems. As you can see."

But Miles couldn't see. "Name the gems!"

Shum cleared his throat and shifted on his feet.

He handed his torch to another troll. "Emeralds," he said. "And rubies, diamonds, sapphires, garnets, a few moonstones."

"Where are the pearls?" said Miles. Mother and Hanna loved pearls.

"Um . . . no pearls, sire. We're too far from the sea here in Uthor."

"I see," said Miles. His own words, but their meaning angered him. He couldn't see the treasure at all. Only gray gold, gray rubies, gray emeralds . . .

He looked about the walls, which were hung with troll armor. The shields and breastplates were dusty. His eyes were sharp enough to see that, at least. He nodded at the wall. "Guards," he said.

The troll guards bowed before him.

"Take the armor from the walls. Polish them. Bring the bludgeons. Sharpen every sword." At his word the trolls eagerly began to take down the armor, enough for a small army.

Miles walked around his treasure pile and spied necklaces, bracelets, all small, all made for troll kings. But though the trolls were only four feet tall, their wrists and necks were thick and no smaller than a man's.

Mine to wear, thought Miles, but he'd have to wait. He couldn't waver from his plan. He'd have the gold taken up to his rooms, assemble the trolls and the banished sylths he'd gathered to train for war, then they'd march against the Shriker. He wanted the pleasure of killing the beast, and he wanted the glory—his blood would taste richer in his mouth than the gullmuth's had. He'd take the killing bite, but he'd have his troll guards armed and ready at his back if he should need them.

Kill the beast.

Break the curse.

Miles sat on his haunches by his grand treasure and thought of Brim, of Mic and Cully—stupid, snotty village boys! *If they could see me now. Rich beyond their dreaming! In command of my own army! Better than that, if Da could see me, or the Falconer . . .* He looked about, his chest swelling. In a flash of torchlight he saw for the briefest moment what the Falconer would see. A giant black dog crouching in a dank underground vault with a pile of money and fifteen ragged trolls. He blinked the vision away and let out a slow growl. The trolls quaked and worked all the faster with the arms.

I'll finish what I began, thought Miles. *Once the Shriker's dead, I'll lead the trolls through the wind wall and march victorious to Queen Shaleedyn.* He felt a wave of pride. Her kingdom. Now that would be worth having. He licked his muzzle and jabbed his tongue through the gap from his missing fang. It was a good plan, but his subjects needed to tell him apart from the enemy. In the pile he spied a long, heavy chain; it might be gold or silver, he wasn't sure. Too large for a necklace. A king's belt? A heavy jewel hung at its base. He pointed to it with his paw. "I will wear that."

No one moved. The trolls were too afraid of him to come that close. He saw that, so he made his order clear. Miles pointed to the two ugliest trolls with his paw. One with a bulbous nose, the other covered in warts. "You and you," he said. "What are your names?"

Both bowed. "Endcust," said the warty one, and the other said his name, "Freeborn," at the same time, so the names blended together, EndcustFreeborn. "I name you Mic," he said to the one with the bulbous nose. "I name you Cully," he said to the warty troll. "You are my personal slaves."

"Aye, sire," both said, falling to their knees and groveling.

"Slaves," said Miles. "Put that chain around my neck."

Miles lowered his huge head so they might reach. Mic and Cully lifted the long, heavy chain and, shaking, put it around Miles's thick neck. They bowed again and backed away.

"Bring this treasure to my rooms, and make the armor ready," said Miles. "We have an enemy to kill." He turned about and was escorted back up to the inner palace, where he planned to curl up on his padded throne, lick his wounds, and eat meat that was freshly killed for him, served on a king's platter.

BEAST TRACKS

BEAST TRACKS

Thus Breal's hope was gone, the hero all but broken, when the wind woman Isparel blew his vessel skyward toward the final battle.

—THE EPIC OF BREAL

HANNA PAUSED AND WIPED THE SWEAT FROM HER NECK. She'd walked all night and rested little through the next day, overcome with drowsiness both from lack of sleep and from the sprite arrows. The tips had been dipped in tamalla. The pungent smell had told her that. It would have been easy enough to carry her off to the Sylth Queen if she had been drugged and dreaming.

In the dusky valley melting snow dripped from the overhanging branches. But the little pushing breeze that had followed her here through the night and day blew warmth across her back. "Am I going the right way?" Hanna asked. The little breeze didn't answer.

371

Swinging her left foot forward, she pressed on, though her legs felt leaden and her body numb. She rubbed her hands and face and ran her tongue over her wind-cracked lips. Yesterday she'd clambered down the steep hill as the arrows whizzed past her ears. The sprites in flight just behind. They would have captured her if she'd gone any other way, but as the air darkened round her, the sprites stopped mid flight, hovering there as she plunged into the wind wall.

She hadn't seen the wall, only heard the blowing, like the moaning of the sea in deep island caves, and when she ran inside, she was surrounded by the singing gales—drawn in and in by the great gust until she was taken up, spun round, and thrown at last against the ground like a wave-tossed body to the shore. She'd gotten up, run more after that, swaying like a drunkard as she ran, but the sprites never flew past the wind wall, never entered the dark land.

A flurry of snow encircled her. She pulled the Falconer's tinderbox from her pack and held it in her open palm. Her throat ached as she looked at the small black box. She could see his veined hand now as he sparked his flint to light the rushlight. A gentle breath pressed her forward, but she longed for the feel of the Falconer's hand on her shoulder. A hand as large and warm as Granda's. She needed his kind touch now and his strength to help her face the shadow vale. Only two days left. How was she to find Miles in the dark vale with no one to help her?

Tucking the tinderbox back in her rucksack, she gripped her bowstring and checked the woodland trail. There were many watchers here. First there were the trees, whose thick, gnarled branches hung overhead. Their trunks weren't tall and proud, as the evergreens in Shalem Wood, but seemed to writhe up from the earth. It was easy in these shadows to mistake them for misshapen giants watching her. Waiting for their moment. Then there were other eyes, more felt than seen, peeking out from thick bushes and around the twisted trunks. She took a breath. Kept walking. There wasn't time to stop or think or worry, only to move.

More lonely hours passed. She spied what looked like caves—dark, open places in the rocky ravine—and headed for them. A beast would seek them out for shelter from the cold, and she might find some sign of Miles there. The far-off mountain peak, which had been a kind of beacon to her the past few hours, was going dark. Twilight already. Tonight and tomorrow, that was all the time she had left to find Miles before it was too late. If he stayed in the beast form through tomorrow's full moon . . .

Hanna didn't finish the thought, which rose up in her mind like a great, dark wave. With all her might she held the wave in place. The full of it would not crash down. She would press it back and back.

Halfway along the slope she stopped and knelt. Tracks. Sharp claws had dug black pits in the snow above four deep impressions left by giant padded paws. Her ears rang with sudden fear. The Shriker's prints. Or were they her brother's? She'd been right to head toward the caves. Light and joy peeked out behind the fear. She touched the muddy snow. "Miles?" There was no way to find out other than to go. She stood again, braced herself, and followed the beast tracks. *Be Miles,* she thought, *be Miles,* with every step, her damp boots leaving small impressions beside the great paws.

Hanna tracked by starlight, and by the moon as it coursed overhead. The valley had felt closed off to the world in the daylight hours, but the shadow realm opened itself to the night, and what light there was fell clear from the heavens.

Searching through the woods, she thought on the tale Granda Sheen used to tell of the serpent Wratheren, who swallowed the moon, and of Breal of Kelleneur, who battled the serpent in the sky. It was a myth from a long-ago time, but it warmed her some to think of Breal, a common man who overcame a giant serpent to rescue the moon.

She remembered how she used to feel when Granda told Breal's tale: how she'd imagined herself doing battle with the serpent to bring light back into the world. But her life had been simple back then, and her longings had been safe beside her mother's hearth. Words from the tale filled her ears, as if her granda walked and talked beside her. *After a full year of chasing the sea serpent Breal gave up the quest and turned his ship homeward, for Wratheren had grown great wings and taken to the sky. And what ship can grow wings? Thus Breal's hope was gone, the hero all but broken, when the wind woman Isparel blew his vessel skyward toward the final battle.*

Hanna paused, the branches about her creaking like so many old doors. She hadn't thought of that part of the tale for a long while. Breal gave up. Breal, the greatest of all heroes, turned back until the wind spirit Isparel came to blow his ship into the sky.

She looked up through the branches and let Granda's words settle into her the way they always did; let them fill her ears, her mind, her heart. If Breal lost hope and still continued on, then she could do the same.

STOLEN

STOLEN

Open as you have before,
Let the traveler through the door.
From this opening begin,
The only way out
Is in.

—An opening spell,
from *The Way Between Worlds*

Near the valley floor the tracks came closer together. The beast had slowed down to a walk, but how long ago had he been this way? Was it a day? Two? Bushes grew in a leafless tangle, and tree roots reached across a patch of ground like bony-fingered hands. Hanna walked around them, passing by a tumble of boulders.

"A girl! A girl!" screeched a voice from a high branch above. Hanna looked up and was surprised to see two giant kravel birds in the moonlight, both black-feathered females with orange plumage on their heads. The sturdy birch branch sagged under their weight.

"Welcome to Uthor!" screeched the bird on the left.

"Turn back!" warned the other.

"She can't, Mok," said the first, hopping along the branch. "Once you come in, you never get out!"

"Hakaw! Hakaw!" they both laughed. The kravels flew upward, then dived down. Hanna screamed and set off at a run. The first bird skimmed past and pecked at her head, while the other tried to pull the rucksack off her back.

"Stop it!" Hanna cried, flailing her arms to ward them off as she ran.

"Stop it!" mocked the kravels.

"Knock her down for me, Tapp!" ordered Mok.

"Knock her down! Knock her down!" screeched Tapp.

Hanna sped up. "Leave me be!" she screamed. "I have nothing you want!"

"Oh! Listen to that!" cried Mok. "She has nothing!"

"Nothing at all! Nothing at all!" screeched Tapp, ramming into Hanna's back so hard and fast that Hanna tumbled over.

"Oh, I'm good. I'm good!" boasted Tapp. She landed on the snow before Hanna and preened the feathers on her left wing. "Take the pack, Mok!" she screeched.

Hanna kicked and shouted, but in no time Mok had flown down and stripped the pack from her back. The birds flew off, Mok's large, dark wings flapping heavily under the weight of her bounty.

"Stop!" screamed Hanna. "Give that back! It's mine!"

"Give it back!" mocked Tapp.

"It's mine!" screeched Mok.

Hanna darted left, then right, then left again as the kravels wove in and out between the treetops. *I'll lose my way,* she thought. *And I won't find the Shriker prints again.* She stopped a moment and leaned over, breathing hard. She knew she should turn back, but she took another breath and plunged through the underbrush.

She had some bread in her pocket, so she wouldn't have bothered to go after the pack with its cook pot and drinking cup. But the Falconer's gift was in the rucksack. He'd wrapped it well, trusting her to bring it to Miles. For that, and that alone, she ran.

Hanna tried to watch where she was going, to know the trees, bushes, the snowy rocks, so she could find her way back to the tracks. But she could not keep her eyes on the woods and follow the kravels' flight at the same time. *Break low branches,* she told herself. *Make a trail back.*

She thrust out her arm as she ran, snapping small juniper branches here and there as best she could while bounding through the snow.

Far in the distance the kravels circled in a slow spiral over a giant fir tree, as if waiting for her. She sped toward the tree. Just then Mok dropped the rucksack. It tumbled down and disappeared into the high branches. Hanna raced up a narrow path to the broad trunk.

"I have nothing you want!" mocked Tapp again. "Nothing at all!"

"Go get it if you want it!" called Mok.

"Hakaw! Hakaw!" they laughed as they flew off.

Hanna put her hands on the rough brown trunk, tipped her head, and looked up. The pack was up there somewhere but far too high to see in the dark. The lowest branch on the fir was more than a ladder's length away. The elm beside it was not close enough for her to jump tree to tree. Aetwan could fetch it for her if he were here. The thought made her feel even more alone. The sprites could fetch it, a sylth or bird, anything with wings. A giant could reach down his long arm and bring it up again.

"A girl! A girl!" the kravels had called, and that was

all she was. She held the trunk, her arms reaching but a fourth of the way around. She gripped the coarse bark hard until the tart fir smell filled her nose. Gone. The Falconer's tinderbox, her blanket, Gurty's wise root, and worse than that, Miles's gift. It was then the wave inside her nearly broke.

Hanna awoke stiff and sore in the hollow of a pine tree. Outside the wind whistled, stirring up little flurries of snow. The last day to find Miles. She would have to leave the pack where it was. There was no way to fetch it. Today she'd find the tracks again. "They will lead me to Miles," she whispered to reassure herself.

Sitting up inside the tree, her cloak wrapped tightly round her, she leaned back against the mossy wood and chewed the breadcrust from her pocket. The dream she'd had just before awaking came back to her then.

She'd seen the Falconer leaning over his table. The old man had his back to her, and he was scribbling with his quill pen. "You're here!" called Hanna. She tried to run to him, wanting to lean her head against his chest. To smell the winterleaf and forest there in his old shirt, and to feel his large hand on her back. Her feet flew, her legs churned, but she couldn't get any closer. She was running in the air. "Turn around," she had called. "Look at me." But the meer hadn't turned. He'd kept on writing.

Inside her tree Hanna hugged her knees to her chest and shivered. "What was it you were writing?" she whispered. More of the dream came back. The meer had laid aside his quill, climbed up in the air, and gone into the roots that hung from his ceiling. Hanna tried to follow, but she couldn't float upward into the air as he had. And she found herself standing with her hands braced on the back of the bent-willow chair. She peered at the table and read the words he'd left upon the parchment.

With her back in the hollow of the tree, she whispered now what she'd read inside the dream: "For Miles in Attenlore."

He wanted her to go back for the rucksack. *I'll go,* she thought. *I'll fetch it quickly, then I'll look for fresh tracks.* The sweetness of having seen the old man again brought lightness to her chest. Hanna crawled outside to the dim morning and crossed the path till she found the fir.

It was well she'd thought to scrape a marking on

it, or she wouldn't have been able to pick the tree out from the many others. She peered through the branches. There. Her dangling pack was dusted with snow. But it was too far up. She might shoot it down. Stepping back, she drew out an arrow, pulled the bowstring taut, aimed, and shot. The arrow flew through the branches nowhere near the pack. Again she tried, and again. One arrow fell back to the snow, two more landed in the tree. *I'll waste all my arrows this way,* she thought as she began to pace. *If only I had a ladder.*

Hanna looked about the trail and off to the sides. After a lot of searching she found a fallen sapling and pulled it slowly along. It was heavy, and she fell with the weight of it twice before leaning it up against the fir trunk and climbing on.

Gathering all her strength, she pulled herself up the sapling until she reached the lowest fir branch. Bracing her foot against the trunk, she reached up higher still. "For Miles in Attenlore," she whispered under her breath as she pulled herself upward.

And he named his children after his enemies.

—THE BOOK OF EOWEY

THE NIGHT'S SNOWFALL HAD FILLED THE TRACKS HANNA had found the day before, and she spent all afternoon trudging through the dim valley seeking more. No time to build a cook fire, she chewed a few dried mushrooms for strength as she walked, glad to have the pack with its gear and food snug against her back again.

Tonight was the first full moon since Miles had formed himself into the Shriker. She had to tell him to change back before it was too late. *Find him. Find him.* The words echoed through her mind with every footfall as her boots crunched through the snow.

Late in the day she came at last upon a new set of

tracks. Heart racing, she squatted down. The paw prints were as round and broad as the well bucket; the weight of the passing beast had set each one deep in the snow. She followed them beneath the whispering boughs, moving with haste as the shadows all around her darkened.

Near the valley floor she came to a sudden stop by a straggly juniper bush. The tracks ahead were even, but there were red splashes on the snow nearby. Blood. Drawing closer, she went down on one knee. New impressions here, coming out of the undergrowth to join the beast tracks. They were shaped like human feet, a little larger than her own. Blood pooled in the heel of one of the tracks. Her throat tightened. "Miles," she whispered.

She rose again, straining to peer through the thick evergreens. He must be close now! She quickened her pace through the deepening snow. The prints, both beast and human, turned sharply to the right.

She'd just changed direction to follow them around the bend when a troll leaped out in front of her.

Hanna froze, stifling a scream. The troll was small, his head no higher than her chin, and his thick body was covered head to toe with mossy green hair that was parted by a long, warty nose.

My bow, she thought, but her hand moved faster than her head, for in a flash she'd plucked Aetwan's troll glass from her pocket.

As soon as he saw the triangular mirror, the troll jumped back and fell to his knees. "Please don't hurt me," he cried in a gravelly voice.

Hanna kept her aim, a small white bead of light falling across the troll's bowed head. "Stand up now," she said.

The troll came to his feet and peered at her through matted hair, though he made sure to keep his gaze above the glass. His eyes were marble black, and he smelled like wet leaf mold.

"Tell me who you are," said Hanna.

"Cully of Uthor's lower dell."

Hanna flinched at the familiar name, thinking for a moment that someone had hexed Cully from Brim and turned him into a troll. But this troll was old, not a boy at all, so only their names were the same. Still, it troubled her.

Cully pointed to the troll glass. "Put it down," he said, trembling.

She peered at his red-stained fingernails, which curved to points like cat claws. "The blood on the snow," she said. "Is it yours?"

"I was going to bring the kill back to him," he said. "All of it." He licked his lips as if recalling the taste of rabbit or fox or whatever it was he'd eaten, then pointed to the troll glass again. "Did the Hound King give you that?"

"The Hound King," whispered Hanna. Not in answer to the troll, but in surprise at the strangeness of the words.

Cully seemed to take it the wrong way. "Oh, I'll bring my share back to him tonight. Tell him. Tell him. I'm the best hunter in the vale!"

Hanna took this in. If Cully thought her to be a spy for the Hound King, whoever that was, she wouldn't tell him otherwise.

He took a step toward the trees.

"Stop," ordered Hanna.

"Don't shine it in my eyes!" pleaded Cully. He pressed his bloodstained hands together. "Don't turn me into stone with your glass!"

Turn him to stone? Who'd said anything about that? Then she remembered Aetwan's words, "Trolls can't look at their own likeness." She gripped the charm tighter in her fingers. Cully's fear gave her a sense of power she'd never felt before. "I'm looking for someone," she said. "I think you will help me."

The troll sighed. "What sort of someone?" He plucked a beetle out of his hair and popped it in his mouth. "I'm not telling on my own folk. But if you want to know about that marsh rat Tinzel—"

"A boy," said Hanna.

Cully swallowed the beetle and gave her a narrow look.

"He may have followed the Shriker into the valley," Hanna added.

As soon as Hanna said "Shriker," Cully fell to his knees, bowed his bushy head, and said, "He killed the mighty gullmuth. Long live the Hound King!"

The shock of his words hit her hard. Hanna tensed as the image of the beast king, a crowned Shriker, formed in her mind. She worked to hold the troll glass steady.

A small bead of sweat ran down her forehead. She wiped it off with the back of her hand. Cully used the split second of her undoing to dart back into the woods and race through the trees.

"Wait," screamed Hanna, bounding through the snow. "Stop!"

She flew through the woods behind the troll until her breath came hard and her throat stung. At a crossing

Hanna stopped, looking left and right. No sign of Cully. She searched the snow. No tracks. She'd lost him. *He was no help,* she thought, to calm herself. *He wouldn't have led me to Miles.* But another thought echoed back through her mind: He might have told her something.

Tired and needing rest, she took none. Instead she retraced her steps and picked up her old trail. At the path's edge she knelt down by the broad paw prints.

The beast was king here. What did that mean for Miles? The question made her chest ache.

It was near midnight when Hanna reached a frozen stream. There in the deeps of the valley she broke the ice and filled her cup. *Find him. Find him,* she'd thought with every hurried step all afternoon and into the night. But she'd failed, and now the moon had risen round and lantern bright over Uthor Vale. Exhausted and heartsick, she drank. As the cold, clear water crossed the back of her tongue, she peered over the rim of her cup and saw two eyes, burning red as coals, watching her from the bushes.

The serpent Wratheren swam the sky,
hungering for the moon.

—THE EPIC OF BREAL

WITH HIS EYES FIXED ON HANNA, THE BEAST STEPPED around the juniper bush. She screamed and dropped her cup. It clattered on the creek stones as she dived for the cedar tree behind her and scrambled up the trunk. He could hear her panting breath. See her fear in the way she clung to the cedar branch. Moonlight fell across the boughs and lit her tangled hair. She was muddy, and her cloak was torn.

Hanna gripped the bowstring across her chest, but the arrows had fallen to the snow beside her pack when she fled. She was alone and unarmed in Uthor Vale.

"You should leave here," he growled. "It isn't safe."

Hanna recoiled at the sound of his gruff words, but she recovered. "Miles?" she said in a trembling voice. "It's . . . it's you. I came so far to find you."

Miles did not reply at first. The troll army was nearly ready. There was no room for Hanna just now. A girl that needed protecting would only get in the way of his plan.

"Your coming here only makes it harder for me. Did you think I wouldn't be able to kill the Shriker on my own?"

"No. It's not that." Hanna tipped her head. "And anyway, that's not why I came."

He saw how tightly she clung to the branch.

"The Falconer said you had to leave the Shriker's form before the next full moon. If you don't change back tonight, you may be lost."

"He said that, did he?" growled Miles. The Falconer had always underestimated him. Miles pricked up his ears at the sound of footsteps crunching in the snow. They were very close by. He lifted his snout. The damp, moldy smell of troll was in the air. "Quiet now, Hanna," he warned. A moment later his servant Mic came toward him, nearly stumbling under the weight of a large platter.

"Your meal, sire," he said, placing the platter on the snow.

"Where's Cully?"

"He didn't ... um ..." Mic tugged his hair worriedly. "He's not back from his hunt yet?" he guessed with a sniff.

Miles peered at the raw boar's flank on his king's platter. "It's not enough," he growled.

Mic backed away, then fell to his knees and bowed his head. "I'll bring you more, sire; I promise. It was all I could carry."

"Yes, more," said Miles. "You and Cully, wherever he's gotten to. But bring it later. I need to be alone tonight. No one else is to come near me." The troll bowed again, his knotted hair sweeping across the snow. Then he leaped up, turned, and hurried back into the woods.

Miles pawed the tray behind the junipers to eat out of Hanna's view. He chomped the raw thigh, reveling in its texture as he gulped it down. When he'd finished, he ran his tongue along his teeth, poked it through the gap from his missing tooth, then lowered his head and licked the boar's thighbone clean, until it was as white as the snow beside it. Meal done, he stepped out from behind the bush again. Hanna was still up in the cedar, but her neck was craning to see him better in the moonlight.

"He called you sire."

"I killed the gullmuth monster. He was larger than the Shriker and stronger, but I was quicker and deadlier. I slew him!" Miles tightened his muscled legs, adding with pride, "The shadow realm is mine now by all rights. Not the Shriker's or anyone else's, though the trolls can't tell us apart without this." He pawed his king's necklace. "Once I've killed the real Shriker, no one in Uthor will be confused about who's king." He stopped short. She would never understand. She was human and mortal and far from him now, much farther than the distance the tree gave her.

Miles limped down to the stream, dipped his tongue through the cracked ice, and drank. Moonlight shone on the frozen stream, too bright at this midnight hour. The gleaming reflection caught in his jeweled necklace. The light from both hurt his eyes. He limped back to the bush and lay down again.

"You're hurt," said Hanna.

"I'm strong. Stronger than anyone else in Uthor.

You should have seen what I did to the monster." He glanced up, expecting to see Hanna's admiring look. But her face showed only shock, and her eyes were hard. He should leave her alone and see how long *she* lasted in this place. But she was just a girl, and powerless. "I'll take you to the valley's edge," he said. "And there I'll let you out." He said this not knowing how he'd lead her through the wind wall.

"Aren't you coming home with me?"

His breath caught. The word "home" piercing his chest like a small, unexpected spear. "I haven't killed the Shriker yet."

"It doesn't matter," said Hanna. "As long as you come home."

That word again. Miles tensed his shoulders. "If I stop the hunt now, he'll win," he snapped. "He'll hunt through Attenlore and into our world forever. Do you want that?"

"No, Miles. But I want you back. You're frightening me. You don't seem . . ." She faltered.

"Human? Is that what you were going to say?" Miles licked his snout. "I'm more than human now." The muscles rippled along his mighty shoulders as he rose. He crossed the stream and stood beneath the tall tree. "Come down, Hanna."

"I won't."

"I am Hound King here, and I order you to come down!"

THE EYE OF THE HEART

*If you walk the way of love,
you will not be lost.*

—The prophet Jynn,
from *The Book of eOwey*

Hᴵɢʜ ᴜᴘ ɪɴ ᴛʜᴇ ʙʀᴀɴᴄʜᴇs Hᴀɴɴᴀ ғᴇʟᴛ ʟɪᴋᴇ ᴡᴇᴇᴘɪɴɢ. It looked as if she'd lost Miles for good. He waited at the base of the tree with shining red eyes, his thick pink tongue hanging over sharpened teeth. Her brother was huddled somewhere under the heavy beast's flesh, but she could not find him, could not see him with the eye of the heart as the Falconer had taught her. She wasn't strong like a meer. She was only a girl. And anyway, both her eyes and her heart were telling her that her brother was a monster.

Hanna wiped her damp eyes. "Do you remember Mother and Da?"

396

"Of course I remember them."

"They've been so worried, Miles."

There was silence below for a time, then he said, "That can't be helped."

"Of course it can. You can come home."

"Not while the Shriker hunts."

Hanna didn't know what to say to that. It would be so much easier to talk to Miles if only she could see him. She felt in her pocket for the glisten pouch. It was for this moment Meer Eason had given it to her, but the pouch wasn't there. She'd left it in the rucksack down by the frozen stream, her arrows scattered on the snow beside it. There was something in her pocket, though, and it was warm. She drew out the smooth stone she'd found at the shore and was surprised to see it glowing softly. Blue light spread across her palm. The light shone upward, warming her cheeks and brow.

"What have you got?" asked Miles from below. His red eyes had gone large, and he swished his tail slowly.

"My stone," whispered Hanna. "It's never glowed like this before." She remembered then how Eason and Olean had said to bring the stone with her. Was this why they'd admired it so?

"Who gave it to you? Was it the Sylth Queen?"

"No. I found it."

"You don't just find a lightstone."

"Well, I did."

"Where?"

"Down at the shore." She gazed into the blue light and saw that it was ever so slightly pulsing.

"Bring it closer," said Miles.

She climbed down one branch but no more. Then she held out her hand. Miles went up on his hind legs and rested his forepaws against the tree to get a better look. The blue light traced along his furry face, his long snout and pointing ears. And in the soft light Hanna saw the wounds all over his body. Not only the long red slash across his foreleg, but the cut on his high cheekbone and the long scar on his side, matted brown with dried blood.

She pressed her lips together, her eyes suddenly moist. "You did a brave thing protecting me from the beast the way you did," she said. "And I'm grateful. More than grateful." A fresh breeze blew about her hand as she spoke. "I owe you my life. But it's enough now. It has to be, because you're in too much danger yourself."

"I'd be in more danger if I changed back to human form."

"No," said Hanna. "Less. The danger's all around you now. It's in the shape you've taken."

Miles snapped his jaws. "Do you think I'd have any chance of killing our enemy if I changed back into a boy?"

Hanna wanted to cry, "But you've become the enemy!" But she knew it would be the wrong thing to say. She shone the lightstone at his side. "Do your wounds hurt?" she asked.

"Aye."

"Come out of the beast and let me bind them."

THE PARCEL

MILES BLINKED UP AT THE PALE LIGHT. "I'M KING HERE. I can have anyone I like bind my wounds."

Hanna didn't reply, but her face dropped and he saw her lip quivering. He looked away. She would never understand everything he'd gone through to protect her, to save Attenlore and Enness Isle from the Shriker.

He pondered his broad paw resting on the rough tree trunk. Even with his many wounds he still had the power to kill the Shriker if he stayed in this form. And he wasn't going to give up the hunt for his softhearted sister.

"Miles?" asked Hanna, her voice trembling. "*Can you change back?*"

"Of course I can," he snarled. "Whenever I want to." It was a lie, and the lightstone seemed to waver as he said it.

A sick fear gripped him and he quickly shook it off. "I'll change back when the Shriker's dead," he growled. Though that, too, wasn't the full truth. He didn't want to give up his kingship, earned through blood and battle, to become a mere boy again. He was rich beyond measure and had a good chance of expanding his kingdom once the Shriker was dead. He didn't want to change back, did he? *No*, he thought firmly, then deeper still, and quieter, *Yes.*

"You don't understand," said Miles, as much to the voice inside himself as to his sister in the high branches.

Hanna held the stone away from her face and wiped her eyes. She was crying, and he guessed she didn't want him to see her tears.

"I was thinking," she said, "how afraid I was of the Falconer when I first brought you to his cottage. Do you remember?"

Miles felt a stirring in his chest. Why must she

bring his teacher up now? He went back down on all fours at the base of the tree.

Hanna shone the lightstone across the snow. "The Falconer sent you a gift."

"Why didn't he bring it himself?"

The soft light from the branch above jeweled the broken ice by the abandoned rucksack. "It's in the pack."

"What is it?"

Hanna shook her head. "Open it."

Miles nosed the pack and tugged a cloth bag out with his teeth. He sniffed the bread and goat cheese and the dusty smell of dried beans through the cloth. Then he went for the pack again, dragging out the sooty cook pot and then a leather parcel tied with twine. It had an odd shape and smelled of winterleaf, the Falconer's favored healing herb. He read the tag penned by the meer: "For Miles in Attenlore."

Miles gently bit through the twine and nosed the leather package open. Brightness shone out. He blinked, only half believing what he saw as his eyes adjusted to the light. The Falconer's silver ervay lay on the soft leather wrapping, glistening in the glow of lightstone and moon.

How long he'd waited to touch those fine silver pipes. To run his fingers along the ancient Othic letters engraved along the side.

"The ervay was his greatest treasure," he whispered. "A gift from High King Steffen of Angalore." He put out his scarred paw to touch the fine instrument; a shadow fell over the gleam, and he placed his paw in the snow again. This was like his dream. But why had his teacher sent it to him here? And why now?

It was considered a high honor to be gifted with a thing so rare. Only a master musician should play an ervay. Miles shook his heavy head. "I don't understand." Looking up, he asked Hanna a second time. "Why didn't he bring it himself?"

His question was met with silence, and he sucked in a sudden breath. A cold shock ran across his back. "He's . . . he's dead, isn't he?"

Miles drew back. "I don't want it," he cried. "Not if it means he's . . . not this way."

A low wind breathed a tune through the ervay. A strange song that was both sweet and haunting. The tune rose up from the snow, filling the night air like a sigh. Miles hung his head. "I don't want it," he cried again.

He looked down at his blood-encrusted paws. Beyond all his mistakes, his anger, his misuse of magic, the Falconer had loved him and believed in his gift.

The tune blowing through the ervay sang hollow through his bones. Deep and deeper. And he heard it for what it was. The song of his own making. His keth-kara.

Miles's eyes welled up. "You saw," he sobbed. "You saw me."

His chest ached as it opened outward. The song broke the darkness like a dawning. He was growing small again, though he felt himself expanding. This could not be so, yet it was so. The thickened hide trembled and slowly shrank away. The weight lifted from him.

He found himself down on all fours in the snow. A long-haired boy in brown rags that hung from his frame. A heavy chain around his neck. He wept at the sight of his own hands.

AZURE ROOT

AZURE ROOT

*The azure is a noble tree, and its
blue root has great healing powers.*

—*Entor's Herbal*

T HE SKY OPENED AND SNOW FELL ACROSS THE MOUNTAIN,
covering Attenlore and drifting down into Uthor Vale.
It filled the Shriker's tracks, rounded the jagged rocks by
the stream, dusted the trees, and filled the darkened air
with cold brightness. From the cedar branch the cry of
"Miles" rang out.

Hanna scrambled down the tree and threw her
arms around him. "You've come back," she cried happily.
"I knew you could do it! I knew you could!"

They stood embracing. Miles felt her arms through
his rags and chilled skin, warm as a healing balm. He
looked down at her damp head. She was so much stronger

405

than he'd ever thought her to be. He lifted her woolen hood back over her head. Blue, even in the night he could see the color. It startled him after having lived so long in a world of black and white.

"We'd better leave here," he said at last. "The trolls will return by morning." He didn't mention the danger they were in. Trolls were the least of their worries, now.

A pang went through him for the loss of his kingship, his wealth, and his power, but he ignored it and turned to rewrap the ervay, knotting the twine with trembling fingers. He wasn't dressed for this weather. His green cape was torn and dirty now. It draped like a defeated flag across his back. Snowflakes thickened and swirled about him as he placed the Falconer's gift into the rucksack. The vale was full of beasts on the hunt this time of night. They would have to move on, and quickly.

"Here," said Hanna, holding out the quiver. She'd picked up the fallen arrows and removed his bow. He took them from her, the wound on his left arm stinging as he did so. "It's not much use against the Shriker," he said.

"It is if you aim well."

He was grateful to her for saying that. She'd always

trusted in his strength and his talent with a bow. But he felt clumsy in his boy's body, and he wondered if he would disappoint her.

A chill wind picked up as they walked against the driving snow. There was little light above now that the moon was half hidden by clouds. Hanna used her light-stone to guide the way, and he saw the beam from the stone was as pale blue as lake water. How strange to be back inside his own skin. His body felt small and weak. His legs lacked muscle; his arms were flimsy as twine, his left one too damaged from the wounds left by the gullmuth and the Shriker to be of any use in a fight; and his nails were soft and insubstantial.

He ran his tongue along his smooth, flat teeth and found a gap on the upper right side. His wounds had all come with him, like the other times he'd shifted back, no surprise there. But why sustain this small loss of a missing tooth from his shape-shift? Was that all he'd gained from the beast?

Trudging on through the flurries, he lifted his face to the night. The air was no longer ripe and thick with telling scents. That power was gone from him. Still, his nose told him one thing, and strongly. "I stink," he said.

Hanna laughed. "Not as bad as Cully."

"So, you met Cully?"

"Aye."

"And did you draw your weapon?"

"I used my troll glass."

Miles stopped. First a lightstone, now a troll glass. "Did you find that on the shore as well?"

"No," said Hanna with a smile. "Aetwan gave it to me."

A ripple of jealously ran up his back. Aetwan had never given him anything with magic power.

Hanna talked as they walked on. "The troll glass worked well enough on Cully. But he was more afraid of the great Hound King. He told me how the Hound King defeated the gullmuth monster."

"It was a real battle, that," said Miles, cheering a little. They climbed a steep grade, sidestepping patches of ice. The terrain flattened out again. The blue light faltered ahead, and he knew his sister's hand must be shaking. When he turned around, he found her leaning against a thick tree trunk.

"It's no good walking," she said. "We can't even see where we're going."

"We can't stay in the open, Hanna." He felt the need to list the dangers, so many wild things wandered here at night, but he saw her pale face in the blue light. And he knew she was worn down.

They would have to hide until daylight. "How long has it been since you slept?" he asked.

"I napped an hour or so last night, I think, cramped inside a hollow tree."

Miles looked around. "I can't say for sure," he said, "but if we're where I think we are, then there's a cave nearby. Wait here," he added.

Miles used the Falconer's flint stone to spark a little fire in the musty cave. Hanna cooked a small pot of soup with the dried mushrooms and beans she'd brought from home.

The bright little fire and the hot soup eased them against the cold, and the hard bread softened when it was dipped in the broth. They ate together in silence. Miles didn't want to speak of the storm outside or of the beast that waited hidden in the valley.

After finishing his soup, he handed his empty bowl to Hanna, careful to keep his arm covered so she wouldn't view his wound. He winced with pain as he broke a stick and added it to the fire. Squatting by the glow, he poked at a bit of kindling here, a dried pinecone there, to keep the flame alive. He remembered with an ache how many fires he'd tended by his teacher's side, how he'd once seen the Falconer herd fire, move the flames this way and that just by positioning his hand, a power he'd asked to have for himself and one not given him.

The meer had held back his magic with good reason; Miles knew that now. He'd mishandled the magic he was given from the start, nearly lost his life—and Hanna's—by doing so, though at the time it had all seemed right.

Miles squinted across the flames. "How did the Falconer die?"

Hanna paused. "He grew ill," she said. "He was very old."

"More than a hundred years, some said." Miles drew his frayed hood back over his head. "I thought he would never die," he admitted.

When their small supper was over and the dishes cleaned with snow, Miles stored them back inside the rucksack. His back to Hanna, he pulled his king's necklace from the pack. He had this bit of treasure with him, at least. He looked down at the jewel in his hand. Even in this dim fire's glow he saw clearly for the first time what it was. Not a royal necklace with an enormous diamond at the bottom, but a heavy chain with a glass bauble. He turned the bauble over in his hand—cheap, ugly, and worthless.

Miles felt a heat rising up his back. He thrust out his arm to break the glass against the rock wall, and Hanna cried out, "Oh. Your arm."

She came closer. "That hurts," she said. "It must."

Miles stashed the necklace in the pack again. "Aye, a little," he admitted.

Hanna fished through the rucksack. He wondered if she would retrieve the worthless necklace again, but she tugged out a small cloth bag instead and pulled a twisted blue root from the pouch.

Azure root. It must be. He'd seen a drawing of it in *Entor's Herbal,* but azures, the most ancient of all the trees, grew in only two places in Noor. He watched her break off a piece and crush it between two stones.

"How did you come by that?"

"Gurty gave it to me."

"An ordinary woods woman?"

"She's not so ordinary, it seems." Hanna worked the stones against the root until she'd crushed it into a fine blue powder, then she spit into the powder again and again until it was a paste. As she washed the wound with cloth and melted snow, Miles bit a stick to keep from screaming out. Hanna gently applied the paste across the raw flesh. Last she bound the wound.

Miles shifted his seat and leaned back against the cave wall. The arm throbbed and stung much worse than before, but he knew the healing had begun. To keep his mind off the pain, he said, "Tell me how you came to Attenlore."

Hanna put the rest of the root back into the little pouch and stored it in the pack. "What do you want to know?"

"The full of it. From the time I left you and the Falconer in the deeps."

It was a long tale. He listened as the snow fell across the mouth of the cave, white flurries from the black sky like thousands of moth wings fluttering down. And he interrupted only once, when she told him of the unicorn.

"I didn't kill her."

"I know that."

Miles leaned forward. "I tried to stop the Shriker, and we fought, but it was too late." He frowned to himself. "Then after, when her body lay in the field, when I was starving for meat . . ."

Hanna sucked in a breath. "You didn't!"

"No, I didn't eat her meat, though I was tempted to."

They both sighed at the same time. He was so glad now that he'd fought the urge to feast.

"The Falconer told Queen Shaleedyn you'd never kill a unicorn," said Hanna. "But she banished us all the same."

His teacher had told the Sylth Queen that? The Falconer had known he wouldn't kill the unicorn, even in his beast form. That comforted Miles some. Still, the Sylth Queen hadn't believed the meer, and she'd banished them. "The Sylth Queen can be cruel," he said.

Hanna turned away.

"What is it?" Her face looked so tired in the fire's glow. "Tell me."

"The Falconer sent me to the Enoch Tree."

Miles shivered at the mention of the twisted tree. "Ah, it's a sorry place."

"It was Queen Shaleedyn imprisoned Enoch in the tree."

"I figured that."

"But did you know the why of it?"

Miles shook his head. Hanna brought her hand up to her chin. She closed her eyes and opened them again, so he could see the fire glossing her eyes with gold. "It was fifty years ago . . . ," she began.

Miles stared at the rocky floor when the tale was done. A long silence followed. He was swept up in his own thoughts so long that when he turned again to Hanna, he saw her eyelids drooping. "I'll keep guard tonight," he said. "You sleep awhile."

Hanna didn't argue, but took her blanket from the pack, curled up, and was out in an instant. Miles kept the fire going as the night hours passed. Outside the snowstorm became a full blizzard. The heavy snow would fill their footprints, and he was glad for that, but the blizzard held other dangers. If there were Shriker tracks outside, they would be covered as well. There would be no way to tell if the beast was tracking them. Snowstorms changed the look of everything. When morning came, he wasn't sure he would be able to find his way out of the shadow realm.

ESCAPE PLAN

ESCAPE PLAN

*If Enoch had come forward and turned
the book in . . . but he tried to cover
his tracks. The boy burned it.*

—THE FALCONER

IN THE CLOSE CAVE MILES POCKETED THE TINDERBOX AND
listened past the keening wind for other sounds. The
rattling of dead leaves, the gurgle of a brook beneath the
snow, and very far away the call of a great horned owl.
He heard them all and knew it was more than a missing
tooth he'd brought back from the Shriker's form. The
quality of sound he gathered from the woods outside
and the layers of it down to the soft clicking of snow-
burdened branches told him he still had the beast's acute
sense of hearing.

He felt for the little patch of fur on his neck
from his first shape-shift. It was still there. If these two

remained, he might still have the increased vision from his falcon's form too. In the dark of night and in this blizzard he couldn't tell if this was so.

Hanna slept on peacefully. But he was too unsettled to let himself sleep. Miles rubbed his dry eyes and gave in to his thoughts. Enoch's stolen spell had been said on the night of the dark moon. He'd failed to break the Shriker's curse and ended up releasing the monster on the world.

Miles's throat tightened. He'd planned to go to Othlore himself and find a power spell. But he wasn't Enoch. He would never have gone so far as to steal a spell. The fire popped and sent up a flurry of sparks. One fell against the back of his hand, and he felt the sting of it before pressing it out. Taking the spell from the Falconer's book wasn't as bad as Enoch's crime, was it? He hadn't stolen the whole book. He hadn't burned *The Way Between Worlds*.

"A stolen spell is never rightly wielded." Shree's words. Miles had miscast the spell on Breal's Moon night. And the pearl path had faded even as he walked along. But he'd put only himself in danger that night. He wasn't like Enoch. He wasn't the one who'd brought the Shriker back.

The muscles down his arms tightened. All was done now and could not be reversed. He and Hanna were lost in Uthor with but three arrows and a knife—useless weapons against the monster.

We're not trapped here, he told himself. *We'll find our way out.* But his heart told him otherwise. He felt how small his hands were, how powerless his human jaw. And if there was a spell to kill the beast, he'd never learned it. *"Now you are cursed, and the thirst for revenge will drive you all your days until your thirst is quenched!"* How could such a curse be broken? And if a way was found, would the breaking of it kill the beast?

Laying another stick on the fire, Miles blew it to a golden flame, the color of the Falconer's eyes, then sat back, deep in thought. *Teacher. What would you do now?*

The storm eased, and they met only light snowfall at dawn when they left the cave. The deep woods looked endless and impenetrable in the shadow vale, but Miles walked firmly on, his bow at the ready and his arrows within easy reach. He watched the woods on either side for trolls and listened for the telltale hiss of skullen snakes, which often slumbered in the trees. His sharp hearing made him keenly aware of the loud crunching noises he and Hanna made on the snow.

They passed an outcropping of gorse bushes, which gave over to aspen trees and pine. Miles stopped and slid his finger along his knife handle, listening for the telling sound of cracking twigs, which would betray the presence of his enemy.

Snowflakes gathered in the creases of Hanna's hood. She swung her hands as she proceeded along the trail. Her fingers were blue with cold. Still, she seemed refreshed from her night's sleep and hiked along at a steady pace. He remembered the pleasant look on her face when she awoke. She'd been so happy to see him that he couldn't bear to tell her his plan.

"Which way?" she asked.

"Straight ahead."

She stopped and turned round. "Are you sure?"

"Aye." He stared into her round face, though he wanted to look away.

"All right, then," she sighed.

"And pick up the pace even more, if you can," he said.

In another mile they entered a small clearing near the place where he'd slain the gullmuth. He looked down, comparing his sister's small tracks with his own as he stepped beside them. He should warn her soon. The pit he sought was somewhere nearby, though he wasn't sure where. Perhaps just off the trail where the trees parted.

A sudden, loud crack followed by a scream stopped him dead in his tracks. Miles looked up just in time to see Hanna break through a layer of branches and slide down into the pit.

"Hanna!" Miles raced forward.

She flung out her hands, trying desperately to grab on to something, but she was swallowed up before he could reach her.

There in the deeps the Darro's
ghost hounds surrounded Rory.

—THE LEGEND OF THE SHRIKER

"GRAB MY HAND," SHOUTED MILES AS HE WENT BELLY down and slid up to the edge of the pit. He reached down the side, but Hanna was too far below. He peered into the dark and saw her clinging to a thin root.

"Hold on," he called.

"I can't. My hand is slipping!"

"You mustn't let go, Hanna! The pit's too deep!" If this was the gullmuth pit he'd heard Perth boasting of, there would be long, sharp spikes at the bottom. She had to hold on. He couldn't let her fall.

"I'll find a way to reach you," he promised.

He leaped up and ran to the trees. He needed a long

branch, but they were all too high up to reach, and there wasn't time to shinny up a trunk. Why hadn't he warned her of the pit? He didn't think it would be so well covered with branches and snow. Oh, she mustn't fall! "Hold on," he cried again. There must be a branch on the ground he could use. He raced through the snow—found none.

"Hurry," moaned Hanna.

Miles tore off his bow and pressed down on the wood. His fingers were stiff, but he managed to unhook the bowstring. Tying it round his ankle and securing the other end of the string to the base of a sapling, he knelt again and dipped the wooden bow down into the pit. Reach for it!" he called.

"It's too far up!"

Miles stripped the pack from his back and dumped it out on the snow. The necklace lay atop the food pouch. It was long, and if he unhooked it . . . He tore open the latch, crawled to the edge again, lay on his belly, and lowered the king's chain down. *Hurry! Don't let her fall!*

"Can you see the chain?"

"Aye."

"Grab it, then, and hold on tight. I'll pull you up."

"It will pull you down if I do."

"Trust me and do as I say, Hanna. Now!"

In the half dark Hanna swung out her left hand and missed the chain, nearly losing her right-hand grip on the root.

"Lower it down farther." She tried a second time, and on the third she gripped it and held on. Miles strained hard against the weight as he tried to pull her up. He felt himself being dragged downward. His left leg stretched out, held fast by the taut bowstring. His sweaty hand slipped on the chain. *Hold tighter! Pull harder!* The bowstring cut into his ankle, sending a sting of pain up his leg. Let it cut him. As long as he could save her from those spikes. His muscles strained with her weight. Gritting his teeth, he redoubled his efforts and pulled back with all his might.

At last Hanna was near enough to the top to reach him. She clasped his wrist. He took her hand.

"Miles!"

"It's all right," he said. "Just hold on to me."

Up a little more and she was out. She crawled from the edge. The chain slipped from his stiff fingers. Before he could grab it, the king's chain tumbled to the bottom, hitting the spikes with a clank.

They sat together a few feet away from the pit, their breath puffing out in quick little clouds. He leaned back on his hands, his limbs quaking. That was close. Too close. He blamed himself for her fall. If he had lost her . . .

Miles untied the bloody bowstring about his ankle.

"It was clever of you to come up with that," said Hanna. "I would never have thought to—"

"Stop it," said Miles. "Why do you always talk yourself down?"

"I was just admiring how—"

"I know what you were saying, but you're wrong. I'm no better than you!"

"You shouldn't shout."

"I can shout if I want to!" He stood on unsteady legs, untied the end at the base of the sapling, and tried to restring his bow. Hard to do with shaking hands. Hanna was right about the noise. It was dangerous to shout here in Uthor with so many creatures on the prowl. But he didn't care right then. He really didn't.

"There's no reason for you to be angry with me," said Hanna.

"I'm not angry with you! Can't you get that through your head?"

"Why are you shouting, then?"

"I'm not shouting! I'm yelling!"

Hanna's face broke into a smile. "Well, all right, then," she said.

They both let out a laugh, and he sat back down on the snow beside her. "The truth is," he said hesitantly, "I knew about the pit."

Hanna's chin shot out. "You what?"

"It's the gullmuth pit," he said quickly. "Reyn and Perth dug it together to trap and kill the monster."

"Who?"

"Two renegade sylths who captured me," he said. "It's a long story, but if you want to know—"

Hanna leaped up. "I could have died!" She turned and started up the trail.

"Wait," called Miles. "Don't leave. I didn't mean for you to fall in. I promise that."

Hanna turned about, sniffed, and wiped her nose.

He cleared his throat. "I didn't think the pit would be on the trail. Only off to the side somewhere. Nor did I think it would be so well hidden, but with all the snow-fall . . . they left the pit unfinished and only half covered, or so I understood. Someone else must have come along and—"

"Why didn't you warn me?" She stepped closer and sat again.

He felt her hot breath on his face. She would hate him for what he had to tell her. He looked down and pressed his stiff fingers against his bloody ankle. Still he felt her gaze.

She dug a small stone from the snow and chucked it at a nearby bush. "If you knew we might be passing the pit as we made our way out of the valley—"

"I wasn't planning on leaving Uthor."

"What?" Hanna leaped up a second time.

"Sit down, Hanna."

"I won't. Not until you tell me what this is about."

"You know what it's about," said Miles. "I won't leave here until the Shriker's dead. I promised myself I wouldn't."

"And what about me? I don't want to stay in Uthor any longer. I want to go home."

He looked up at her flushed face, expecting tears. But he was met with a fierce look.

"If I don't kill him once and for all, he'll go on

hunting creatures in Attenlore. He'll come to our world to devour people. He'll come after you again."

"I don't care!"

"Don't you? What if you knew for certain that he would kill again? What if he were to come after Tymm?"

Hanna took in a surprised breath, as if the Shriker truly had turned on their little brother. "Would he?" she whispered.

Miles set his jaw. "He might—if I don't stop him."

Hanna slowly sat back down. "I don't want to have to face this."

"Neither do I, but for some reason it's mine to do."

"Not yours alone. The Falconer said it was our story from the beginning. Yours and mine." She looked down at her hands. "He told me it was ours to finish."

Miles felt a sudden warmth across his face, like the old man had just breathed on him. "He trusted us to do it, Hanna. We shouldn't let him down." He crept to the edge of the pit and looked over. Enough morning light now to see the long, sharp spikes at the bottom. He shuddered and hugged himself.

"This would kill the Shriker sure," he said, his back

still to Hanna. "It's well covered with branches and leaves. And with the snow on top it's twice hidden."

Hands on hips, he turned. "I have to lure the beast here somehow."

A stirring breeze sent a flurry of snow between them. Hanna gave a single nod. "I will be the bait," she said.

"No," he insisted. "I'll not let you risk your life again. You're to hide away while I take care of him."

Hanna brushed the snow from her muddy cape. "You need me."

"I don't. Really, Hanna."

"You do. I'm the one he's wanted all along, Miles. And . . . ," she added in a low voice, "I know how to call him."

He stepped forward. "How?"

She looked up, her eyes blue and green—pale sky, fertile earth—a readiness in both. "Trust me," she said. And she wouldn't say more than that.

They worked together to pull down two evergreen branches to cover the hole made by Hanna's fall. Then they gathered snow from a nearby hillock and scattered it as best they could across the top. Miles stood back to admire the work. The pit was completely hidden once again. Surrounded by thick lines of trees, it took up the entire walking path, so the monster would be sure to fall in.

When all was ready, Hanna placed herself near the pit at the edge of the thick tree line. She stood on the far side, feet apart and head up, facing the long, broad path that led up the valley. Miles hid behind the pine tree to her right.

Hanna looked at him. "Ready?"

"Are you sure you want to do this, Hanna?"

"Aye."

Miles pulled his bowstring taut, aiming just above the pit. "Ready," he said.

Hanna curled her small hands into fists. Her blue hood fell across her shoulders as she lifted her chin. Head back in the falling snow, she called out, "RORY SHEEN!"

The name echoed across the valley and was answered by a howl.

THE TRAP

THE TRAP

The Darro was used to poor souls in their last earthly moment begging to be spared.

—THE LEGEND OF THE SHRIKER

DOWN THE DARKSOME VALLEY THE SHRIKER CAME. Moving like a blackened stain over the snow. The stain grew ever larger as he bounded along the slanting hills toward the little glade where they stood.

Hanna moaned.

"Keep your place now, and don't run yet," warned Miles. He watched her swaying slightly to the left, but her boots stayed put, half hidden in the dirty snow. The wind sang all around her, blowing her hair and cape sideways, like a blue flag fringed in brown. Behind the broad tree trunk Miles caught the tail end of the breeze and smelled the snow on it.

The baying wind, the charging beast. These two seemed the only things moving down the valley, and both rushed toward Hanna. The Shriker was less than a quarter mile away now, leaping over the boulders, weaving in and out between the trees, knocking down the smaller saplings as he ran. The sound of the name, Rory Sheen, had him hurtling through space like a dead star flaring down to its last orange coal. Two coals. His burning eyes. His ears pressed back against his head. His great paws kicked up the snow as he rushed toward Hanna.

Miles held his bowstring and pressed his cheekbone against the feathered fletching.

"Steady, now," he whispered, as much to Hanna as to himself. Even as he said this, he locked his knees to keep from running away.

Pounding through the hardened snow, the onrushing beast suddenly filled the path before them. His broad back eclipsing the view of Shalem Peak behind. His red jaws opened, his thick tongue flailed.

"This is it," whispered Miles.

The Shriker hurtled forward, leaped high in the air, and landed on the snow before Hanna. His paws hit the ground with a thunderous crack as the branches went out from under him. His legs suddenly disappeared. Then his body, then his head as the artifice collapsed under his weight. He howled as he fell to the bottom of the pit.

There was a thud, followed by a loud yelp, then came an ominous silence.

Miles held his breath and waited. At last he crept out from behind the tree. Bow in hand, he tiptoed to the pit and looked over the side. No sound at the bottom and no movement from the huge black form. He turned to Hanna, smiling. She raised her fist and screamed with fear and triumph. Miles threw down his bow, and they embraced, dancing round and round near the edge of the pit.

"We did it," called Hanna with a laugh.

"Aye, we did!" Miles's heart drummed with victory, so loudly he thought Hanna might hear.

"You were brave!" said Hanna.

"And you!" He looked into her smiling eyes, then wiped the smudge of dirt on her cheek.

"Home now," he said delightedly. "We'll leave the valley straightaway and look for the passage back to our world."

"Home," sighed Hanna. "I'm ready. More than ready."

He was picking up his bow when he heard a low rumbling sound from the depths of the pit. Hanna turned to him, startled. Just then a giant, bloody foreleg stretched out and clawed the ground near his feet.

"Look out!" screamed Hanna.

They both leaped back as the top of the Shriker's head suddenly appeared.

"Run for it!"

The beast was halfway out of the trap. They raced into the trees. How could he have survived the fall? The sharp spikes at the bottom?

Miles scrambled over a fallen tree, kicking hunks of rotten wood up into the air as he leaped down again. Hanna climbed the log and stood atop, ready to jump down. On the trail below the Shriker was in chase, dragging his bloody hind leg across the snow.

"Come on, Hanna," Miles called. "His leg's broken. We can beat him!"

Hanna leaped down onto the snow, and they took off running again. The Shriker was fast, even on three legs. Miles looked back as they passed an outcropping of boulders. The beast was gaining on them.

"Move!" shouted Miles.

The snow gave way underfoot. Miles grabbed Hanna's hand, pulling her along. "Hurry!"

Hanna tugged his arm the other way. "Look!" she cried. "The passage! I see it!"

"Where?"

"Over there!"

Miles pivoted and joined Hanna in a mad dash toward the blackened entrance. A hole like the one he'd tumbled into long ago after his battle in the deeps. *Be the way out! You must be the way out!* They tore through the gorse bushes and threw themselves into the passage. Hanna halted so suddenly in the darkness that he knocked her down.

"Come on," urged Miles, stooping to pull her up again. Hanna drew the lightstone from her pocket. The soft blue beam filled the tunnel. They followed the beam, walking as fast as they could under the low ceiling. "Out the other side and we'll be home," said Miles.

The tunnel broadened, and the low ceiling soon gave way to a higher one.

"I'm not sure," said Hanna. "This may not be . . ."

A deep roar filled the passage. Hanna jumped back and grabbed Miles's arm.

"He can't get in," said Miles. "It's too narrow for him." But even as he said this, his ears were filled with the terrible sound of the Shriker's paws, digging into the earth after them.

"The way out," Hanna puffed as they scrambled through the tunnel. "This has to be the passage. It can't be just a cave." But no sooner had she said this than the passage ended in solid rock. Miles stretched out his hands and touched the cold granite. He looked left and right for another opening. A hole large enough to crawl through. Anything!

Hanna kicked the stone wall with her boot and pounded it with her fist. "Let us out!" she screamed. "I want to go home!"

A loud snuffling noise came from behind them and more digging. It was like the sound Da's sheepdog made when he hunted for moles. Nosing the earth and digging furiously, only this time they were the moles!

"What now?" cried Hanna.

"I'll think of something," snapped Miles, but they were trapped here and he knew it. "Give us your stone." He turned the beam toward the entrance. The beast's head and shoulders were in. The monster pushed and pushed against the earth. His red eyes narrowing on them, he snarled, exposing yellowed fangs. Miles and Hanna pressed themselves flat up against the wall.

"I'm sorry," said Miles.

"I know."

They held each other, bodies trembling as the stench of the Shriker's breath filled the cave. One more mighty push and he would break through.

Earth and rock tumbled from the low roof as he lunged for them. A larger chunk fell on his head, a blackened tree root cut across his muzzle. Suddenly there was a thundering crash.

Miles dived for Hanna, covering his head and hers as the roof came tumbling down.

BROWN EYES

BROWN EYES

Where the one self meets the other,
In the beast eye spy your brother.

—SONG OF THE SYLTH QUEEN

MILES FELT FOR HANNA IN THE DARK. "ARE YOU ALL right?"

"I'm cut, but not badly. Is he . . . is he dead?"

"Wait." Miles passed his hand along the floor, seeking Hanna's lightstone. He felt only damp earth and rough rocks at first. Then, reaching far to his left, he found a smooth stone, which warmed to light as his fingers passed over it. He held it between them and saw the blood running down Hanna's cheek. Tearing a corner from his cape, he pressed it to her head. "Keep pressure on it," he whispered. Miles leaned back and wiped the sweat from his neck.

A low breathing sound came from the other end of the cave. The breath was followed by a deep rumble, like waves crashing far out to sea. Was the beast creeping nearer in the dark? With shaking hand he held out the glowing stone.

The Shriker lay flat under the fallen roof less than twelve feet away. The beast's head was visible, his huge front paws, and part of his back. The rest was hidden under the rubble.

"He's pinned down," whispered Miles.

"He might shape-shift and get out that way," said Hanna.

Miles raised the stone to shed more light on the far end of the cave. Blue light flickered over the stones and dirt across the Shriker's spine. Miles narrowed his eyes and shook his head. "I think he's trapped."

Hanna pointed to a small opening in the rock, near the Shriker's bloody side, which revealed a glimpse of sky. "Do you think we can get past him?"

The roof was only partly fallen above them, though the entry ahead was shut off, and there was room to stand and walk right up to the narrow opening. Miles held the shining light on the slit. Outside snow was falling like flung pearls, but the crack looked too small to crawl through, and even if they could, the way out passed too close to the Shriker. Miles was trying to think of how to answer Hanna's question when the beast opened his eyes. The lids were covered in a fine gray dust. The orange fire behind the irises had gone out, and the large eyes were now an even brown.

"Hanna," whispered Miles.

"Aye?"

"He's dying, I think."

The Shriker's tongue slid out of his mouth. He panted, trying to lift his chin from the floor, but he couldn't move.

"It will be over soon," said Miles.

Hanna took his wrist. "It'll be over for all of us," she said. "We're trapped here."

He could feel the fear in her grip, and he didn't want to look at her. "Don't be giving up now, Hanna. I'll think of something." His eyes still wandered along the body of the beast, only half visible under the rubble. Something about the way the Shriker lay crumpled on the ground troubled him. He circled around the feeling, unwilling to climb fully inside of it.

"Tell you what," he said. "I'll shape-shift small enough to get through the slit, then I'll go find someone to help dig you out."

"Who?"

"I'm sure I can make my troll servant Mic bring his pick and shovel if I shift back into something fearsome."

"No," said Hanna. "It's too dangerous. You only just left the Shriker's form behind."

Miles held his breath. Let it go. He felt too constricted in this small space, and he wanted out. "It's our only chance, Hanna."

"No. Don't leave me alone with him."

"I'll kill him for you, then. All right?" He handed her the lightstone. "Hold it on him for me." Miles dug his bow and quiver out of the rubble beside him and examined the arrows. One was split in half from the fallen rock, but two were still intact.

The great beast heaved a sigh. Miles aimed straight for the Shriker's eye. How big the eye was. The size of his fist. And how brown. His aim faltered when the lightstone leaped to the beast's ear, half hidden in the tangled roots.

Miles took a deep breath. His sweaty palm slid on

the bow. He tightened his grip, pulled the bowstring back, and tried again. The soft beam wavered. It was then he saw it. A small shape, but real. He was sure of it.

"Hanna," he said.

"Please hurry," pleaded Hanna. "I'm holding it as steady as I can."

"Look," he whispered, his heart pounding in his chest.

"Look at what?"

He gazed deep into the beast's brown eyes to a small shape trembling in the soft blue beam.

"The dog," he whispered. "Can you see the dog?"

"Now you are cursed, and the thirst for revenge will drive you all your days until your thirst is quenched!"

—THE LEGEND OF THE SHRIKER

HANNA LOOKED PAST MILES AND SAW NOTHING BUT THE Shriker lying prone under the rubble. Miles lowered his bow and heaved a breath. "Do you remember?" he said. "The story that started all of this?"

"Aye," she said, fear still creeping across her flesh. "Why won't you kill him, Miles? I can't bear to look at him anymore."

"It's the words the Darro said when he cursed Rory's dog. Do you recall them?"

She leaned against the wall. The words? She'd heard the Darro's curse before, but she couldn't think of it now. Not with her head pounding so. Not with the close, stale air all around her. "Finish him," she pleaded.

Miles reached out his hand. "Give me some water."

"Now?"

He waited while she pulled the water pouch from her pack. She poured some into the metal cup, spilling a small rivulet down her sleeve before she filled it brimful. Bending low, Miles cupped his hands around hers for a moment. This was the cup she'd dropped into the streambed when she saw him in the Shriker's form. They held the metal rim together. Hanna felt a tugging in her chest. What was it? What did he want? She gazed up for reassurance and read a wild look on her brother's face that sent her heart to her throat. "Miles?" she whispered.

"Trust me," he said before taking the cup.

He turned his back to her. She leaned against the rough stone and waited for him to drink. The wall was cold and unforgiving, but it was the farthest point from the beast, and so she clung to it. She watched Miles's shoulders rising, falling as he breathed. A fine gray dust coated his hair and the torn green cape at his back.

"Do it," she whispered. "Kill him now."

He didn't drink. Didn't move to lift his bow. The

cave walls seemed to close in around her like a tomb. She couldn't bear the wheezing sound coming from the far end.

What was he waiting for? She wanted to leap up and scream, "Grab your bow and finish this!"

Just then Miles broke the stillness. In nine steps he closed the gap between himself and the Shriker. His shadow crossed the Shriker's head. He was near enough to lean forward and speak into the creature's ear, but his steps were speech enough.

Hanna's chest constricted. "Miles?"

He didn't turn to look at her, but placed the cup by the Shriker's mouth, then slowly stepped back. The Shriker blinked and lifted his head an inch from the floor. He sent his long pink tongue out for the drink and lapped the water from the cup. The metal cup wobbled as he drank.

"What are you doing?" cried Hanna.

"Wait," said Miles, his back still to her. "I saw something. I'm sure of it."

The Shriker took another drink, and the cup tipped over with a clatter. The beast looked up at Miles. The boy's reflection caught in his eyes, and in the soft brown gaze a shining speck of light. The head fell. And a last, long breath eased out.

Miles went down on one knee, his torn cape falling to his side. "It's over," he said.

Hanna brought her fingers to her face. Dead. He was dead at last. She touched her chin, her lips. All numb.

The only sounds in the cave were those of breathing. Her breath. Miles's breath. And then . . .

In the shadows Miles reached out his hand. "Come on, boy," he whispered.

Hanna peered around her brother. Whom was he speaking to?

A small, dry wave of dust crossed the cave. As the air cleared, she saw a creature emerging from the shadows.

A black bear hound limped out of the fallen rocks. He was no bigger than Hewn's dog. A fine gray dust covered his furry coat. Soft ears down and brown eyes to the floor, he lowered his head and stood trembling in the rubble.

"It's all right," said Miles. "I won't hurt you."

THE DOG

THE DOG

*He was a loyal hound, always
looking to please his master.*

—THE LEGEND OF THE SHRIKER

THE DOG TOOK A STEP CLOSER. TAIL HANGING LOW AND legs wobbling, he stopped again and looked at Miles fearfully.

"Come on, boy." Miles held his outstretched hand in the air between them and waited. His heartbeat pounded in his ears. The sound seemed to fill the cave, as if he were trapped inside a drum.

"Miles," whispered Hanna. "Where did he come from?"

Miles pointed to the place where the Shriker's body had been a moment before, with his head tilted sideways and his jaw open in death. The beast was gone. Only dirt, cave stones, and a tangle of roots and branches remained.

"I . . . I don't understand," said Hanna. "What have you done?"

"The curse is broken, Hanna."

"How do you know? What if it's a trick? What if he just shape-shifted and—"

"Quiet now. Don't alarm him." Miles kept his voice calm, speaking to her in the same soft way that he was calling to the dog. "It's no trick. He hasn't shape-shifted into a dog any more than I shape-shifted back into myself."

He closed his eyes. How could he tell her what he knew beyond knowing—what he felt? "It's something else, Hanna. A . . . returning."

"I don't understand."

"He's just a dog," said Miles. "The way he was before the Darro put a curse on him."

He could hear his sister's quickened breath behind him. "But the curse was forever."

"You forgot the words hidden there when the Darro said, 'Now you are cursed, and the thirst for revenge will drive you all your days until your thirst is quenched.'"

Even in the dim beam that came from the light-stone he could see her screwing up her face in thought. But when she spoke again, her mouth was hard. "And that was all?" she spat. "Someone just had to give him water?"

"No, Hanna. That wasn't all." He wiped his hands on his torn shirt. The dog stood with lowered head before him, and his sister cowered near the inner wall. How could he explain it to her? He'd seen the dog inside the Shriker just before he died. And it was like seeing himself huddled in the darkness. He'd known that dark place and how it was to live inside it. A lost place of strange powers tethered to anger, the way a dog is tethered to its master.

"There's another kind of thirst," he said. "The water was only an act of kindness. Only a beginning." He wanted to say more, but he faltered. This knowing was hard won. He could not put his new understanding into words for her, and anyway, she was still trembling.

Miles went to her and touched her shoulder; it felt hard as a small rock. "Hanna," he said. "Look at him. What do you see?"

She lifted the lightstone and shone it on the dog.

"He looks like . . ." She moved the blue light along his backbone, down the crouching legs, along the bushy tail that swished hesitantly. "Like Hewn's bear hound, Kip. Like . . . an ordinary dog."

"The curse died with the Shriker," said Miles. "He's only a dog now."

He could see by the look on her face that she was still uncertain. It would take more than words to convince her, and he decided not to press her. He looked into her eyes, the blue and the green, still holding on to their fear. "Do you think you can help me?"

"With what?" she asked warily.

"If you're ready, we could start to dig our way out."

*But Rory's dog, who loved his master
beyond all measure, leaped into the fray
and fought the beasts to save his master's life.*

—THE LEGEND OF THE SHRIKER

IN THE CLOSE CAVE HANNA WORKED WITH MILES. THE dog dug beside them, and in an hour's time the hole at the cave entrance was large enough to squeeze through. Hanna was the first to climb out. She came to a stand and stretched. How good it was to be free again! Throwing her arms out wide, she ran down the snowy hill just to feel the crisp wind blow across her face.

The shadow realm was deep blue, and the trees stood like sentries along the hill, but high overhead she could see the orange-streaked sky, and close to the mountain peak pink clouds flew before the setting sun. The clouds were far away, but her eyes drank in the

449

colors, and she could almost touch the light they brought with them. Eyes still to the sky, she gulped in the clean air. Her task here was done. Miles was back, the Shriker dead. All that was left to do was to climb out of Uthor Vale and find the passage home.

Miles came down the hill, broke the ice in the shallow streambed, and refilled the water pouch. Hanna watched the dog beside him lapping up the rippling stream.

"How thirsty he must be," said Miles. The dog looked up and wagged his bushy tail.

"What will you do with him?"

"Bring him with us," said Miles. "We can't leave him here in Uthor."

"Why not?" She kept her eyes on Miles, still kneeling at the stream. Her stomach tensed as he reached over and patted the dog's head. How could he trust him like that? So easily and so soon? The dog had helped them dig their way out of the cave, but any hound would dig like that to free itself.

"He's ours to look after now, Hanna," said Miles. "Besides, it's too dangerous for him here."

She rocked back and forth on her heels. *Tell him the*

dog must stay. Tell him now. She looked into the creature's brown eyes. They seemed soft, even kind, but how could she be sure?

Miles came to a stand. "There's no trail to take us out from here, but if we keep walking upward, we may get out of the valley before dark." He wiped his brow, smearing a long brown streak across his forehead. "Do you think you can walk that far?"

Hanna picked at the dirt under her nails. "I'm strong enough." Her muscles were sore from all the digging, especially her arms and back. Her head throbbed under the bandage, and she didn't feel strong in the least, but she wanted out of Uthor Vale more than she wanted rest.

Miles turned and gazed up into the trees along the valley's edge. "We'll have to walk with care," he said. "There may be some skullen snakes in those trees, though with luck, we won't awaken them."

Hanna nodded. She hadn't run into any skullens so far, and in an hour's time, maybe two, they could be free from this valley. "Let's go on," she said.

Miles shot her a quick smile. "Aye, let's get out of here and find the passage home."

~

They were still walking two hours later when the sun set behind the high ridge. Hanna couldn't yet tell how far they were from the valley's edge. Darkness had fallen over the mountain, and the intertwining branches of the ancient oaks obscured both moon and stars.

She gripped the lightstone and held it steady. Up ahead Miles walked in the pale horizon of the beam. The dog trailed behind him. Head up, ears cocked, he scanned the thick forest, peering through the tangled hawthorn bushes along the trail.

Hanna kept close behind the two, sensing the presence of life all around her, though she could see none. Bracken, browned with the cold, lashed her legs as she walked. Her skin pricked as she passed a hollow-eyed stump. She gazed at the gnarled wood, the twisting trunk that ended branchless and broken halfway up.

A crackling sound at her left made her jump back. The dog wheeled round, ears twitching. Suddenly he leaped past a hawthorn bush and raced through the woods.

"Come back!" cried Hanna.

Miles swung round. "Quiet," he whispered. He

narrowed his eyes and pointed up at the broad tree limbs. "Skullens," he mouthed.

Suddenly the branches began to move. Green slit eyes opened. A soft hiss passed from tree to tree as long, sinuous bodies twisted through the boughs.

Miles drew his bowstring and quickened his pace. "We should have lit a torch," he said. "Skullens are afraid of fire."

The hiss grew louder.

Hanna's flesh went cold. She wanted to dive under a rock and hide, but there was no shelter here.

"Come on," called Miles.

They took off up the trail. Hanna's feet sank in the snow as she ran. Overhead the branches stirred with life. Trees to the left and to the right, before her and behind, all hissing like a kettle close to boiling.

She'd flown past the thickly huddled trunks and had nearly caught up with Miles when a giant skullen lowered itself down before her. Hanna froze, the skullen's yellow green scales shining like armor in the lightstone's beam.

"Run around it!" shouted Miles.

Hanna skirted the giant snake and darted through

the birches. Another unfurled in front of her. Blinking yellow eyed. It opened its fanged mouth.

Miles drew his bow and shot the serpent on her left. But as she raced past, another fell directly before her head and swiftly coiled itself around her middle.

"Help!" she cried.

Up ahead Miles was pounding a snake with his fists. His bow had fallen on the ground. "The knife!" screamed Hanna. "It's in the pack!"

The skullen tightened its grip around her waist and began to coil around her legs. Hanna kicked its thick hide and tore at it with her nails. The thing was all muscle and bone. She couldn't even scratch it!

On the trail above she saw Miles tear the knife from the pack. He raised the blade and cut a long gash down the snake's side. The slit ended at the creature's throat. The skullen stiffened and fell dead at his feet.

"There!" he shouted, kicking himself free.

"Hurry!" cried Hanna. The snake squeezed her chest. She could barely breathe. She pushed against the thick-skinned beast with the flat of her palm. "Toss me your knife, Miles!" she called. The muscles in her arm tensed as she tried to push against the skullen's heavy body.

Miles raced toward her. She had one arm still free. She could stab the skullen if she had the hunting knife. "Throw it!" she screamed.

He was about to toss the weapon when another snake dropped down suddenly, attacking Miles from behind.

Hanna kicked and struggled. The skullen squeezed her chest—tight, tighter. She let out a garbled scream as her feet left the ground. It was drawing her upward!

There was a cracking sound from below as the dog bounded through the undergrowth. With a loud "Woof!" he leaped in the air and snapped his jaws, tearing the corner of Hanna's cape. The dog tumbled backward, rolled head over paw down the path, then jumped up, shook himself, lunged forward, and leaped again. This time he sank his teeth into the skullen's flesh.

The serpent writhed, swinging Hanna and the dog back and forth. Blood ran down the dog's face as the serpent swung outward; still he did not let go his hold. At last the snake let out a loud hiss and fell from the tree. All three hit the forest floor with a thud.

Hanna sucked in a ragged breath. Just above and to her right the dog had the creature's neck. He shook and shook until the serpent's neck broke with a loud *snap!*

Hanna pried herself free from the coils and rolled away, gulping in the crisp air. Pulling herself up to her knees, she saw Miles fighting the longest skullen of all on the path ahead.

The dog raced over to Miles, who was madly slashing at the skullen coiled around his middle. He hurled his full weight at the viper and had him in his jaws.

"That's it, boy!" screamed Miles.

Hanna rolled across the snow; a second skullen was lowering toward Miles and the dog. She grabbed the bow and shot the skullen. The arrow plunged into the snake's head. The serpent fell from the branch and dropped onto the snow.

Meanwhile, the dog held the other skullen's neck tight within his jaws. Miles freed his arm, swung it round, and plunged the blade into the skullen's side.

A low hiss filled the woods as the rest of the skullens withdrew from the battle.

Hanna waited until the last sound disappeared. She swallowed, sat back gingerly, and touched her bruised side. The dog abandoned the skullen's body, circled Miles, then lifted his nose and sniffed the air warily.

"It's all right, boy," said Hanna. "I think they're gone."

"Aye," said Miles. "We fought them well. I think they'll stay clear of us now." He slid his knife along the snow to clean the blood from the blade.

Miles looked up and smiled at Hanna in the soft moonlight. "We showed them, didn't we?"

"Aye," said Hanna. "The three of us."

The dog padded over to her. She took a handful of snow and gently washed the serpent's blood from his furry coat.

Wratheren had the full moon in his jaws,
and all the sky was dark. Then Breal
took out his sword and slit the serpent's
throat to free the moon.

—THE EPIC OF BREAL

THE TREES CHANGED FROM BIRCH TO CEDAR AND PINE. No hissing noises came from the high green branches, but Miles heard other sounds. First a soft whisper, like a brush against a drum. *Swish, swish.* And later as they trudged through the snow, the sound deepened and broadened. *Husssh! Husssh!* So that even Hanna heard it and shivered.

"That storm sound," she said.

"It's the wind wall you're hearing." Miles looked left and right; even this far down the path the evergreens were swaying.

"I came through it when I entered the vale," said Hanna.

458

"Aye, getting in may be easy enough. But the wind wall imprisons everyone here."

He wanted to say, "We'll find a way through," but he wasn't sure it was true. Miles walked faster, taking his worry with him. None but the Shriker had ever broken through the wall—he and the renegade sylths Reyn and Perth, who had crept out in his wake.

The dog brushed past. Nose up, ears back, he bounded ahead, a black fur patch against the white snow.

Whoosh! The wind wall lifted them both from the ground and swept them up in a great wave, like toy boats on a stormy sea. The wind surged upward, and hard as they tried to swim against it, the gale was stronger. Together they flailed and kicked like drowning souls; Miles's legs, Hanna's arms, waving in the deafening roar.

Whoosh! The wind flipped Miles over, and he tumbled down until he landed on his back in the snow. Head spinning, Miles lay looking up, sucking in breath after breath. Through the blowing wall stars swirled above as if he were looking up from the bottom of the sea. At last he pressed himself to an unsteady stand. A few feet away Hanna tumbled down and fell into a heap.

From somewhere behind them the dog leaped out. He circled them and ran off again. Feet flying, they took off after the black shadow that darted this way and that across the snow.

No gusts swept them off their feet as long as they followed the dog. He seemed to know the way out, not by sight or smell, but by another sense altogether. Whatever led him on, they followed in his path, panting as they ran. Great gales blew up beside them, but they raced through the wind wall unhindered, as if the sea had parted for them.

The dog veered left in the half dark. He stopped, sniffed, then trotted to the right. Miles kept hold of Hanna's hand and followed. With a final gust and a gentle push the air about them broke. The clear night warmed. The air stilled. Miles stopped, took a breath, and turned about.

"We've broken through," said Hanna, leaning over to catch her breath. Miles gazed back at the great, invisible wall, which he could still hear but not see at all. He patted the dog's soft head. "He got us out."

The wind wall calmed before them. A soft blowing sound came from it now. A breeze at play and no more than that. They turned together to face the moonlit woods of Attenlore.

"Beautiful," whispered Hanna.

Miles leaned against the rough boulder and took the wooden bowl from Hanna. Inching closer to the sleeping dog, he dipped the crusty bread in the warm broth and ate hungrily. After an hour of walking they'd stopped to rest beneath two tilting boulders.

He lifted his eyes to the starry sky. He would never return to Uthor Vale, not for the trolls' great treasure, which he'd need an army to steal, nor to rule the beasts and shadow folk who dwelled there. All of the power he'd had in Uthor Vale felt like a dark dream now.

"Tomorrow," he said, "we'll seek the passage home."

"Aye," said Hanna. "We're sure to find it."

Miles tore a bit of hard bread. "Searching it out may not be easy. We'll have to travel in secret." He didn't say more. Hanna knew the dangers they faced.

Hanna ran her hand along the dog's soft black fur. "I was wondering what to name him." She tilted her head so the moonlight caught in her hair. "I was thinking on Breal."

"Ah," said Miles. "The great warrior who hunts Wratheren."

"And pulls the moon from the giant serpent's mouth. It was always one of my favorite tales."

"It was Granda's favorite, I think." Miles looked up at the moon. It was just past its fullness, and a small part was darkened now.

Miles reached out his hand, and the dog gave it a lick. The dog had killed more than one serpent in Uthor, and he'd saved both their lives. "It's a big name, Hanna."

"He's been through a deal of trouble."

Miles traced a scar that ran from the dog's left ear down to his cheek. "I wonder how much he remembers?"

"Oh, he remembers battling the snakes, I'm sure." Hanna's eyes beamed. "And taking us through the wind wall." She rubbed his furry back. "I wonder how he knew the way."

Miles thought he knew. The Shriker had broken through the queen's wind wall before, and some small part of that memory was still inside the dog. But Miles hadn't been talking about the skullens or about finding the way through the great wind wall. He'd been thinking on the long years the dog had spent as the Shriker. Still, he said nothing. He didn't want to break even the smallest piece of Hanna's joy. She'd come to trust the dog, and he wanted that for her. It was good to see the fear gone from her eyes.

Hanna curled up beside Breal and put her arm across him. With a wide yawn she said, "Let's rest here a while longer."

"You go on," said Miles. "I'll keep watch." The queen had many spies, and there were wild creatures in the woods. With their last arrows used to kill the skullens, they were down to his simple hunting knife for protection.

"I won't sleep long," promised Hanna. "I'll take the second watch."

Soon she and Breal were fast asleep, breathing in and out in rhythm as if they'd been together from the start.

Miles drew closer to the fire. It might be that Breal did not remember the Shriker and bore no shame for what he'd done under the curse. If that was so, he was lucky for all that. Miles shuddered with his own memory of living in the Shriker's form. He wrapped his cape about his shoulders. Still the thoughts swept through him in a series of cold waves. The hunger he'd felt. The glorious, strange power. But strongest of all he remembered the anger that had eaten away at him night and day while he was lost inside the beast.

Wild creatures hunted to live, but it was more than hunger that had driven him. He'd been thrilled at the look of fear in his prey. And every time he'd killed, he'd drunk in the last desperate look in the creature's eyes before he tasted blood. If he'd managed to stay the Hound King and trained the troll army to do his will, the anger and blood thirst would have grown into a war. Uthor against Attenlore. Troll against sylth. The queen had been angry with him. She'd sent her spies to hunt him down. For that he would have taken her throne.

The larger plan had been forming in his mind since he found the treasure trove filled with weaponry. And the only thing that had stopped him . . . He looked over at his sleeping sister and lifted the hood over Hanna's head to shield her from the cold.

Breal's paw jerked in his sleep. Miles stroked his side, the fur soft and warm. He wanted to shrug the memory off. Tell himself he'd been enspelled. And that he'd left that creature self when he crawled out of the beast, but he knew it had been in him long before he shape-shifted, and the anger had come from his own darkness. He shivered, thinking how far the Shriker's curse might have taken him if Hanna hadn't come.

Hours passed beside the boulder. Miles slept and woke again with the setting of the moon. He built up the fire until the rucksack cast a small, dancing shadow across the ground. Stretching, he rubbed his arms, then pulled the leather package from the pack. With stiff hands he slowly unwrapped the ervay. The sylth silver gleamed in the fire's glow. He could touch it now if he wanted to. The instrument was his.

Hand hovering over the flute, he hesitated, then softly ran his fingers along the smooth metal, surprised to find that it was warm. There was one who'd seen his gifts and known the music and the magic that warred within him. He pictured the old man's face now. Age-worn brows above the ever-twinkling eyes. *You saw me.*

Miles trembled. A slow stream of air escaped his mouth, but he held his hand steady and didn't lift the ervay to his lips. Not now. Not yet. He would wait for the song.

At dawn they arose and saw a circle of light far down the snowy hillside. The lights turned, shining diamond bright, like a gathering of stars.

"It's come," whispered Hanna. "The passage home."

Breal stood and shook himself.

"It's not like the dark passage I came though," said Miles.

"But I told you I came through a bright passage like that one," she said, pointing down the hill, "the last time I entered Attenlore."

Miles grinned. "I'll race you."

The three of them flew downhill, snow showering behind them in small flurries. The morning air was sweet. The brightness ahead was dazzling with the snow mirroring back the light. Miles and Hanna ran full of hope and laughter, with Breal not far behind, so it wasn't until they were nearly right up to the lights that they saw the shining wheel was not the passage they were seeking, but a gathering of swirling sprites, and by then it was too late.

The sprites surrounded them, their bowstrings taut, arrows pointed and ready.

Breal raised his hackles, drew back, and barked.

"Hush," warned Miles, giving Breal a pat. They'd come so close to escaping, but he should have known the queen would find a way to trick them. He squared his shoulders. "You needn't put us to sleep," he said. "We'll come with you to face Queen Shaleedyn on our own."

We follow the law of the Old Magic. . . .
Break it and our punishment is swift.

—THE SYLTH QUEEN

THE SPRITES HOVERED WITH MILES AND HANNA OVER the Sylth Queen's courtyard, which stretched out from the mountainside like a broad stone balcony beside the tumbling waterfall. The courtyard was encircled by giant marble columns that looked as if they were both tree and stone. *Like the stone tree in the meadow*, thought Miles.

The sprites darted back and forth, then hovered over the central fountain. Hanging free in the air beside Hanna, with the sound of the falling water in his ears, Miles only just had time to take in the sylth palace, the glimmer walls cut shining from the sheer mountain rock, as the sprites flew down and placed him on the ground. The sound of wind and water filled the quiet courtyard. Miles knelt on the hard stone. The queen might accuse him, but he would be ready. He tugged Hanna's hand, and she knelt beside him, waiting.

The castle doors opened, and Queen Shaleedyn, borne up on her throne, was carried to the marble dais. The sylths stopped their wandering. Heads bowed. Miles knew this, though with his own head down he could not see the others.

On her flowered dais above, the queen presided over all, surrounded by her armored guards, whose breastplates shone like mirrors. Miles took in a slow breath, the silence growing heavy on him. Was the queen waiting for him to speak? Or must he wait for her to begin? He always felt so confused before her.

Clearing his throat, he peered through the throng. As his eyes adjusted to the bright sunlight, he saw hundreds of spiderwebs strung between the marble columns, each with a red or violet spider jeweling the center. He squeezed his sister's hand, and she blinked as she took them in. He hoped his hunting knife could cut through spell webs.

Far to the right Breal crested the steep trail that led to the courtyard and stopped behind a broad white column, his tail wagging slowly and uncertainly. By the look of his position, he was just out of the queen's view. *Stay your ground, boy,* thought Miles. *Come no closer in.*

He was still sending his silent thoughts to Breal when Wild Esper flew into the courtyard, the breeze in her wake lifting Hanna's hair, stirring the sylth's tunics and gowns, and blowing back Miles's coarse cloak. Esper swept over the branched marble columns, a swirl of cool, bright color, her sky gown and cloud-spun hair streaming out behind.

There was a whooshing sound as she turned about in the courtyard and decreased from a gale to a softer breeze. As the air settled, the wind woman diminished until she was no larger than the Sylth Queen. Gathering her blue skirts, she landed gracefully and stood beside Shaleedyn's throne.

The queen greeted Esper with a single nod. The two so near together seemed like sisters, though Shaleedyn's raven hair differed from Esper's white. Both faces had a fierce beauty, and they had a brightness to their eyes—the queen's violet, and Esper's glacier blue. Wild Esper leaned in close to whisper in Shaleedyn's ear.

The queen frowned and turned her gaze on them. "Miles Ferrell, come forward."

Miles stood and stepped closer to the dais. Hanna moved up beside him, though she hadn't herself been called.

Queen Shaleedyn fingered her sapphire necklace. "You have done well with the sylth gift we gave you on the night of Breal's Moon."

Miles was startled by the queen's compliment. *It's a trick*, he thought, *she'll start by flattering me and entrap me if I soften to it.* He stiffened his back. He had something to say, and he must say it now before he lost his nerve.

"I know why you sent the sprites to capture us, and I say now before everyone here that I did not kill the unicorn."

Queen Shaleedyn looked away, but Miles caught sight of the tear rolling down her cheek.

Esper spoke. "The queen knows you did not kill Neurreal. I blew in near the end of the battle and saw you defending her unicorn."

"Why did you wait so long to tell her, then?" asked

Hanna suddenly. "She blamed Miles for the unicorn's death and banished us from Attenlore when we came here to find him."

It was too bold a thing to say to the wind woman, but Miles didn't blame his sister for saying so.

Wild Esper did not take offense. Instead she seemed pleased. "I see you've found your courage, Hanna," she said, "and that is well. But you must remember we wind spirits cannot always steer the mighty gusts we ride. We are but wind riders. I rode into the queen's realm as soon as the way opened."

Miles and Hanna glanced at each other. The look of surprise on Hanna's face matched his own. He'd always thought wind spirits like Wild Esper—or Noorushh, who rode storm winds over the sea—had the power to control the winds they rode.

He cleared his throat and faced Queen Shaleedyn again. Her cheek still glistened, but she'd wiped away the tear.

"If you know I didn't kill the unicorn, then why did you bring us here?" he asked.

The queen did not answer him at first.

Miles clamped his mouth shut, waiting.

At last the queen replied. "We tried once before to use a boy from your clan to kill the Shriker, but the boy failed us."

The queen was talking about his great-uncle Enoch. The ugly story was still fresh in his mind. He crossed his arms. He'd felt sorry for the queen only a moment before when he saw how much she still missed her unicorn, but his heart hardened against her now that he knew the truth.

"So," he said in a trembling voice. "Enoch failed to kill the Shriker for you, and so you used *me* to do it." He couldn't hide the resentment in his words. He didn't want to hide it.

"You can put it that way if you like," said the queen. "I needed the beast destroyed. Only a human boy of your clan could hunt the Shriker down. You played your part well, Miles Ferrell."

The story fell into place before him. The queen had given him the power. The wind woman had blown him to Uthor, and the queen's wind wall had kept him prisoner there until he'd done the deed. They'd used him for their purpose, and they didn't seem to care about the danger they'd put him in. They'd used Hanna, too, pressing her toward Uthor with no magic to help her through the dangers.

An angry shiver raced up his spine. "How did you know I would be strong enough to carry out your plan when . . . I was lost," he said with a gulp. "Nearly lost inside the beast! What if I hadn't . . . what if Hanna hadn't come to bring me back? I would still be trapped in Uthor!"

"But you're not, are you?" said the queen.

"You shouldn't toy with people like that!"

Hanna tugged his cape. "Quiet," she pleaded. "She may turn you to stone or—"

"I don't care!" He shook Hanna off.

Queen Shaleedyn smiled bemusedly. "You wanted the power we offered you."

"Aye," he admitted. "But I didn't know then. It was more power than I had a right to. More power than I could control, and I nearly . . ." He stopped midspeech to fight the sob rising up his throat. Clamping his teeth tight, he pressed it down, down.

"You asked for sylth magic, and we gave it. The gift of magic is rare, and it comes with a cost. If we wanted you to kill the Shriker in return"—she tipped her head—

"that's a fair enough payment. The Old Magic is satisfied."

"You shouldn't have to pay for a gift," Hanna blurted out, then slapped her hand over her mouth. Wild Esper laughed, tilting her head back, so the sound of the laughter blew all about the courtyard.

Miles swayed on his feet. The weight of what they'd done to him, what he'd done to himself, dizzied him.

There was a strange tingling in his fingers. He glanced down and saw a dark, furry head. Breal had padded up and was licking the back of his hand.

"Go away, boy," he whispered, but Breal licked his hand all the more and wagged his tail.

"Whose dog is this?" asked the queen.

Miles wiped his nose on his sleeve. "Ours," he said, but it came out in two voices, for Hanna had said "Ours" at the same moment.

Shaleedyn studied them from the dais. "Where did he come from?"

"He came from nowhere at all," Miles blurted.

"I see," said Shaleedyn. "A handsome bear hound— and strong, I can tell." She looked him up and down. "If he came from nowhere, you would give him to me if I asked it of you."

"No," said Miles.

"We couldn't," cried Hanna.

"Wait." Wild Esper blew across the courtyard, and flew in a small whirlwind around the three of them. Settling back beside the throne, she turned to the queen. "It's him," she said. "The beast."

There was a loud intake of breath all around the courtyard, and many of the sylths backed away from Breal.

"It can't be!" said the queen.

"It's not him," said Miles. "Not anymore."

Queen Shaleedyn touched the spider broach that clung to her gown. The little velvet legs twitched. "Did you or did you not kill the Shriker?" she demanded.

"No," said Miles.

Her eyes went hard as she came to a stand.

"That is," said Miles, "the Shriker died in the cave after I gave him drink."

"You . . . quenched his thirst?" The queen sat again. She seemed to reel for a moment, then took hold of herself. "Why did you do this?"

Miles could not find a quick answer. Would she believe him? The words of change were hidden in the

Darro's curse, but they never made sense to him until he saw the dog inside the beast. Would the queen understand that? Even Hanna had struggled to grasp his reasons.

"This dog," accused Wild Esper, her white hair blowing up above her head. "Tell us the truth."

Miles put his hand on Breal's head. "The truth is . . ." He bit his lip. How could he put it into words? "The truth is . . . the curse is broken."

"The dog that remains must be destroyed," demanded the queen.

"No!" Both Miles and Hanna went down beside Breal and flung their arms around him.

"He's just a dog now," cried Hanna. "Nothing more than that!"

"He won't be harming anyone ever again," said Miles. "I promise you."

Queen Shaleedyn rose up beside Esper. "The Shriker terrorized Attenlore for three hundred years. He slew my people. He killed my unicorn! We cannot abide that he should live. The Old Magic must be satisfied." She fixed her gaze on Breal and lifted her hand.

Miles held Breal fast in his arms. "Wait! We'll give

you anything for him," he said. "Anything you ask." His heart beat wildly. "I'm to blame for breaking the curse. Punish me if you like, but leave him be." Breal started beside him as if he understood what Miles was trying to do. He licked Miles's cheek and thumped his soft tail against Miles's back.

"You're not the one I would punish, boy."

"The one you want to punish is dead," said Miles. "Our dog is innocent."

"I have a lightstone," called Hanna, pulling it from her pocket. "It's yours, only leave him be."

The queen raised her brows. Wild Esper stepped forward and looked down at Hanna. "If you have been favored with a dragon's tear that warms to your touch," said Esper, "then we cannot take it from you."

There was whispering in the air, the words "dragon's tear" and "lightstone" breaking in small waves all around them.

Miles drew his ervay from the pack and held it above his head. "Take my ervay." The silver caught the sunlight and shot a bright beam across the courtyard to the queen's high throne. A sigh rippled across the crowd.

"An ervay is made from sylth silver. Beautiful indeed," said Shaleedyn. "And rare." A long silence followed. Even the warbler ceased his singing, so the only audible sound was the far off waterfall and the burbling of the fountain. Miles touched Breal's soft muzzle. Was the queen weighing his offer? Would she set Breal free?

At last she shook her head. "I do not require your ervay. I can have one made for me if I like."

Miles lowered his gift. What now?

Wild Esper whispered in the queen's ear. The queen nodded, her cherry lips rising to a half smile. She looked at Miles and Hanna. "If this is but a dog now—and a harmless one, as you say—you must prove it to us."

"How?"

"First you and your sister must step away from the beast."

Miles looked into Hanna's frightened eyes, then back to the queen. "What will you do to him?"

"You won't kill him," said Hanna.

"A test," said the queen, "but you must do as I command."

Miles gave Breal a tender hug. "Good boy," he

whispered. Then to his sister, "Do as she says, Hanna."

Hanna released her hold, and they both took a single step back. Miles felt for the knife in his pocket. He'd defend Breal to the death if he must.

"Neither of you are to touch him," warned Wild Esper. "No matter what occurs, you're to stay well back."

On the dais above, both queen and wind woman lifted their hands, palms facing outward. The sylths backed away, some gathering behind the fountain, some clinging to the marble pillars. Sprites flew back as well, leaving Miles, Hanna, and Breal alone to face what magic might come.

Knife hilt in one hand, Miles tucked his free hand in his armpit, fighting against the urge to reach for Breal, not only for the dog's comfort, but also for his own. He could see Hanna swaying beside him, her breathing quick and shallow as a trapped nestling's. "eOwey protect us," she whispered.

The wind woman and the queen began to hum. A mild breeze stirred up. The breeze twirled faster and faster, lifting hair and gown and glistening spiderweb. The swirling wind moaned, and the moan swelled to a roar as the Sylth Queen and wind woman chanted:

"Beware the one that walks between
The world of men and lands unseen.
Danger waits within his dwelling,
Wake him and there is no telling.
Sight unheard
And sound unseen,
We call the ghost
Of Rory Sheen!"

"No!" cried Miles and Hanna.

Blackness spun in the center of the screaming wind, and the water in the fountain darkened. Birds fled. The sylths moaned, drawing farther back. Then from the gaping core of the sudden storm a ghost came flying upward. Gray and tattered as a torn sail, he hovered in midair between throne and fount. His face had a darkness all around it, as if he'd brought the grave soil with him. He looked at both wind woman and queen, his hollow eyes gleaming like wet stones. The ghost turned about, slow as a salt-boned man. When he saw the dog below, his jaw fell agape, and he began to scream.

Miles covered his ear with his free hand, but kept the other on his knife. Beside the fountain Breal stood tense. The fur on his neck bristled as he pressed his ears back.

"It's all right, boy," said Miles. "He can't hurt you now." Breal didn't seem to hear him. His lip curled upward in a snarl.

"Stay back, boy." Miles tried to sound soothing, but fear roughened his voice. If Breal leaped at Rory, the queen would strike him dead for sure. Miles worked to keep from rushing forward and grabbing Breal by the neck.

The ghost clawed the air, a rust color seeping from his mouth and neck, like old blood stained with time. Breal inched forward—his snarl rising to a growl.

"Leave him be, boy," Miles urged softly. "He's dead and gone. He doesn't even know your name."

Breal lowered down on his haunches, his muscles tense and ready.

"Do something, Miles," cried Hanna.

"Breal!" said Miles. "I call you by name!"

The dog turned his head a moment. Eyes full of anger. Face confused.

"There's a good boy." Miles let go his knife and put out his hands. Fingers spread wide. Palms upward. He went down on one knee. "Come, Breal."

Breal whipped his head around and gave the ghost three ear-shattering barks. Then he turned his back on Rory Sheen and ambled over to Miles.

"Ah," said Miles, "there's a good fellow."

Breal wagged his tail and licked Miles's face.

In the air above them the ghost began to crack. Bit by bit he broke apart, the falling pieces clattering against the stone courtyard. The shards lay in a gray brown pile like shattered pottery. A moan passed through the crowd and then a sigh.

In the silence that came after, Miles watched the pile that had once been Rory Sheen crumble to a fine dust. It swirled up overhead and blew into the far-off sky.

Hanna knelt beside Breal and put her arms around his neck. "Ah, you're such a good dog, you are." She kissed his soft ear, and Miles placed his hand on Breal's noble head.

"So," said Queen Shaleedyn, "you named him Breal."

"I didn't," said Miles with a grin. "It was Hanna did that."

The queen conferred with Esper, then lifted her hand. "By this test," she said, "I claim the truth. The Shriker is dead. The Old Magic is satisfied."

One by one the sylths came out from behind fountain and pillar. First there was laughter, then there was cheering. Sprites flitted about like shooting stars.

"The Shriker's dead!" they all shouted. "Long live Breal!"

In such hours as these a world is born.

—WILD ESPER

WILD ESPER CARRIED MILES, HANNA, AND BREAL FROM Attenlore to Enness Isle, world to world, which was only a whisper and a breath apart to her. She placed them by Shree's red-leafed maple on the high mountain cliff. Miles stood between Breal and Hanna. Together they watched Esper blow back out to sea. The sun was setting, and the clouds over Turnbow Bay were trimmed in vermilion.

"I wonder, will we see her again?" said Hanna.

"It's sure we will," said Miles. He ran his hand along Breal's head, relishing the taste of clean mountain air on his tongue.

On the cliff top Gurty came around from behind the Enoch Tree and dropped her garden spade. "Miles!" she cried. "You're home at last! Give your old Gurty a hug." She embraced him, holding him a bit overlong for his taste.

"Well, now," she said, taking a step back. "You've grown taller, boy." Gurty looked past him and blinked. "And where'd you get the dog?"

"It's a long story."

"Aye, there's many a long story up here on Mount Shalem, and I've been in one or two myself."

Miles looked from her soiled garden gloves to her eyes, which held the bright color of morning grass, but it was Hanna who spoke his thought. "It was you, wasn't it? You were the green-eyed girl who left Enoch for another."

"Ah, well, I was young then," sighed Gurty. "And your great-uncle Enoch had a dark power in him that drew me in and pushed me away all at the same time."

Miles knew all too well what Gurty meant.

"I come here spring through fall to mind the soil around the tree and make what amends I can." Gurty turned to gather up her digging tools. Hanna knelt down to help in the gathering, and Miles stepped around the far side of the Enoch Tree.

On the back side of the gnarled oak he ran his hand along the rough bark, and a glint of white caught his eye. There seemed to be a piece of crystal rock wedged into the trunk. Miles gripped the edge and tugged. When it was loosened enough to pull free, a long, sharp fang came out.

Shuddering, he dropped the fang as if it were a fiery thing, then he went down on one knee to retrieve it. The Shriker's fang lay long as a dagger across his open palm, and he trembled in the wake of its finding. He touched the tip. Sharp as an ice pick. Then he fingered the smooth curve to the base. He'd run his own tongue over a fang like this not so long ago.

Breal came up beside him. Miles slipped the great, long tooth inside the rucksack before Hanna or Gurty could turn about and see the thing he'd found. He stood again and stepped around the trunk. No wind blowing across the high cliff, but the tree began to sway.

"Look," cried Gurty. The oak gave a shudder. Slowly the old man stepped out of the tree. First one leg, then the other, then the full of him.

Miles's heart pounded in his ears as Enoch stood blinking in the afternoon light. The old man's lean face and deep-set eyes were so much like Granda's. When he took a step, it seemed as if Miles's own granda were stepping toward him.

Breal's hackles went up. A low growl rumbled in his throat.

"Easy, boy," whispered Miles.

A look of fear shadowed Enoch's face. He turned and went down on his knees before Breal, his hands upturned like a beggar.

Ears pressed back, Breal slowly padded up to him. He sniffed Enoch's head, his cheek, then stood quite still over the kneeling man. Enoch put his arms around Breal and rested his head on the dog's thick neck.

Enoch wept. Miles wanted to step toward them but found he couldn't move. Breal moved instead, after the old man's sobs had broken over him in waves. It was a small thing and a great thing all at once, and it took only a moment. Pulling his head back just far enough, Breal licked the tears from Enoch's cheek. The old man had been held in the tree fifty years for his crimes, and fifty years was a good long time to pay for all. Breal's kiss said so, and with his kiss Enoch's sobs subsided.

At last Enoch wiped his nose on his ragged sleeve. He hugged the dog again, then stood unsteadily and looked about, eyes wide, as a new babe views the world. "Which one of you freed me?" he asked hoarsely.

Miles thought of the long fang he'd pulled from the back of the tree. "I may have," he said.

Enoch looked long across the few feet between them as if seeing Miles for the first time. He touched his fingers to his brow and gave a slight nod. It was a meer's greeting, and Miles felt it like a small flame passed from man to man. He thought to say, "I'm not a meer," but Enoch was speaking.

"Tell me your name."

"Miles." He did not say, "My granda was your brother." He could not say it. Not now. Not just yet, for there would be too many tears behind the words and too much talking after. *Next time*, he thought, and he knew the moment he thought that, there would be a next time, and a next, with his great-uncle home.

"eOwey sent you at last," said Enoch. "How long I've prayed for it."

He put his hand on Breal's head. "What is your name?" he asked, as if the dog might speak.

"He is called Breal," said Hanna.

Enoch's eyes brimmed, the unspilled tears adding their own sheen. "I never thought I'd stand among human folk again." He looked at all of them. "And your names?"

"I'm Hanna."

"Hannalyn." He said her deya name with a respectful bow.

"How did you . . . know?" asked Hanna.

"It's long I've lived inside a tree. I'm honored to meet thee, Hannalyn."

Hanna's eyes shone.

Gurty took a step forward, pulling off her garden gloves. "I think you know my name."

Enoch squinted. "Gurty? It's you, isn't it, my green-eyed girl?"

"Aye."

Enoch put out his hand. She reached for him, and in midair their smallest fingers met. Their touch had a sound to it, or so it seemed to Miles, the sigh of leaves rustling in the wind.

Breal nudged Miles with his cold, wet nose. "Aye," whispered Miles. He nodded to Hanna, and they left the couple alone on the cliff.

They reached the broad meadow with the rocky outcropping that overlooked the sea. Miles stopped and leaned against the giant's-head boulder, where his own story had begun so long ago on Breal's Moon night.

Beyond the edge of Enness Isle the ocean shone violet. One day soon a ship bearing saffron flags would sail across Turnbow Bay and dock in Brim Harbor. Passage for him, passage for her; for Hanna had told him what the meers said to her by the well, and he guessed she may well accept Olean's offer to study on Othlore. He didn't share his thoughts, but let them pass. The meers' ship would come in its own time. Right now he wanted to be home and felt the wanting of it in his bones. There was only one thing left to show Hanna before they left the meadow.

Miles clapped his hands. "Here, Breal."

Breal ran through the grass, panting happily. Miles went down on his knees beside the boulder. "Come close by, Hanna," he whispered. "There's something here for you to see."

Miles gently lifted Breal's soft lip to show his missing fang. Then, with his other hand, he hooked his mouth with his forefinger and pulled back his cheek to show his own gap. Hanna looked from mouth to mouth. The missing teeth were in the very same place.

Miles let go of his lip. "Do you see?" he asked with wonder.

"What does it mean?"

"I'm not sure, but I missed the fang as soon as I changed into the Shriker's form, though I could never remember when it had come out." He reached into the rucksack and drew out the long tooth: a dog's fang, only much larger. It could only have come from the Shriker. Miles nodded toward the cliff. "I found this in the Enoch Tree while you were busy helping Gurty with her tools."

Hanna gazed at it with wonder. "Aye," she breathed. "Shree said the Shriker attacked Enoch, but before the beast could kill him, the Sylth Queen took her own revenge—"

"And the Shriker lost his fang when the man went all to wood," finished Miles. "It must have been like that."

Miles scratched Breal behind the ear. "It was a

member of the Sheen clan that had to break the curse. The queen knew that, and since Enoch had failed, it came down to us." He said "us," not "me," and he meant it, for he'd come to see that Hanna had played as much a part in the breaking of the curse as he had. He looked at her tired face, saw the cut across her brow from the cave-in. "You were brave to search Uthor for me," he said. "I never told you that."

In the long silence that followed, Hanna leaned against the giant's-head boulder, her arms crossed, thinking. "The Falconer said it has always been our story. Yours and mine."

"Aye." Miles slid the Shriker's tooth back into the rucksack. "But we didn't do it alone. Granda armed us with the tale. The Falconer helped, Wild Esper, and Shree. Even the queen helped in her way."

"And all the while Gurty tended the tree," said Hanna. "And Enoch was praying for his freedom."

Miles looked round the mossy boulder. His heart filled up like the sea itself, and he knew a song would come, someday, a song that might touch the way he felt just now. And he had the Falconer's ervay to play it on when it came.

The sun had gone behind Mount Shalem. A lone falcon caught the last rays on his wing. The trees in the woods below were tinting blue with twilight, but here and there patches of red and gold could be seen where the maples grew among the evergreens.

"Well," said Miles, "are you ready, Hanna?"

"Aye. Mother, Da, and Tymm will be glad to see us."

They started down the grassy slope.

"Come on, Breal," called Hanna.

Breal rushed ahead and led them down the path toward home as if he'd always known the way.

GLOSSARY

Abathan	Peace
Akabree tha	All praise to you
Attenlore	Otherworld name for Enness Isle
Braughnoick	Old man. The term is often used in a derogatory way.
Breal	Legendary hero who killed the serpent who swallowed the moon
Brodureth	The Oak King of Oth
Darro	Death's messenger
Deya	Tree spirit
Dreamwalker	A sleepwalker with dreams that can foretell the future
Elandra	Obey
Eldessur	You are called.
Eldessur Kimbardaa	You are called. Come home to yourself.
eOwey	One who sang the universe into being, also called the Maker.
Ervay	A flute with two pipes made of sylth silver
Eryl	Human male. Term commonly used by deyas
Esper	A wind spirit or wind woman, also called Wild Esper

Essha   Listen with understanding
Evendera kalieanne. Mosura tan ahanaad.
                          Magic spell roughly translated as:
                          I call the moon to place a pathway at my feet.
Eyeshala   The beautiful afterworld of the souls

Grandtree   Ancient tree that houses a deya
Gullmuth   Huge woolly mammoth with birdlike head

Hessha elandra   Hear and obey

Isparel   Wind spirit of the east

Kalass   Stay back or keep away
Keth-kara   The pure self-sound eOwey sings as each
                          individual is formed
Kith   Friend or spirit friend
Konor-duvan   The creation chant
Kravel   Ravenlike black birds. Females have orange
                          plumage on their heads.

Leafer   Healer, or one who uses herbs to heal
Lyn   Human female. Term commonly used by deyas

Meer   Literally "one who wields magic." A title
                          given to one who has studied magic with
                          meers and is blue-palmed.
Mishtar   Hero who fought alongside dragons and
                          eventually helped to negotiate an end to the
                          dragon wars.

Noor	Name of the world
Noorfest	Holiday celebrated at winter equinox
Noorushh	Wind spirit who rides the sea winds
Oth	Name of the magical Otherworld
Otherworld	Another name for Oth
Othic	Ancient language formed when Noor and Oth were one world
Othlore	Island where meers study magic
Shriker	Name of the cursed dog, a shape-shifter who is out for revenge
Skullen	A type of giant snake that lives in the trees of Uthor
Sqyth-born	One whose eyes are different colors, usually one blue eye and one green. Also called *sqyth-eyed.* The word *sqyth* was formed from *sqy* (sky) and *-th* (from *ear-th* or *O-th*).
Sylth	Winged fairies of Oth that are human size
Taberrell	The largest of the dragons, with blue-green scales and golden chests
Tamalla	Herb used to bring on a state of calm or help one to sleep
Terrow	Smaller dragons with golden scales
Thool	Dark brown drink served hot and sweetened like cocoa
Tygoss	Wind spirit from the southern reaches
Wratheren	Legendary serpent that swallowed the moon